The Darkling Mage

Mages of Asterheim Book 2
The Darkling Mage

Steven D. Jackson

Published by Vulpine Press in the United Kingdom in 2024

ISBN: 978-1-83919-565-5

www.vulpine-press.com

For the Emperor

Prologue

A steel-grey eye watched the boy enter the smoke-choked tavern, his clothes torn and his feet unshod. Like so many others, a refugee. Many had come through; many had been lost along the way. So many more never set out on the journey, and that was the greatest tragedy of all.

Sir Rivan Dirkling made no attempt to attract the boy's attention. He turned his gaze to his cup, a rough thing of old wood still brimming with the ale he'd purchased hours before at the start of his long vigil. He deliberately ignored the face looking back at him, poorly reflected in the brown liquid and lit only by the dancing flames of the tavern fireplace to his right. Like the cup, it was a rough face, atop an aged body encased in old steel and faded livery. He had no need to be reminded of his scars, his gnarled features, the fact that one of his eyes was a milky colour no damned mage seemed able to fix. Once his remaining hair had turned white, he'd started avoiding mirrors altogether.

Propped up next to the old knight was a shield; a bit rough and a bit chipped, the enamel faded and worn, and no longer proudly displaying the sigil of House Orswell. It had been painted grey, much like the little grey shields dotted around the city, each one positioned so as to point the way to the next. A simple trail, if one knew where to look for it, and of course it was one of the better kept secrets in Asterheim for very good reasons. Those who needed it eventually found it, provided they survived long enough to ask the right questions first.

It wasn't a perfect system, Dirkling thought as he drank deeply of his cup, but it was better than the alternative.

'Excuse me,' said a thin voice. Rivan looked up at the boy and tried to summon what he hoped looked like a reassuring smile.

'You the new apprentice?' the old knight asked, loudly enough to be overheard and with a healthy dollop of scorn.

'I...' the boy faltered. His face was pale, his hair long and dark, falling over his forehead into his eyes in an untidy mess. He was thin, his collarbone clearly visible through the ragged tear in his shirt. Dirkling had seen that tear before. Only one thing caused it; someone managing to escape the grasp of a strong man with a poor grip.

The knight took another slurp of his ale and grimaced. It really was dreadful. He glanced at the boy's feet; they were filthy and were either bleeding or had only recently stopped.

'Astrid!' he yelled at the barkeeper's daughter, who looked up with a long-suffering stare. 'Two more ales!' She didn't respond. He didn't care. It was all for appearances anyway.

'Out with it, lad,' he said gruffly, still talking louder than was necessary and hoping the boy would understand what he was trying to tell him. 'Are you the new apprentice or did I just order myself two drinks?'

'I...I'm the apprentice,' said the lad. His eyes were wide, darting left and right as though either frightened of who might see him or looking for an exit. Probably both.

'Then sit down!' Dirkling blustered. 'You standing there is making me nervous.'

The boy pulled another bar stool across to the table with a frankly alarming amount of effort. Rivan peered at him.

'You'll need some more meat on those bones, boy, if you want to be useful.' He'd tried to make it sound light, but he'd meant it.

The lad offered a wan smile and rested his scrawny elbows on the table, looking around fearfully.

'It's just a tavern, boy,' said the knight, gently, 'you're safe.' Then, more loudly, he added, 'Bring us a pie, Astrid!'

Astrid ignored him.

'So,' Dirkling said quietly, turning back to the skinny boy and fixing him with a stare. 'Tell me why you're here.'

'I…I followed the shields.'

'Yes, I know you did. Good. But before that?'

'I heard about the shields from Molly Dell. She runs the Heaven An'Dell place.'

Dirkling nodded and smiled. 'Best brothel in the city. Best named one anyway.' He took a swig of his ale. 'Why is it you all seem to know the working girls?'

'We all?'

'Lads like yourself. Lads who need the Grey Shields.'

The boy smiled and shrugged. 'I met Molly a year or two ago. She was working a street near where I lived with my dad and brothers.' A spasm of pain crossed the boy's face and he bit his lip.

'Go on,' said Rivan. 'It helps to talk.'

Astrid appeared from nowhere, carrying two ales and a steaming pie with a large knife sticking out of it. She slammed it down on the table and stalked away, flinging her long red curls back over her shoulder as she went.

'Thank you!' called Rivan at her retreating back and looked at the boy with a grin. To his surprise, the lad smiled back and reached for the ale with a grateful nod.

'She did what they all do,' he said, resuming his tale, 'laughed and flirted with my dad and my brothers as we walked by. But I caught her eye and I think, I think she just knew. She's used to men reacting to her a certain way, I suppose.'

'Hard not to, when it's Molly,' said Rivan with an appreciative smile.

'So when lads like *myself* don't...' The boy shrugged and took a slurp of his ale. He nodded appreciatively at Dirkling.

'I went to find her after that. Turns out, quite a few *lads like me* end up making friends with the girls and for the same reason. So Molly's was the first place I went when...when I left.'

'You want to talk about that?'

'Not really. My dad found out about me. Doesn't matter how.' The boy looked away into the distance, his voice starting to choke a little. He took a deep drink of his ale.

'He kicked you out?' asked Dirkling.

'No. The opposite. Locked me up, said I'd stay there until I straightened out. I managed to get away after a while. And Molly told me about the Grey Shields, but didn't say what they meant. Just that it's a safe place for us.'

'It is. You're going to work in the Citizenry Guild.'

'You're not serious.'

'Very serious. Congratulations.'

The boy stared at him, open-mouthed, before smiling such a wide and earnest smile that Rivan Dirkling forgot for a moment that the end of his glorious service to House Orswell had come to

4

this. Babysitting the unwanted children of the worst parents in the city.

He reached for the knife and started hacking at Astrid's over-baked pastry. After all, the boy certainly wouldn't be strong enough to do it. Few in Asterheim would be.

'What's your name, lad?' he asked between grunts of effort. Flecks of pastry and splatters of gravy coated his faded sleeves.

'Tyler,' said the boy.

Chapter One

In the empty silence of the night-shrouded fortress, the young mage made his choice. Pale fingers reached out towards the ancient books, hesitant at first, and heavy with a dread sense of finality. Alakis jerked his fingers back with a hiss as tiny flashes of lightning danced for a moment beneath the skin, a legacy of pain lingering even now.

By his side, Alakis could see Dominitia. His friend and constant companion these last painful months, she was standing with her eyes closed, whispering softly, her own fingers moving with her words. The lightning beneath his skin subsided again as a feeling of relief washed over him and he sighed, his shoulders sagging. Dominitia opened her eyes and looked at the books, the process of calming his attacks now so routine that she barely even noticed she was doing it. The terrible burning and flashing would begin, she would soothe him. Over and over. Probably for the rest of their lives, if she stayed with him that long.

'I'm sorry,' he muttered, as he did every time. Dominitia gave a short smile, barely glancing at him. He looked at her for a long moment. He was fourteen now, and she at least three or four years older. But she was beautiful, with long dark hair and big blue eyes, and he was not. The terrible lightning storm that had engulfed him during the attack on Hilda's Barbican months before had never truly left him. It had taken his hair and drained his skin of colour. Even his eyes seemed to have been washed out.

Dominitia would never see him as he saw her, he knew that. Not unless he could fix things. He looked back at the books, heavy tomes arranged neatly on the shelf of the tutor who had lived and worked here. These were the books Sophine had used, he was sure of it. These were the books that held the keys to the powers that she and her friends wielded and denied to anyone else.

A melancholy sigh escaped him as he pulled the first two books from the shelf and dropped them in his bag. Perhaps the knowledge within these tomes could help him, and perhaps not, but he owed it to himself to try whatever the cost.

'It's in here, Dominitia—' he said, grunting with effort as he heaved another heavy book from the shelf. 'The power to fix me. To fix everything.'

'Nothing fixes everything,' his companion said timidly. Alakis ignored her, as he always ignored her more cowardly comments. Beautiful she was, but her beauty was marred by her constant nervous worry. The fear she carried around like a shackle upon both their wrists had only grown more profound as the months had passed. He did not blame her, as such, but she hadn't suffered nearly as much as he had and sometimes her relentless, damaged dread got on his nerves. He felt the lightning rising again and tried to calm himself.

Since the destruction of the Senate and the exodus of the mages, fear and mistrust of magic users had deepened in Asterheim. It was well known that a mage had brought the ancient building, the seat of all power in Astregoth, to ruin with sorcerous flames and that half the senators had barely made it out alive. Some insisted that it had been the mages who had saved the city from the ambitions of

Lyoris Mountebank, others spoke of darker conspiracies and alliances. Unfortunately, even with the restoration of the Senate, the absence of most mages from the city now meant there was little opposition to the loudest and cruellest voices. Those voices often belonged to the dispossessed and leaderless priests of the Sacred Circle, and the senators who resented the new regime.

And for those very few mages who had made the decision to stay, thinking the fall of the short-lived Echelarch would improve things, the situation had only grown bleaker. To keep things from escalating the new Rector of the Barbican, Sophine, had insisted that the few remaining mages in residence at the fortress keep a low profile and had expressly forbidden any and all delving into the past. Into the only secrets that could help Alakis.

And so it had come to this. Sneaking around the ancient fort in the dead of night and stealing the knowledge he needed. He and Dominitia would take them far away, learn what they needed, and return to rid the city of the chaos that had—

'Alakis.' A soft voice, sad but brittle. A voice he knew well. His fingers jerked in sudden agony as lightning flashed within them and he almost yelped. With an effort of will, he mastered his fear and lowered the bag to the floor, turning slowly to regard the shadows from which Sophine had been watching him the whole time.

'Come to say goodbye?' he asked as lightly as he could, the flashes of pain and light robbing his tone of levity and leaving him sounding bitter.

Sophine didn't move from the shadows.

'I came to ask you to stay,' she said in a quiet, dangerous voice. Alakis's mouth twitched in a false, mirthless smile.

'You know I can't,' he said, gritting his teeth as a spear of light illuminated his skull from within. 'I can't live like this anymore. I've tried.'

'Just a little longer, Alakis, please. We're close.'

He turned away and went to pull a smaller, darker book from the shelf, but his fingers stopped short of the black leather. He felt rather than heard a soft voice in the back of his head, sighing in ghostly, sibilant sounds as he looked at it. He gulped and grabbed the book next to it instead and pulled it from the shelf. He thrust it into the bag with all the violence he itched to do to the world in general, trying to ignore the whispering entreaties of the darker book.

'Not close enough,' he growled, turning back to face the Rector of Hilda's Barbican and hefting his bag. The book on the shelf continued to hiss in his mind; he could feel it fumbling at the back of his skull. 'You're too busy with your politics and your teaching to care what happens to me. Well, I've done my part. I've waited. But you couldn't fix things. So now I'm going to fix them myself.'

'Don't do this.' Sophine's voice was a whisper in the gloom, a soft promise of fear like a cold breath on the back of the neck. 'If you leave now, you'll expose us all to danger.'

'We're already in danger. We have been since you and your friends destroyed the Senate. How long do you think before a purge begins?'

Sophine took a step forward, the pale light of the chamber catching her gaunt face, the worry-lines etched permanently around her eyes. Her thick black hair was a tangled mess.

'I can still stop it, I just need—'

Alakis cut her off, waving a dismissive hand as he headed to the door.

'No. I will stop it. You had your chance. And all I ask is that you stay out of my way.'

The door slammed shut, inches from his face. Flashes and tingles spat and tiny arcs of lightning danced across his eyes as a surge of adrenaline pumped through his body. He turned slowly, determined not to yelp or wince at the short, stabbing pains. He looked at Sophine.

'You don't want to do this,' he said.

'I know.'

'Open the door.'

'You know I can't.'

The moment lengthened, filled only by the soft wordless sighs of the book that refused to be ignored. There was nothing more to say. Alakis relaxed his grip and let go of his control.

A searing bolt of pure energy, blue-white and impossibly bright, leapt from his abused fingertips and flew at Sophine without him even needing to direct it. Tiny forks jumped from the main beam to the floor, to the ceiling, jerked and crackled across the stone walls and ignited the draperies. The lightning bolt exploded against Sophine's invisible shield and enveloped it, coruscating energies snapping and spitting as they writhed against one another. Alakis turned and blasted the heavy door, exploding it into fragments as though it were made of pottery. He grabbed Dominitia and ran through, pulling her along after him.

'Where are we going?' she gasped as they ran, her voice interrupting his concentration as he tried to conjure a portal.

'Anywhere!'

'Alakis, wait!'

'We don't have time,' he shouted irritably. The hissing of the abandoned dark-leather book was near-frantic in his head, almost impossible to ignore.

He gestured desperately at the darkness and a yawning hole into nothing screeched painfully into being. He winced as a cold wind seemed to blow from within it. Something inside the aching darkness at the centre of the black portal gave a hideous scream, or maybe it was just the wind.

Behind him, he could hear the sounds of someone yelling at him to stop. They only had moments left. He motioned at Dominitia to jump.

She shook her head, her eyes wide and terrified and her body rigid with terror. He hesitated, casting one quick at the foreboding, hastily conjured portal. His hand clutched the bag tighter and he gritted his teeth, wanting to shake her violently by the shoulders.

He hesitated for a brief moment, caught between the portal and Dominitia, but only a moment. He could not stay. He now had the means to fix himself, Asterheim and everything else Sophine and her friends had ruined. He couldn't lose it now. He had to go, with or without Dominitia.

He turned from her and leapt into the roiling darkness, hoping she'd follow him just one more time.

**

In the silence of Master Thomas's old study, Sophine slowly sat up, marvelling that she was still alive. Her robes steamed, the skin beneath hot and sore to the touch. In spite of everything she hadn't thought Alakis would really do it, not really. He was just a kid after all, a frightened boy with a terrible affliction. He wasn't a killer.

Except that he was, of course. He had killed plenty of soldiers and entranced citizens on the night of the siege of Hilda's Barbican, a prisoner within his own body screaming as elemental energies used him as a conduit to wreak terrible destruction on anyone within reach. It had changed him, broken him. But he hadn't been in control then. Today, he'd *chosen* to attack her.

Her eyes drifted to the book from which Alakis had recoiled. She had heard something emanating from it, a ghostly whisper, as Alakis had escaped. Now it was silent. She shuddered; he'd taken all her books except the one she avoided even looking at. The one that still whispered to her every now and then, which she oh-so-resolutely ignored but somehow never quite managed to put somewhere far away from her. Her eyes lingered on it a moment, its plain black binding seeming strangely dark like a void in the world.

'Curse you, Alakis,' she muttered unconvincingly, as she got to her feet. She knew she was angry with herself more than the afflicted boy. After all, from Alakis's point of view what choice did he really have?

She strode bitterly from the room, determinedly ignoring the now suspiciously silent lone book on its dusty shelf.

***

The matter before the Senate was one of extreme banality. A simple decision regarding who would have the right to tax trade moving in and out of the city. The choice was between the Travellers, who had responsibility for the roads and gates themselves, or the particular Guild to which the relevant trader belonged. The Travellers could do the actual collecting more easily, of course, but the paperwork afterwards was not something they were suited for. The individual Guilds would easily be able to handle the paperwork, but they lacked the presence and infrastructure to actually collect the money.

Lady Ariene Gloriana perched on a stool at the centre of the dais, around which rose the tiered seats of the newly constructed Senate building. It wasn't quite as opulent or beautiful as Asterheim's former house of central power, because it had been raised quite hastily for mainly utilitarian purposes, but it served. High white stone walls, a dome at the centre, on the underside of which someone no doubt planned to paint something epic and inspiring, and seats arranged in a semi-circle spreading from the dais up. The further back you were, the higher and thus more removed from the action. Gone were the overlooking boxes and galleries from the old building, which had traditionally been used for the noble families to conduct private business that more often than not ended up official policy before long. A new start, supposedly, had been the intention.

Ariene snorted and shook her head, adjusting her position on her deliberately uncomfortable stool. Had she still been as frail as she had been only months ago, she was fairly sure she'd have fallen right off it by now and someone would have brought her a cushioned chair. As it was, restored as she was to relative youth and health, everyone thought it was perfectly fine to let her suffer. She looked over at Amir Barten, balancing precariously on a similar torture device with far more grace than she was managing. He looked at her, his dark skin seeming to gleam in the bright light reflecting off all the stone. He smiled; a nice smile she thought, albeit forced. It was a smile that said, "This is fine, don't worry, everything is just fine."

13

Which of course meant it wasn't, because the new start had very quickly begun to resemble business as usual and the infighting had picked up exactly where it had left off, with just one big difference – she and Amir were on the same side. Jointly appointed caretaker leaders of the Senate in the wake of the Lyoris Mountebank debacle, the two of them had tried to steer the city back to normality. Some senators had prospered by this, others had seen opportunity in it, and others saw opportunity in opposition. And now everything, from crop rotation to Guild workforce regulations, was filtered through the various factions and their interest in the only thing that mattered: power.

Ariene sighed and looked at the unpainted ceiling.

Politics. Like wine, a taste could be fun but any more was just asking for a headache.

With a rustle of silk, Ariene got off her stool and held her arms out for silence. She was fairly sure, constitutionally speaking, that she had no right or authority to officiate but since she was here…

'Lords and ladies of the Senate,' she said, long practice carrying her voice across the chamber with ease, 'I believe we have picked this issue apart for long enough. Will the Travellers concede that they do not have the capability to account for collected taxes?'

There was a grudging murmur of agreement from her own supporters, the Travellers Guild amongst them.

'And will the representatives of the merchant guilds concede that they cannot collect those taxes themselves without oversight?'

Another grumbling assent, this time from all around.

'Then I propose that the Overseer sends a delegation to meet with Lord Barten'—she suppressed a grin as Amir stiffened by her side—'and that the merchant guilds do the same. Together, you can find a suitable solution for fair administration of these taxes without us all having to shout over each other.'

'My lady, you are wise beyond your years,' said Lord Aresbrook, her long-time ally, slyly from his seat in the second row of chairs.

'My years are far more than they appear, my lord,' she smiled back.

'All in favour?' Amir barked, clearly less than happy with her for volunteering him.

There was a general chorus of consent, though decidedly lacklustre in some corners. Ariene allowed herself a small sigh of relief; she hadn't misjudged the boredom in the room after all. Even her enemies had been happy to agree with her just to put the tedium to rest.

She stepped cautiously down the dais, holding her skirts up in case the fabric snagged her feet. She was met by a young man, dark of hair and as troubled of face as only the young can be. He was dressed in a dark jacket worn open over a lighter shirt and was hopping from foot to foot as though agitated.

'So serious, Rigel,' she admonished with a smile, linking her arm through his. 'You're far too handsome to be frowning all the time, dear. One day you'll be old and you'll have plenty of time for frowning. Try a smile.'

'What do we have to smile about, my lady?'

She suppressed a sigh at his tone.

'That we're alive, perhaps? Healthy? The sun's out? Pick something.' She waved a hand around as though to encapsulate the whole world. 'Honestly, young people.'

'We got nowhere today, Ariene. How will we ever get a constitution written if all the Senate ever does is bicker over…what even was that about?'

'Taxes, dear. Money. What's it ever about?'

'Exactly!'

Ariene sighed and decided not to reply as they made their way out of the Senate surrounded by the bustling forms of friends and enemies. Rigel was right, of course; the grand plan to create a new constitution to protect Asterheim from the rot that had allowed Lyoris Mountebank to rise had stalled. Things had gone back more or less to where they had been before, except with no veiled throne giving the whole thing a sense of solemnity and righteousness. Now politics in Asterheim was precisely what it looked like; a room full of self-interested people refusing to get things done in case it benefitted their rivals.

Even so, the view outside was worse.

Through the heavy double-doors of the new building a crowd could be seen. Common folk in dirty clothes, merchants too lean for their finery and pleading mothers sheltering their children behind skirts patched many times over. All of them pressing forward, trying to make themselves heard over the general murmur of voices and the shouts of the desperate. Men in mail and armour were keeping order, trying as gently as possible to keep the petitioners from swamping the emerging nobles and guild officers.

Ariene and Rigel made their way past, keeping their heads down, until a young woman who couldn't have been more than Rigel's own age broke through the line and flung herself at his feet, clutching at his hands with desperate twitching fingers.

'Please, my lord, you're a mage, help us!'

Rigel stood, aghast, staring at the woman gripping his hand as she begged. She had a heart shape, like a birth mark, just under her right eye.

'The crops are failing, lord,' she pleaded, 'my children are starving! Bring the mages back, lord, please!' Her eyes were round and pleading, but once she spotted Ariene her gaze hardened into a particularly poisonous glare.

'The houses are collapsing in the old Commercial Quarter,' shouted a man, gesturing vaguely at Rigel, 'surely you can—'

'The children are dying!' shrieked a near-frantic woman, her arms around two crying toddlers. 'They're getting sick and you're healing *her!*' She pointed at Ariene, glaring with eyes maddened by grief and fear.

'I…I'm sorry,' Rigel cried, backing away from the kneeling woman with a look of horror on his face.

'Come, dear,' Ariene said softly, steering him away. 'There's nothing you can do right here right now except lose your sense of perspective in a tide of emotion.' He let her guide him to their carriage and sat in silence as they pulled away, leaving the pitiful sight of the crowds behind.

'We can't let this continue,' he said eventually. Ariene nodded.

'No,' she said, watching the city go by out of the window. Their city. Her city.

'No, we can't.'

***

The hooded man watched the departing carriage with satisfaction, surveying the rest of the crowd as he did so. The young woman had remained on her knees, hands reaching theatrically for the retreating carriage as it left. A bit much, he'd thought, but otherwise she'd done well. The woman rose to her feet and dusted off her knees, turning to look right at the shadowy recess in which the hooded man stood. He smiled ruefully and fished out the bag of coins as she sauntered over. He tossed it to her and she caught it smartly.

'Easy afternoon's work,' she smiled, looking at him with her big, mischievous eyes. 'Anything else I can do for you, my lord?'

The hooded man chuckled. 'I think you've done enough, Andine. I barely have enough silver left for lunch.'

The working girl pouted attractively and slipped the pouch into her robes.

'Too bad,' she said, arranging her clothes and everything beneath them in a seemingly random but skilfully revealing manner. 'Remember me the next time you want a performance like that though, won't you? I thought I was pretty good.'

'Very good,' he said, his eyes moving over her body. 'You know, I find I'm not that hungry after all.'

She smiled prettily.

'Oh?'

'You're very manipulative, Andine.'

She raised an eyebrow.

'*The crops are failing*,' she breathed in mock-desperation, one hand on an ample breast.

'Alright, alright,' he allowed. 'So am I.'

She slipped a hand into his with a lascivious grin.

'This way then, my lord, let's see if we can't perk those crops of yours up...'

***

Dominitia ran through the twisted streets of Terminheim, the close wooden houses and their dripping thatch sodden with rainwater. Her boots splashed cold mud up her legs but she paid it no heed, desperately pressing on through the thick shadows of the night. The darkness flashed and growled as lightning cracked the sky, forks of arcing brilliance illuminating the now-permanently roiling clouds obscuring the stars. The storm had not abated in days and, she was sure, nor would it now.

She only had the vaguest idea of where she was, and where she was going. Since they arrived in Terminheim only a few days ago, she and Alakis had been staying at the palace of the Lord Governor in the centre of the stony city. She had believed Alakis at first, when he told her they had to remain inside for their own safety. But she'd seen nothing of him and her door had been locked, and as the storm had built outside so too did her fear that something terrible was happening. And then she'd tried to leave...

A crackle of something up ahead, in the thick darkness of the unlit streets. Dominitia stopped and ducked into a doorway, her skin crawling as it touched the rain-soaked wood. Terminheim was as far from Asterheim as it was possible to go whilst still being in Astregoth, and the people and customs had proven very different. Even their buildings were crude and ramshackle, built of the rough, ugly stone from which so much of the city was constructed. Only the houses and residences were different, made of wood and thatch, presumably because it was less bleak than cold stone. The people seemed, to her at least, simple and superstitious. Labourers and stonemasons for the most part, pleasant enough, but dedicated to their craft and interested in little else.

'Dominitia.' The voice belonged to Alakis, but she couldn't see him. A bull-shouldered man lurched from the shadows, hefting a large hammer. He paused, and in the brief light from a flash of the constant lightning splitting the sky, she could see the slack features and empty eyes that had so terrified her in the palace as she'd fled, plastered across the faces of the Lord Governor and his household, the guards and servants.

The slack-featured man turned and looked at her, seeing her perfectly despite the gloom. She stepped forward, trying to summon some courage.

'Let me go, Alakis,' she said as bravely as she could manage, pulling her robes closer around her. The big man's face did not change, but he shook his head in a disturbing, jerking manner.

'I can't,' Alakis said through the man-puppet. 'Not yet. Stay with me, just a little longer.'

'I won't tell anyone what you're doing, I promise. Haven't I been by your side all this time?'

The man-puppet nodded stiffly, its glazed eyes still holding her.

'You have. That's why I've spared you. Don't you see? I don't want to hurt you. Stay with me.'

Dominitia briefly considered lying to him, pretending to agree and then fleeing again, but the man-puppet's eyes were on her and she knew Alakis would see through any deception as easily as through his conduit.

'What you're doing here is wrong,' she said sadly, 'surely you know that.'

Alakis did not reply, but she sensed a slackening of the Terminheimer's shoulders, almost a weakening of his hold. A thought occurred to her, and she started to mutter the words she used to calm her mind and thus his.

'Don't do that, Dominitia!'

She ignored him, flexing her fingers as she focused her will as she had time and again to ease Alakis's affliction. The man-puppet blinked and coughed, dropping his hammer in the muck. He looked around and peered at her.

'You alright out here, lass?' he asked gruffly, rubbing at his eyes. 'I think we ought to get somewhere warm. This is no night to be out.'

She gaped at him. She felt sick. Was this why Alakis hadn't wanted her outside the palace? In case she ran into his puppets and started releasing them? Exactly what did he have planned for this place?

Dominitia turned and fled, heading through the alleyways to what seemed like a town square. An open space edged by the typical depressing forms of Terminheim's blocky stone buildings, and beyond the short, squat city walls.

'Dominitia,' said a voice to her left. Alakis's voice. She started, jumping back, as a man lurched into sight from the shadows.

'Dominitia,' said another. To the right. And another, and another. A chorus of strangers with one voice, repeating her name as they walked into the square. More emerged from the alley behind her.

She stumbled and ran; a few steps left, a few right, hysteria welling up within her. Alakis's puppet army moved closer still, repeating her name in a cold, dead whisper.

Dominitia screamed.

Chapter Two

Rigel held the thick wooden door of the tavern open for Ariene as she gingerly picked her way over the threshold, clutching the fabric of her dress so it didn't trip her. Rigel resisted the urge to shake his head or roll his eyes; this was one of Ariene's foibles that she seemed strangely unable to let go and she could be prickly about it. He looked determinedly away as she glanced at him, peering into the gloomy tavern. Of the nine or ten tables he could see, most were empty. A few young men sat around one clutching cups of ale and looking thoroughly miserable, and they barely glanced up as Rigel and Ariene passed.

'At least there's plenty of work,' said one of the boys as they passed within earshot. 'I don't think my master and I have ever been so busy.'

'For sure,' agreed one of the others, 'plenty of walls and houses to fix up now the mages are gone.'

A third snorted.

'Well, good luck finding some food to spend your wages on then, when the harvest fails.'

Rigel sighed as they sat down, adjusting his shirt, which was now a little too big for him. Ariene looked around, seemingly oblivious to the conversation they'd partly overheard.

'A charming place,' she said, just loudly enough to be heard by the plump, bustling woman heading their way in a stained apron. The woman smiled broadly, a little desperately, Rigel thought, as she reached them and began what Rigel was sure was her usual, well-rehearsed welcome.

'So good to see you, what may I—' The woman broke off and her eyes widened, before she stammered an apology and hurried away, almost knocking over a stool as she went. She vanished behind the bar into the kitchen, from whence she could then be heard near-hysterically yelling at her unseen husband that, "The Echelarch is here!"

'…You sure it's her?' came the muffled reply, followed by a loud clang and a much clearer yelp.

'Of course I'm sure! It's her! Sure as I'm a maid!'

'You ain't been a maid for—'

Another loud clang and a yelp, and a man appeared rubbing the top of his head and scowling. He was an older man, balding, and dressed in stained leather trousers and an open, equally stained shirt. He peered at Ariene through rheumy eyes and made an awkward bow. The woman appeared behind him and made a clumsy attempt at a courtesy, not helped by the fact that she was still clutching the frying pan that she had evidently been using for emphasis during her discussion with her husband.

'Your Ladyship,' said the fat woman, the expressions crossing her face now a peculiar mix of fear and excitement. 'It's not often we have such honoured guests staying with us…'

The youths at the other table had fallen silent and were watching in amazement, nudging each other and muttering words like 'Gloriana' and 'Senator'.

23

'Please,' said Ariene, holding up a hand from which, Rigel noticed, she had deftly removed her rings. When she had managed that he had no idea, but he could just see the gleam of gold and fabulous wealth hiding in the shadows of the hand she kept out of sight in her lap.

'I am no Echelarch,' Ariene said evenly. 'Merely an old senator out for an afternoon stroll, and hoping you might have some wine and maybe some—'

'Pie,' Rigel said quickly, 'ale and pie, is what we mean.'

Ariene glanced at him uncertainly and then smiled at the couple, who were still staring with their half-manic grins fixed in place.

'Ale and pie. Yes. Just what I was hoping for.'

All at once the woman came to life and clouted the husband again with the pan.

'Pie and ale! Did you not hear the Echelarch?'

The man flinched away from her and scurried away.

'I'm so sorry your Echelarchy but it's just we're not used to…' Something seemed to dawn on the woman then and she cut herself off with a gasp. 'Oh no, I'm not sure we have any pie,' she said, 'I'll have to go and check. I'm so sorry it's just that the prices are so high now and people don't come in so much and it all started back when the mages left…'

The woman seemed to be unable to stop herself now, words tumbling out as she gave her story about surging prices as crops and produce dwindled, customers staying away to save their own money and the whole horrible cycle going on and on. Ever since the mages had gone, the grim reality of how mercurial nature could be was biting everyone in Asterheim.

Rigel let his senses drift as the portly woman spoke. Little glimmering silver threads manifested across his vision, showing him the lines of the barkeeper's lifeforce as it flowed around her body. He was so accomplished at this particular use of his power now that he could do it idly, but even so it still retained a small vestige of the thrill it once had. He watched the gleaming strands pulling at the corners of her eyes, glittering around her waist. He realised that, plump though she seemed, this lady was considerably slimmer than she had been not long before. The frantic pulsing of the shining web spoke of a hunger that had not been sated for days, of a body consuming itself. He pulled back, horrified, the desperate hope on the woman's face now anything but comical.

Ariene made some kind of conciliatory comment and the woman left them alone, hurrying back to the kitchen to prepare whatever it was they would be served from the available scraps.

'She's starving,' Rigel said quietly. Ariene looked down at the table.

'The city is,' she replied. 'If we can't get a grip on this, it's going to get much worse.'

He didn't reply, struggling to master his emotions as the tragic desperation on the barkeeper's face refused to leave his mind.

'I'm making a mess of this, aren't I?' Ariene's tone was subdued.

'No,' he said automatically.

'I am. The common people think Amir and I are the new Echelarchs. We've done it again. Torn one tyrant from his throne only to utterly fail to replace him with anything better.'

Rigel didn't reply for a moment, tracing the grooves in the old, gnarled wood of the table with his fingertips.

'It wasn't a revolution you started, Ariene. You inherited this mess from Lyoris Mountebank and now you're just trying to fix it.'

'Am I? Because it feels very much like nothing's changed. The fantasy of a throne still lurks in the background and every day that

Amir and I behave like we belong on one, it becomes more real. Whatever our actual position might be; presidents or principals, kings or Echelarchs, our supporters want us where we are because they think it raises them above their opponents, and our opponents want us there until they can take it for themselves. No one is going to let us step down gracefully or return us to a republic.'

Rigel grimaced.

'And people always blame their leaders,' he said darkly, remembering the woman with the heart-shaped mark and how she'd stared at Ariene with such hatred. 'Never mind that you actually helped the mages. There would be none at all if it hadn't been for you.'

'That's what it comes down to, isn't it?' Ariene muttered. 'Mages. As soon as the mages left, it all went wrong.' She shook her head ruefully. 'For goodness' sake, we must have been better at this before. How did people cope before mages?'

'By living in caves and being eaten by wolves,' Rigel sighed. 'We haven't had to fend for ourselves for centuries.'

'The stories say they managed alright during the Purge,' Ariene said doubtfully.

'You mean the stories written by the priests before the people turned on them and asked Hilda to bring the mages back?'

Ariene didn't reply. From the kitchen, sobbing could be heard amongst the clatter of empty crockery.

'We have to fix this,' she said.

'I know.'

'That woman was right. We need the mages back.'

'I know.'

She looked at him with a pained, apologetic expression. He sighed.

'I know,' he repeated. 'I guess we're going to Ceresheim then?'

'Not we, Rigel. I'm needed here. Amir can't hold it all together alone.'

He groaned.

'Great. Just me then. I'll make the trip to a place I've never been, leaving you in a place where half the people hate you and the other half will very soon if you can't magically fix everything, and try to persuade a city prospering under a huge influx of grateful mages to hand them back?'

Ariene nodded and smiled broadly at the approaching red-faced, puffy-cheeked barkeep carrying two large cups of frothy brown ale. She plonked them heavily on the table and wiped her eyes, giving them such a shaky smile that Rigel was convinced she would burst into tears at any moment.

Ariene made no move to take the ale, and Rigel couldn't help but smile at the studied expression of polite gratitude she had automatically assumed at the sight of it. He doubted she'd had a frothy cup of tavern ale in many, many years. If at all.

'You know,' Ariene said to the woman, peering at the ale, 'that looks to be just about the best—' she groped for the word.

'Tankard,' Rigel said blandly.

'—tankard of ale,' Ariene continued, with a grateful glance at him, 'that my old eyes have ever seen.' She reached up for the woman's hand, as though to shake it, but Rigel saw the barkeep's watery eyes widen as she felt the shape of what Ariene was pressing into her palms. Ariene did not let go but held the woman's gaze.

'Be wise with this,' she said softly, 'I can't help everyone, but I'll be damned if I don't do what I can.'

The woman pulled her hands back and looked quickly at the rings with an expression so shocked it would have been comical, had it not been so tragic to behold.

'And stop hitting your husband,' Ariene added.

'Yes, my ladyship, your lordship, yes my lordyship...' the woman tried to back away, bow to them, courtesy, clutch her newly acquired lifeline and talk all at the same time. She succeeded simply in falling over the stool she'd knocked over previously, which broke the spell. She picked herself up with surprising speed and disappeared into the kitchen.

Left alone, Ariene and Rigel sipped their ale. Rigel put his down with a grimace. It wasn't the worst he'd tasted, but it wasn't far off. Ariene forced another mouthful down and replaced her tankard with a slow, deliberate movement.

'Well,' she said eventually, 'I suppose everything tastes bitter if you pay enough for it.'

He laughed.

'You know I wish I had a little book sometimes, so I could note these things down when you come out with them.'

She peered at him.

'Are you saying I'm wise?'

'Very. Esteemed even.'

She scowled.

'Cheeky wretch. Don't you have somewhere to be?'

'Ceresheim, apparently.'

'That's the one,' she reached for the ale and took another sip. 'Bring back some wine won't you, dear? If this is all the people of Asterheim have to drink, there'll be civil war within weeks.'

'Seems to be growing on you,' Rigel remarked as she drank more.

'Don't be absurd, dear. This is merely penance for my grotesque act of guilty charity.'

Rigel smiled gently.

'It's okay to be charitable sometimes, Ariene.'

She shook her head and forced more beer down.

'If one's only motivation for an act of charity is to feel better about oneself, then it is an act of selfishness.'

'Which requires penance in the form of beer?'

'In this case, yes.'

'Then I think we'd better have another round.'

Before she could protest, he signalled the barkeeper and gestured for two more, ignoring the horrified look on Ariene's face.

***

'Have you tried just talking to the Ceresheim Senate?' asked Thaniel later that night. They were sitting around the excessively grand and tastelessly opulent table that had once belonged to Lord Balderwin, Sophine's erstwhile tormenter, which was now their dinner party venue of choice. Every week, Thaniel, Rigel and Sophine would join Lady Gloriana and occasionally Amir Barten for a meal and a catch-up. Technically, it was purely a social event, but in practice a gathering of the three most powerful mages in the city and the two most influential senators was far more akin to a political council than anything resembling frivolity.

Thaniel had dressed for the occasion in a white shirt that was too big round the arms and a tight waistcoat of red satin. He liked the way the sleeves flapped, he said, and was given to gesturing excessively to demonstrate their quality in that regard.

Sophine was more circumspect, in dark trousers and jacket, with her long black hair pulled back in a ponytail. She had been picking disinterestedly at her food with a troubled expression until now, roused by Thaniel's comment, she looked up.

'Witan,' she said. Thaniel blinked at her.

'What?'

'Ceresheim has a Witan, not a Senate.'

'What's the difference?'

She stared at him.

'One's a Witan,' she said, without a trace of a smile, 'and the other's a Senate.'

'Asterheim's where the Senate sits,' Rigel added. He was still wearing his clothes from earlier but had made an effort to tame his hair, at Ariene's urging. 'Ceresheim and Terminheim have their own councils, but they're subordinate to the Senate.'

'Supposedly,' said Ariene with a wry smile. She was pulling at a bread roll, picking ever smaller bits off it without actually eating anything, Rigel had noticed. 'In practice, I think a lot of what the Senate orders is treated as advisory at best. Not that I'd know for sure, never having visited.' She cast a sidelong glance at Rigel, catching him watching her fingers. She dropped the bread.

Thaniel picked up his wine glass and took a sip.

'Even so,' he said. 'Couldn't you talk to this Witan? Ask them to send some mages over…'

Rigel sighed heavily.

'As it happens, that's the plan.'

'It is?'

'It is. I'm going to Ceresheim myself. After today, we realised we just had to do something and apparently messages from us to Ceresheim haven't been answered.'

'We can't seem to make contact at all,' added Ariene, with a look at Sophine. 'Communication is as big a problem as food. Without mages to send instant messages or ensure the crops ripen...'

Sophine met her gaze without flinching. She slowly reached for her wine glass, without breaking eye contact.

'They're unavailable, Ariene. They're too young, too vulnerable and too...'

'Innocent?' said Ariene with a raised eyebrow.

'Don't start, you two,' Thaniel put in, the note of levity in his voice ringing decidedly hollow. This was a conversation they had had many times, and it never ended well. Sophine's new recruits at the Barbican were mostly children, virtually untrained and only just beginning their journey towards becoming mages.

Sophine ignored Thaniel.

'Even if they could be taught the basics of agromancy, Ariene,' she said, 'what happens if one of them has the wrong unguarded thought or feeling just when they're connecting to the roots beneath a field of vital crops? The whole thing could be lost. It's too risky.'

'Riskier not to have any food at all,' Rigel muttered.

'That's a bit dramatic,' Sophine smiled dismissively, taking a deep swallow of wine. 'It's not like there's no food. There just isn't as much and the guilds are charging too much for what they distribute.'

'Anyway!' Thaniel said brightly, nudging Eric who was sitting next to him, largely forgotten by everyone else. Eric looked up from the book he was writing in, his dark eyes startled.

'Sorry, did you say something?'

31

'I was just going to suggest we could give Rigel something for the Citizenry office in Ceresheim, an introduction letter or something?'

'He's going to Ceresheim?' Eric looked confused.

'I'm going to ask some of the mages who settled there to come back,' Rigel said, smiling at Eric. He liked Eric; he tended to make Thaniel less annoying.

'They'll need reassurances,' said Sophine. 'They'll need to know the madness Lyoris started died with him.'

'We have records of the abandoned properties,' said Eric thoughtfully. 'We could make up some lists of as-yet unclaimed assets and you could take them with you. Perhaps the offer could be anyone who returns gets one, or free lodging at the Barbican if Sophine can arrange that, and licences from Ariene as patron of the Guild.'

Thaniel beamed proudly and gave Eric a kiss on the top of the head. Sophine rolled her eyes.

'Some kind of payment too perhaps,' added Ariene. 'I'll talk to the Senate.'

'When are you going?' asked Thaniel.

'Soon as I can, I had planned to go tomorrow but it sounds like I need a couple of things from you guys first.'

'It won't take long to get you that letter and the asset list,' said Eric. 'I'll get on it tonight.'

'Tomorrow,' said Thaniel. Eric sighed.

'Fine, tomorrow.'

'It's a good thing one of you takes this Citizenry business seriously,' said Rigel. 'I'll probably be meeting with Lord Orswell in Ceresheim, he'll want to know it's in safe hands instead of…you know…'

'Thaniel's,' said Sophine with a sly grin.

'Hey!' Thaniel protested weakly.

'Aw, you know it's true though,' said Eric, turning back to his book. Rigel tried to see what it was he was doing, but it all looked like numbers and lists to him.

Ariene was wiping her hands despite, Rigel was sure, having eaten nothing at all. He knew her well enough to know she'd be heading to bed shortly.

'Wait,' said Sophine, waving at Ariene, 'there's something I think we should discuss.'

Ariene, not used to being waved at, stared at Sophine expectantly.

'You remember the kid, Alakis?'

Rigel frowned and munched a piece of bread.

'Was he the one with the lightning, that night at the Barbican?' He remembered the boy, how he'd sat sullen and miserable after the attack, but not much after that.

Sophine nodded.

'When the boat left, he was on it. But he came back. He was…afflicted.'

'Afflicted?' Ariene reached for a wine glass, her face watchful. Rigel began to worry; if Ariene thought something serious was coming it probably was.

'He couldn't control the lightning. It was still in him. Under his skin, flashing and burning. It had taken his hair and all the colour from his skin…'

'Sacred Circle,' breathed Thaniel. 'That poor kid.'

'I was trying to find time to look at ways to help him,' said Sophine, pushing a chunk of potato around her plate, 'but I never really managed it. I've been so focused on getting the Barbican running and meeting all the people I needed to make it work…all the administrators and teachers were gone so I had to—'

'We know,' said Thaniel gently. 'You've done amazing work to get that place running, Soph.'

She nodded and looked down at her plate.

'I didn't do enough to help him. And then he left.'

'He left?' Ariene's tone was hard. Sophine did not look up.

'A few days ago. He took some of the forbidden books from Master Thomas's old study and left with them through a portal. A badly conjured portal, maybe a dangerously conjured one.'

'Dangerous how?' asked Rigel.

'Sometimes you can create pathways that go…through places you shouldn't go,' she said. 'You never know what passing through a place like that could do to you.'

'Where did he go?' asked Ariene, taking a large sip of wine.

'That I don't know. I tried to reach out to him, mind to mind, but he was blocking me. Until last night.'

Sophine reached for her glass and took a sip. She didn't look up.

'I saw a glimpse of his mind before he blocked me again, and it was…unlike him. Full of bitterness and rage. I saw an image of darkness and death. That friend of his, Dominitia? I think she's in terrible danger just being near him. Wherever he's gone, he's dangerous and angry, and has access to those books with all their forbidden knowledge. He could kill himself or worse.'

'Much worse,' said Rigel. 'We have to find him.'

Sophine shook her head. 'I'll find him,' she said. 'You have your job in Ceresheim. Ariene has hers with the Senate and making sure this city doesn't implode. And Thaniel needs to sit around looking pretty.'

'Only thing he's good for,' added Eric, scratching away with his pen. Thaniel leaned over and whispered something in his ear that made him giggle.

'Ugh,' said Sophine, rolling her eyes again.

There was a knock at the door, and one of the former Balderwin servants poked her head in.

'Lady Ariene? A messenger just came from the Senate. There's been an urgent petition from the Messengers' Guild and Lord Barten has called a dawn session to hear it.'

'Thank you, dear,' said Ariene, rising smartly to her feet. 'Goodnight, everyone. And if I don't see you before you leave, Rigel, good luck in Ceresheim. Bring us some mages.'

Rigel offered a shaky smile.

'No problem,' he said, suddenly feeling very sick.

Chapter Three

Ariene arrived at the Senate as the sun was starting to come up. Her eyes were itchy and raw from lack of sleep, despite having managed about four hours. She wondered, not for the first time, if she should ask Rigel to just make her a young woman and be done with it. She'd always thought excessive vanity a weakness of character, but the young had advantages beyond appearance that could not be denied. Not that they knew it until those advantages had faded into memory and they woke up one morning aged forty, with a stiff back and clicking joints.

The Senate was quiet today. Not everyone, it appeared, had decided Lord Barten's dawn session was worth getting up for. A few of her friends and colleagues sat yawning in their chairs, giving her a weak smile as she passed by to the dais in the centre.

'Not many in today,' she remarked to Amir with a smile as she reached her own chair. He grimaced and rubbed at his bald head. He was wearing a well-fitting dark tunic, and she noted that some of the buttons were in the wrong holes. Stress radiated off him in waves.

'Some made it,' he said darkly, nodding in the direction of a cluster of senators sitting together on the right-hand side and staring grimly at the joint caretakers on the dais. There were at least fifteen of them, and Ariene groaned at the sight.

'Oh come on,' she sighed, 'yesterday it was taxes, and today it's messages. Nothing is banal enough for them to just stay at home, is it?'

'Seems not,' said Amir, making to sit down but then standing again with a wince. His injury from last year was still painful sometimes, despite Rigel's best efforts to heal it. Either the fact that the wound had been sustained in the dead-zone of Stonegate castle or from a blade held by the mage-priest Kahin kept it from responding fully to the mage's power. Amir had almost weekly sessions with Rigel to keep it from opening up again. It disturbed Ariene a little how much they had grown to rely on the nervous boy she'd met on the bridge not so long ago, but it wouldn't be forever. Soon they'd be able to retire from this stressful life and—

'I call the meeting to order,' said Amir, his voice carrying easily across the relatively empty chamber. 'We have an emergency petition to hear from the Messengers.' He gestured at a young woman sitting in the front row of chairs, alone. She was wearing riding clothes, a leather jerkin and trousers. Her long red hair was pulled back with a leather band from a pale face, and she gripped a piece of paper with shaking hands as though it could fly away at any moment.

Ariene frowned. The girl looked thoroughly terrified.

'My…my lords,' the Messenger stammered as she got to her feet and turned to face the senators. 'I bring official word from the Guild that…that…'

'It's alright, dear,' said Ariene from behind her. The girl looked over her shoulder with wide, frightened eyes. 'Why don't you turn around and talk to me?' said Ariene warmly. 'Never mind this rabble.' She waved a hand airily in the direction of the rest of the chamber and grinned.

The girl sniffed and smiled, turning her back on the gathered senators and looking once again at her paper.

'Be sure to speak up though,' said Ariene. 'Pretend I'm profoundly deaf. It's fun, I used to do it a lot.'

'She certainly did,' growled Amir, with a broad smile.

That made the girl laugh a little, and she started again.

'The Messengers have decided that they will no longer be carrying messages of any kind by road between Asterheim and Terminheim. Any messages for Terminheim will be—'

'What?' called a senator from the cluster of people forming the anti-Ariene brigade. 'We can't hear you over here.'

'Then come closer, my lords,' Ariene called back. 'There's hardly anyone here today so there's no need to sit so far back.'

There was a general muttering and grumbling from the assembled lords of Asterheim as they pushed their chairs back and made their way closer. The girl stood and waited, still not turning around, still clutching her paper.

'Now then,' said Ariene with a calmness she did not feel, 'what's all this about Terminheim?'

'Why are we discussing Terminheim?' blustered a fat senator in red, sitting amongst the opposition party.

'Because the Messengers no longer want to go there, Jarethin,' said Amir.

'Ha! I don't blame them,' said the fat Lord Jarethin, 'there's nothing there except rocks and ice and beards. Savage place.'

'A vital partner,' said Ariene evenly. 'Does Asterheim have any Stonemasons anymore? No. Our quarries are dilapidated ruins since our people collectively decided such things were beneath them. We import all our stone from Terminheim like we import all our grain from Ceresheim. We can't live without either. Not to mention—'

The fat senator waved a pudgy hand and looked away. 'This discussion is beneath me,' he remarked.

'Then I pity it,' said Ariene lightly. There were some chuckles from the senators on the other side of the room. Jarethin went the colour of his outfit. The man next to him, a strikingly handsome man with a trimmed dark beard and bright eyes, smiled suddenly. Ariene immediately wished she was twenty years younger.

'That's it,' she muttered, 'I'm having Rigel finish what he started.'

'Hm?' said Amir, glancing at her and then at who she was looking at as the laughter subsided. 'Not Creswell, Ariene, come on.' He shook his head.

She ignored him, turning her attention to the Messenger girl.

'My dear, why don't you tell us why your Guild is against Terminheim all of a sudden?'

The girl raised her head and looked right at Ariene. Something in her eyes chilled Ariene's blood.

'It's a place of ghosts and death,' she said in a dark, fearful voice, 'you needn't even take my word for it. Stand on the eastern walls on a clear night and you can see the flashes in the sky.'

The elderly Lord Aresbrook made a choking coughing sound and inched himself forward in his chair, which had been especially fitted with wheels.

'My lady, may I speak?' he asked in a wheezing voice. Ariene glanced at her old friend and sighed.

'Lord Aresbrook, you know you don't need my permission. I am not the Echelarch.'

'Well, constitutionally,' began the old man, who had been patron of the Lawyers for longer than anyone could remember. Ariene waved her hands at him frantically.

'Alright, alright, we don't need to get into it,' she said. 'Just…speak.'

'As you command,' he said with a mischievous smile. 'Dear girl, are you telling us that the Messengers have lost their courage over a lightning storm?'

The Messenger turned around and looked at the elderly senator.

'This is no ordinary storm, sir. It's a storm that surrounds the city and has not passed in days. The roads on the approach to Terminheim are impassable. Some are flooded, others blasted by lightning or caught in an endless gale that knocks men from their horses. It is no longer possible to reach Terminheim at all, and even if someone could find a way through, no one would go.'

'And why is that?'

The girl straightened and held his gaze.

'Would you?'

Silence greeted this challenge. Aresbrook looked puzzled, then nodded slowly and wheeled himself back.

The fat Lord Jarethin arose, with some difficulty, from his seat. The handsome young Lord Creswell was obliged to discreetly change seats in order to give him more room.

'The Senate should not accept this outrageous dereliction of duty from one of its most vital Guilds,' he pronounced bombastically. 'Based on nothing more than superstition and fear of getting wet from the sounds of it. As the Lady Ariene pointed out earlier, Terminheim is an important trade partner and communications must be kept open.'

'That's absurd,' said Barten, giving up once more on lowering himself into his seat. 'If they cannot reach the city then it would be better for them not to waste any further time or resources trying.'

'Mages?' asked someone from Ariene's supporters. 'Could some of the new mages not—'

'There are no new mages,' said Ariene, more harshly than she'd intended. 'Those youngsters at the Barbican are too young and not properly trained.'

'Perhaps,' said Lord Creswell smoothly, rising to his feet and looking slyly at Ariene, 'one of our few *remaining* mages could go to Ceresheim and bring some back? Then we could keep some lines of communication open through them.'

Ariene decided he wasn't actually all that handsome after all.

'As it happens, I have tasked my mage with that very burden, my lord,' she said. 'He will be leaving today and I hope he succeeds. In the meantime, I trust the Senate will approve my suggestion of a substantial payment for any who do return.'

Lord Creswell smiled broadly and bowed, sinking back into his chair and crossing one well-formed leg over the other. Ariene deliberately looked away from him.

'That expense, which the city cannot afford in these difficult times, would not be necessary if you hadn't let them all sail away...' began the fat Senator Jarethin. And so the debate slowly sank into the usual angry exchanges and surly imprecations as those opposed to Ariene and Amir continued their campaign to suffocate any meaningful action in the Senate.

Ariene sat on her chair and sighed.

It was going to be another long day.

***

'Wouldn't it be easier to just open a portal?' said Thaniel, jerking his head away as the horse flicked its tail at him. Rigel stopped struggling with the saddle strap and looked at him for a moment.

'To Ceresheim?'

'Sure,' Thaniel shrugged.

'Who do you think I am? Hilda? I've never even been to Ceresheim. I only have a vague idea of where it is.'

'South?' said Thaniel, lifting a saddle bag.

'Yeah, south. Like the sea. And mountains and bandit camps. Sharks. Holes in the ground.' He took the bag and hesitated, looking at the strap.

'You need to tighten that,' said Thaniel.

Rigel looked at him darkly.

'That supposed to be helpful?'

'Well, not *unhelpful.*'

'Then,' grunted Rigel, as he pulled the strap, 'I've got...' He jerked it again. 'News for you...'

The stable was empty, besides them and the large brown horse who seemed decidedly unimpressed by the two of them and their bumbling attempts to saddle him. A thick smell of hay and manure hung heavily in the air, and Rigel was secretly amused at how carefully Thaniel was trying to move around to avoid getting anything unpleasant on his boots. They'd spent the morning getting the provisions together, after collecting Eric's list of properties and Ariene's promise of Senate support, and now they were at the city walls near Fishers Road.

'It's going to be strange, you not being here,' said Thaniel heavily, as he handed one of the last bags over. 'Don't be too long, okay? I don't think I can handle Ariene *and* Sophine all by myself.'

Rigel snorted as he tied the last of the satchels to the strap. He gave the horse a quick look, worried that it was being overburdened, but if the horse even noticed the weight on his back yet he gave no sign. The destrier chomped away at some hay as if the two boys weren't even there.

'You sure you need a horse that size?' Thaniel asked, peering at the animal with something between fear and awe.

Ariene's household had many stables around the city, this one included, and the disturbingly young stableboy had insisted they take Roan because he was "the best". And he certainly was the biggest. A huge, muscular brown horse clearly bred for war but who seemed, here at least, not to have the irritable restless demeanour of most destriers.

'He's probably got—'

Whatever Thaniel was going to say was lost as the shadows on either side of them erupted with incoherent screams and the unmistakable shriek of steel being pulled from scabbards.

Rigel barely had time to turn his head before the first man was on him, grabbing at his shoulder with one rough hand, the other raising a gleaming blade. Rigel's thoughts were a jumble, with nothing but the dull realisation he was about to die penetrating his shocked mind.

The horse, however, did not hesitate. With one terrifyingly fast movement, its long head snapped to the side and its mouth opened. Its blunt teeth closed on either side of the assassin's face with tremendous force, tearing skin and fracturing bone. Roan jerked his head back, taking most of the shrieking man's face with it.

43

Rigel's assailant fell back, clutching at the ruins of his face and making the most hideous keening wail Rigel had ever heard. He looked around as another figure in black was thrown high into the air to crash against one of the thick timbers supporting the stable roof. He fell to the ground with an unpleasant crunch and did not move.

'I got the other one, too,' Thaniel said calmly, pointing beyond Rigel into the shadowy recesses of the stable. He flexed his fingers, looking altogether too pleased with himself.

Rigel nodded shakily and took another slow step back from the horse, who was now once more chewing on his hay without a care in the world. Roan regarded him with wide, innocent horse-eyes and flicked his tail nonchalantly. Somewhere on the other side of the horse, a man with half a face was wailing and sobbing, staggering around blindly and calling for his mother. The horse blinked slowly and chewed his hay. One foot idly pawed at the ground where something red and wet was splattered.

'That,' said Rigel, not daring to take his eyes from the animal, 'is one dangerous horse.'

'Only if you're a bad guy,' said Thaniel brightly, standing horribly close to the murderous beast and slapping it genially on the neck. Rigel felt sick.

'Than…should you be that close to—'

'Roan. His name's Roan.' Thaniel rubbed the horse's massive head affectionately, seeming not to notice the blood on his fur. 'And you'd better show him you're grateful for him saving your life, or he might get offended.'

Thaniel moved away as Rigel came towards the horse and gingerly stroked his neck.

'Thanks, Roan,' he whispered shakily, 'thanks, boy. That guy nearly had me.'

The horse made an indignant whinnying sound.

'I mean it,' said Rigel, realising he actually did. 'I really am grateful. I've just never seen a horse do...that.'

Roan shook his head so his ears flapped. Rigel laughed, for a moment forgetting that a man with horse teeth-marks in the scant remains of his face was lurching around screaming just a few feet away.

Patting the horse one last time, Rigel headed around to where Thaniel was clumsily trying to heal the assassin's face, giving the horse's teeth a wide berth as he did so.

'Move over,' he said, giving Thaniel a shove. His friend straightened up and made an "all yours" gesture shortly followed by another, less friendly, gesture. Rigel barely had to concentrate anymore to see the silvery threads and lines that indicated another human's life energy, so it took less than a few seconds to see the sobbing man's gleaming but violently broken network of forlornly flailing threads and start to tie them together. The man's cries became sobs, became whimpers, and finally faded to nothing as he slipped into unconsciousness. Thaniel returned to stand by his side.

'He's never going to be pretty is he,' his friend remarked. Rigel shook his head.

The man's face was no longer a bleeding ruin, but it was a hideous mass of scars and thin skin over deformed bone. The bite had taken huge chunks of flesh that the body could not simply 'heal'. He would live, but he was forever changed.

'One of his eyes is missing,' said Rigel. 'I didn't realise that. Maybe if we could find it, we could put it back...' he turned to look over at the red mass by the horse's foot. Roan was watching him, chewing his hay. Rigel had only managed to take a single step when the horse, without breaking eye contact, lifted up a hoof and brought it firmly down on the remains of the man's face. Roan snorted and looked away.

Rigel stared, open-mouthed.

'That's not possible,' he breathed.

'What?' said Thaniel, still staring in fascination at the sleeping man's face. 'Did you get the eye?'

'I...I don't think the horse wants us to get the eye.'

Thaniel looked at him.

'You feeling okay?'

Rigel thought for a moment.

'No. No I'm not.'

Thaniel smiled and clapped him on the shoulder.

'Let's get a drink then, before you go. We literally just nearly died and I'm pretty sure I killed those other two guys. It's been a tough morning.'

Rigel fought and won a brief battle against a rising feeling of hysteria.

'It has, hasn't it?'

As they turned to leave, Rigel spotted something on the floor, frighteningly close to the bloodthirsty horse's hoof.

'Hey, Roan?' he said, knowing he sounded crazy and not caring. His mind was full of chomping teeth and bits of face. 'There's something there by your foot that I think might mean something. I just want to get it, okay?'

Roan gave no sign he'd understood, merely watched Rigel with those big brown innocent eyes as he crept closer and bent down, down, past those big teeth to the floor. He plucked up the little leather pouch and opened it, ignoring the smell coming off it.

'Nice,' said Thaniel, peering at the coins in the pouch. 'Drinks on them, then.' He reached in and fished out a small piece of folded paper.

'Just numbers,' he said, giving it a glance. 'Probably a receipt for payment.'

Rigel's heart sank a little.

'Nothing else on it? No signature?'

'No. Oh wait…a little shield with someone's arms on it, but it's very badly drawn.'

'Guild insignia, maybe,' said Rigel. It wasn't much to go on but it was something.

'I'll take a look later,' replied Thaniel. 'When you're well on your way. For now, free drinks!'

'Free drinks,' Rigel said with a half-smile. 'And a lifetime of horrific nightmares!'

Thaniel laughed.

'Only you could make free drinks a bad thing, Rige.'

***

Thaniel marched into the reading room in the Citizenry Guild and stomped around, kicking off his boots and muttering to himself. He dropped his travelling cloak on the back of a chair and then paused, feeling eyes on his back. He looked around. Eric was watching him with a raised eyebrow from across a large desk. A dusty book was open in front of him.

'Eventful morning?' asked Eric simply.

'Very!' Thaniel said, pulling back a chair and flopping into it. 'Nearly got murdered by three men in the stables!'

Eric frowned.

'Why would anyone want to murder you?'

Thaniel blinked, then laughed.

'You don't think I'm worth murdering?'

Eric looked back at his book with a smile.

'Well, you're loud,' he said, dipping his pen in an inkwell, 'you leave clothes everywhere and have far too many shoes…which you also leave everywhere.' He tapped the pen to get the excess ink off. 'But I wouldn't say that makes you worth murdering.'

Thaniel glanced at the cloak on the back of the chair.

'Everyone does that,' he muttered, looking surreptitiously around to find his shoes. One was by the window. The other was not.

'They really don't,' said Eric, scratching something in a margin. 'You know, I think people are actually leaving the city more than they are entering it. We've had so many requests for references from guild offices in the outlying towns and way fewer citizenship applications this year. I think the younger people are just leaving.'

Thaniel shrugged.

'Things are bad,' he said. 'Life's probably better outside the city.'

'Very bad news for us,' said Eric. 'We need to talk to Ariene. The Senate needs to get its act together or things will get worse.'

'I'll mention it when I see her,' said Thaniel. 'I need to tell her about this morning anyway.'

Eric didn't reply, scratching away at his book.

'About being nearly murdered,' Thaniel added, peevishly. 'I need to tell her about that. Remember how I said I was nearly murdered?'

Eric gave him a smile.

'But you didn't, did you?'

'What?'

'Get murdered.'

'Well, no.'

'Great,' said Eric absently, peering across the table at something. 'That's great. Can you pass me that list of exit visa applications?'

Thaniel sighed and made to pick up the piece of paper when the door opened and a strongly built middle-aged man with one milky eye walked in, followed by a thin boy with wide eyes and bits of what had to be pastry in his hair. The man clanked when he walked, encased as he was in what appeared to be an antique set of dull steel armour.

'My lords,' said Sir Rivan Dirkling gruffly. He always said everything gruffly.

'We're not lords, Sir Rivan,' Eric said warmly, rising to his feet and clasping the older man's hand, 'as we tell you every time.'

'And as I tell you every time,' the man replied, 'yes, you are.' He turned away, as though the matter were settled, and practically shoved the thin boy into the room. 'This is Tyler,' the gruff man continued, 'he's very pleased to meet you.'

Rivan looked at the boy with an expectant stare. The young man looked from the knight to Eric, to Thaniel and back, before finally finding his voice.

'I am,' he said, nodding his head. 'Very.'

Eric moved past the knight to offer the boy his hand.

'Tyler, was it?'

'Yes, lord.'

'It's just Eric, Tyler. Lord Orswell is the lord of this place.'

'If you say so, lord.'

Eric sighed and looked accusingly at Dirkling.

'He's one of Molly's,' Dirkling growled, ignoring the accusation, 'she always was one of the best.'

'We'll take your word on that, Rivan,' said Thaniel with a smile.

The big knight snorted a sound that could have been a laugh. A gruff one.

'You don't know what you're missing, boys, believe me.'

'I do.' Eric shrugged. Rivan cocked an eyebrow at him, and Thaniel almost fell off his chair.

'Well, I had to be sure, didn't I?' he said simply.

'Didn't visit Molly though, did you,' Rivan muttered, a little defensively.

'It wouldn't have been Molly,' said Tyler brightly, as though happy to have something to add. 'Andine was the one with the rich clients. Lords. Well, one Lord anyway. Called her the goddess of love.'

Thaniel snorted.

'Why?'

'She has this mark on her face, looks like a heart,' said the boy. 'She's very pretty.'

A heart. Thaniel paused. Where had he heard of a heart-marked face before?

'This Andine, Tyler. Which Lord did you say was her client?'

'I don't know lord; I never caught his name.'

'What did he look like?' asked Sir Dirkling in his low, gravelly voice.

'Gorgeous,' said Tyler with shy laugh, pushing his hair behind his ears. Pastry flecks fell to the ground. 'Slim, young, trimmed dark beard. Nice hair. Long legs.'

That didn't sound like any lord Thaniel knew, but then the Senate was very much not his arena.

'Thank you, Tyler. Sir Dirkling, please take him to the offices on the second floor and they can get him his accommodation sorted. We'll find a job for you tomorrow, Tyler, okay?'

The boy smiled gratefully as the big knight steered him out of the room.

'Why the interest in this handsome lord, Thaniel?' asked Eric blandly.

'I'm not sure yet,' said Thaniel slowly, rising to his feet. 'Just a feeling that something isn't quite right.' He fished the little piece of paper out of his pocket and stared at the badly drawn sigil on the note.

'I'm going to the Senate.'

***

Ariene was sitting in one of the lower tier chairs in the now empty Senate building when he found her. Thaniel approached her cautiously. She may not be a horse, but she could bite just as painfully.

'Ariene?' he asked gently.

'Hello, Thaniel,' she sighed, not looking round.

He sat down in one of the chairs a row or two behind her and put his feet up on the back of the chair in front.

'Rigel leave in the end?' she asked, finally glancing his way. She made a tutting sound at the sight of his feet, at which he grinned.

'He did. Eventually,' Thaniel said with a grimace.

Ariene frowned. He spoke before she could ask him anything; he wanted to get this straight in his head before all hell broke loose.

'Can I ask you something, my lady?'

Her eyes narrowed.

51

'Are there any lords in the Senate who you would describe as gorgeous? Young, slim with dark hair and a trimmed beard. Long, shapely legs?'

Ariene laughed.

'I think you should stick with Eric, personally. He's much more your type.'

Thaniel smiled.

'What do you mean?'

'He lets you be you, and you're a handful. No senator would.' She rose to her feet in a rustle of Senate gown silks. He moved to meet her as she made her way to the stairs that led out of the building and took her arm in his.

'The secret of lasting love,' she said, 'is letting the other person be who they are, whether that's who you would *prefer* them to be or not. Politicians want to shape the world, including their spouses and lovers. Which is why none of us are ever happily married for long. Divorce, misery or murder, that's the usual fate of a politician's love life. Often all three.'

Thaniel chuckled politely, knowing full well that Ariene had in fact been happily married for many years before her children had died, shortly followed by her husband.

'I'll have to tell Rigel to add that one to his book,' he said. 'But, Ariene, did that description match anyone here?'

She stopped and looked at him.

'You were being serious, then?'

He nodded.

'I'm sorry, dear, I assumed you'd come to cheer me up and it was all empty banter.'

He smiled thinly.

'I guess it often is with me.'

She held his gaze.

'I'm sorry, Thaniel. I haven't forgotten who destroyed the poison beneath the Senate and saved us all from Lyoris.'

Thaniel looked down, remembering Sophine's remarks at dinner the night before and how Eric had agreed.

'I think some people have,' he said.

'The description actually matches Lord Creswell, Thaniel. The patron I think of the Fishers, if memory serves. Why did you ask?'

'Creswell,' Thaniel mused. 'Apparently, he makes use of the services provided by a young woman named Andine. A woman with a heart-shaped mark on her face.'

Ariene's gaze sharpened.

'The one who accosted Rigel and me, who riled up that crowd. So she wasn't a mother at all.'

'Probably not.'

'It was a performance then, likely orchestrated by Creswell. But why?'

'I think I know,' he said bitterly, fishing the paper out of his pocket. 'Whose sigil is this, Ariene?'

She peered at it.

'I couldn't be sure, but it looks like three wavy lines and a blob that could be a fish. And if it was, then it would be Lord Creswell's sigil.' She looked at him, her eyes like flints. 'Where did you get this, Thaniel? What are you not telling me?'

Thaniel sighed and ground his teeth, levitating the offensive piece of paper up into the air. He held it there for a moment as he gathered his thoughts, before ripping it into hundreds of tiny pieces with a jerk of his mind.

'Rigel and I were attacked today, just before he was due to leave. In the stables. Three men followed us and tried to kill us. I found this on one of them.'

Ariene nodded slowly, barely reacting at all to the news that they'd almost been killed. Thaniel shuddered at the steel in her soul; just what was friendship worth with a person so dreadfully pragmatic?

'Creswell actually asked me to send Rigel to Ceresheim today,' she said. 'First the ploy with the girl to plant the seed, then raising it in the Senate. He wanted Rigel to leave.'

'Wanted him *isolated*,' growled Thaniel. 'Vulnerable. They weren't after me, then.'

'No. But they probably ran out of time waiting for him to be alone. I stupidly told them he was leaving today, so they knew he'd get away if they didn't attack when they did right there in the stable. You saved his life, Thaniel, just by being there.'

'The horse saved his life,' Thaniel muttered.

'What?'

'Never mind. I think it's time I had a little talk with this Creswell.'

'No, let's take some time to think—'

'I'm done thinking,' said Thaniel, cutting across her and bounding up the stairs. 'No one attacks my friends like that and gets away with it.'

'Thaniel, stop!'

'Contact Sophine,' he called over his shoulder, 'she needs to know what's going on.'

He ran up and out of the Senate, his hatred and anger at this Creswell person boiling inside him. He reached the stairs and was about to leap down them when he hesitated. He turned around with a sigh.

'Ariene,' he shouted, 'where does Creswell live?'

Chapter Four

Sophine was a master of the darker magic available to a powerful mage; portals, illusion and peeling people like oranges. Rigel had a knack for slowing time and healing, not to mention handling Lady Gloriana, which was a powerful ability in itself. Thaniel did not excel in those areas.

Thaniel excelled in telekinesis and pyromancy.

The huge wrought iron gates of the Creswell estate exploded off their hinges and flew high into the air, crushing an ornamental fountain as they fell heavily back to earth. Fire sputtered and sparked across his fingers, unbidden and unconjured but manifesting purely in response to his foul mood. Up ahead, courtiers in purple livery ran for the safety of a moderately-sized mansion and Battlemasons assigned to Lord Creswell charged, with pikes held at their waists.

Thaniel snarled his contempt and knocked the soldiers back with a careless flick of his right hand. Pikes flew from hands. Soldiers stumbled; some fell. Most understood their limitations and fled. Two did not. He let them get close enough to see his face and then unleashed a jet of flame that billowed in a roaring wave from his outstretched fingers. They turned and ran before the curtain of fire reached them and Thaniel let them go; his fight was not with soldiers.

He stalked angrily around the fountain, a flicker of guilt crossing his mind at the destruction. Up ahead the great double doors of the mansion stood closed, and he briefly considered smashing them too but restrained himself. He knew nothing about Lord Creswell, whether he had a wife or a family. He didn't want to terrify any children, only their father.

With an act of will, he calmed the flickering flames dancing around his fingers and breathed in deeply. Then he knocked on the door, not knowing what else to do.

Before long there was the sound of a heavy iron bolt being drawn back, and the door opened a crack. An old man peered out with wide, frightened eyes.

'I'm here to see Lord Creswell,' said Thaniel pleasantly. 'Please tell him that if he doesn't present himself here, I shall be inserting the blunt end of one of those pikes'—he turned and pointed to the pile of abandoned weaponry behind him—'into his murdering backside before sundown.'

The old man stared at him with wide eyes, his mouth working soundlessly as he tried to process an appropriate response. Thaniel looked pointedly at the evening sky and the lengthening shadows.

'He doesn't have long,' he remarked. 'Better deliver your message or your lord won't be sitting down for a very long time.'

The old man vanished behind the heavy door. Thaniel heard him fumbling with the bolt before abandoning it.

Thaniel stood back and looked at the mansion. Not as opulent as Lady Gloriana's sprawling manse, but obviously the home of a rich and important person. Probably one looking to become richer and more important, because of course that was the whole point of being rich and important, wasn't it?

The door opened and a very attractive man stepped out, looking very pale and indignant. He was wearing a loose-fitting shirt and dark trousers, with no boots. His eyes were blue and his short hair black, a trim beard around his chin. Thaniel tried to look menacing but had to fight an urge to smooth his hair down and smile.

'You're Creswell?'

'I am,' said the man haughtily, pulling at his shirt sleeves and trying to look regal.

'I'm Thaniel. I'm the mage who destroyed the Senate. Rigel's friend. You remember Rigel? You tried to murder him today.'

The man did not flinch.

'Funny,' he said flatly. 'I don't recall trying to murder anyone *today*. Is it Friday already? Where does a week go?'

Thaniel let flame flicker around his hands for a moment.

'Don't play with me,' he growled. 'I know it was you.'

'Prove it,' the man snapped.

Thaniel's hand swept up before he was conscious of moving it. The startled lord rose into the air with a choked cry and hovered, clutching at his neck a few feet above the ground. Thaniel could feel his teeth grinding together and tried to relax, but did not release Creswell.

'I don't have to prove anything, dimwit,' he snarled. 'I know it was you and I'm not here on anyone's business but my own. So let me be very clear.' He paused, watching the man's feet kicking wildly as his face turned purple and his eyes bulged. Creswell's hands clutched at the empty air around his neck, ripping nasty-looking tears in his own skin as he tried in vain to release the telekinetic stranglehold.

Thaniel let him drop. Creswell collapsed in a heap, heaving and spluttering and coughing on the ground.

'Let me be clear,' he repeated in a voice of deathly calm. 'Keep your thugs away from Rigel. In fact, just keep them at home. If I decide you're up to something, I'll be back.'

The gasping lord did not reply, still coughing and hacking on the ground. Thaniel turned and stalked away, giving the cracked stone of the fountain one last glance.

'Such a shame,' he muttered.

***

The road to Ceresheim had so far been cold, hard and extremely brutal on the backside. The massive destrier was no dainty palfrey, picking its way over the ground with a nice smooth gait. Instead, Roan strode like a titan, as though continually surprised and annoyed that the earth did not simply smooth itself out beneath his hooves. In his saddle, Rigel was constantly rocked and knocked about, but he dared not say anything. He was still convinced the horse could understand him; if not word for word, then certainly his demeanour, and he had not forgotten the faceless man and his hideous screeching.

By the end of the second day, Rigel had decided that sleeping rolled up under a hedge simply wouldn't do, and he'd found an inn to spend the night. Roan had seemed unimpressed by the stable, and had fixed Rigel with a flat, unfriendly stare when he gave the pale-faced stable boy a warning about the destrier's temper. Now he was in the main hall, eating a thin broth and drinking a thin ale, propped up on a stool by himself in one corner of the large room.

All around the smoke-choked inn sat travellers of various kinds, sitting alone or in small groups, muttering or playing dice games. A huge fire burned in the chimney hearth at one end, and the whole place was lit by the shadowy orange flames hungrily devouring four massive crackling logs.

The man behind the bar was rubbing a filthy rag over a well-used tankard, peering at it critically as he made small talk with the patrons.

'How about you, friend?' he asked, sparing Rigel a quick glance. Rigel looked up from his broth.

'Sorry?'

'Where are you from?'

'Oh, Asterheim,' he said, taking a sip of ale.

The barman looked at him more closely as the people closest to him went quiet and someone a little further off started making whooping, laughing noises. Rigel blinked and looked around.

'Asterheim, you say,' said the barman with a smile and a shake of the head. 'Well, you might want to keep that to yourself around here.'

'I…can see that,' Rigel said with a smile, glancing at the people looking at him. They turned away and went back to their muttering, but he could feel eyes on him nonetheless.

'The capital's not really popular out here,' said a woman, plopping herself down onto the stool next to him and planting an empty flagon on the bar. 'Another, please?' she slid a coin across the gnarled wood towards the barman, who barely looked at it as he reached for the flagon and turned away.

'I'm Sindel,' she said. She was about his age, with a huge mass of curly brown hair which hung past her shoulders, but she was much bigger than him. Where Rigel was slender and in his opinion, shapeless, she was curvaceous. She had a round, rosy-cheeked face which reminded him of a hedgehog when she smiled, and when she crossed one leg over the other on her stool, he found it hard to look away from the curve of her ample...

'Rigel,' he stammered, looking back at his ale and trying to remember how to speak.

'So where are you going, Rigel from Asterheim? I'm on my way to Ceresheim, as it happens. I have an appointment with a Thane.'

'A what?'

She laughed, a cascade of mischievous mirth that made him smile.

'A Thane. One of the four Grainlords? The people who rule the four Thane-holds...am I making any sense?'

'Probably,' Rigel smiled, 'I just don't know anything about Ceresheim.'

'So where *are* you going?'

Rigel looked at his drink.

'Ceresheim.'

Sindel paused and stared at him.

'You're going to Ceresheim and have no idea about the Thanes or the Thane-holds?'

He offered a weak shrug. She raised an eyebrow, then flung her hair back behind her head with a flourish that made her cleavage bounce. Rigel looked away, feeling fire in his cheeks.

'Staying here tonight?' she asked, taking the flagon of ale the barman had returned with. Rigel nodded.

'Good. Me too. So...'

Sindel proceeded to explain the layout of the country he was riding into, which he hadn't even thought to open a book about before he left. Feeling like a moron, he listened as best he could.

Ceresheim was evidently divided into four rough mini-kingdoms each ruled by a Thane, colloquially known as the Grainlords, although of course Ceresheim grew all kinds of agricultural produce besides grain. Until recently, these Thanes had maintained their wealth and status by reminding people periodically of the delicate and unpredictable nature of agriculture. Burned or raided crops meant higher prices, which coincidentally made the Thanes richer, so it was in everyone's interest to pay up to ensure the Thanes' *protection* of those crops.

'Pay now,' said Sindel, with a "what can you do" shrug, 'or pay more later.'

There had always been a saying in these parts that there were no raiders in Ceresheim.

'Only Thanes,' said Sindel with a wry smile.

And so the Thanes had maintained their own warriors, ostensibly to protect the fields and silos, but also to project their power and wealth – and also to raid the stores and fields of other Thanes, as the endless internecine squabbling continued its dance. In the centre of the country stood the walled city of Ceresheim itself, a relatively small place since most of the population lived outside working the fields and living under the Thane of their district. Within the walled city was the administrative government and the guild offices, some churches for the Sacred Circle and the Speaking Hall, where the Thanes would meet as equals and address the Witan, which was the body of common people who supposedly made the laws governing the realm under the supervision of the Moderator who lived in the palace nearby.

'He was nobody,' said Sindel, gulping down half her flagon without blinking. 'Just a figurehead really, lord of the common folk with no power to oppose the Thanes. Until the Mages came.'

When the massive galleon containing almost the entire Mage population of Asterheim had turned up off the coast of Ceresheim, things had changed. Given employment by the Moderator and housed in the Mage Guild within the city walls, the mages had set to work fireproofing crops and increasing yield by a ridiculous factor. Ceresheim had always had mages, of course, but never in such great numbers.

'So what happened?' asked Rigel, enjoying the tale as much as the speaker.

'The Thanes got weaker,' she shrugged. 'So many crops that the prices fell through the floor and no amount of phantom raiders could stop them. The Moderator and his people in the city got richer, because Ceresheim was exporting so much to Asterheim. And now the balance of power is all wrong. People like me are out of work.'

'Like you?'

'I was a soldier, a Prefect in the Grain Guard for Thane Cuthbert. But who needs Grain Guard when a mage can make the crops indestructible? Now, I'm freelance.'

Rigel frowned.

'Freelance?'

'I take contracts, assassination or investigation. Whatever I can get. Sometimes I talk to a man, get his guard down. Then my partner cuts his throat.'

Rigel gulped and leaned back a little.

'You...do?'

Sindel laughed uproariously, her hair shaking like autumnal leaves in a stiff wind.

'Well, no. But I do take contracts. Work is hard now, which is why I'm going back to see Cuthbert. We deserve better, and he has enough left to make it easier for us.'

He signalled the barman for more ale and tried to look nonchalant.

'Why did everyone react like they did when I said I was from Asterheim? Isn't Ceresheim getting rich off the capital now it can't grow its own crops?'

She stood up from her stool and stretched. Rigel once more averted his gaze. She laughed.

'Because, silly, the Moderator has been sending word to the capital for months asking for help. A few Battlemasons around here would stop the Thanes bullying people with their disgruntled soldiers and disaffected thugs. There are some who think the Thanes are actually planning to set themselves up as kings, take over completely. But there's been no reply; Asterheim isn't helping.'

'That's strange,' he said, frowning at his drink, 'we haven't received anything...'

She paused, studying him.

'And you would know, would you? Just who are you, Rigel from Asterheim?'

He looked at her, this time in the eyes.

'I'm one of the mages who brought down Lyoris Mountebank, destroyed the Senate and saved the city. I've been assisting Lady Gloriana to hold everything together since. And I'm bringing a petition from her to Ceresheim, asking the mages to return.'

Sindel blinked at him, open-mouthed, for a moment. Then she nodded slowly.

'Well then, perhaps we ought to ride together tomorrow. The roads can be dangerous for important people.'

He smiled.

'You'd protect me?'

She didn't return the smile, but nodded.

'With my life. I think you're the one we've been waiting for.'

**

The sun was beginning to rise as Rigel made his way to the stables. The bed had been comfortable, warm and dry and he felt better than he had for some time. As he left the inn, he saw Sindel leaning against one of its wooden walls. She was standing on one leg, the other bent with her foot resting against the wall behind her. She had on tall riding boots that reached almost to her thighs and a leather jerkin that was belted around her ample waist. Rigel blinked at the sight of five slender blades in a belt buckled around her upper thigh. She had a similar holster on the other leg, and two more thin knives sheathed in a leather bracer around her wrist.

'You, ah. You have a lot of weapons there, Sindel.' He knew he sounded stupid saying it but couldn't think of anything else to say.

She shrugged and pushed away from the wall, moving with an easy rolling grace.

'It's a dangerous road, Rigel. Like I said.'

He smiled and hefted his little overnight bag onto one shoulder. Together they walked towards the stable, Sindel a few paces in front, just as a thought struck Rigel.

'Oh by the way, my horse is—'

Someone tall and stealthy emerged from the shadows to his left, where they had been concealed by the wall. Sindel spun round, lightning fast, her hand snapping out and her fingers pointing like darts at the man who was crumpling, stumbling back into the wall, with a thin blade lodged in his throat.

'Wha—' began Rigel, as Sindel whirled again, lithe as a dancer, her other hand whipping up from knee to forehead and this time he could almost see the gleam of the sun on the blade as it flew like an arrow into back of the hooded man who had very nearly reached him with a wicked dagger upraised in one meaty fist.

Rigel fell back with a strangled cry, falling in the mud and dropping his bag. Spare clothes and a toothbrush fell out into the still silence of the now motionless, filthy yard. He propped himself up on one elbow and stared at them, at their unassuming, blithely normal innocence. He'd almost died, leaving nothing behind but a toothbrush for teeth that would never again have been brushed and spare clothes for an almost abruptly dead body. This very moment, this very minute, had very nearly been his last. He should be a corpse right now, cooling in the morning sun.

'Are you alright?' Sindel asked, peering at him. He hadn't even realised she'd walked over to him.

'You...' he began, breathing hard, his head swimming. 'You weren't...'

'I wasn't lying,' she said with a wink and a sly smile. 'I said you were the one we'd been waiting for. I just didn't tell you I meant, you know...' She gestured at the two men she'd just skewered with her tiny, vicious blades. 'Me and them.'

'Then why...?'

She reached down to offer him her hand, and Rigel noticed one of the thin knives from the wrist bracer was missing. Somehow that struck him as terrifying, so he didn't reach up. She shrugged and turned away. A blade on her thigh was also missing. She knelt by the body of the hooded man who had almost reached Rigel and rolled him over. Rigel looked away.

'You're on a mission I happen to feel good about,' she said, grunting with effort. Rigel did not look up.

'I want to help you complete it,' she continued. 'And besides the guy who paid us for this didn't pay much. Not enough to split between three anyway,' she laughed lightly. She rose to her feet.

'That was a joke,' she said.

Rigel got to his feet and started picking up his now-mud splattered clothes. He peered at his toothbrush.

'You should probably get a new one,' Sindel remarked. 'That one's dirty.'

Rigel almost lost it then but managed to keep from breaking into hysterics by a pure effort of will. He looked at the dangerous, beautiful woman who could apparently move twice as fast as him despite looking twice as heavy.

'So when we first met, you were planning to kill me?'

She shook her head.

'Only when I'd verified you were the one on the contract,' she said seriously. 'Professionalism is important. Plus, I did warn you.'

He thought back to her remarks about cutting throats.

'I suppose you did.'

She shoved a blade back into its thigh holster and crossed to the other corpse.

'Aren't you glad I'm here now?' she beamed, looking like an adorable hedgehog. Rigel felt his knees weaken at the sight and mentally kicked himself. She collected her blade from the man's throat with horrifying nonchalance and turned to the stable.

'Watch out for the horse!' Rigel called on impulse.

She looked round quizzically, sliding the blade into her wrist holster.

'He...he bites. He's a biter.'

'Me too,' she winked.

***

Later that night, a group of like-minded men and women of the city met in the Seven Buckets tavern. Each was a noble of some standing, united in common purpose yet divided, as such worthies typically are, by self-interest. The youngest of them had elected to attend this evening wearing a brightly coloured scarf around his neck and appeared to have no intention of taking it off.

'You look like a peacock,' remarked a corpulent man of advanced years and many chins, who had long since decided that men without a decent man's paunch or receding hairline were not to be trusted and certainly not liked.

The young lord adjusted his scarf and wheezed some kind of a reply.

'What?' asked one of the two women of the group, an elegant lady in a beautiful emerald-green gown which looked horribly out of place in the rush-floored, spilt-ale-smelling tavern.

'I was strangled,' the man squeaked eventually, with a grimace of pain.

'By the mage,' growled the fat man.

'He knows, then,' remarked the woman in the emerald dress.

'Unless he does this sort of thing for fun,' said a third man.

'You know what he does for fun,' grinned the second woman. That set off a round of chuckles and comments of an off-colour nature.

'We have no choice then, my lords,' said the corpulent, chin-faced man. 'And ladies,' he added, with a nod to the two women. 'We must accelerate our plans.'

'Is that wise?' asked the woman in emerald. 'The first one got away and this second one is more dangerous than we thought.'

'I think that shows what little choice we have.'

'Agreed,' wheezed lord Creswell, wincing at the effort.

'Very well then. We strike at the pretty-boy. Any word from your cutthroats along the road?'

The woman in green snorted.

'I'll leave cutthroats to you, Senator. Those in my employ are of a subtler stripe.'

'What does that mean?'

She shrugged.

'It hardly concerns you. He's out of the city, so *she's* vulnerable.'

'Not until the pretty-boy is gone too, she isn't,' said the heavy-set man.

'And the girl,' added the second woman. 'She's more dangerous than either of them.'

'Alright. Let's move quickly on both of those then. This could all collapse if we don't push on.'

The conspirators talked of dark things well into the night and left beneath a gleaming moon.

Chapter Five

Sophine could never quite get over the fact that she was a teacher. Standing now in her old classroom, dictating principles and warnings to students like her old masters had, made her feel old and sometimes like an imposter, as though she had no right to be there at all. She often felt like the door would burst open at any moment and someone would drag her to the Rector's office for misbehaving.

Except that *she* was the Rector now. A Rector with no teaching staff, a load of inherited employees from cooks to cleaners, and a handful of untrained mage students who could barely levitate a stone.

She paced around the brightly lit room, looking down at the children reading the pages she'd just asked them to turn to. It was a glorious day outside, and she knew precisely how many of the words the kids were looking at would be absorbed by their over-excited brains. Even she wanted nothing more than to go and sit in the courtyard in the sunshine and relax, to calm her mind and her nerves before she eventually had to start searching for Alakis again.

She felt a stab of minor irritation at the thought. Finding Alakis was so far proving difficult. He didn't seem to be anywhere in the city, though she still had to try the south-western area down by the military quarter. It was a time-consuming process because she couldn't very easily direct her search. From within the confines of her mind she could receive visions of what she wanted to see, but it was largely passive. She had to almost focus on different areas, street by street and building by building, and the frustration of the search made it hard to maintain focus. She wondered if it would be faster to just go door to door.

Alakis had snatched most of her best books too, which hadn't helped. She'd read most of them already and learned a few things, but it wasn't the same as having something to flip through for ideas. He'd left the unpleasant, dark-leather bound one which sometimes hissed if you walked past it. That one she was sure contained some very dark things and was forbidden for a very good reason. Why Hilda hadn't just burned the lot of them she wasn't sure, although if the ancient mage had done so Lyoris Mountebank's scheme would have actually worked and they'd have an Echelarch right now.

Which at least would mean there was someone doing *something* at the top.

'Miss Sophine?' asked a small boy at the front of the class. He was a thin child of maybe seven years, sent to the Barbican by parents so destitute and fearful that they assumed he'd have a better life here. She felt a fiercely powerful need to make that a reality, but an equally deep fear that she could not.

'Yes?' She had not yet learned all their names and hated herself for it.

'My page tore,' he said with big, wide eyes, holding a ripped piece of paper in one small, trembling hand. A hush fell over the class as other eyes turned to him, some sympathetic and others no doubt cruelly eager.

'Oh dear,' she said, overly seriously, slowly crossing to stand by him. 'And how did that happen?'

71

She held his gaze as she took the book and the paper from him, then turned away as though considering his fate.

'I was trying to turn the page,' he snivelled, 'and it had something sticky on it...'

'It had something sticky,' she repeated, 'or your hands were sticky?' She looked back over her shoulder at the boy who did, indeed, have something on his hands. The boy looked at them, and Sophine let the moment last a few more seconds before she turned back and replaced the book in front of him.

'I don't see anything wrong with this book,' she said with a shrug, turning away nonchalantly and pretending not to notice the other kids straining to see the newly healed page, the big smiles on some faces or the disappointment on others.

The boy looked up in wonder as she sat back behind her desk and started flipping through papers with nothing on them. She wanted very much to grin and wink and laugh with them, but that wasn't her role.

As the whispering and excited muttering began to grow, Sophine stood up again and looked through the window.

'Alright, I think that's enough for this morning, don't you? Go on out and play. And remember what I said, the first person to lift a stone...gently,' she added, with a stern look, 'and show me will get to wear their Barbican robe first.'

She only had a few robes, because the tailors were horribly expensive at the moment and she didn't want to be seen splashing too much cash around. Lord Balderwin still had plenty of gold in his basement, but the last thing she wanted was for thieves to decide the Barbican was wealthy.

As the kids pushed and shoved and ran through the door, completely ignoring her half-hearted requests to do the opposite, she leaned forward and put her head in her hands.

'What are you doing,' she whispered to herself. 'What…are you *doing*?'

'There was not a teacher ever to live who didn't ask herself the same,' Ariene said, from the doorway. Sophine groaned.

'Charming,' said Ariene. 'Are you really that pleased to see me?'

'I can't see you,' she muttered, 'I'm not here. I'm on a beach somewhere with a glass of something strong and fruity.'

'Alone?' asked Ariene. Sophine could hear her moving into the classroom, her silky gowns rustling.

'Very,' Sophine replied. She looked up as Ariene perched herself on the nearest desk.

'How are they doing?'

'They're coming along.'

'And they aren't up to lifting rocks yet?' Ariene's voice was bland but Sophine could hear the accusation in it.

'There's a lot to learn first,' she said, sitting back in her chair. 'You have to understand the theory first, then you have to try to believe that theory. It's not as easy as you think.'

'I never said it was easy.'

'No but you act like they can be hurried along. They can't be. I've said it before.'

'Well perhaps they could be focusing on something else…'

Sophine sighed and stood up. She began to walk around the room gathering up the books.

'Like what, Ariene? What do you want them to do now? Make enough crops grow to feed the city? Put out the fires in the commercial quarter? Or maybe just fix the endless squabbling of our useless, paralysed Senate?' This last was said with such venom that she surprised herself. She glanced around guiltily, but if Ariene had taken offence, she gave no sign.

Instead, the older woman gave her an innocent smile.

'Why, could they?' she said blandly. Sophine scowled and added another book to her already too-high stack.

'Feel free to help me,' she said, still scowling. Ariene did not move.

'You're doing well. I've always said you're a very capable young woman.'

Sophine gritted her teeth, stepping to her right to rebalance the books.

'Thanks,' she muttered. She started to manoeuvre the stack onto one of the desks.

'I think I already know the answer to this,' the senator said from behind her, 'but I don't suppose they would be able to send messages to the Messengers Guild in Terminheim?'

The books toppled and crashed messily to the floor. Pages came loose and scattered around the room like a flock of startled birds. Sophine stood and looked at them, then looked accusingly at Ariene. The senator did not move, and merely looked at her expectantly.

Sophine stalked away, muttering darkly to herself. She dropped back into her chair behind the desk and shoved her long black hair past her ears.

'Terminheim,' she said, looking back at Ariene. 'Why would you be asking me to send messages there?'

'The Messenger's Guild refuse to send anyone,' she said. 'There's a storm out there, somewhere between us and them, and it's apparently so frightening that they daren't make the journey while it's still there.'

Sophine snorted a short laugh.

'That doesn't sound likely. Could it be that it's just too expensive to finance long distance trips at the moment?'

Ariene smiled faintly.

'It could indeed. I've not known them to be so jittery before though. Could you look into it?'

'Well, I'll add it to the list.'

'The list?'

Sophine sighed.

'Yes. Of things I have to do. There are lots. I need to get these kids learning, keep them fed, warm.' Ariene started to interrupt but she pressed on. 'I need to think up ways of rehabilitating the image of mages, and of course, I need to find bloody Alakis.'

Ariene nodded slowly.

'Alakis,' she repeated. 'The young man with the lightning.'

'The very one,' Sophine gazed out of the window.

'Lightning,' Ariene mused. 'You don't suppose he's in Terminheim...'

Sophine looked at her sharply.

'Causing that storm?'

'Is it possible?'

It was. It was very possible. Unpleasantly, worryingly possible, in fact.

She nodded slowly.

'I'll look into it,' she said. 'It's a very long way though. I can't even reach the edge of the city without difficulty, so I'll need to...' she glanced at Ariene. 'I'll need to read up on it.' Her thoughts strayed to that dark, hissing book as a tingle of excitement danced up her spine.

'Let me know how you get on,' said Ariene, looking pointedly around at the forlorn heap of books. 'I'd better leave you to it.'

'You're too kind.'

'I know. It's a failing.' Ariene smiled and swept from the room, leaving her wondering just what kind of trouble Alakis had gotten himself into. To conjure a portal, when she was fairly sure he had never done so before, from the Barbican to Terminheim…that shouldn't have been possible. Not a stable one anyway.

'Alakis,' she muttered, 'what did you do?'

***

Sophine was pacing around the dark, relatively empty storage room at the Barbican, placing little candles in a geometric pattern that she found pleasing but which, to her knowledge, contained no arcane power. She knew that there were some arrangements of physical things, patterns and alignments of various substances and objects of significance or history which could be used to create reflections in the ethereal realm beyond theirs. Like causing ripples on the surface of a pond which echo into the depths, and call to the dark things that squirm with blind, hungry eyes down below in the lightless murk.

She had no intention of doing anything of that sort, though the idea wouldn't leave her mind as she placed the candles in jars to keep them upright. How did anyone discover such things in the first place, if not by accident? She stood back, looking around at her pattern and then out of the single window to the moonlit city outside.

'Right then,' she said aloud, trying to sound more decisive than she felt. She sat down and waved a hand at the candles, feeling a tiny thrill of satisfaction as they flared into sudden life and surrounded her with a warm, flickering glow. No matter how often she used her abilities, it never seemed to stop being fun.

She looked into the dancing flames, letting her eyes drift past to the rippling shadows beyond them, letting her mind calm and relax. Then she closed her eyes and reached out.

'Show me,' she muttered, focusing on Asterheim first. The southwestern side. The military quarter. A vision swam before her, dark streets and moonlit shadows, revellers in taverns and soldiers sharpening blades. People sleeping and…not sleeping…in brothels. She dismissed that area and focused on the next street, the vision moving through alleys and over rooftops. Frustration began to build again, making the visions ripple and lose definition. She tried to conjure the image of Alakis's face and direct her visions towards it, but the emptiness she felt as the visions flowed and floated around the city told her what she already knew.

Alakis was not in the city.

The visions melted and faded away, leaving her surrounded by candles and the jagged shadows they cast on…

She frowned at the book lying on the floor by the door, bathed in shadows and gleaming orange firelight.

'Where did you come from?' she muttered, rising to her feet before she realised which book it was.

The dark-leather tome with the unpleasant hissing. She froze, looking at it.

'I didn't bring you here,' she said to it. The book did not reply, for which she was very grateful.

Had one of the kids brought it up to the storeroom? A prank of some kind? Maybe. Possibly. Almost certainly not.

Sophine could hear a faint hissing whisper at the back of her mind, like the sigh of a ghost trying to speak but worn down by centuries of soul-draining weariness. She shook the thought away and flicked a hand at the book, sending it sliding into the shadows out of sight.

'I'll have to find a box for you,' she said. 'One with a very big lock.'

Putting the forbidden book out of her mind, she sat and refocused her thoughts.

'Terminheim,' she said, this time reaching deeper inside. When the fallen mage-priest Kahin had cast his spell on her, she had been at the mercy of her emotions. Anger, fear and pain had unlocked a wellspring of energy within her that she'd been able to turn to her advantage particularly in conjuring portals and shields. She'd even managed illusions, with the help of the less forbidden books that she'd devoured in the latter days of that terrible time. Since then she'd learned to tap that spring of energy without the emotion, but it always helped to start with the face of the man she'd hated more than any other.

The gloating Lord Balderwin, the unpleasant pig of a man who had chosen her as his mage only to renege on his promise and who had come to a violent, bloody end at her hands. His face appeared before her eyes, and the tiny flicker of hatred that came with it was enough.

A flush of heat, then a rush of tingling potential. Sophine smiled into the candlelit room and took a deep breath.

This time her visions were faster and clearer, the images spilling and dancing across her mind. From the confines of the room in which she sat, she saw the boundaries of the city flying past, the great walls beneath her, the road stretching out beyond over fields that gave way to barren rocky ground and at last to the mountainous region that Terminheim called home.

She gasped as her vision exploded into white light. Crackling energy and darkness blocked her sight, along with an echo of fear she felt within her heart. Alakis's face wide-eyed and scared, flashed into her head, just a glimpse and then gone. Sophine fell back with a cry as the vision vanished, blinking into the dark room which smelled faintly of smoke. All her candles had gone out.

'Well,' she said in a shaky voice, trying to quell the trembling in her limbs. 'I guess you're in Terminheim then.'

Her eyes strayed to the shadows in the corner of the room, where the dark-leather book lurked. An idea began to form, and she pushed it firmly aside.

Without a backward glance, she strode from the room.

***

'I really wish you hadn't done that,' said Ariene lightly, pouring tea from one of the fabulously expensive teapots with the outrageously thin, egg-shell pottery for which the long-departed Lord Balderwin had no further use. She delicately stirred the golden-brown liquid with a silver spoon.

Sophine had chosen not to attend this evening's dinner, which had cast a shadow over Ariene's mood. Lately relations with the prideful, brooding girl had been more strained than usual, not least because of the Senate's repeated requests to rush the young mages into service – requests that Ariene did not think were entirely unwarranted, given the fractious state of the city. With Rigel away in

Ceresheim and Barten handling his own affairs, tonight it was just Thaniel and herself. Ariene tried not to let her worry show, but it wasn't easy. If their unofficial ruling council fractured, the fragile system they were holding together could come falling down around their ears.

'To confront a senator in his own home is one thing, but to assault him is quite another.'

Thaniel made a snorting, huffing noise as he reached for one of the small cakes piled up on a gold-rimmed plate.

'I'm almost a senator myself,' he said, splitting the cake in half and reaching for the butter. 'So that just makes it politics.'

Ariene took a sip of the tea, looking around the opulent but dimly lit dining hall.

'Seems strange to be here without Sophine,' she remarked. 'It would be like being at Orswell's mansion without you. How odd that you both ended up caretakers of the houses of great lords.'

Thaniel regarded her, chewing his cake.

'Alright,' he said, 'we're only caretakers. Not senators. I did say "almost".'

She nodded lightly and replaced her cup on its saucer. She winced at the tiny crack she heard. Thaniel grinned.

'How many is that now?'

She sighed. She'd lost count.

'Absurd to make a plate so thin,' she said, carefully lifting the cup to inspect the saucer beneath. A forking, hairline crack was running through the centre, branching off to the edges. She poked it with one fingernail and a piece fell out and tinkled to the tabletop.

'As I was saying,' Ariene said, sitting back in her chair. 'You are not a senator and there are those out there who resent that two of the most notorious characters in the city are living like lords in the abandoned mansions of the formerly mighty. Some are suggesting the entire affair with Mountebank was staged by those notorious characters with the ultimate aim of raising themselves to the Senate.'

Thaniel snorted a laugh, crumbs flicking to the table from his grinning mouth.

'I know,' she conceded, 'absurd. But not long ago it would have been too absurd to even suggest. Now it is being suggested. You see how things are worsening. If they think you're going around attacking senators who oppose you, you'll do that one thing that no politician ever actually wants to do no matter what they claim.'

'And what's that?'

'Unite the Senate.'

He chuckled.

'I'm serious,' she said with a smile, reaching for a pastry mostly out of guilt that the servants had gone to the trouble of preparing them. 'A government united is a terrifying prospect, because it's almost always united out of fear and scared people are not to be trusted with power.'

Thaniel nodded and chewed. She wondered if he really understood what she was saying; he was never the most politically astute of the mages. Thaniel's gift to the group was his heart, where Sophine's was her power and Rigel's, his mind. But hearts, famously, had a hard time listening to reason.

'Don't give them a reason to come after you, Thaniel. That's what I'm saying. I wouldn't want to lose you too.'

He looked up with a flicker of a frown.

'I know,' he said, 'but don't worry about me. I'm pretty sure I can handle anything they throw at me.'

81

'But I can't,' she said, letting her worry slip through her features. 'Without Rigel, I'm already a little exposed. I have enemies lining up to wrest this caretaker position away from me.' She gingerly reached for her teacup and took a tentative sip.

'I don't care about the power,' she said. She stretched her arm out to replace the cup but then thought better of it and sat with it in her lap instead. 'I would give it up in an instant if I thought the city could prosper under anyone else. But with most of the senators working day and night to control the chaos in their own Guilds and households, the only people looking to advance themselves for the leadership are the wrong people.'

'The wrong people?'

'The self-interested. People who want power for power's sake. Not people with the interests of the city at heart. So until there's a suitable alternative, I can't let go. And there won't be one while the chaos continues. And so my enemies are interested primarily in keeping the chaos going, which ironically enough keeps me in place. Sooner or later, they will get tired of waiting.'

'They couldn't remove you, Ariene. Not without your cooperation.' Thaniel said it with such innocent confidence that Ariene's concern deepened all the more.

'These people are not patient or reasonable, Thaniel. Creswell is one of them, but there are others worse than him. More desperate. I'm sure they're emboldened now Rigel isn't with me. Having someone who can stop time and heal any wound around you makes it hard for anyone to put a knife in your back.'

Thaniel grimaced.

'I guess,' he muttered.

'And now he's gone, all I have is you.'

'And Sophine,' he said without much conviction. Ariene did not deign to answer that, letting the echoing silence of Sophine's inherited dining room speak for itself.

Thaniel shifted a little on his chair.

'I'll be careful,' he said, grabbing another cake. 'I promise.'

***

The sun was warmer as they progressed further south, and Rigel found himself thoroughly enjoying his trip. Sindel was great company, laughing and joking constantly and looking fantastic all the while. Around them, the countryside was beginning to flatten out, and the road began to pass through fields of tall crops gently swaying in a pleasant breeze.

'You know, my parents probably live around here,' he said suddenly, as they crested a small hill and looked down on the final leg of their journey. Sindel gave him a peculiar look.

'You don't know where your parents live?'

He shrugged, expecting to feel a familiar twinge of regret and sadness that had been so useful to him when he'd first begun to access his powers. Somehow, he did not. He smiled at her.

'I actually don't. Does that sound strange to you?'

She looked away, out over the green and yellow land dotted with small villages, and in the distance, the unmistakeable outline of a walled city against the blue sky.

'A little,' she said soberly.

'They kicked me out when I was small,' Rigel said, gazing out at the country of Ceresheim. 'One too many mouths to feed in the Wheatly household.'

'Wheatly,' she mused.

'Farmers,' he shrugged. 'I was sent to Asterheim to be a mage, but I was never much good at it.'

She laughed.

'And yet here you are, mage to the Echelarch herself.'

'She's not an Echelarch. She's just taken over from the old Echelarch.'

Sindel looked at him flatly. Roan flicked his ears and snorted.

'Alright, alright you two,' he sighed. 'Ariene would never let herself be crowned, let's put it that way. And I'm only her mage because I found her dying on a bridge one night and'—he wiggled his fingers—'that was that. All because some crazy man was trying to provoke a war with the mages to force the Senate to make him Echelarch.'

'You don't see it do you, Rigel?' Sindel said, clicking her tongue to get her horse moving again. 'That story you just told me is more interesting and impressive than most people around here could even imagine. And look at you, with your court-mage clothes and nice hair. If you walked into your parents' house right now, they'd think you were royalty. They wouldn't be far wrong.' She trotted slowly away.

Roan followed along after Sindel's horse without waiting for Rigel to tell him to, which was just as well because his powers of speech and thought had been temporarily replaced by a nameless, warm feeling in his stomach. He stared at Sindel's brown hair bouncing lightly with the rhythm of the horse's movement and thought it was the most amazing thing he'd ever seen in his life.

So intent was he on trying to think of something to say that wouldn't make him sound like a complete idiot that he almost didn't notice the large wooden building to their left and the soldiers filing out of it, until Sindel's horse abruptly stopped. Roan shook his head irritably and snorted.

'Halt,' said a bored-sounding man leaning on a long pike that he was probably supposed to be brandishing.

'Name and business,' said another. This one had a few patches of metal plate sewn on his leather clothing and seemed to be in charge. He was every bit as bored-sounding as the other sentry.

'We're here to see Cuthbert,' said Sindel from atop her horse.

'That's *Thane* Cuthbert,' said the sentry in charge, without much conviction.

'If you say so,' Sindel shrugged, 'but it's a lousy Thane who can't pay his men. I haven't been paid for months.'

The pikeman peered at her through a squint that probably came from standing around in the sun all day.

'If you're one of Cuthbert's, what are you doing out there?' he jerked his head back the way they'd come.

'Tried to make it freelance,' Sindel sighed. 'Not much work out there either. So I figured I'd see Cuthbert while I'm here.'

The sentry with the poorly sewn armour plates glanced at Rigel and wiped his nose on one leather-clad arm.

'And you?'

Sindel jerked a thumb at him.

'Messenger from Asterheim. Bit of paid protection work.'

Rigel found his tongue at last.

'Waste of money it was too,' he spluttered, as haughtily as he could. 'Not a soul on this road for the last twenty miles. I shall be speaking to the Thane about stopping his brigands hiring themselves out with tales of highwaymen and bandits to unsuspecting—'

The pikeman chuckled and spat on the ground.

'Might try that myself,' he grinned, 'sounds like easy money to me.'

'Very,' said Sindel, 'but it doesn't pay much. Messengers don't carry cash.'

There were general murmurs of agreement at this nugget of wisdom and before long they were being ushered through. As he went by, the pikeman turned to his superior.

'Not what we're looking for, sir?'

The other sentry made a dismissive noise.

'No. He'll be a single traveller heading to the city. Some kind of mage. If he even comes.'

Rigel rode on as unhurriedly as he could, hoping the sudden fear that had gripped him didn't show. When they'd gone a little further and he still didn't have an arrow between his shoulder blades, he relaxed.

'Someone knows I'm coming,' he said to Sindel. She turned her head and gave him another of her mischievous winks.

'I did,' she grinned.

Chapter Six

Eric looked up from his work as someone knocked on the open door of Lord Orswell's study. Maurel, an older woman who had been a servant of House Orswell since she had been old enough to walk, looked in at him with a bland, prideful expression. Eric had always liked Maurel. She was a lowborn person who took great pride in having done well for herself, and who spoke with a deliberately refined, polished voice but could never quite shake her tendency to drop the odd "h" or "t". The overall effect was quite charming. She was in charge of the servants at Orswell's mansion and took her position very seriously, always with her chin tilted up and her nose in the air, walking around in her governess's gowns with careful, steady paces of studied dignity. Her long grey hair was always carefully arranged on top of her head like some kind of tightly woven hat.

Eric suddenly realised he was shirtless and wearing only a bathing robe he hadn't bothered to tie up. He instinctively pulled the edges around his body and tried to look dignified as his cheeks reddened.

'Sir,' said Maurel, her dignified expression not changing, 'there's someone 'ere to see you.'

'There is?' Eric replied, glancing at the large candle in the corner of the room. It had burned down most of the way. 'It's way past midnight. Nearly morning.'

'Yes sir, 'e says he's from the Guild but 'e looks far too young.' One eyebrow twitched on her haughty face and he was sure he detected a hint of disapproval in her eyes. He straightened, tugging at his robe which refused to cover his torso properly.

'Whatever you're thinking Maurel, don't. I'm not having secret visits from mystery boys while Thaniel's away.'

'I should think not,' Maurel replied with a sniff, as though it was the furthest thing from her mind, yet he thought he saw a flash of relief. 'Shall I send 'im in then, this mystery boy?'

Mistree boi...

Eric laughed and made a flapping motion with his hand.

'Yes, yes alright. Give me a few minutes to—' he gestured at the papers scattered around on the desk. 'Then send him in. Is there another chair in here?'

Maurel turned her head ever-so slightly and pointedly looked at the three chairs lined up neatly along the side of one of the bookcases by the door, where Eric had placed them to make room for more paper.

'Oh,' he said, sitting back and pondering the mess.

'May I suggest the library?' said Maurel.

Lyie-breh...

'Master Ormond often received visitors there. He had similar tendencies to you.'

Eric raised an eyebrow.

Maurel's eyes widened and she began to splutter. All trace of the refined voice vanished.

'I meant the paper, sir! And y'know...mess...'

88

Eric held up a hand and laughed.

'I know, Maurel. I'm playing with you.'

She stopped spluttering and cleared her throat, clasping her hands before her.

'Very amusing sir, I'm sure.'

Shoo-er...

Eric adopted a contrite expression and apologised again, holding his hands up in surrender. Maurel tilted her head up, eyebrows raised and eyes down, the perfect expression of quiet, offended dignity, and swept from the room in a rustle of cotton.

Getting to his feet, Eric picked his way over the piles of paper and grasped at the sides of his bathing gown, trying to get hold of the soft belt that was supposed to be looped through the little rings around the waist. He found it as he padded his way to the large library doors, pulling the robe closed and tying it up before he entered.

'Eric!' called a voice down the hall to his right. Someone was walking towards him, a shadow in the dimly lit corridor.

'Tyler?' he said as the boy came into sight. Tyler smiled warmly, the grin a little too wide and his eyes slipping past Eric as he waved. Eric took a step back and gagged; the smell of stale beer on Tyler's breath was overpowering.

'Tyler, what are you doing wandering the mansion at this hour? You need to be in bed.'

'I do,' nodded Tyler, swaying a little. 'I went out with some of the boys from work...'

'I see that,' Eric agreed, glancing down the corridor behind Tyler. He could hear Maurel's refined voice but couldn't make out the words. 'Look, Ty, it's not a good—'

'I wanted to thank you,' said the youth, his eyes starting to fill with tears. 'You saved my life, you saved—'

'I know, I know,' Eric said, one hand on the door to the library, 'and I was happy to. Anyway, it was Sir Rivan who...' the voices were louder now. His guest was on his way. 'I have to go now Ty, okay? You go to bed, alright? You need to be in work tomorrow...'

Eric was reasonably sure that Tyler would not be in work tomorrow and he knew full well it didn't matter, but he had to say something. The boy nodded and breathed out heavily.

'I love you,' he said thickly. Eric blinked.

'I...love you too, Tyler. Now go to bed.'

The boy stumbled away, making strange hiccupping sounds and squeaking half-formed words in an emotion-choked voice. Eric rolled his eyes and stepped into the shadow-wreathed library, pulling the door closed behind him and crossing to the candelabra on the table. The moonlight was just about sufficient to navigate by, but he still struggled to light the candles.

'Where's Thaniel when I need him?' he muttered, just as the door burst open and someone came charging at him through the pale moonlight, stumbling as he came.

For a moment Eric thought it was Tyler, but the shape running at him was too big, too aggressive and too loud to be the quiet boy from Citizenry. Behind the charging figure Maurel was shrieking, all trace of her refined voice gone as she called for help.

All this ran through Eric's head in the instant it took to turn around, and then the running man was upon him. But Eric knew the library, and the assailant did not. Eric jumped to the side on pure impulse, and the shadowy figure crashed into the desk on which the candelabra stood. The man let out a growl that was far more anger than pain, but by then Eric was running. He whipped past the door, grabbing the frame as he did to aid his turn, and pelted down the hall.

Maurel was hurrying up the corridor as he ran down it, holding her heavy skirts up and calling to him. He just had time to see her wide, terrified eyes slide to something behind him before something heavy crashed into his back and sent him flying a metre through the air before he landed heavily on the carpeted floor. He looked round, scrabbling to his feet as the man who had tackled him leapt up, only to be smacked solidly on the head by a long cane-like weapon wielded by Maurel and which she had evidently been keeping in her dress. The assailant turned, swiping with his hand as though to ward off the next blow, but Maurel swept her cane low, the heavy wood crashing into the man's knees. He snarled with pain as something gave an unpleasant crack; Eric couldn't tell if it was the man's knee or the cane, but he didn't wait to find out. He leapt on the man's back and tried to get an arm around his neck, but the intruder was bigger and stronger than Eric and he was flung again to the ground. Maurel was jabbing with her cane, making incoherent snarling noises, when the man grabbed it and threw it behind him. The cane clattered to the ground and the man smacked Maurel across the face with a cruel, backhanded blow. Eric screamed as she fell, and the man whirled, grabbing at him and crashing his forehead into his face.

Brilliant white stars exploded against an ocean of infinite blackness, and Eric's world went dark.

***

Tyler crouched against the wall in the darkness of the corridor, watching the big man heave Eric onto his shoulder and make off

91

with him down the hall. He had been drunk a few moments ago, and he was fairly sure he'd said some very stupid things to some people, but the specifics were a blur.

But then the world had gone mad and an intruder had burst in, and suddenly sobriety had returned in a surge of adrenaline. He'd watched as Maurel tried to fight the man off, the bravery she'd shown almost enough to make him join in…but only almost. He was no fighter, and nor was Eric. Few of Lord Orswell's lost boys were fighters, though none of them were strangers to violence.

Tyler gritted his teeth and tried to think through the surging adrenaline and the beat of his heart, not to mention the lingering fog of alcohol.

Rising to his feet on shaking legs, Tyler carefully trotted down the hallway after the retreating figure. Maurel was pushing herself upright, her nose bloody and her eyes fierce.

'Maurel,' Tyler whispered, dropping to her side and casting a fearful look down the hall. 'What can I do?'

'Kill 'im,' snarled Maurel, groping in the dark for her cane, 'quick, before he gets away.'

Tyler shook his head, relief that she was alright warring with panic at what she'd said.

'I can't! I'm not a fighter!'

She made a slightly disgusted noise and got to her feet, clutching at the heavy folds of her dress.

'Well, I ain't a runner,' she hissed. 'So run. Follow 'im. Find out where 'e's taking Eric. If he gets away…'

Tyler nodded and swallowed hard.

'You can do this, boy,' Maurel said, looking at him sternly. 'Don't fail him.'

Tyler ran off down the hall, skidding to a halt as he reached the stairs leading down. The big man was crossing the reception room at the foot of the steps, heading for the door. Tyler carefully sneaked down the stairs, clinging to the ornate banister at the side. The intruder hauled the front door open and trudged out, still holding the unconscious Eric over one shoulder. Tyler moved as fast as he dared, creeping over the faded carpets and peering through the door.

The big man had draped Eric over the back end of a horse, face down, and was busily unfolding a rope, presumably to tie Eric's hands and feet to keep him from falling off. Tyler felt a surge of terrible pity and briefly considered charging at the man, but dismissed the idea. He would end up dead and Eric would still end up tied to a horse.

Instead, Tyler crept along the crunchy road to where Lord Orswell kept his stables, hoping the man would take a few minutes to tie Eric securely. He quickly untied a horse and led it slowly to the edge of the stable. He could just about make out the figure of the man in the moonlight, swinging up into his saddle. Tyler glanced at his own mount; it had no saddle and he had no time to get one. All it had was some reins, by which its master had tied it to the wooden beam of the stable. Grimacing, he leapt up on its back, cursing and struggling and holding handfuls of its mane to haul himself up. The horse, thankfully, didn't seem to mind, just gave him a stare of unfriendly disapproval.

'Come on,' he whispered, 'let's go.'

***

Eric gasped as cold water splashed onto his face and soaked his body. He jerked awake, aware first of the hideous cold and then, moments later, of the equally hideous pain in his forehead. He closed his eyes and moaned in distress.

'Morning,' said someone with a rasping voice. Eric opened an eye.

'Who are you?' he asked the man with the cropped dark beard and blue eyes, standing in front of him in an emerald-green jacket. Gold rings glinted on his fingers and a silken scarf was tied around his throat.

'My manners!' the man laughed in that wheezing voice, crouching down in front of him. He had a nice face. He also didn't seem to be much older than Eric himself. 'I am Lord Creswell. Joard Creswell. Pleasure to meet you.' He put a hand to his neck and winced, as though the effort of speaking hurt.

'And you,' croaked Eric, blinking at the pain in his head as the memory of what had happened to him sluggishly reappeared. He tried to move and found he was tied to his chair.

'Where am I?' he asked, squinting around. He was in a large room, wide and well lit. It smelt faintly of smoke. The floor was wooden, as were the beams holding the roof and the staircase off to the left. But much of the wood was charred and blackened, and the floor was a mess of broken furniture and other debris. Shutters were closed over the windows, but they let in plenty of light and he could tell from the soft breeze that there was no glass in the windows.

'An old tavern,' said Creswell, rising to his feet and tugging his scarf. 'It's been abandoned a while as you can see. There was a fire and I just couldn't justify the expense of refitting it all.' He grimaced. 'Times are hard for us all.'

'Some more than others,' Eric remarked, with a glance at his bonds. He was suddenly aware that he was wearing only his bathing gown and that it was now soaking wet. He shivered.

Creswell looked at him.

'Cold?'

Eric nodded.

'Well. I'm sure that's as bad as it will get. There's no reason to hurt you, is there?' His tone was light, but Eric could hear the danger in that silky voice.

'You already hurt me,' said Eric.

His captor nodded slowly.

'And for that I apologise. But you see, I was hurt too.' He indicated his neck as his tone turned hard. 'Your Thaniel paid me a visit yesterday.'

Eric felt a terrible chill race through his body.

'He blames me for trying to kill a friend of yours,' said the senator. 'Which of course I did, but his...assault on me left me with no choice but to take steps.'

Eric was now shivering in earnest, and not just because of the cold.

'Steps?' he said, trying to keep the conversation going and absolutely terrified of what might come next.

'Steps to ensure he would cooperate. He's forced our hand, you see Eric. Shown himself to be a danger.'

'Thaniel's not dangerous,' Eric said without thinking.

Creswell snarled and yanked the scarf from his neck. An ugly purple bruise seemed to ring his entire throat, sliced in places by deep red gashes that looked very much like they'd been made by fingernails. Eric was appalled.

'Thaniel did that?'

Creswell replaced the scarf gingerly.

'Mostly,' he muttered. 'And now you see how precarious your position is, Eric. If your Thaniel doesn't do as he's told, I'm afraid it will go badly for you.' He offered an unpleasant grimace in place of a smile.

'This won't work,' Eric said, with complete confidence. 'You should set me free. Thaniel is…protective…of me. When he finds me, you're done for. Let me go now and I won't say anything.'

Creswell looked at him with amusement and gestured at someone behind Eric. Four men stomped their way into view, each one big and muscular and violent-looking. Eric recognised the face of one; he'd glimpsed it as it smashed its way into his forehead. An ugly face with a scar over one eye.

'I'm afraid that's not going to happen, Eric. We aren't likely to be interrupted here. Besides, if Thaniel stays out of our way, then you'll be alright. Mostly.' He gave a small, apologetic shrug. 'One of these fellows seems to think he has a score to settle with you though, so I wouldn't imagine it'll be entirely plain sailing.'

Eric started to shiver anew.

Creswell turned to the thugs.

'Nothing permanent,' he said. 'We need him alive and whole, for now.'

The scar-faced thug gave an evil grin and looked at Eric with eyes that promised pain.

Tyler headed for the gaudily-painted building in the middle of the crowded street, his plan still forming as he walked.

This was one of the busiest streets in all of Asterheim, he was sure. Wide and reasonably well-cobbled, it cut straight from the harbour, down past Portgate Castle and into the heart of the market district, around which the Noble Quarter sat. Anyone getting on or off a ship was fairly likely to find their way to the market area and thus to this arterial route at some point, and so the street and those branching from it were always rammed with travellers, merchants, thieves and of course, working-girls.

Tyler had almost been giddy with relief when the thuggish man had turned this way from Orswell's mansion instead of crossing one of the bridges over the river. He knew this area; he had spent time here after fleeing his father's house all that time ago, and the half-burned inn to which Eric had been taken wasn't far from...

'Heaven An'Dell,' he said aloud with a shaky smile as he came closer to Molly's den of delights, in which he had spent so long before he'd managed to make contact with Sir Rivan. He admired Molly and owed her a lot. He'd asked one of the girls one evening how she'd managed to turn Heaven An'Dell into the incredible success it was, and the story had never left him.

'Well,' the thin girl in the tight dress had said with a preening flourish, 'word is, Molly managed to get herself named in the will of a very wealthy, very old and very grateful client some years ago.' She nodded with wide eyes and a broad, admiring grin. 'Used the money before she could be killed for it,' she gave him a knowing look. 'Wise girl,' she added. 'Bought three houses along the busiest road in Asterheim and the shops beneath them, knocked all the walls through and reinvented the place. And now look at it! The biggest entertainment parlour in the city.'

And what an entertainment parlour it was. It had a tavern and kitchens on the ground floor, a stage for dancing and theatre on the first, bedrooms on the rest. Molly's girls were the best in the city, they liked to say. Certainly they were the best dressed, best fed and best paid.

Tyler smiled as he approached the red-painted façade and stepped up to the beautiful girl leaning seductively by the door. She had long blonde hair which she was twirling playfully, looking up at him through long lashes.

'Good *morning*,' she said with an uncertain smile and just the right tone to suggest that whilst she was clearly a working-girl, she was, in spite of herself, attracted to and interested in the young man before her. Tyler was impressed; she had to be new but she was very, very good.

'I'm here to see Molly,' he said. The girl pouted, abruptly shifting gears into full-blown seductress.

'I can give you anything she can,' the girl said, pressing herself closer to him and tilting her head back to emphasise the height difference between them. He could smell her light, pleasant perfume. 'And between you and me, sugar,' she added with a salacious smile, 'I can do much better.' She touched his arm gently.

Smell, touch and power. The three key ingredients, besides the obvious, to unlocking a man's arousal. Tyler had heard all about it from the girls, but never been the subject of it before. He had to admit, this girl was a master of her trade.

'I'm…flattered,' he said with a smile, 'but—'

Instantly the girl's smile vanished and her eyes hardened. He held up his hands and backed up a step.

'I'm Tyler,' he said. 'I lived here for a while; Molly took me in.'

'Did she now?' the blonde girl said flatly, her eyes gleaming with suspicion. She folded her slender arms.

'The grey shields, do you know the grey shields?'

She rolled her eyes and let out a heavy breath.

'Oh you're one of the *boys*,' she said ushering him closer. 'Well, get inside then. Molly's on the first, rehearsing.'

He squeezed past her through the doorway into the warm, pleasantly lit tavern area. A few people were in, drinking at the tables and standing around talking to the girls in their implausibly bright, low-cut dresses. It being the middle of the morning, he was surprised even that many were here. He jogged to the stairs and headed up, ignoring the curious eyes that followed him.

The first floor was a wide-open space with a stage at the end. Tyler knew from experience that the room actually extended a lot further behind the stage for all the dressing rooms and storage areas, but he sighed in relief that he wouldn't need to navigate that dark warren, because right there on stage, stood Molly.

The owner of the establishment, Madam of the brothel, director of the theatre and saviour of lost boys was looking glorious. She was wearing a modestly-cut, armless blue satin gown that reached the floor and shimmered as she moved, her dark skin gleaming under the light of what had to be a hundred candles. Molly's jet-black hair was a wonder, a huge mass tightly bound into long, thin pleats that cascaded down her back and reached beyond her waist, around which she wore a belt of gold that glimmered in the light. A gold necklace encircled her slender throat, made in a sunburst shape. She turned as he crossed the room, a heart-breakingly beautiful smile like the sun coming up crossing her face.

'Tyler!' she said, striding to the edge of the stage and stepping delicately down to meet him. He saw a flash of her thigh as it escaped the slit in the dress and smiled; there was a knife belted to the thigh.

'Hi Molly,' he said with real warmth, taking her hands in his, 'I've missed you.'

'Oh really?' she said with a blithe, wide-eyed look, 'I barely noticed you were gone.'

He copied her expression. She exaggerated hers. They both started to laugh.

'You look amazing,' he said, stepping back and looking her up and down. She twirled slowly, hips swaying.

'Oh, I know,' she said, running her hands down the material. 'I'd say the same but…honey. You look dreadful.'

He copied her twirl, swaying hips and all.

'I know,' he said. She laughed. He grinned and looked at the floor then up to the stage, where three people wearing peculiar outfits that looked a little like sheep were doing some kind of dance and counting loudly.

'I need your help,' he said, looking back at her. She gazed back at him.

'I thought as much,' she said.

'A friend of mine is in trouble.'

'Friend?' she winked. He smiled and shuffled his feet.

'No, not like that,' he said. 'An actual friend. He's been kidnapped. They're holding him in the burned-out tavern a few streets away.'

Molly stepped away and started to pace.

'Honey,' she said softly, 'you know I'd do anything for you. But my girls can't risk busting someone out of—'

He held up his hands.

'I'm not asking you to bust him out. I'll do the busting…'

She looked him up and down, hands on hips.

'Girl,' she said flatly. 'You aren't serious.'

He smirked.

'Aren't I always? Look, I just need to get in there. He's locked in with four muscle-heads. I'm sure the girls can get them to come out and,' he made a jabbing motion with his hand, 'I jump in. We'll be gone before they—'

Molly shook her head, sending her tight pleats shaking. He saw she had little bands of gold worked through the mass of long tendrils.

'No, honey. My girls do that and those muscle-heads will know they were a distraction.'

Tyler stared at her, lost for words. She looked away, with a heavy sigh.

'Listen. How about this? Get them in here. We'll get the key, slip it to you. They'll think they left it behind and that he escaped.'

He groaned.

'But how do I get them in here?'

She smiled.

'Oh honey, one thing I know is how to drum up business.'

Chapter Seven

Eric was coming to again; he could feel it. The dark cocoon of warm bliss was fading, replaced by the shivering cold and the throbbing pains all over his body. He tried not to groan but couldn't help himself.

'Hey there, princess. You're awake,' said the gruff, phlegmy voice of the man who had broken into Orswell's.

'We tried the water on you again,' said another. This one had a nasal voice and always seemed to hover in the background, enjoying the show as the larger one hit him. 'But you didn't wake up. We were worried for a minute.'

'We certainly were,' said the gruff one. 'Wouldn't want to hurt you now, would we?'

Eric didn't trust himself to reply. His lips felt large and swollen, and he was fairly sure he'd bitten his tongue at some point. His ribs ached from the repeated punches, and the throb in his forehead still hadn't gone away. They didn't seem to need any encouragement to hit him, so he tried to keep quiet hoping they might think they'd done some permanent damage.

He heard a long, thin moan, realising only a moment later that he had made it. Something wet and warm trickled down his neck.

'Looks like you could do with some more,' the gruff one chortled. 'Haven't learned to keep quiet yet have we?'

'Lay off him, Benio,' said one of the two men who had so far not left the table in the far corner. 'He's had enough.'

'I say when he's had enough,' yelled the gruff one, Benio, crossing to Eric and holding his chin in one hand. 'Looks fine to me. Still got all his teeth even!'

'Creswell—' said the man at the table blandly.

'Creswell said not to kill him!' shouted Benio. 'Never said nothing about not having no fun.'

'That's a lot of double negatives,' someone with Eric's voice said dreamily.

Benio stood up and looked at him with an incredulous, infuriated expression. Eric felt sick as the realisation he'd spoken filtered through his throbbing head.

'What did you say?' the thug growled.

Eric tried to reply but the thug was turning away, startled by a banging sound. The two at the table stood up, reaching for knives. The three of them walked carefully towards the door, followed by the smaller one with the nasally voice.

'Hey, open up,' someone was calling. The thugs opened the door a crack.

'What do you want?'

'I was hoping you could help me...'

'What.' said the man from the table very slowly and deliberately, 'Do. You. Want?'

'Well,' said the voice. It was a strangely familiar voice, but Eric's pain-fogged mind couldn't figure out who it belonged to. 'I have this pouch of gold, see...'

The thugs made a noise that sounded like a collective intake of breath and opened the door wider.

'...I got it off a merchant,' the voice continued. 'I was going to have a morning at Molly's down the road, but the girl on the door won't let me in.'

The thugs cackled cruelly at this.

'She says I'm too young. But I thought if someone came with me...? And I'm guessing you fellas wouldn't mind spending stolen money seeing as how you're hanging out in the old tavern...'

'Wouldn't worry me,' said Benio, his grin clear from his voice.

'Me neither,' said the man from the table.

'I'll buy you all the ale you want,' said the voice. 'And anything else you want. Come on, please?'

'What do you think?' said Benio, closing the door a little.

'We could just take the money,' said the nasally voiced one.

'I heard that,' the voice called. 'You're not getting a penny until we're in Molly's. I'm small but I bet I can run faster than you.'

The man from the table glanced at Eric, and he let his head loll forward as though falling unconscious again.

'He's not going anywhere,' the man said. 'We can have an hour or two spending this fool's coins. Creswell won't care.'

Benio actually let out a little whoop of happiness and pulled the door open. The four men stomped out, slamming the door. Eric heard a key turn in the lock and wondered what had just happened, drifting back into the oblivion that the sudden silence granted him.

An hour or so later, he heard the key turning again and swam back to consciousness, moaning at the pain as the door opened and light flooded the room. Someone was running towards him, touching him gently, making little cries of horror and gasps of distress. Something tugged at his arms, or at the ropes holding them, as someone grunted with effort.

'Am I dreaming?' Eric slurred, wondering what else it could be. No one knew he was here. No one who had the key would be rescuing him. Nothing made a whole lot of sense. He flopped forward, sliding off his chair and falling to the cold wooden floor. The hard, cold ground felt good, but then someone was dragging him painfully along it. He tried to bat the hands holding his feet away.

'Stop it Eric, I'm trying to rescue you!'

'Tyler?' The voice finally had an owner.

'Yes, it's Tyler, now stop squirming and—'

'Tyler, I've been kidnapped,' he yelled suddenly, the thought occurring to him that he needed to get help. 'Tell Tyler!'

'I...I am Tyler,' the voice said. The pulling started again and Eric tried to roll away.

'Oh, to hell with his,' Tyler muttered.

Eric shrieked as cold water splashed over him, jerking to sudden wakefulness and leaping to his feet.

'Circle's balls, that's cold,' he shivered. He peered at the person holding the bucket next to him.

'Tyler?'

His rescuer let out a frustrated sigh and hurled the bucket aside.

'Yes, it's me. Again. Now come on,' he came forward and draped Eric's arm around his shoulders, helping him out of the abandoned tavern and into the cool morning. People marching up and down the street paid them little mind, but Tyler gave a particularly fearful glance at the Heaven An'Dell bordello.

'Oh, wait,' Tyler said suddenly, dropping his arm and fishing a key out of his pocket. Eric watched as he ran back to the tavern and put the key in the lock from the inside, then closed the door.

'So I escaped all by myself? With the key?'

Tyler nodded, his face flushed and serious.

'Yes, you did. Now let's get you back to Orswell's.'

'No, they'll look for me there. Take me to Balderwin's.'

'Who?'

'Never mind. Hail us a carriage and I'll direct us from there.'

***

Thaniel had always been a night-owl. Or so he told people to justify his late mornings. In truth, he just liked to sleep. He loved the sensation of being tucked up in a warm bed, hovering on the edge of consciousness. Anyone who leapt out of bed the moment they were awake was strange and alien to him.

The sun was streaming through the window of the bedroom he used when he stayed over at Balderwin's, and he opened his eyes grudgingly. The night before had been a strange one, with Ariene warning him about not making enemies in the Senate and neither Rigel nor Sophine being there. He liked Ariene, of course, and they'd been through a lot together. But it was still odd having dinner just the two of them. He'd made his excuses and come upstairs relatively early, and stayed up reading by candlelight, only now hoping that Ariene hadn't noticed the glow under the door when she'd gone to bed herself.

Something was nagging at his mind as he dressed, pulling on a long white shirt with baggy sleeves and a tight-fitting waistcoat of black satin. He couldn't shake the feeling that Eric needed him for…something. It wasn't a pleasant feeling. He pulled on his long black boots and cocked his head to one side, listening.

The faint crunch of gravel and pounding of hooves were getting stronger. Someone was coming up the roadway to the mansion, and in a hurry. Thaniel left the room and headed down the stairs, fluffing his blonde hair up as he went. It very often went flat on one side when he slept. He reached the front door just as someone knocked on it.

A servant girl appeared behind him and he gave her a smile and a quick, dismissive wave. He opened the door and gasped in sudden shock.

Eric was standing on the doorstep, leaning heavily on the boy from Citizenry. His face was a swollen mess of red flesh and purple bruises, and a nasty cut on his head was bleeding freely down his neck and soaking the thin material of the bathrobe he wore.

'Eric,' Thaniel whispered in horror, reaching for him and bringing himself up short when Eric raised a hand.

'Don't touch, Than,' Eric said, smiling with half a mouth. 'This feels worse than it looks.'

'That…doesn't seem likely,' he said as lightly as he could, stepping aside and letting the boy guide Eric into the house. The servant girl was still hovering in the background. Thaniel looked at her.

'Could you get some clothes and towels, please,' he said with an evenness he didn't feel. 'Take him to my bedroom,' he said to the boy. 'Tyler,' he added as the name finally drifted through the shock clouding his brain.

They went slowly up the stairs, Eric leaning heavily on Tyler for support, before stripping off the soaked bathrobe and collapsing with a grateful groan into the bed. The servant girl appeared at the door carrying a bundle, and Thaniel indicated a chair in the corner with an apologetic shrug. She placed the bundle down and vanished. Thaniel reached over and pulled the duvet up over Eric's shivering body, but the words died in his throat when he started to speak. Eric's eyes were closed, his breathing deep and even; he was fast asleep.

Thaniel turned to Tyler and steered him from the room and down to the dining room.

'Tell me,' he said, in a flat, deathly voice. He could feel the fear and anger boiling up inside him, the initial shock and horror giving way to more visceral emotions.

Tyler explained everything. How they were attacked in the mansion just before dawn, the nerve-wracking ride through the city expecting to be noticed at any moment. The plan with Molly.

'And then he told me to hail a carriage and bring him here,' he concluded. 'So I did.'

Thaniel was motionless in his chair, digesting the story in silence.

'Creswell,' he said softly. 'You're sure the men said Creswell?'

'Absolutely,' said Tyler. 'They were standing right in front of me. He said: "We can spend this fool's coins for an hour, Creswell won't mind". Why, who's Creswell?'

Thaniel rose to his feet and kept rising, his anger becoming rage, his rage becoming fury. He was only vaguely aware he was floating a few inches off the floor, his whole world becoming a red tempest of fiery wrath.

'A dead man,' he snarled.

***

In a modestly-sized tavern, burned and charred and filled with the detritus of squatters and rats' nests, four small-time hired thugs were arguing. One, a big man with a cruel scar on his face, was in the middle of demanding an explanation from a small, rat-faced thief with an irritatingly nasal voice, when the ground seemed to vibrate beneath them. The damaged walls of the fire-ravaged tavern trembled slightly, and the thugs turned as one towards the street-facing wall and the door they'd thought they'd locked an hour or two before.

Something was happening to the wall. Something impossible. The wood was moving, rippling like liquid, flowing upwards like a slow-motion waterfall in reverse. The scar-faced thug blinked and took three steps back, convinced he was hallucinating, as solid wooden beams peeled up and melted back on themselves, flowing up and round. The door ran like wax under a flame, vanishing to leave nothing but a hole to the street, which widened further still as the wall continued to flow away like the tide.

Outside, people were running and screaming; merchants and peasants, women and men all fleeing the area around the melting tavern, and from the horrifying sight that the widening hole gradually revealed to the thugs within. A blonde-haired man was floating two metres off the ground just beyond the rippling hole in the wall, his arms bent at the elbows and his hands upturned like claws. A pale nimbus of silvery light played around his hands and gleamed from his eyes, and his face was set in an expression of unmistakable hatred as he looked at the four criminals.

The rat-faced thief with the nasal voice tried to run, scurrying with surprising speed, making for the gaping hole. A finger twitched on the right hand of the floating apparition, and the thief's legs were ensnared in liquid wood. He screeched as the strange substance wrapped itself around him to the waist and solidified, crushing his lower body with the sudden weight of metre-thick timber. For a moment the man writhed and flailed, his arms flapping ineffectually at the immovable mound of solid wood, before he gasped and drooped, his skin grey and drained from massive blood loss.

The other thugs did not run, but that did not save them. A few minutes later, when the screams had ceased and the people in the street ventured closer, all that was left were arms and hands sticking up out of peculiar mounds of smooth, thick wood and stone.

***

On his second trip to Lord Creswell's mansion, Thaniel did not bother to knock. A blast of force sent the heavy wooden door flying back into the interior to crash heavily against the stairs that led up to the second floor. The rich, thick carpet was torn by the impact but Thaniel did not notice. People were running – some were servants, who scurried past him fearfully, and some were soldiers, who ran towards him with blades bared. He sent them flying with a twitch of his thoughts, the rage swirling within him stoking the fires of his power to new heights. He was only vaguely aware of the soldiers confronting him; his mind was set on the master of the house.

A spear flew at his face, beautifully cast. A perfect throw. He turned it around mid-flight and sent it back to its owner. Someone screamed.

He floated up the stairs, hovering a foot or so from the floor. The house was large, with paintings on the wall and statues and cabinets filled with curios. He noticed none of it.

At the top of the stairs, he found his quarry. The well-dressed lord with the nicely groomed beard and pleasant eyes was in the process of running from his room to see what the disturbance was. He froze at the sight of Thaniel, rising like a demon to greet him.

'My lord,' said Thaniel. 'I said I'd be back.'

Lord Creswell stumbled backwards and turned to run, but Thaniel stretched a thought towards him and pulled him violently into the air by his fashionable neck-scarf. Creswell gurgled and choked, grasping at the scarf in vain. He slowly rotated back around to face Thaniel.

'You tried to murder my friend,' Thaniel said, his voice barely above a whisper. 'Then you kidnapped the one person in this world who means even more to me. Should I take it personally, my lord? Did I do something to offend you?' He let the man drop as more soldiers appeared behind their lord. He flung them into the walls with lashes of telekinetic force and let them crumple unconscious to the floor.

'We only,' gasped Lord Creswell, the bitterness in his voice coming through despite his ruined throat. 'We only wanted…the best for…the city.'

'Kidnap? Murder?' replied Thaniel, his fury reigniting anew, his voice rising with every word. 'Torturing an innocent in some rat-infested hovel?' He was near-screaming now, the light around his hands gleaming brightly. 'I'll show you what's best for the city you low-life, stinking degenerate!'

A long piece of metal tore itself free of the banister at his merest thought and flew across the room towards the open-mouthed senator. It rammed up into his stomach and lifted him bodily into the air, bursting through his back and stabbing itself into the ceiling. Creswell hung pinned to the roof like a tangled puppet, his struggles weakening with every second. Thaniel floated down to the floor and fell to his knees, his vision clearing as the heat drained from his mind. The light around his fingers flickered and died. By now all the servants and soldiers had fled, leaving him in silence.

He stayed like that for a moment, breathing hard, trying to make sense of what he'd done. Ariene's face floated into his mind, saying something about not making enemies in the Senate. His lips twitched in a mirthless smile.

'Too late,' he whispered. His eyes strayed to the impaled form of the senator hanging from the ceiling. He felt no regret at having killed the man, but the sight still filled him with shame. He'd lost control, and now who knew what would happen?

Thaniel reached inside himself, calming his beleaguered mind and willing flame to arise on his fingers. He looked again at the gruesome body and the metal railing pinning it. He made his decision.

The flickering flame leapt from his fingers to the thick carpet, catching hungrily and rapidly growing. Smoke began to fill the hall as the fire built, stretching up to caress the walls and ignite the heavy drapes. Expensive paintings started to blister in the heat, the oils running just before their frames caught fire. Thaniel trudged slowly down the stairs, flinging a few more flames to be sure.

As he left, the mansion was burning in earnest, a blazing pyre which he knew would not entirely erase his actions but might at least mask them for a time. He turned his eyes to the dancing conflagration.

'Sorry, Ariene,' he whispered.

***

Ariene was in what appeared to be a deep conversation with the rotund bar-maid when Sophine arrived at the tavern around midday. The place was virtually empty except for a few sour-faced boys drinking at one table, and the grey-haired senator in her glittering gown of green silk at another. A cup of ale was in front of Ariene and, as Sophine crossed to the room, the bar-maid poured more into it from a jug she carried.

'Well, this is a surprise,' Sophine said with a smile as she sat down. 'Since when do you drink ale?'

Ariene lifted her cup with mock-horror and peered into it.

'Lucile!' she cried, 'you told me this was wine!'

The plump lady giggled, pouring more ale into a second cup she'd pulled from who knew where and placing it before Sophine.

'Oh Ariene,' Lucile said with a bright smile and a shake of the head. She turned and walked off towards the table with the sour-faced boys, who started to sing an off-colour song as she approached.

Sophine watched her go with amusement.

'Oh *Ariene*,' she imitated quietly, grinning at Ariene. 'You have a new pet, I see.'

'So cynical,' Ariene said, taking a sip of the murky liquid in her cup. 'It doesn't hurt to make new friends.' She grimaced at the taste and peered at the ale suspiciously. 'Even if it does require a certain amount of sacrifice.'

'How did you even know about this place? You aren't a tavern-girl.'

'I am many things, Sophine,' Ariene said archly. 'Though it was Rigel who brought me here.'

Sophine laughed, rolling her eyes.

'Surprise, surprise,' she said. She tasted the ale and almost spat it back out. 'Wow. Now I see how spoiled we are at Balderwin's.'

'Indeed,' said Ariene. 'It always pays to remind oneself that there's a whole world out there, and foul ale is only one of its many delights.'

They sat companionably for a few moments, listening to the rowdy yelling of the half-drunk sour-faced boys. Eventually Sophine looked up.

'I asked you to meet me because I tried to see into Terminheim,' she said softly.

'I suspected as much,' Ariene replied. 'It's not often I get a luncheon invitation from you these days.'

'I know. I've been busy.'

Ariene sighed.

'Me too. So. Terminheim?'

Sophine took a swill of the ale and tried to put into words what she'd experienced.

'Alakis is there, I'm sure of it,' she said, when she'd recounted her attempt to reach Terminheim. 'The storm, that's him too. Wherever he is, he's not letting me see him, whether deliberately or...' she shrugged. 'It might just be the legacy of the spell Kahin cast. His emotions might be reacting and forming a barrier, maybe that's causing the storm too. I'm not sure.'

Ariene pondered this in silence as she looked around the tavern. One elegant nail tapped the side of her cup.

'Should we be worried, do you think?' she asked.

Sophine hesitated.

'I don't know. He could be a danger to himself, and I guess the people there might be afraid of the storm like our Messengers, but otherwise I don't think that—'

Lucile returned then with a plate with what looked like some very hard biscuits and two slices of bread. She put it down between them with an apologetic look at Sophine, then she bustled away, yelling at the boys to keep their noise down. They shouted some choice things back and she threw her dishcloth at them. Laughter ensued.

'I don't suppose your students could help you,' Ariene said lightly, reaching for a biscuit.

'Don't start,' said Sophine. 'And no they couldn't. They haven't the slightest idea how to—'

'Alright alright,' Ariene sighed, waving a hand. 'I just wanted to check you couldn't somehow…' she groped for the words, '…combine powers.'

Sophine smiled the indulgent smile of long-suffering professionals confronted by the hopelessly ignorant.

'No we can't *combine powers*,' she said. 'And even if we could, they're only children, Ariene. You can't expect me to let you or the Senate use them in any way at all. I refuse on principle.'

Ariene munched her biscuit with a pained expression. Sophine could hear the hard crunches even from her side of the table. She winced, glancing at the biscuits.

'You're very protective of them,' Ariene said eventually, wiping at her mouth with a napkin. 'You see yourself as a mother to them, don't you?'

'Some of their parents had no choice but to send them,' Sophine acknowledged. 'Their mothers thought they would have a better life with me than they could offer, and I can't imagine the grief that must have caused them. That puts me in a motherhood role whether I like it or not – so yes, I do.'

'And that's why this has been so consuming for you,' Ariene said. 'I see that now.' She looked down, and Sophine thought she saw a glimmer of an unshed tear in the corner of one eye.

'You…had children…didn't you?'

Ariene sighed and dabbed delicately at the eye that had betrayed her.

'I did. Two boys. Both died in their sixties. That was over ten years ago now, not long before my husband passed.'

'That must have been hard,' Sophine said, not knowing what to say or do with this unexpectedly tender moment.

'I was an old woman by then,' Ariene shrugged. 'I fully expected to join them. I felt more anger than sadness because they were both likely political killings. Never proven of course. And then I got my second chance, and I haven't really thought about them since. They're still waiting for me, somewhere. And maybe that's why I am the way I am now.'

'How do you mean?'

'Politically. I'm trying to change politics, make it more reasonable. We got rid of the Echelarch and now it's our chance to work together...'

Sophine gave a quick snort of laughter.

'So you're mother to the city now?'

Ariene paused and looked at her, taking a fierce bite of a biscuit.

'Perhaps I am. Keeping it calm, keeping it together. Trying to stop it falling apart like a wayward family. Mother of the city,' she nodded, chewing loudly. 'There are worse positions.'

'Well then, as its mother,' Sophine said with a weak smile, 'couldn't you organise a delegation to Terminheim? The Messengers won't go but someone could. I'm very worried about Alakis and we should try to figure out what that storm's all about...'

Ariene waved a hand, looking like she'd suggested building a house out of eggs.

'I can't do that, Sophine. Remember, I'm only overseeing things. Someone would have to propose it and the factions opposing me would refuse. It would never get approved, and I can't suggest it myself or I'll be accused of acting dictatorially when I'm trying to create order.'

Sophine took a deep drink of her ale, her eyes steady on Ariene's. She didn't like this meek indecision coming from the woman who had defied death itself to save a city.

'So what can you do then? Watch like an indulgent mother while nothing gets done and chaos reigns?'

Ariene's eyes turned hard.

'You think this is chaos?' she said with a flare of her old strength. 'Wait until I step away and then I'll show you *chaos*. I'm holding order together and you could at least show some gratitude…'

'No,' Sophine said, her temper rising. 'Order is *control*, and control is *power*.' She banged her fist on the table for emphasis. 'A leader without power can't create order, and the Senate isn't just going to going to hand it to you.'

Ariene regarded her for a moment, looking wrong-footed.

'What do you mean?' she asked carefully.

'If you want order, Ariene, you need power. The senators have no need of a nursemaid, they need a leader. And the city has no need of a mother, it needs a *queen*.'

Sophine stood up from the table and dropped a coin onto it.

'Think about what I said.'

She left Ariene sitting in silence and stormed away.

Chapter Eight

The palace of the Moderator, supposedly the head of the government of Ceresheim and leader of its people, was barely half the size of Ariene's mansion in Asterheim. Made of brick, unlike many of the buildings in the city of Ceresheim (except those of great importance), it was obviously supposed to look impressive, but to those who had spent any time in the capital it fell rather short.

Rigel had tried to hide his surprise as they passed through the city walls, rising no higher than those of the Barbican and no thicker either, and made their way through the city at the agricultural heart of Astregoth. Modest buildings and the occasional stone monument stood along unpaved roads and streets of earth and soil long since turned to hard, cracked mud. Even the few remaining churches of the Sacred Circle were diminutive.

'Where is everyone?' Rigel had asked, as they proceeded across a large market square towards the Moderator's palace.

'The residential areas are over there'—Sindel had waved one hand vaguely east—'for the guild workers and suchlike. But most people live outside the walls where the work is. And the space. Who wants to be trapped inside walls all the time?'

Rigel had pondered this as they passed unchallenged through the gates of the palace into a large courtyard, again unpaved and uncobbled. It was like some country estate in the middle of a city and struck Rigel as very peculiar.

Now Roan and Sindel's smaller horse idly chewed hay in a stable nearby, and Rigel was waiting for someone to answer the door. Flickering candlelight gleamed through the windows on the ground floor of the mansion, which were overgrown with vines and other vegetation, but those of the first and second floors were dark.

Eventually the large wooden doors creaked open and a young man smiled broadly at them, ushering them into a large wood-panelled hallway decorated with heavy, faded tapestries. A large chandelier hung overhead, in which maybe half the candles burned, casting dim light across the oppressive hall. A staircase with a tired-looking reddish carpet swept up from where they stood, splitting in two as it made its way up to the balcony encircling the room and leading, presumably, to those dark rooms on the first floor. The young man, dressed in a blue velvet jacket and trousers that Rigel thought looked absolutely hideous, crossed to a door on the left and opened it for them.

'This way, please,' he said in a high, nasally voice, 'his lordship will be down shortly.'

Rigel and Sindel shared a look as the courtier closed the door behind them.

'He didn't ask us who we were,' Rigel said.

'Or who we came to see,' she added, pacing around the room. Paintings were hung on the walls, all of dour looking men in purple robes. Thankfully there were windows, through which the sunlight managed to penetrate the oppressive gloom created by the heavy wood of the walls.

'Were they all Moderators?' asked Rigel. 'There must have been fifty of them.'

119

'At least,' she replied. 'They don't tend to last long. Holding the balance of power between four Thanes is a risky business.'

The doors flew open and in marched a very short, very stocky man, in a tattered shirt and trousers of a nondescript dark cloth, carrying a gleaming bundle of purple cloth under one arm and a sceptre of a strange shape that caught the light in one hand. The man, who had not one hair on his head that was not growing from his chin, flung the sceptre onto the long, heavy table in the centre of the room. It made a horrible clanging sound and rolled a little, though not enough to fall off, and Rigel could see it was gold moulded in the shape of a crop of some kind. Some type of grain, maybe. The man dropped the bundle of purple fabric onto a chair and sat heavily in another, regarding them with hooded, watchful eyes. His beard, Rigel could now see, was extraordinarily long. The man had apparently draped it over his shoulder to keep it out of his way, so Rigel had no idea how far down his back it reached and found he really didn't want to know.

Sindel made a short, unconvincing attempt at a bow which Rigel tried to copy. The man did not move, watching them for long moments before finally stirring and gesturing to the almost comical, forlorn shape of the sceptre on the table.

'My rod of office,' he said, in an extremely low voice that made Rigel blink in surprise. 'And my glittering gown of state,' he continued, patting one meaty hand on the rustling bundle on the chair. 'Impressive, are they not?'

Rigel looked at Sindel, not sure how to respond. She gave no indication that she had any ideas to offer.

'You're from Asterheim,' the man continued in his low, gravelly voice, 'a mage, I believe.'

Rigel nodded.

'And I am Thorius Stalkreaper, Moderator of Ceresheim. Which, if you are who I suspect you are, makes this a state visit.'

'My lord,' Rigel said tentatively, 'this is not an official visit. No word was sent of my coming...'

The short man's eyebrows rose.

'And you're wondering how it is I know who you are?'

Rigel smiled weakly.

'Sit, boy.' The man indicated one of the many seats around the room and gestured at Sindel too. 'Lady, sit.'

They sat.

'I know who you are because Moderators do not last long in this city,' the gruff man growled, flicking stray bits of his long, wispy beard back over his shoulder. 'You learn fast that the way to survive is to know as much about what's going on with the Thanes as you possibly can before one or other of them either wants your help, wants you dead, or some mix of the two that eventually sees you dead. I was educated in Asterheim, boy. I did my time in the Senate, and that experience, while grim, has resulted in me lasting longer than many of my predecessors.'

'I don't understand, lord,' Sindel said. 'How did the Thanes know he was coming?'

'And just who are you?' the short, muscular man with the penetrating eyes asked.

'I was contracted to kill him,' Sindel said. 'Someone in the city wanted him dead. I didn't get a name.'

The Moderator gave Rigel an appraising look, then clapped his hands twice. Rigel jumped in his chair.

'So this one was hired to kill you and someone was warning the Thanes to watch out for you,' the Moderator said contemplatively. 'You must have something very important to say.'

'I do,' said Rigel eagerly, nodding. 'I—'

The door opened and the courtier in the horrible blue outfit came in carrying a large bottle of wine and three glasses. Rigel waited while the youth arranged the glasses and filled them, trying very much to ignore the fact that Thorius Stalkreaper's eyes did not leave him the entire time. He shifted uncomfortably.

'Your name, boy,' the Moderator said as the courtier left. 'You did not tell me.'

'Rigel,' said Rigel, feeling sheepish. 'And that's Sindel.'

The Moderator gave no indication he had heard or cared, simply watched him with those hooded, intense eyes.

'You see, boy, I have sent many messages to Asterheim. Many petitions. Our need here is great. You arrive amidst something of a war. A silent war, fought beyond sight. No one is drawing blood in the streets, but in the shadows...well. That's another story. It will not be long before it all becomes public though I fear. The Thanes are desperate. My position is untenable. And the capital is silent.'

Rigel tried to say something but managed only a short cough. He wondered what he was supposed to say.

'And yet here you are,' said the Moderator, 'a boy of less than twenty if my eyes do not deceive. A young man with no title or rank save that of Mage, here not to help me but to ask something of me. Am I right? How am I to take this if not as an insult?'

'Lord,' said Sindel.

'Silence!' boomed the Moderator with sudden intensity that shook the table. The glasses rattled and the wine danced. Rigel jumped again.

'I...I'm here on behalf of Lady Ariene Gloriana,' Rigel said, his heart thumping and his blood pounding in his ears. 'I do not know anything of any messages from Ceresheim—'

122

The Moderator looked away and put one hand on the arm of his chair as though to rise.

'But I am Lady Gloriana's mage,' he continued fast, 'together with Lord Barten and my two friends we know everything before the Senate at any time. We effectively rule the city.'

Thorius looked at him again.

'Do you now?'

Rigel looked down at his knees.

'I don't mean it boastfully. I mean, if you are sending messages to Asterheim, they are not reaching the Senate. Someone is blocking them.' As he said it, he could feel the truth of it, and on the end of that thought came another.

'Probably the same someone who wanted to stop me coming here,' he said. 'Someone wants this chaos, both here and in Asterheim. Our messages to you have been unanswered too.'

'There's chaos in Asterheim?'

Rigel grimaced.

'Yes, sir. The lack of the mages has sent everything out of balance. As you know, before communication dried up we were buying food from Ceresheim at a huge rate because our own crops aren't enough. Buildings are dilapidated, there are no healers. The city's in crisis.'

The Moderator nodded slowly, reaching for his glass and taking a surprisingly dainty sip, holding his beard flat to his chest with the other hand.

'So that's why you're here.' He took another sip, looking contemplatively at the paintings on the wall.

'Yes sir. I need to speak to the mages who fled the city and make them an offer to return.'

Thorius stood up from his chair and moved to the window, holding his glass thoughtfully.

'I don't think so,' he rumbled in his rough voice.

'You…don't?' Rigel glanced at Sindel, who looked back at him with hard eyes. She lifted one hand to one of her wrist blades, loosening it a little in its sheath.

'The mages are the best thing to happen to Ceresheim in years,' the Moderator said, turning back to them. He sounded almost regretful. 'I can't let you take them away. Not when the power of the Thanes is finally being broken. If they can be humbled, and true power restored to the city and to me as its representative, then we can have genuine peace here. We can prosper. But for that I need Asterheim's Battlemasons, and I need the mages. Once the Thanes are dealt with, perhaps you can have your mages back.'

Rigel rose to his feet, a surge of anger sweeping away his awkward caution.

'That's not good enough, sir. Asterheim is dying and it is your capital. The Senate requires that you let me speak with the mages.'

Slowly, deliberately, the Moderator placed his glass carefully on the table. He put his hands behind his back and looked at Rigel with calculating eyes.

'And if I refuse?'

The courtier burst into the room making a ghastly, keening wailing noise. The double doors banged heavily into the walls and bounced on their hinges.

'Thorius!' he yelled, 'Thorius, look—'

Something thudded into his back and the courtier collapsed to the floor, gurgling. An arrow protruded from between his shoulders. Rigel jumped back, aware of Sindel tensing at his side. The Moderator moved slowly behind the heavy table as more men shoved their way into the room, armed with short blades and heavy clubs. One had a crossbow and a very unpleasant smile on his face.

'My Lord Moderator,' drawled a large man in a fur cloak over heavy leather armour. A short, wide-bladed sword was belted at his side. Like the Moderator, he was bald or shaven-headed, but his beard was thick and blonde, and threaded with rings. 'I heard you had received unwelcome visitors. My apologies for the…mess.' His eyes drifted to the courtier on the floor and then to the smiling man with the crossbow.

'Not unwelcome, Thane Sidric,' replied the Moderator, not moving from behind the table.

'But not invited,' replied the Thane, looking with interest at Rigel. 'So you're the one, are you? You don't look the sort to evade cutthroats and checkpoints, but still. This one doesn't look much like a king, does he?' he jerked his head at the Moderator with a flash of a toothy smile.

'Only a Moderator,' said Thorius, sitting down and picking up his wine. Rigel could see the liquid trembling slightly in the glass. 'What do you want, Sidric?'

'It is my duty as Thane to ensure the continuity of our constitution, Lord Moderator,' said Sidric, with obviously false sincerity. He placed one mailed hand over his heart. 'When I receive word that you, our esteemed leader, are being visited by agents of a foreign power, I feel it necessary to protect you.'

'I need no protection. This young man is here from Asterheim, hardly a foreign power. You are here unlawfully.'

Sidric sucked his teeth and waved a finger.

'There are no raiders in Ceresheim, Lord Moderator. Only good people looking out for their country. You see,' Sidric's tone turned hard. 'I have it on good authority that he is acting contrary to the interests of Ceresheim, and is, in fact, a traitor to Asterheim on top of that.'

'Your authority does not extend to this hall, Sidric. I am lord here.'

The big Thane made a show of glancing around the unimpressive dining room.

'And so you are, lord. But I am acting in the interests of Ceresheim,' he paused, glancing at his men. 'And I have the swords.' He smiled, pointing at Rigel. 'Kill that one,' he said, 'and bring the Overseer to my fort. For his own protection.'

The crossbowman died first, a slender blade lodged deep in his eye socket before he had the chance to even think about raising his weapon. The man to his left shrieked and fell sideways, clutching the terrible gash a whistling blade had opened in his throat. Blood sprayed, but there were too many even for Sindel's deadly skill.

Five, six men rushed at them, yelling war cries and holding weapons aloft. The Thane was turning away, uninterested in what must have seemed to him an inevitable victory. Three more soldiers on the other side of the table were reaching for the Moderator when Rigel unleashed his signature power.

Taking the tension and fear, the panic and the anger that had arisen within him and funnelling it outward, Rigel directed it at the very essence of the material world itself. The natural order bent and flexed against the terrible strength of his mind, bucking and heaving as he suborned it to his will. Time slowed, stuttered, stopped. He could feel it almost as a pressure against a shield, as though they were on the inside of a bubble of gossamer thin web, outside of which the vast ocean of time itself roiled and crashed in its fury.

Droplets of blood hung suspended like perfect gleaming rubies; motes of light gleamed on blades held motionless in place by men who screamed silent battle-cries from frozen mouths. The Moderator's wine glass, its delicate edge hovering just above the heavy wood of the table, remained whole merely fractions of a second from fracturing. Sindel's third blade, its lethal edge caught mid-arc, glinted in the sunlight.

'How...what...' Sindel breathed, looking around in wonder. She reached up to the wrist-blade she'd thrown with expert precision at one of the charging men and tugged at it. It did not make even the slightest movement.

'Can I get that back?' she asked, as though focusing on the banality of reclaimed possessions was the most she could cope with at that moment.

'No, it's stuck,' said Rigel, secretly pleased to finally be able to show off his favourite ability. 'Nothing that I haven't deliberately moved out of the flow of time will move.'

'But aren't we in the flow of time? We're moving and they aren't.'

He shrugged.

'I think we're the ones outside of time. Out there'—he gestured at the charging men and the retreating Thane—'everything's normal. They're just waiting for us.'

The Moderator moved slowly around the men reaching for him, touching them and their weapons in fascination.

'These people were not taking me anywhere for long – look at them,' he muttered. 'This one is actually thrusting.' He flicked the wicked-looking dagger.

Sindel shrugged.

'I don't think any of us were supposed to survive this,' she said, 'so don't take it personally.'

'Sidric,' said Thorius, shaking his head. 'Cuthbert, I could understand, he's been so vocal lately. But Sidric. What was his plan I wonder? To say he had me in his fort and hope no one noticed I was never seen again?'

'It's been done before,' said Sindel. 'I guess Sidric got fed up waiting for one of his rivals to make the first move.'

'Moderator,' Rigel said, wincing at a spasm of pain, 'we don't have long before I have to release them. Where can we go that no one would think to look for you?'

'Nowhere really,' Thorius grumbled, stepping around the men to stare into Thane Sidric's unseeing eyes. 'This is one of the more secure buildings in the city. Or was until…'

'Until?'

The Moderator sighed.

'Until the mages came with Lord Orswell. He set himself up in a mansion across the city near the lake. The mages were so grateful that they raised it in about three days. He's their hero now. His place is the unofficial Guild office for the mages, and I suppose he's their patron.'

'Orswell,' Rigel smiled. 'Thank the Circle, we'll go there then. Quickly, before I have to drop this bubble.'

'Bubble?'

'Never mind…let's just go.' He moved to scoop up the body of the courtier, not knowing if he was dead or dying. The Moderator waved him away, lifting the boy with surprising strength and heaving him up over one shoulder.

They made their way gingerly around the Thane's men, Sindel actually clambering over the top of one of them, using him like a climbing frame when there wasn't enough room for her to squeeze past. Thankfully, they had burst through the front door in much the same manner as they had the door to the dining room and so the fugitives were able to simply run through. They were some streets away from the mansion when Rigel finally let the churning ocean of time crash back over them.

'Will they chase us?' asked the Moderator, looking fearfully over his shoulder as he lay the arrow-struck courtier down.

'Doubtful,' said Rigel, rubbing at his head. The relief was immense. 'To them, we literally just vanished into thin air. They'll have no reason to think we've gone in any particular direction.'

'You're a very dangerous young man,' remarked Thorius.

'Thank you, sir. Now, let's see if this poor man's got any life left in him.'

Rigel knelt by the courtier and closed his eyes, reaching for the second sight he had first encountered that night on the bridge with Ariene. The darkness began to swirl, tiny motes of dull light glimmering like candlelight half-seen through thick dark clouds. Gradually, they resolved themselves into something like the shape of a man.

Only the very faintest gleam of silvery threads floated through the unseen space within the young man's body, a quickly draining network of light now confined to the head. The courtier couldn't have more than moments left. Rigel sucked his teeth and concentrated, channelling as much of his energy as he dared into the depleted web of life energy. Almost as an afterthought, he yanked the arrow out of the man's back and threw it away.

Gradually, slowly, the web began to glow brighter, slowly starting to expand outwards as it reacted to his presence. Tentatively, it rippled across the body, forging connections within connections until glittering capillaries of brilliance spread throughout the emptiness.

In the real world, the ghastly hole in the body began to heal, a healthy flush returning to the grey, cooling skin. All at once Rigel fell back, gasping, just as the youth sat bolt upright and vomited messily all over him.

Rigel made a disgusted strangled noise and scrabbled backwards like a crab. He made to wipe the filth off his clothes, but then thought better of it and simply sat, gagging at the smell, his hand waving frantically in the air.

'Sacred Circle, I'm so sorry,' moaned the young man, looking at himself and what he'd just done in horror. 'What...where am I? Am I dead?'

'Not anymore,' said Sindel. The youth blinked at her.

'No, no, not dead,' said Rigel between short, gagging sounds of disgust. 'I can't heal the dead. You weren't far off though.'

The Moderator reached for Rigel's hand, then withdrew it when he saw the state of the hand. He straightened, nodding his bald head.

'As I said,' he rumbled in his gravelly voice. 'Very dangerous indeed.'

***

Lord Orswell's house was situated in the far northern end of the walled city, on land that Thorius explained had once been a cemetery.

'A storm blew through once, some years ago,' the Moderator said with a shrug. 'Ripped up the earth and knocked most of the monuments down. Bodies and corpses everywhere, and no one could tell who was who anymore. The Thanes held a council and decided to burn everything for health reasons and the land was just left unused. It was thought unlucky by most people.' He smiled wryly. 'Not unlucky for Orswell, though.'

The mages had wasted no time in raising the colossal palace, which now housed many of them and served as their Guild, their fortress and their embassy. It was a sprawling site on five floors, made of a strange dark material which looked smooth as stone but reflected no light from the now setting sun. The entrance boasted pillars and stairs that were clearly inspired by the Senate building in Asterheim, flanked left and right by long walls containing the wings of the mansion, which looked as though it could house hundreds of people.

'What is this made of?' asked Rigel in fascination, touching a smooth pillar. The cold, unyielding material was a dull, dark hue, but had hints of white and green here and there. He looked closer at one white patch and jumped back, snatching his hand away.

'That's a worm,' he said.

Thorius laughed.

'Probably. The whole thing was raised from the earth. Your mages were not all builders, but there were enough to direct them. It was quite a sight. Hundreds of people all'—he wiggled his fingers in the air—'with the builders and stonemason types barking orders. They lifted the ground itself, bodies and all I suppose. And worms. Turned bit by bit into blocks, then into a building, and held it there with sorcery.'

'It's like a palace of black stone,' put in the pale-faced, blue-velvet clad courtier, 'but someone's painted it to look like a tilled field after a tropical storm.'

Rigel turned to look at him.

'What's your name, friend?'

'Ceolnbert.'

Rigel hesitated, unsure if he could get his tongue around those sounds.

'Call him Bert,' said the Moderator. 'I do.'

'I'm really sorry I threw up on you,' said Ceolnbert.

'It's okay. I'm sure Lord Orswell will lend me something. Maybe you too.'

'I didn't get any on me,' the courtier protested, looking at his blue velvet sleeves.

'No vomit,' said Sindel from behind him. 'But from where I'm standing your jacket has seen better days.'

The youth looked confused for a moment, then laughed.

'Oh right. The arrow.'

'The arrow,' agreed Sindel. 'Such a little thing. So easy thing to forget.'

'A trifle,' nodded the Moderator. 'Hardly worth mentioning...'

'Alright alright!' said Ceolnbert, following Rigel up the steps towards the large wooden doors of the mages' palace.

'Where did they get the windows,' said Rigel, knocking on the doors. 'And wood for the doors?'

'Window and door shops, I imagine,' said the Moderator. 'This is a city, you know. It may not be as big as your *Asterheim*—'

The door swung open and Lord Orswell stepped out with a wide smile on his face. Rigel tried to hide his shock at the sight of the man who had saved them from certain failure a few months before. Orswell was fatter, greyer and happier than Rigel had ever thought he could be. His shiny jacket was bright green, and his hair was oiled.

'Rigel! I thought that was you. I happened to be in the library upstairs and caught sight of the Moderator walking this way with a fellow I knew I recognised from somewhere and it turns out—'

Orswell trailed off and sniffed, his smiled fading.

'What is that dreadful smell?'

Rigel shuffled from foot to foot.

'Ah, that's me, sir. I, eh…have some vomit on me.'

Orswell peered at him, then at the unmistakably lethal Sindel with her blades. Finally, he looked at the Moderator.

'You look terrible, Thorius,' he said lightly. 'Something tells me this is not a social call.'

'We're in trouble, Ormond,' replied the shorter man in his rumbling voice. 'Sidric tried to kill me.'

Orswell's eyes flicked to Rigel.

'Something to do with you, no doubt?'

Rigel gave a short, weak laugh.

'Maybe.'

Orswell sighed.

'You can take the mage out of Asterheim…' he said, shaking his head. 'You'd best come in then.' He held a hand out as Rigel made to step through the door, barring his way.

'Not you, Rigel. You take that filthy stuff off before you come in here.'

'But it's cold!'

'You're a mage, heat yourself up.'

Rigel stared at him hatefully and gingerly reached for his sleeve.

'It seems to me,' said Lord Orswell, plucking a grape from his bowl and rolling it between thumb and forefinger, 'that you don't really have time to be sitting here talking to me.' He popped the grape into his mouth and sat back, looking thoughtfully out of one of the very large windows which, by virtue of being on the fifth floor, overlooked the whole of Ceresheim city. The ball room was stupendously large, running almost the entire length of the east wing, but sparsely furnished. A few desks and tables sat along the edge of the room, at which small groups of well-dressed people sat talking in plush seats. The rest of the room was filled with large round tables that could fit perhaps six to eight, though besides their group none of these were occupied, and at one end was a stage on which some people appeared to be rehearsing something. A few paintings and draperies hung from the walls, but it still had the feel of being unfinished.

'Thane Sidric will be unlikely to just go home and shrug his shoulders, I would think, or am I wrong?' Orswell looked at the Moderator.

Thorius made a small nod in reply, sitting stiffly in his chair. Rigel had the distinct impression that the more the small man saw of Orswell's palace, the less he liked it.

'Might need to do something about that then,' the former senator said, waving a hand at a servant who came hurrying over. 'Food please,' he said, 'something simple and fast.' The servant scurried away.

'You've done well for yourself here,' Thorius finally said, looking out from under his heavy brow at the opulent room.

'Thanks to the generosity of Ceresheim, my lord,' said Orswell politely, but Rigel caught the patronising undercurrent to his words. You could take the man out of the Senate...

'I think perhaps we have been over generous. You run this place like you're a Thane yourself.'

'Not at all, sir. Merely patron of the Guild of Mages, who have proven themselves so...helpful...to Ceresheim of late.'

The undercurrent was now more of an overcurrent, and Rigel squirmed.

'Lord Orswell,' he said, 'you're still patron of Citizenry in Asterheim, too.'

That seemed to surprise the former senator. His eyebrows rose and a faint smile played about his lips.

'And how do they fare? My lost souls still plugging away at their visa applications and what-not? The boys who followed me here are now in various administrative positions within the Guild and very much enjoying Ceresheim's more relaxed attitude to life. Or so I hear.'

'They're doing well, lord. Eric and Thaniel have it well in hand.'

Orswell smiled broadly and actually clapped his hands together in amusement.

'Marvellous! And they're still together?'

'Oh yes. Very.' Rigel rolled his eyes.

'How wonderful. Well, you can tell them that I'm no longer alone either, as it happens. And he's a wonderful cook, hence this,' Orswell patted his stomach. 'And how about you, Rigel?' His eyes flicked to Sindel, sitting by Rigel's side.

Rigel felt his cheeks flush red and hot. He looked away. Orswell, to his credit, sat back in his chair and changed the subject.

'In any case, Sidric will need to be dealt with before this gets out of hand.'

'You can't just march in there and kill him,' Rigel said.

'*He* can't march anyone anywhere,' growled Thorius. 'I'm the Moderator, not him.'

'Of course, sir. I just meant I need to know a few things first.'

'Such as?' said Orswell, ignoring the Moderator's discomfort.

'Who he's been in touch with in Asterheim. There's a plot of some sort, and I need to warn the Senate about it.'

The Moderator laughed gruffly at that.

'He's hardly going to tell you that.'

'No,' agreed Rigel. 'I'd need to look around his private chambers.'

'Out of the question,' Thorius said. 'If I march a load of soldiers up there and demand entry for you...'

Orswell laughed.

'What would happen, Thorius? Sidric will try to kill him again? He'll come after you? We already know that's his intention. You have no choice but to act first.'

'What if...' said Sindel, pausing to push her long hair back over her shoulder. 'What if we snuck in there tonight, found what Rigel needs and dealt with Sidric at the same time?'

'You think you can do that?' asked Orswell doubtfully.

'I *know* they can do that,' Thorius growled. 'You should have seen what happened at the palace. That woman had two men dead before you could blink and then he...he...'

'Did something with those wiggly mage fingers of his, I'm guessing,' said Orswell with a smile.

Rigel nodded, silently horrified at how simple it had been to decide to murder a man.

'And what about my request, lord?' he asked, looking sidelong at Thorius. 'I need to speak to the mages, to bring them Asterheim's offer.'

'Asterheim's offer?' said Orswell slyly, with an eyebrow cocked.

'Well, Ariene's offer.'

'That's what I thought.'

Thorius stood up from the table and moved towards one of the large windows.

'I don't like it,' he said, his tone suggesting that anything he didn't like shouldn't exist at all. 'But taking out Sidric will stave off chaos here for a while and open up communications with Asterheim, so it's only fair that I should let you try to stave off the chaos there too. Very well. Do this, and I will permit you to address the mages.'

'You're very gracious,' said Lord Orswell blandly, with a glance at Rigel that spoke volumes. Rigel nodded back; either way, that look suggested, the mages would hear what Ariene wanted them to hear.

'Am I coming?' asked Ceolnbert suddenly, looking up from the bowl of fruit and cheese he had been forcing into his face for the last half hour. Rigel frowned at him.

'Of course not,' he said.

'Oh, good,' said Ceolnbert, reaching for a pear.

Orswell and Rigel shared a bewildered look.

Chapter Nine

Sophine slammed the heavy wooden door of her office behind her and trudged heavily to her desk, flopping into the plush, leather-cushioned chair behind it and putting her boots up on the heavy wood. Some papers fluttered and scattered away from her careless feet and she watched them with disinterest.

The meeting with Ariene earlier that day had not gone well and the rest of the day had been difficult too, on a much more mundane level.

She sighed in frustration, silently cursing Ariene. The old woman had refused to send anyone to Terminheim, and seemed determined to keep up this farcical pretence at running the city through this caretaker role she'd been given. Before long, Sophine was sure, Ariene would have to take charge properly and burn out these opposition senators making life difficult for everyone.

There was a knock on her door, and a timid laundry-worker poked her head in.

'Rector? We need more soap for the laundry and the chef says he can't plan next week's meals because some of the food deliveries haven't arrived…'

Sophine waved a hand, cutting the woman off mid-flow.

'Thank you,' she said, with a smile that felt false even to her, 'I'll get on that tomorrow. Could you maybe make a note and—'

The woman's face fell and Sophine instantly regretted her words. The laundry lady couldn't read. If she'd been less distracted by Terminheim and Ariene she'd have remembered that.

'I mean, let's have a meeting tonight and we'll decide what to do. Round up the chef and the cleaners, and all the other staff, and let's…let's talk about what we all need.'

The laundry-worker nodded.

'Thank you, Rector,' she said, and vanished.

'I can do this,' Sophine whispered into the empty room. 'I can manage this place. I just need to deal with bloody Alakis first.'

Something caught her eye then, perched at the edge of her desk, looking for all the world like it belonged there.

The dark-leather book.

Sophine scowled at it, reaching across the desk for the creepy volume and ignoring the whispering in the back of her head. It was surprisingly heavy for a relatively small book, and her hands tingled as she touched it.

'You seem to think you have the answers,' she muttered at it, 'so let's see…'

She flipped it open.

The book vanished. Sophine blinked at the space where it had sat. The wooden desk seemed…different. Where once it had been a sea of papers on dark, heavy wood it was now a clear surface of light yellowy timber. She looked up.

Her office was gone. She was in a wooden hut with a thatched roof, sitting on a rough wooden stool before a simple table. The hut was small and featureless, the windows dark and the door shut beneath the heavy thatch. A fire burned in a hearth not far from where she sat.

Opposite her sat a pale-faced woman in a peculiar outfit. She wore a mail shirt of heavy rings over a steel breastplate, her arms and legs encased in tight fitting metal armour with narrow points at the corners. Over this she wore an open traveller's cloak, with its hood down.

The woman's armour, clothes and hands were all the same pale, colourless hue as her face. She glowed faintly, as though lit from within by some strange ghostly light. Across her knees she held a thin-bladed sword, which shimmered with a similar glow.

But it was the chair on which the woman sat that drew Sophine's gaze. It was an inky black shape, softly undulating as though made of compacted dark mist. Small tendrils of wispy darkness floated and sighed around it, seeming to writhe and squirm at the touch of the glowing woman. It was hissing in that now-familiar half-heard ghostly whisper.

'Where am I?' asked Sophine, her words sounding thick and ponderous as though she was speaking through heavy air. The hut and the woman had a strange, dreamlike quality to them, made all the stranger by the flickering flames in the hearth. They leapt and spat like normal fire, but a hundred times too slowly, and they made no smoke.

The apparition did not reply. It did not even seem to see her. Sophine stood up with difficulty. Moving in this strange vision was not easy, her body responding only sluggishly to her mind's commands. She slowly made her way across the room, her clothes floating around her as though underwater. The woman in the living chair of rippling smoke did not look up and did not notice her, but an echo of some half-heard word drifted towards Sophine and seemed to emanate from the motionless ghost.

'Hilda,' it whispered, repeating endlessly, flowing in and out of the very edge of hearing.

'Hilda...Hilda...Hilda...'

Sophine reached out to touch the inky darkness of the chair-like shape, suddenly sure this was an image of the legendary mage who had ended the Great Purge. Her fingers were almost within touching distance of the gently swaying tendrils of darkness, when the woman's empty eyes flicked to lock on Sophine's.

The spell was broken. Sophine sat alone in her office, looking at an open book. She blinked, trying to make sense of the peculiar vision.

'Hilda,' she said softly running a finger tentatively down one page.

'You're in there, aren't you,' Sophine mused. 'Some part of you.' She calmed her mind, seeing past the book's physical form. Something was definitely inside it, a gleaming mote of light.

She knew without doubt now that this book had belonged to Hilda, and that the great mage had found a way to imbue it with a fragment of her mind. Her essence. Nothing sentient, but something that retained Hilda's essential being outside of her body. The vision she had seen and the strange behaviour of the book suggested a measure of living power within it, an echo of the person who had put it there so long ago.

'Master Thomas,' she chuckled to herself, 'you old scoundrel you...'

They'd been taught that the mind was all. Mage craft was about mental discipline, above all else. She'd already discovered that those particular lessons were specious at best, given the power she and the two boys had gained through emotion during the Kahin conflict, but this...this was a revelation still further. The concept of a fragment of a person living on beyond their death suggested the existence of a true *soul*. A spirit of a person as separate to the body and the mind as distinct from its physical shell.

'So many possibilities,' she said, wondering about Terminheim. A mind within a body did not have the power to direct itself reliably over such distance, and anyway, she couldn't get past the disturbance surrounding the city. But a mind *outside* the body, a consciousness free of its physical shell, well...

Information sighed and floated in her mind as she traced the pages of the invaluable work of the great mage and understanding began to dawn. Sophine gasped with the revelation, grinning broadly as her heart began to beat faster.

'Can I speak to you?' she asked, addressing the book directly. She felt a whisper of something beyond hearing but undeniable nonetheless. It felt very much like an answer. Her heart leapt and thudded within her chest and she had to suppress the urge to pump her fist in the air.

'I need to see further,' she said. 'Show me how.' She raised her finger and flipped the pages, wondering if they were turning more of their own accord than her movements. She stopped and peered down at the page she'd come to.

'Well now,' she said, with a glance at the leather binding. 'Would you look at that.'

***

Eric moaned as his eyes fluttered open and turned towards Thaniel, a tired smile making its way across his almost-healed face. It hurt Thaniel's heart to see the bruising on that face, the angry red around the eyes he saw in his dreams and ached for when awake.

He'd done all he could, but he was not a healer like Rigel. He had sped up the process considerably, using the remaining embers of his cooling rage to lend him the strength to push Eric's natural healing processes along at unnatural pace, but Eric still had a way to go. Cosmetically, at least.

'How do you feel?' Thaniel asked, touching Eric's face gently.

'Better,' he said. 'Much better actually. Did you...?' he shook a hand free of the covers and wiggled his fingers. Thaniel nodded.

'Did my best. You still look like you picked a fight with a brick wall though.'

Eric smiled.

'That's me, a fighter to the end.'

'You'd best believe it,' grinned Thaniel. 'You took a harder beating than anyone I've ever known and lived to tell the tale.'

Eric's eyebrows rose.

'Is that *fighting* where you come from?'

Thaniel shrugged.

'You got me. I don't know anything about fighting either.' His voice rang hollow as he thought back to his short-lived but extremely violent rampage of only a few hours ago.

'Than?' Eric said guardedly, reading his expression with ease like he somehow always did. 'What are you thinking?'

'Nothing,' he said brightly, reaching out to adjust the duvet covers. Eric shifted and pushed himself up to a sitting position. Thaniel sighed in frustration.

'You should rest—'

'Tell me, Than. What did you do?'

Thaniel hesitated for a moment, not knowing how to say it. He looked away.

'I...went to the tavern. Tyler told me which one. I don't really remember how I got there.'

Eric sighed, reaching out to touch his shoulder.

'Tell me.'

'I killed them, Eric,' he said, relieved that his voice didn't crack. He sounded strong, confident. Like he regretted nothing. 'Creswell too.'

Eric winced and sucked in a breath through his teeth.

'Oh. Did anyone see?'

Thaniel let out a short, mirthless bark of laughter.

'I may as well have sold tickets,' he said. 'I wasn't thinking.' He fully expected Eric to say something like "Clearly not" or "Obviously". He could practically hear the words in his head. Instead, Eric surprised him.

'Doesn't matter,' he said. 'They'd have known it was you regardless.'

'Who?'

'*They*. Them. Whoever they are who thought you were such a threat.' He smirked and gave a short chuckle. 'I guess they were right.' The eyes Eric turned on Thaniel then were full of fierce pride.

'Thank you,' Eric said thickly. 'Thank you for doing that for me.'

Thaniel grinned and shook his head.

'You do surprise me sometimes.'

Eric shrugged.

'The key to a lasting relationship, I hear, is to keep surprising the one you love.'

Thaniel laughed, absurdly pleased that the disappointment and recrimination he had fully expected, and fully felt he deserved, had not come.

'You remember that first day we met?' he asked. 'I fixed that wall in Orswell's estate?'

Eric nodded.

'I learned something today. I can do the same thing in reverse.'

'Knock a wall down?'

'*Melt* a wall down,' he said.

Eric snorted and rolled his eyes.

'Well I'm sure *that* will come in handy.'

'It might!'

'Uh-huh.'

As Eric slid his legs out of the bed and stood up, Thaniel heard the crunch of carriage wheels and hooves outside. He made himself look away from the tantalising form of Eric's naked body and went to the window.

'Someone's coming,' he said.

Eric made a quiet chuckling noise.

'Oh, you think?'

'I do,' said Thaniel distractedly, his eyes on the carriage. 'I really do.'

The carriage was coming at speed, practically sliding to a halt in a cloud of dust in the courtyard at the front of the house. Ariene Gloriana stepped quickly out of the carriage before the horse had even stopped moving and marched with swift purpose towards the doors, holding a shawl around her shoulders that billowed in the wind behind her.

'It's Ariene,' Thaniel said softly. 'And I don't think she's very happy.'

***

In the space of only a few hours, Sophine felt that she'd learned more than in years of study at the Barbican. Her fingers had found the pages she'd wanted without effort, as though the tome were helping her along. Given that it had managed to appear close to her a few times over the last few days, she was not particularly surprised. There was a sentience to the book, some half-formed consciousness that seemed to obediently help her when she needed it, possibly the legacy of the tiny piece of Hilda's mind embedded within it.

Her mind, or her *soul*.

She still had no idea why the great mage-lord would have done such a thing, let alone in a work as dark and dangerous as this one. Perhaps to warn off the wrong people from using it, perhaps to help the right people to use it. Either way, it was a mystery.

That the book itself was inherently fearful had been clear to her long before she'd started reading it. Even Alakis had shied away from its ghostly whispering and the sensation of cold it seemed to carry with it, leaving it on the shelf when he had fled. But the content did not seem wrong in and of itself, though undeniably dangerous in the wrong hands.

'If one can allow for the existence of a soul,' Sophine read aloud by candlelight, snuggled up on her plush sofa in her office with a blanket around her, 'beings of similar form and substance to a human soul must also be assumed to be possible. And since we have proof of the soul through confirmed astral projection and the art of mind-fragmentation (discussed below), we must conclude that such beings exist either within our realm but beyond our ordinary perception or beyond our realm entirely.'

She shuddered at the thought. Demons. Angels. Things of energy and emotion beyond our understanding. No wonder the priests of the Sacred Circle had wanted all this suppressed.

From there the book became more heavily academic. The discussion of the soul moved on into other theories and concepts, the idea of transference of souls and the movement of minds between bodies being particularly disturbing. Necromancy, that most forbidden and feared witchcraft, was openly considered as a natural evolution of soul-theory. If beings had souls, then they could be implored to return to a body after death. The possibilities, it seemed, were bound only by the imagination of the sorcerer. That, and her strength of will.

She flipped back to the page she'd started on, which was a discussion of how to actually embed a fragment of consciousness in an object. She traced the wording with her finger, going over it until she was sure she had the concept firm in her mind.

'Mistress Sophine?' the head chef knocked on the door and peered in at her. 'Are we still meeting tonight?'

She looked up, startled. She'd almost forgotten her management meeting. The sun had set, so she only had an hour or so left.

'Of course, of course,' said with a reassuring smile. 'I'll be there in about an hour.'

He thanked her and left, leaving her groaning in frustration.

'It's now or never then,' she muttered, swinging her legs off the sofa and reaching for the little bowl of stones she'd collected from the courtyard.

'I'm sure I mentioned,' said Ariene, in a light tone which did not at all match the angry gleam of her eyes, 'that attacking senators in their own home was likely to cause difficulties for us all.' She finished pouring the tea, this time into thick mugs she'd had brought from the servants' quarters. She stirred them in ponderous silence.

Thaniel and Eric sat on one side of the long dining table, holding hands underneath it. Ariene stood on the other side, handing out the mugs. Then she sat down and gave Thaniel a flat stare.

'Did I not?' she asked.

Thaniel felt Eric squeeze his hand and raised his chin a little.

'They took Eric. Tortured him. If it hadn't been for the little lad from the Citizenry Guild—'

'Tyler,' said Eric.

'If it hadn't been for Tyler, he'd still be there. And we'd be sitting here reading demands from them.'

She stared at him with wide, uncomprehending eyes.

'Demands?' she repeated.

'Yes, demands. They took him to force me to, I don't know. Stay out of their way? I expect their demands would have been to leave the city. The country, even. I don't know. And when I refused, they'd start sending me things to show me how serious they were...' his voice was choking, turning into a hoarse squeak as he felt tears arising. Eric squeezed his hand again.

'I'm sorry,' she said, looking at Eric. 'I didn't know. Did they hurt you? You don't look too—'

'Thaniel healed the worst of it,' said Eric. 'I'm alright now. Still sore and my ribs are a bit suspect, but I'm alright.'

She sat back and sipped her tea. The mug looked absurdly large in her delicate hands.

'The Senate heard reports from Battlemasons stationed in the Noble Quarter,' she said softly. 'Reports of a floating mage with blonde hair burning down Senator Creswell's mansion. I thought it was just about Rigel. Seemed somewhat overkill, to put it lightly.' She smiled weakly. 'Doesn't seem to be overkill now.'

'It doesn't?' Thaniel asked, surprised.

She smiled again.

'I could tell you stories of retaliatory hits on rivals going back many, many years,' she said. 'Kidnapping and extortion are a dangerous game. You have to be sure no one knows where you are, otherwise things get very messy.' She gestured at Thaniel. 'That's what happens. I think if the people behind all this are honest with themselves, they'll have to admit that Creswell's mansion going up in flames was always a possibility when kidnapping a mage's husband.'

Thaniel started in his chair, almost knocking over his tea.

'We…we're not married,' he said, glancing at Eric who was looking steadfastly forward.

Ariene didn't appear to notice his jerking movement or their sudden awkwardness, merely stirring her tea with a faint smile.

'Oh yes, that's right,' she said mildly. 'Now, where was I? Ah yes. We heard the reports, so I left immediately to come here and berate you in my best "*I'm so disappointed*" voice. But I doubt that even my supporters will be able to stop the Senate voting to have you both dragged before them on charges of arson and'—she peered at Thaniel with questioning eyes—'murder?'

He smiled weakly.

'I'm afraid so.'

She waved the admission away and continued to ponder her cup.

'Creswell's body hadn't been recovered at the time, so no one was sure. I suspected though, as I'm sure did any of his odious friends in the Senate. In any case, I would think you have less than an hour left before a battalion of Battlemasons appears to arrest you.' She looked over her shoulder through one of the large, opulently curtained windows. 'Sadly, it seems you will have to flee after all, Thaniel.'

'I'm sorry, Ariene,' he said. 'I really am.'

'As am I,' she sighed. 'With you in hiding, I'll be truly alone. In a sense, they've won already. I don't know what I'll face in the Senate without my gallant protectors to shield me from the veiled threats and the less veiled threats, but I don't think it'll be long before they strike.'

Thaniel tried to think of something to say, but came up short.

'Never mind,' Ariene said, replacing her mug on the table and rising to her feet. 'I've fought battles in the Senate before and come out alive. I'll just have to do it again. You two need to pack and get out of here before the Senate's enforcers arrive.'

'Where can we go?'

'There's only one place you'll be safe,' she replied with a doubtful look, 'and even there I'm not sure quite how safe. Hilda's Barbican, with Sophine.'

Eric gave a short laugh.

'You don't think they'll think to look for a mage…at the headquarters of the Guild of Mages.'

She dipped her head in acknowledgment of the point.

'I'm sure they will,' she allowed. 'But you'll be safer there than anywhere else. Very few would dare tangle with that girl. At the very least, they'll think twice before coming.'

Thaniel nodded and went to grab a bag.

***

Sophine was unimpressed when Thaniel and Eric told her their tale later that evening. She sat in her plush chair behind the Rector's desk, looking at the two boys who sprawled on a sofa against the wall. Thaniel had only been in this room once in all his time at Hilda's Barbican, after getting in trouble for smashing a window with a careless flick of telekinesis when he was supposed to be reading something about crops and how they grow. He smiled faintly at the memory, looking around the room.

The Rector's office was much larger than Master Thomas's dingy cell, and much better lit. It had long windows running along the top of the wall near where it joined the roof, which, despite not permitting a view of any kind, allowed the light in. The wall hosting the windows was made of cold, grey stone, and was one of the original walls Hilda had raised when the Barbican was first built. It exuded a sense of history and permanence he found calming, in stark contrast to the mess of the rest of the room.

Sophine's office was a confusing jumble of books and bits of paper. Her desk, long, heavy and obviously very old, was piled high with various bits of clutter. The bookcases lining the room were no longer neat and tidy, the books having fallen over on themselves when key tomes had been removed by careless hands and not replaced. Thaniel scrunched his toes on the thick rug, which seemed to be the pelt of some unknown animal with white-grey fur. He'd taken his boots off precisely to see how it felt on his feet.

'How long do you think, until they come here?' Sophine asked from her seat behind the desk. She was looking paler and more gaunt than usual, if that were even possible, and her hair seemed darker as though to enhance the contrast. Her voice, however, was as commanding as ever.

'Ariene thought they'd be at Balderwin's within the hour,' said Eric, squirming in the soft cushions of the sofa. He looked as though he might fall asleep at any moment. 'So if they go and don't find us, maybe another few hours to report back and send someone out here?'

A flicker of alarm crossed Sophine's face.

'Hours?' she said. 'I thought we were talking days...'

Eric made a noncommittal noise and closed his eyes.

'He's right, Soph. We don't have long.'

'Well, you can't very well stay here,' she said. 'If a wanted mage is found at the Barbican of all places it could mean the end of everything I've built here. My students...' she trailed off with a frown. 'You can't be here, Thaniel.'

'We can't go to Orswell's,' he protested. 'That's as obvious as here, but without the protection.'

'Why do you need protection anyway? Can't you go and tell the Senate what this Creswell was up to? Defend yourself there.'

'If we do that then we might pull Ariene down with us,' he said. 'This is all about her.'

Sophine gave him a dark look at that, but didn't comment. She rose to her feet, picking up a stone from a pile on her desk and weighing it in her hand.

'I've been…reading…lately,' she said, very clearly picking her words with care. 'Reading about different kinds of abilities.' She looked at him, as though to gauge his reaction. Beside him, Eric let out a small snore.

'What kinds of abilities?' he asked, thinking he knew the answer. His eyes strayed to a thick book sitting on her desk. At first glance it seemed to be made of smoke and he jumped at the sight. Then he realised it was just very, very dark. Sophine made a small, involuntary movement as though wanting to move the book out of sight before realising it was too late. She looked back at him.

'I was trying to see further,' she said. A little defensively, he thought. 'Trying to find Alakis. We think he's in Terminheim, but I can't reach it. Even with the book,' she turned her head slightly towards it, as though only managing not to look at it with great effort. 'Even with the book, I can't quite find a way to get through. It's surrounded by something I can only describe as a storm. A storm both here in the real world and beyond, in the ethereal. I can see lightning and hear…something. I can feel pain and sadness and terrible, terrible anger. It's like a rage-storm surrounds the city and stops me getting in, but I'm sure he's there. And I'm sure he's in danger.'

She hopped up onto the desk and pushed her long hair back away from her face, holding up a stone.

'Something I've learned is that it's possible to divide a person's consciousness and bind a shard of it to something temporarily.'

Thaniel felt a thrill of danger shiver through him.

'Their consciousness?' he asked flatly.

She looked away.

'Perhaps that's not the right word,' she allowed. 'Their essence. Their vitality…'

'Their soul,' said Thaniel. 'That's what you're talking about isn't it. Sophine, this is dark magic, really dark. Souls and life-forces...'

'You're being superstitious, Thaniel,' she said, a little too quickly. 'I'm only talking about imbuing an object with a fragment of your awareness, which fades in time. I'm not talking about necromancy and manipulating souls.'

He hesitated. Sophine was powerful, yes. Ambitious, certainly. And more than willing to look into the darkness if she needed to. But she was also much smarter than him, better educated in these areas and ultimately, she was his friend. She deserved his trust. He exhaled and gave her an apologetic smile.

'I'm sorry,' he said. 'It's been a very, very long day and I've done things today that I'm not proud of. I guess I'm over-compensating with the right-and-wrong thing.'

'The holier-than-thou thing, you mean,' she teased with a flash of her old self.

He grinned and shrugged.

'I guess. So, you were saying?'

'I was looking at communication over long distances,' she said, holding up her stone again. 'And if a person imbues something like this with a piece of their soul'—she grinned at him as he narrowed his eyes at her—'their immortal, life-essence soul spirit—'

'Alright, alright!'

'—then whoever is carrying it around can contact them through it. Not proper contact, not like I'm talking to you now. But enough to make the other person think of them, know that they need to speak to them, maybe even locate them. It's like having a torch that the other person can see when you need them to.'

'Now that sounds useful,' Thaniel said. 'We should all have one for all of us.'

'We really should,' she smiled. 'But here's what I'm thinking.' She pointed at herself.

'I can't see into Terminheim and can't go there because...because of my responsibilities here, and I'm worried about Alakis.' She pointed at him. 'You need to get out of the city for a few days while the Senate looks for you, and you have nowhere to go.' She raised her hands, palms up.

'Road trip to Terminheim,' he said. 'Interesting idea. And why do I need the stone?'

She sighed and rolled her eyes, flipping the stone over to him. He caught it, just about. Beside him Eric muttered something and carried on snoring.

'Because I can get you close enough to Terminheim using a portal, but I can't bring you back unless I know you want to come back and where you are. The stone will do that.'

'You can only get us close?'

She nodded.

'The storm stops me seeing in, and if I can't see in, I can't make a portal, can I? Not a stable one, anyway. And you'll want to take a few days before you get there, just in case you actually can't get through that storm or things are...bad. We need to give the Senate time to conclude you're not here before you come back and tell me what this storm really is.'

'Okay, so we go through your portal, make our leisurely way to Terminheim and see what's going on. See if we can find Alakis and help him out if he's in trouble. Then we come back through the storm and call you on the stone to come get us?'

'Yep,' she said. 'Should work, shouldn't it?'

'Sounds exciting,' he said. 'Soon as this one wakes up,' he gave Eric a gentle shove, 'we'll get going. Do you have a stone ready?'

She nodded at the one in his hand.

'I was practising,' she said. 'Give it a try.'

Thaniel held the cold stone and regarded it thoughtfully. He had no idea what to do.

'Sophine?' he said to it.

'Yeah?'

'No, I was…I was talking to the stone,' he said, suddenly convinced this was all an elaborate prank to make him look stupid.

She shook her head and laughed.

'Don't talk to it,' she said. 'Just…think at it. Connect with it, like we used to when we were students.'

Thaniel looked at her dubiously and held the stone up before his face. He quietened his mind, letting the room swim out of focus and the sound of silence fill his thoughts, vaguely amused at how easy it was to do this now he wasn't a student anymore and no one was grading him. He pushed the thought aside and let serenity come.

The rock in his hand seemed to glimmer, a small mote of gold light swirling inside it. He focused on it.

Sophine, he whispered inside his skull.

'Oh wow,' Sophine said loudly, one hand flying to the side of her head. 'That's weird. That's really weird.'

Thaniel blinked and looked at the stone as the real world flowed back into his mind. It was just a stone.

'It was like I suddenly had this crazy, intense urge to talk to you,' Sophine was saying, the words tumbling out like she was an excited schoolgirl. 'I could see you in my head, smell you even. And even with you sitting right there it was as though I hadn't heard from you in ages and just *had* to contact you.'

He looked at her, laughing lightly.

'It worked then.'

She grinned, her hand on her chest.

'Oh yes, it worked. It definitely worked.'

'And it'll reach you from Terminheim?'

She nodded with a shrug.

'I don't think distance really matters with this kind of magic.'

Something about that sentence felt decidedly off to him. A chill crept down his spine for the second time in this one conversation, but he chose to ignore it.

'We're ready then,' he smiled. 'We'd better pack.'

Chapter Ten

Thane Sidric's fort was a wooden building perched on a hill, surrounded by a high fence of sharp wooden stakes. Around the hill was a ditch filled with foul-smelling water at the bottom of which, Sindel assured Rigel, lurked more sharp wooden stakes.

'So there's no sense trying to climb up,' she said. 'One wrong move and it's straight in the ditch you go. Even a scratch from those stakes would probably be enough to kill you; they dump corpses right in that water, so it's about as close to liquid plague as you can get.'

Rigel could well believe it, too. The stench from the water was almost overpowering as they crossed the only bridge under the meagre light of the newly risen moon. The portcullis gleamed dully up ahead, looking very heavy and very impassable. Sindel stopped just in front of him, and he bumped into her. He jumped back, his mind suddenly blazing with thoughts of soft flesh and the smell of her hair.

'Shh,' she said, looking round sharply. He hadn't realised he'd said anything.

Get a grip, he told himself, hoping that the stirring sensation in his stomach would fade and kicking himself for not being able to control his suddenly screaming hormones.

'Any closer and they'll see us,' Sindel said softly, peering up at the cloud-shrouded moon. The bridge was not lit, the torches standing dark and forlorn on either side. They could just about make out the gleam of metal on the ramparts above them as soldiers wandered along the walls and, as sentries often did, failing to actually look where they were supposed to after long years of having nothing to look at.

'Are we close enough?' she asked.

Rigel got himself under control and looked at the portcullis, wishing Sophine was here. Even Thaniel was better at portals than he was.

'I...I don't know.'

'Well, try.'

'I don't think I should,' he said, knowing how peevish he sounded but not being able to help it. 'If I get it wrong, we could pass through somewhere we don't want to pass through, or pop out inside the wall or something.'

Sindel made a frustrated sound and reached up to her shirt. She took one of her blades and sliced at the material, making long gashes in the material and nicking her skin in the process.

'Sindel what—' Rigel cried in alarm, but she shushed him and he fell silent. She glanced down at her handiwork, gave a short nod and shook her hair over her face.

Then she ran screaming at the portcullis.

'Help! Help me please!' she yelled, waving her arms desperately. Rigel stood in stunned silence, watching her retreating figure as soldiers ran to open the gates and raise the heavy iron bars. Just then, the moon slipped past the cloud cover and lit him in a silvery brilliance.

'Hey, you!' cried one of the soldiers, now tending to the hysterically sobbing Sindel. 'Stop right there!'

Rigel hesitated, not knowing quite what the part was he was supposed to be playing. Not knowing what to do, he ran across the bridge towards the gate.

'Hold it!' yelled the soldier, now joined by two others, each brandishing long spears pointed right at him.

Two strangled yelps were followed by heavy crashes of armour, and the first soldier with the spear turned around just in time to receive a thin blade through the forehead. He too slumped heavily to the ground and lay still. Then Sindel appeared between the two remaining spearmen, her hands outstretched on either side as though embracing old friends. They froze, clutching their ruined throats, before collapsing in ungainly heaps. Sindel flicked the stiletto knives to clear the blood from them and returned them to their thigh holster with a practiced, graceful motion.

Five men dead in the time it had taken Rigel to reach them. He stood and looked in unabashed awe at Sindel, her bushy hair floating lightly in the night air, her skin gleaming in the moonlight.

'If you're finished staring,' she said, with a flicker of a smile, 'it won't be long before this is noticed.' She gestured around them. 'Let's get the corpses in the ditch and the gates closed before anyone sees.' He nodded, caught somewhere between wanting to declare his eternal devotion to, and running screaming from, the unbelievably lethal woman standing before him.

When the bodies of the unfortunate men had sunk silently below the still water and they'd pushed the heavy wooden gates closed enough to hide the fact that the portcullis was raised, they slipped into the shadows of the fort.

Long gangways led to raised lodgings for soldiers, small wooden buildings turned out to be stables. Here and there tired-looking men wandered, some wearing chainmail and some just with a sword or axe belted on their hips.

'Not many,' Rigel whispered in the gloom, watching a man with a tankard stagger through the darkness towards one of the campfires burning further off.

'Times are hard,' Sindel replied from the shadows to his left. 'The Thanes are struggling to keep their men. Some are joining the Moderator's staff; he's the one with the money now. That's why they'll be making their move before long, they can't afford to wait.'

They slipped past one drunken sentry and through a heavy door, into a corridor that led away into the shadows.

'We're in,' Sindel whispered. 'This is the keep, so Sidric must be around here somewhere. Can you locate him?'

Rigel nodded, calming his mind and reaching for the passive connections with the world around him that were considered, in more civilised circles, to be the basis of all mage abilities. He thought of his old tutor, Master Thomas, and how he'd despaired of Rigel ever mastering the serenity needed to access these sanctioned powers.

'Just look at me now,' he muttered.

'What?'

'Nothing.'

He could sense the presence of Sindel beside him, feel the beat of her heart and the sound of her breathing. The rise and fall of her chest—

He gritted his teeth and forced his mind away, into the quiet shadows around them. A few dully gleaming souls, heads fogged with alcohol and belonging to men with little on their minds,

161

flitted across his senses. Nothing in their immediate surroundings. His mind floated up the stairs, into chambers devoid of servants and faded tapestries...

'I have him,' he said. 'Up the stairs, second door on the right. A large, square room with weapons and armour...he's fighting some-one...no he's alone. Practising. Angry. He has a sword and a shield.'

'Impressive,' whispered Sindel, kissing him lightly on the cheek. 'Well done.'

Instantly the serenity vanished and he was standing in the dark with his heart pounding like mad in his chest. He turned his head, sensing her face inches from his own. He could feel her breath on his lips. Without thinking, he moved his lips towards hers.

'Easy there,' she said, moving away. He felt a light hand on his chest and a lead weight inside it.

'I'm sorry,' he stammered. 'I don't know what—'

'Not now, okay?' she said gently, taking his hand in the dark. 'We have work to do. Second door on the right, up the stairs.'

They crept along, and Rigel was grateful for the darkness. He felt like a fool and part of him didn't want her to see his face ever again. And of course, part of him very much did.

The stairs creaked as they ascended, a tired sound that spoke of a fortress once glorious and now almost derelict. The air was thicker up here, choked with smoke from a fireplace somewhere not far away, perhaps in the room where Sidric was sparring.

Rigel hesitated, thinking of the man whose mind he'd briefly touched. He was odious, of course, but also desperate. Half glimpsed thoughts of Sidric's family, his life, swirled around Rigel. The legacy of his forefathers. All of it in jeopardy and only this grubby alliance with someone in Asterheim offering any hope of—

'Do we have to do this?' he whispered. Sindel turned to him, concern flickering across her beautiful face.

'I can't do it,' Rigel said. 'I'm not Sophine.'

Sindel blinked at him; she had no idea who that was or what he was referring to.

'Rigel, you do this and Ceresheim will be safe again. The Moderator, the mages, they'll all be safe. And Asterheim needs you to make the arrangements for their return. You can't do that with Sidric in the way.'

'I know, but...'

She moved closer to him in the gloom, placing a hand on his chest.

'Trust me. We can fix everything, together.'

'Together?'

'Why not? The city will need a representative from Asterheim, and who better than you? Stay here with me.'

'With you?'

'With me. But first, Sidric.'

Rigel nodded, the guilty ache in his stomach not going away but somehow not weighing him down quite so much anymore. He followed her as she moved away towards the door, gathering his thoughts.

The Thane was stripped to the waist when they burst through the door, standing in a room lit by candles and holding a sword in one hand. A heavy wooden shield was strapped to the other. There was nothing else in the room but figures made of sacks of straw and dressed in mail, most of which had deep gouges and cuts.

Sidric did not hesitate. They had barely entered the room when he threw his blade with surprising speed for a man of his size. Sindel yelped and flung herself backwards as the heavy sword whipped towards her and buried itself in the wall inches from her head. Sidric had already grabbed a spear from the rack beside him and was charging before Rigel could even think.

Telekinesis was Thaniel's speciality, but even Rigel could throw a decent blast. Sidric was rocked back, his spear snapping as it took the brunt of his hastily flung ball of shapeless force. The Thane let the momentum take him, rolling backwards and coming up right next to the weapons rack.

'You,' he growled, finally getting the chance to look at his assailants. He reached for a long, thin-bladed sword without taking his eyes off them. The shield on one arm did not seem to encumber him at all. 'Impressive trick back at the palace.' He began to move, his feet never crossing, his sword held in a defensive posture. 'I've always hated mages,' he added, 'nothing honourable about your kind.' He slid his feet again, and Rigel only then noticed he had come closer. Something about the way he moved, head carefully poised, made it seem he wasn't moving at all.

Rigel took a step back, yelping as his back met the wall. Sidric smiled thinly, his eyes never leaving Rigel's.

The Thane ducked and spun suddenly, whipping his shield arm round to cover his body. Two thin blades smacked into the wood. Rigel glanced at Sindel, catching her eye as she hesitated with a third blade held in one hand.

Sidric straightened, slowly, his eyes darting watchfully between the two would-be assassins. He kept the shield half-raised, the slender sword hovering with the tip pointed at his enemies. He slid closer.

Rigel felt an icy sensation creep up his spine. The Thane would close the distance in a few moments and seemed equal to Sindel's lithe speed. They were in serious danger.

'Rigel,' said Sindel in a quavering voice, her eyes flickering between them. She leapt and rolled, a beautiful fluid motion that no one who hadn't seen her move before would have thought she could execute. She somehow flung three blades as she leapt, an impossibly skilful throw, but Sidric swept the shield to meet them nonetheless. The heavy wood caught one inches from his face, another glancing from the steel boss in the centre, and the Thane snarled in sudden agony as the third ripped into the meat of his thigh. He did not drop the shield but lowered it enough to regard Sindel with murderous eyes.

'Got any more?' he growled, pulling the stiletto from his leg and throwing it aside with a contemptuous gesture. It clattered to the floor by Rigel's foot, and he grabbed it instinctively, feeling pathetic and useless and not knowing what else to do.

The Thane exploded into motion, powering forward with a practised lunge clearly designed to break an enemy shield. Sindel's eyes widened and she tensed to leap, but it was already too late.

Rigel screamed, throwing one arm out in sudden horror. Time crashed against his abruptly erected, emotion-fuelled barrier of will. The Thane's charge froze, the solid steel boss of the shield less than three feet from Sindel's motionless, horrified face.

'No,' Rigel gasped, feeling the weight of time crushed against his mind. 'No no no!' Sindel was not outside the time-flow. He'd only placed himself outside and he knew very well that both Sindel and the Thane would be like statues if he tried to move them. He'd wasted his chance.

Giving vent to his frustration, Rigel turned and thumped a hand against the solid, unyielding wall. The dull light of this timeless realm glinted on the thin blade he held, and he looked at it with dawning hope. He let go of the stiletto, letting it float away from

165

him and following it towards the motionless figure of the charging Thane.

'I'm so sorry,' he said to the unseeing man's snarling face. 'I don't have any choice now. I didn't...I don't...' He stopped talking and sighed heavily. He glanced at Sindel, her face a heart-breaking study in terror.

'I can't let you kill her,' he said, and the words felt right. Final.

The floating blade rose up, its lethal edge poised, until its tip touched the Thane's sightless eye. Rigel stepped to the side, his hands on Sindel's shoulder and ready to push.

Then he let time crash back down like the crushing waves of eternity.

The Thane screamed as the momentum of his charge plunged the blade deep into his brain. Sindel fell to the side as he staggered, the shield missing her by inches as the big man crashed into the wall and then collapsed, lifeless to the floor.

Rigel ran to Sindel and knelt by her side, his hands fluttering like panicked birds, wanting to touch her but not knowing where or how.

'Are you okay?' he asked, over and over, in a breathless voice.

She sat up, rubbing at her arm, peering at him.

'Took your time,' she said with a crooked smile. He stared at her; the joke so bad that he was momentarily stunned into silence.

Then she reached out and cupped one hand around his neck and pulled him closer. Rigel's mind emptied completely as she kissed him, feeling his body respond in a way he'd never experienced before. He was filled with a need, an insane need that cared nothing for the fact that he'd just murdered a man and that his corpse was cooling on the floor by his feet. But then she was breaking the kiss, gently pushing him back, and nothing made sense anymore.

He blinked and breathed as his mind started to come back to life.

'I'm okay,' Sindel said. 'Thank you for saving my life.'

Rigel made a series of sounds that he had intended to be words, and then gave up.

'Let's go,' she continued, getting smoothly to her feet. Rigel tried not to stare at her legs, the curve of her waist.

'Come on,' she said, tugging at his arm. 'We have to find his chambers and get hold of those notes.'

'What if there aren't any?'

'We'll deal with it.'

They made their way out of the chamber and down the hall, bypassing several drunken soldiers on the way who barely looked at them twice. The Thane's personal chambers were thick with smoke but well-lit due to the toasty fire burning in the hearth.

As it turned out, there were lots of notes. Thane Sidric had a whole chest full of notes. And letters from and to Asterheim that had never made it past his fortress. Sindel quickly rifled through them as Rigel sat on the Thane's bed, his head in his hands.

'This would be faster if you helped,' she said lightly, over her shoulder.

'I can't,' he replied. 'I'm sorry. I can't get his face out of my head.'

She paused, straightening up.

'You've never killed anyone before?'

Rigel shook his head.

'Not like that anyway. I've been attacked plenty, and people have died, but I don't think it was me who killed them. And I've never done anything so…coldly. I'm a healer. I defend people and heal people. I don't kill them.'

She looked at him appraisingly.

'It's not often you meet someone with real principles,' she said. 'Everyone I know has killed people.'

'Me too,' Rigel said glumly. 'Now I have too I guess.'

'To save me,' she said.

Rigel snorted.

'Yes, but we literally went in there to kill him.'

'True,' she shrugged. She turned back to the chest, bending over in a way that made Rigel's heart thump and his stomach stir. He looked away again.

'Here it is,' she said eventually, appearing at his side and handing him a piece of crumpled parchment. He scanned the letter; it was signed by seven senators of Asterheim that he recognised and other names he did not. His heart sank.

'This is bad,' he said.

'How bad?'

'Thane Sidric wasn't just being paid to keep messages from reaching Asterheim,' he said. 'He was stopping food being sent too. He must have silos full of food meant for the capital. These senators want the city starved.' He scanned the page again. 'Here it is, it's all in return for the backing of the Asterheim Senate when Ariene is overthrown. I guess they were offering to make him sole leader here if he could just keep Asterheim starving long enough for them to take power. And part of that meant stopping the mages coming back. They said I might be coming and to look out for me. I wonder if that means they were pushing Ariene to send me here.'

'Asterheim politics makes my head hurt,' said Sindel with a sniff.

'Consider yourself lucky then,' he replied, 'it actually kills some people.'

***

The little town was called Rock's End, according to the man tying up his horse at a nearby stable as they walked through the gates. Thaniel looked around, glad to be within the walls of the town and away from the ominous sight of the bleak storm clouds on the horizon.

They had stepped through Sophine's portal into countryside very different to what they were used to. Asterheim was surrounded by fields. Grass, wheat, corn and a hundred other crops, in better times at least, vied for space and were split by sturdy roadways. This place was mostly hard ground underfoot, stones and rocks and dirt rather than grass, and the area around it seemed barren of all life. About a day or so to the east, where the ground was even rockier and mountainous, Terminheim sat beneath the now-perpetual storm.

'How do people live here?' asked Eric, looking around the little town with undisguised dislike.

Thaniel laughed.

'Listen to you, city-boy. Haven't you ever been outside Asterheim?'

'You know I haven't,' Eric said, a little defensively.

'Most of the towns in the country are like this,' Thaniel said. 'Wooden palisade, if they have one at all. A gate designed to keep out wolves or bears rather than armies.' He nodded at the wood-built buildings around them with smoke rising from brick chimneys. 'Mostly muddy streets and filth,' he added with a smile, thinking of his own village to the south. 'Some might have a brick-built fort somewhere if they're lucky, but what we're used to? With the stone and the opulence and'—they skirted round an old woman pushing a cart that seemed to be filled with mud—'and space. That's what's unusual.'

'It's horrible,' said Eric.

'No, just different.'

'If you say so.'

The scent of something delicious floated on the air, making them both pause.

'Wherever that's coming from, I want to go there,' said Thaniel.

'Agreed.'

The inn was a thatched, wood-built building not far from the stables where they'd learned the name of the town. The delicious smell was coming from whatever it was they had cooking for the evening meal, and Eric looked stunned when the man behind the bar said they couldn't have anything for a few hours.

'They don't just have food lying around in case someone wants it,' Thaniel said in a hushed voice. 'They make a big pot of something at the same time every day so as not to waste anything. Yesterday's leftovers are probably in it.'

Eric wrinkled his nose, and Thaniel laughed. He spoke again to the owner and was rewarded with some bread and cheese.

'This will do for now,' he said to Eric, passing it along. 'We have a room now too.' He dangled a key in front of Eric's face.

'How long are we staying?' Eric asked, glancing around the smoke-filled inn and doing a very bad job of trying not to look too disgusted.

'Probably just tonight and tomorrow night. Then we'll head off and see if we can get through that storm.'

Eric looked crestfallen.

'That's…a long time.'

Thaniel stepped closer to him with a suggestive smile. He dangled the key again.

'I'm sure we can find a way to pass the time.'

Eric rolled his eyes.

Chapter Eleven

There was a crude, scarecrow-like sculpture of a man slumped against the damp wall of the prison. It looked like it had been fashioned from iron railings and bits of wood. Lengths of metal wire that had to be from fences were tightly wound around the limbs as though to hold them together, and a battered old chainmail shirt had been forced over the torso. The head was an old metal bucket, upturned. Someone had rammed a steel rod of some sort through the top of it and down into the torso. Two holes had been crudely stabbed into the bucket, in a vague approximation of cruel, empty eyes. The jagged apertures stared at Dominitia sightlessly, filled with shadows.

Dominitia tried to look away from the unpleasant mannequin, but she could feel its watchfulness. Nothing was animating it, not yet, but she had a horrible feeling it would come to life at some point to fulfil some ghastly command by its maker.

She leaned back against the cold stone wall. One thing she'd noticed about Terminheim was that they used a lot of stone. Everything seemed to be made of it, except the dwelling huts. And yet, despite the abundance of stone, nothing was beautiful. Nothing was artistic. The buildings were squat and flat and brutal, purely functional. Even the Lord Governor's palace had been a cheerless series of square rooms and massive stone pillars. Only the wooden hall had seemed pleasant, hung with draperies and even boasting a threadbare carpet. She supposed that was why the people preferred to live in wooden huts, if the alternative was a square chunk of cold stone.

'Who are you?' asked a groggy voice from her side. Dominitia turned her head and looked through the metal bars of the unfurnished cell in which she sat. There was a man looking at her from the next cell. They were the only two people in the prison, not counting the motionless scarecrow thing on the floor in the corridor. She could hear the rumble of the perpetual thunder outside and see the odd flash of lightning through the large, gaping cracks in the stone wall. Most of the prison building seemed to be a derelict ruin, except, of course, for the part with the cells.

'I'm Dominitia,' she said simply, looking away again.

'I'm Vorn,' the man replied. 'Do…do you have any food?'

She snorted a short laugh and shook her head.

'I don't remember getting here,' said the man. He rubbed his head and winced. 'I was returning from the quarry in that terrible storm and then…nothing.'

She looked at him.

'You'd been away?'

'A week or so,' Vorn said, getting to his feet and stretching. 'I saw the storm rolling in and thought it was probably time to come home.'

'You missed a lot,' Dominitia said.

'What do you mean?'

She snorted that laugh again.

'I came here with a boy. Alakis.' Out of the corner of her eye she saw something twitch. She glanced at the scarecrow thing, but it was still. 'We're mages. He had a…condition, and we were

173

hoping to find a cure. But he conjured a portal, and something went wrong. When we came through, he wasn't himself. He had changed. His condition was changed. It's like it had become almost infectious, directed outwards instead of inward. And he was different too.'

The man stared at her.

'I need to go,' he said. 'My family...'

'You won't make it,' she said sadly.

He was quiet again, watching her with wide, frightened eyes.

'He locked me in my rooms,' she said, talking mainly for herself, 'and then the storm started. I tried to leave then, when I realised how far he'd gone. But he wouldn't let me. The soldiers from the palace have either been killed or enslaved, along with the Governor and his family. From what I saw when I tried to run, the people he hasn't infected yet are confined to their homes. He has his slaves patrolling and...' her eyes strayed to the scarecrow. 'And I think there's worse out there.'

Vorn looked around fearfully, then frowned.

'These cells aren't locked,' he said with a laugh. 'Look!' He pointed at the door to her cell, which was standing wide open. 'What are we even doing wasting our time here?' He took a step towards the open door.

'Stop,' Dominitia said softly, her eyes on the mannequin. 'The man who brought me here told me I could leave anytime I wanted. He said if I was so desperate to leave, he wouldn't stop me.' She shook her head bitterly. 'He knows what a coward I am.'

'Who? Who was it that brought you?'

She shrugged.

'Alakis. It's all Alakis.' She gestured vaguely around them.

'This is ridiculous,' said the man. 'How do you know you're not just going to sit here and starve yourself to death out of fear? That thing could just be an old bucket on a few bits of...' he peered at the figure. 'What is it even made of?'

'Whatever he found lying around the palace, I think,' Dominitia shrugged. 'Something's warped him. Whether it was what he found in those books or something that broke his mind in that hideous portal, I don't know. But I do know he's gone. That...person in the palace making these things'—she gestured at the mannequin—'that's not the boy I knew.'

'Well I'm not waiting around,' said Vorn. 'I'm going.'

She didn't reply, hating herself for the fear that kept her silent and motionless, watching him with wide eyes.

Slowly, the prisoner edged towards the unlocked door of his cell, reaching a hand out to grasp the cold metal bars and swing the gate wide enough for him to step through.

The bucket-headed figure jerked, a tiny spark of bright white energy snapping across the wires of its right arm. Then it fell back, motionless again. The man froze, one hand on the bars still.

'Don't do it,' pleaded Dominitia, her voice a tiny squeak in the darkness.

'Circle save me,' cried Vorn, pulling the door wide.

All at once the twisted figure of wire and wood blazed, tiny arcs of lightning leaping between the warped wires holding it together. Its ghastly eyes gleamed, lit from within by snapping flashes of blue-white lightning. The impossible marionette jerked to its feet like a puppet pulled up on a string as the man made a dash through the open door. One of the puppet thing's disjointed arms snaked out, impossibly fast, whipping a length of twisted wire that tangled itself around the fleeing man's leg. He tripped, crashing hard to the stone floor, screaming. The monstrous thing lurched towards him, tiny arcs of energy leaping from the debris of its body to the cell bars. Its gait was like that of a children's puppet, bouncing along on its implausible legs. The bucket head blazed with dull witchlight; its empty, pitiless eyes staring.

Vorn was still screaming, frantically trying to free his leg from the possessed wire as the half-floating, soulless marionette pulled him back along the stone floor. It reached down for him with talons made from jagged pieces of pipe and nails, sparking with forks of corrupted light.

Dominitia leapt to her feet and ran, just as the screaming reached a new, fevered pitch and turned into liquid gurgling. She didn't think, couldn't think, and just fled as fast as she could, turning the corner and leaping over piles of rubble. Behind her, something crunched and the screaming stopped, and that made her run all the faster.

Up ahead, she could see flashes of light in the diseased sky and prayed the hole in the wall would be big enough for her to squeeze through.

***

The ballroom of Lord Orswell's sprawling mansion was full of mages. The tables and desks had all been cleared away to make room, and hundreds of people milled around laughing and clinking glasses. Rigel peered around the curtain in front of the stage and gulped.

'That's a lot of people,' he said.

Orswell clapped him on the shoulder.

'You'll be fine. They'll love you.'

'It's not me they need to love,' he fretted. 'What if they won't come back?'

'You can't expect them to, really,' said Orswell gently. 'Some have a good life here, others had a bad life there; some just like the sun and living in a palace. Asking them to go back to a starving city from which they had to escape isn't likely to go down well.'

'I have to try.'

'I know. Are you ready?'

'No.'

Orswell smiled faintly.

'That's the spirit. Here we go then.'

Lifting the curtain, the former senator strode onto the stage and lifted his arms high. The assembled mages cheered and whooped, and their host gave a short bow.

'Friends,' he said, his voice echoing nicely across the room. 'I have someone very special with me tonight who wants very much to speak with you.' There were some laughs and jokes at this, but Rigel was too nervous to hear them.

'Please give a big welcome to one of the mages who saved us from Asterheim and brought down the tyrant Lyoris Mountebank, Rigel Wheatly!'

The crowd was clapping loudly and heartily as Rigel forced his legs to carry him up onto the stage. Faces beamed at him and hands waved. People called out encouraging things he barely heard.

Orswell was retreating out of sight, back into the shadows of the curtain, and the clapping was fading. Silence fell.

Rigel stared out at the assembled crowd and swallowed.

'Hello,' he said. 'I'm Rigel.'

There was some laughter at this and some angry shouts in his defence.

'Rigel!' called someone in the crowd, a voice he recognised.

'Master Thomas?'

'Over here!' His former tutor was standing in the middle of the room, waving one arm frantically.

Rigel made a short, sharp sound that wasn't quite a laugh and grinned broadly.

'That's my teacher,' he said, pointing at Master Thomas. 'Give him a hand, everyone!'

The crowd started clapping and cheering again.

'I couldn't have got us all out without him,' Rigel laughed. 'And I can't tell you how great it is to see a familiar face. Asterheim isn't the same without its mages.'

The smiles started to fade, the faces clouding.

'I'm here to ask…' he trailed off. These people needed a reason before he could ask them anything. He owed them that.

'I'm here to tell you what's going on there,' he said. 'Back home. Last night I went to the fortress of Thane Sidric and discovered correspondence between him and some members of the Senate. They had a plot to starve the city, to keep it on the edge of chaos. None of the messages sent between either city were to get through, and the food being paid for by Asterheim – food they had to pay for because the crops can't grow reliably enough without mages – was to be prevented from leaving.'

'Outrageous!' someone shouted. Others took up the cry and started shouting their displeasure. Rigel held his hands up, his heart pounding violently in his chest as though about ready to jump out and run off somewhere less stressful.

'The result of this is that Asterheim is starving, and the fragile grip on power that Lady Gloriana has is starting to slip. I think they want to isolate and overthrow her, and for that they are willing to let the people suffer.'

There was shocked silence at this pronouncement. Rigel pressed on.

'I know some of you have friends there, family. People you care about. Some of you don't. Maybe some of you thought you had been abandoned or forgotten, but you weren't. The houses you left behind are under the care of the Citizenry Guild. I have guarantees from them to show you can have them back, and a commitment from the Senate to pay you compensation.'

'From Lady Gloriana, you mean,' someone said. 'But she's about to be overthrown, you said.'

'Not if I can help it,' he said fiercely. 'I'm heading back as soon as I can to help her. Those commitments will be honoured.'

People started murmuring and talking over one another. Rigel raised his voice.

'I know Asterheim did you wrong. But Lyoris Mountebank did us *all* wrong. He poisoned everything he touched, but now he's gone and your city needs you. The buildings are crumbling because there's no one to work the miracles you've perfected here.' He held his arms out to encompass the beautifully wrought palace in which they stood. 'The people sicken and die without healers; the crops die to a stiff breeze or a cold snap. Fires run unchecked through the older quarters. We need you.'

Many faces in the crowd had turned away, looking at the floor or the windows. Anywhere, but at Rigel.

'I know it's a lot to ask,' he said, 'and I know you've got no reason to believe me. You've had no word in months, it must have felt like staying here was your only choice. But please, those of you with the power, stretch out your minds and see for yourself.

179

Asterheim is dying, and only you can save it. That's all I came here to say.'

He turned away and trudged back to the curtain, ducking under it and down the steps.

No one clapped.

***

Dominitia's leg was bleeding freely as she stumbled over the last of the chunks of rock that had once been the walls of the prison. The squeeze had been tight, but she'd managed to get through. The puppet-thing was still inside, and she dared to hope she might—

Her foot caught a stone and she tripped, stumbling and unable to catch herself.

She fell into a person, who gripped her with strong hands and steadied her. She looked up into a bearded face, thankful beyond measure that the eyes looking back at her were concerned and frightened rather than the slack emptiness of one of Alakis's slaves.

'Easy there,' said the man as she stepped back and collected herself. He had a pleasant voice, rough and warm. He was wearing a black leather coat with a hood, pulled up against the thrashing rain, as were the three other men standing with him. Each held a large pickaxe like he knew how to use it, and they wore expressions as grim as the dark sky above.

Dominitia pushed her soaked hair behind her head and was about to speak when one of the men spoke first, shouting to make himself heard over the rain and the rumble of thunder.

'Where's Vorn?' he called.

Dominitia shook her head and pointed back at the ruined, crumbling prison.

'We saw him taken,' said the first man, his expression now turning even darker. 'Been waiting for nightfall…'

'He's dead,' she said, shaking her head again. She wasn't completely certain of that, but it seemed a very good guess.

'What happened?' asked the second man.

She turned to glance at the prison wall and was about to speak when a faint gleam of light appeared against the stone. The words died in her throat as first a scrap of what looked like old wire materialised through the wall, followed by the jagged edges of broken furniture and the gleaming rim of a bucket.

Dominitia stumbled back a step as the men around her raised their axes and closed ranks in front of her. The twisted mannequin was half-way through the wall, moving slowly but inexorably, phasing through the solid stone as though it were water. Its blazing eyes turned towards them as one of the men charged, yelling an incoherent bellow of challenge. The axe crunched into the top of the bucket, splitting it almost in half, and the hideous marionette toppled, falling the rest of the way through the stone wall and jerking on the ground with sparks of escaping energies. The man hefted his axe and brought it up for another swing, but the demon-puppet whipped one taloned hand up, horrifyingly fast, and tore through his body with a sound like ripping paper. The man screeched and dropped his axe, falling back and holding his arms across his ruined stomach. The nightmare scarecrow lurched forward, just as the other would-be prison-breakers ran to help their friend.

Dominitia looked around in desperation, searching for something, anything, that could help. The thing was not invulnerable, as they'd seen. If she could just—

There!

A large, jagged lump of stone, blasted perhaps from the prison building by one of the flashing forks of lightning, lay not far from her. She hesitated, glancing at the men hacking and yelling, locked in mortal combat with the whirling, silent marionette. One man shrieked, impaled on a limb made of railings and wire.

She forced the sight away, reaching within her to the serenity she'd been taught was the key to all mage abilities. Her mind refused to quieten, adrenaline and fear combining to rob her of the calm she needed. She gritted her teeth and repeated her mantra, focusing on the words as though they were a spell. It was the same litany she'd used many times to help Alakis, just her own personal way of reaching calm and passing it to him. Her heart slowed, her breathing steadied. She felt the rock's presence near her feet and reached for it with her mind, asking it to lift itself into the air.

The yells and crashes were louder now, threatening to shake her resolve, but she only needed moments. She dared a peep through her closed lashes, and the spinning, clacking death-machine turned towards her. Crackling energies spilled from the broken bucket, tiny reflections of the tormented sky above.

Dominitia screamed as the empty eyes found her. The rock slumped back to the ground with a soft crunch. The two remaining men jumped aside, out of the reach of the flailing limbs, but one was too slow and an ugly tear ripped its way through his leg, almost shearing it from his body. The man fell back, screaming, with the jagged talon still embedded in his leg and the puppet-thing was pulled off-balance. The last one gave a final below of desperate defiance and brought his axe down hard on the monster's head. The bucket sheared in half, the two pieces clattering to the rocky floor as the rest of the insane body collapsed in a burst of escaping light. The crackling lightning vanished, a thin mist-like steam rising from the now-inanimate collection of household implements and industrial detritus. The man with the ruined leg moaned a long plaintive wail. Dominitia got to her feet shakily and crossed to him, moving his stunned, staring friend out of the way. She knelt by the wounded man's side, reaching again for the serenity that had deserted her and trying to will the man's body to heal itself.

His moans became less desperate as the pumping blood slowed and the torn flesh started to knit. She held on for a moment, but the madness of the last few minutes was catching up with on her and exhaustion was close behind. The mindset she needed vanished and she sat back, gasping for air. The wound wasn't healed by any means, but it was all she could do.

'He should live,' she said shakily, as the man with the beard helped her to her feet. 'I'm sorry, there's not much more I can do. I'm no healer.'

'You're a mage?' he asked in some bewilderment, his eyes straying to the carnage around them.

She looked away.

'My patronage was bought by the *Farmer's* Guild,' she said, a little defensively, 'back before the attack. I'm better at crops. Fertilisation, growth. It's similar to healing but...' she shrugged helplessly and gestured at the destroyed sentry-puppet. 'I'm no fighter.'

The man nodded as though he understood, but she doubted he knew anything about the different disciplines of mage-craft. Out here, at the end of the world where only strength and stone mattered, mages were few and far between.

Thunder rumbled in the eternally tormented sky, flashes of brilliant light showing them glimpses of the nearby streets. A few figures walked aimlessly through the night, moving with a tell-tale lurch that marked them out as Alakis's slaves. A group of them wandered past the other end of the prison, slowly patrolling with slack features. They disappeared down a dark street.

'We should get inside,' said the bearded man, watching them go. 'What's your name?'

'Dominitia,' she said.

'I'm Soren. Vorn's brother.'

'I'm sorry,' she replied, not knowing what else to say.

He nodded and cleared his throat gruffly.

'Come on,' he said, turning away. 'We have a house not far off; we've been getting people together where we can.'

'What people?' she picked her way over the stony ground, trying not to trip.

'Miners, stonemasons. Anyone who can use an axe, which is most of the men here.'

Dominitia stopped, her heart skipping as she saw another heap of old wire and pieces of broken things arranged in a man-shape. It was propped up against the wall of a house on the other side of the deserted street, looking forlorn in the rain. Its head was another bucket, smaller than the other one but with similar eye holes crudely carved into it.

'There's another one,' she hissed. Soren looked to where she was pointing and nodded slowly.

'They're everywhere,' he said. 'But until tonight I'd never seen one move.'

She thought back to the patrolling slaves. The two were probably connected. If the slaves were alerted, perhaps that alerted the fence-fiends. They moved away, carefully making their way through the dark, rain-soaked streets. Every other street had a crumpled mannequin propped up somewhere, motionless in the thrashing rain.

'What's your plan for these people you're getting together?' she asked, thinking she already knew the answer.

'We're going to fight back,' the younger man said.

'Against those?' she almost laughed, eyeing one of the terrifying puppets.

'What choice do we have?'

She digested this in silence, listening to the rain and the thunder. Somewhere close by, lightning struck the ground with a terrific explosion, sending chunks of stone and rock flying.

What choice indeed?

***

Rigel was downcast that evening, as he sat across the table from Sindel in the middle of a relatively empty tavern not far from Orswell's. A candle burned in a little pewter jug between them, and a bowl of stew remained untouched before him.

'You tried your best,' Sindel said, swirling wine around the edges of a roughly made cup. 'Did you really think they'd all get up and pack their bags the first time you spoke to them?'

He shrugged.

'Maybe,' he said. 'I just thought, after all the trouble people went to trying to stop me even trying, I would have a shot. As it was, no one need have even bothered trying to kill me. Those guys at the inn, Thane Sidric...'

'Give it time,' she said, reaching over the table to grasp his hand. Little shivers of excitement flashed through his body at the touch and he grinned.

But then the smile faded.

'I don't have time,' he said. 'I can't waste any more time trying to talk sense into a load of people who don't want to hear it. Ariene is facing a well-organised conspiracy, and without me there to help her...'

Sindel smiled.

'Don't you think she can handle herself?'

He laughed.

'Ariene? More than any other person I know. Except maybe you.' He smiled all the wider when she looked down, almost shyly. She squeezed his hand and let it go, crossing her arms.

'Then maybe,' she said, looking up at him through long, pretty lashes, 'maybe you could stay here. With me. I wasn't joking when I said it before.'

He sighed. Looking into those lovely eyes, he could almost see himself doing it.

'I can't,' he said. 'I'd love to, believe me. But I can't. Maybe when this is all over, we could—'

She stood up from the table.

'Wait, where are you, what are you...'

She shushed him and came around the table, holding her hand out again as she stood looking down at him. His eyes were level with her chest, and he tried very hard not to look as he took her hand.

'Come with me,' she said quietly.

'W...where?' he stammered, reaching up for her hand.

'Upstairs,' she said. 'I don't want you leaving without us getting to know each other. And who knows – maybe I can persuade you to stay.'

'Maybe you, what?' he asked in vague disbelief, with a tongue that suddenly felt at least three times bigger than it should have been.

'Come on,' she said, rolling her eyes. She tugged him out of his chair and towed him to the back of the tavern, tossing the man behind the bar a coin as she went. The man caught it with a grin and a wink at Rigel, who smiled back with wide-eyed, empty-headed happiness as he was led up the stairs.

Some time later, Rigel lay on his back looking up at the wooden frames crossing the ceiling and the crumbling plaster between them. Sindel was beside him, her hand on his chest, her fingers lightly brushing the thin wispy hairs growing there.

'I think I understand now,' he said softly, still staring at the ceiling.

'Hm?'

'Why people do such strange things for love.'

She smiled.

'For love, or for...' She slid her hand down his body. He squirmed away.

'No no, no more,' he laughed. 'I honestly think it'll fall off.'

She sighed in disappointment, rolling onto her back. The bed shifted alarmingly as she did so.

'So have I persuaded you?' she asked. 'Can you stay? Just a little longer?'

Rigel pondered this in silence for a moment. He wanted very much to say yes. After all, there was no reason why he couldn't keep at the mages, get some of them moving. Send messages to Ariene now that the roads were safe for messengers again. Asterheim would get its grain, maybe some mages would return. There was no real reason for him to go back.

And yet.

'Ariene's in danger,' he sighed. 'Those senators have done this much to weaken her; I doubt they'll just sit around letting things get better. She needs me.'

'Why you?' asked Sindel, petulantly. 'Isn't she Echelarch now? Can't she gather up some Battlemasons and make them protect her?'

'She could, definitely. But you don't understand. Politics doesn't always work that way. She...she needs me. And I owe her.'

That was the essence of it, after all. Ariene Gloriana had saved him from an ignominious fate and raised him up to the exalted position he now held. She had taken responsibility for three clueless mages being hunted by a psychotic priest and fought beside them to free Asterheim. They had a bond, and he couldn't turn his back on that now.

'Then I'll come with you,' Sindel said sadly. 'Part of the way, at least.'

Rigel turned to look at her.

'What do you mean? Can't you just stay with me?'

She shook her head slightly, sending her brown curls shaking prettily.

'This is my home. I have family here. Once I square things with Cuthbert, I'll go back to being a captain in the Grain Guard. Especially now Sidric isn't deliberately making things difficult. I couldn't live in Asterheim, Rigel. Not as some housewife to a great mage of the court.'

'It wouldn't be like that,' he began. She turned over and kissed him, then placed a finger on his lips.

'Let's not speak of what we both know couldn't be,' she said sadly. 'Let's just enjoy what we have.'

Her eyes turned mischievous as her hand began to travel south again, and this time he let it.

Chapter Twelve

It was hard to gauge the passage of time in the perpetual gloom beneath the roiling storm blanketing Terminheim. The previous day, Soren had insisted they needed to get back to the place he called the 'Warehouse' before nightfall. Now, it was apparently morning, but Dominitia wasn't at all sure how anyone could tell.

The Warehouse was actually a large collection of buildings and wide-open industrial yards, about a mile across, all designed to efficiently get a piece of stone from the quarries in the mountains beyond Terminheim to the roads leading away from it. Large storehouses, partly built of stone themselves and supported in the upper reaches with wooden beams, contained the finished cut-stone blocks and were the closest to the roads. Dumping grounds further to the north were full of unpolished rocks of all shapes and sizes. In between were wood-and-steel cranes, wagons of various sizes and strengths and whole buildings full of racks upon racks of heavy tools.

Dominitia was perched on an uncomfortable wooden stool in the building the burly Terminheimers referred to simply as "Social". She was holding a cup of herbal tea that a young stonemason, not quite as big and burly as the other, bearded men surrounding them, had made her. The heat of the cup was welcome; she hadn't noticed how cold her fingers had got during their desperate run for the Warehouse. The Social was warm, mostly, she was sure, due to the press of bodies, which also explained the smell. She tried not to wrinkle her nose as she sat and listened to Soren, who was perched by her side on another, no more comfortable stool.

'So we figured, the Warehouse is all rock and mountain on the north side, and mostly walled off in the south, so we could probably make a stand here. Most of the Blanks are soldiers or palace folk from uptown, we reckon, so they don't know the Warehouse. Any wander in, they don't wander out.'

'Alakis will notice if you keep killing any patrols that get in here,' Dominitia said with a shudder. She took a sip of her tea.

'He might,' nodded Soren. 'Or he might not. Very few find their way in. They're Blanks, after all.'

The Terminheimers called Alakis's slaves "Blanks" because of the empty look in their eyes. Dominitia thought it was as good a name as any.

'Young lady,' said an older woman, casually holding a long heavy tool with a very sharp spike at one end, 'Soren said you could help us. What is it you can do?' She had white hair and a stern look, and if the weight of the cruel-shaped tool bothered her she gave no sign.

Dominitia wanted to crawl into a space beneath one of the plentiful rocks and not come out.

'I can't do anything,' she said, in a squeaking, pathetic voice she hated. 'I'm a farming mage, I work with plants.'

'You're young,' the woman replied haughtily, 'too young to be so specialised. Surely you—'

'I work with plants because I can't work with anything else,' Dominitia said, feeling even more useless. 'I don't fight, I can't throw fireballs and I can't defeat Alakis. I'm sorry.'

191

'That's the second time you've mentioned that name,' said the woman. 'Is he the one responsible for this?' She gestured around them.

Dominitia nodded. Beside her, Soren put an arm around her shoulders.

'She came here with him. They were staying at the palace, and then she ran when it all began.'

The woman nodded and pulled a stool over. She arranged herself on it and clicked her fingers in the air. The general murmur of voices quietened and bearded faces turned their way.

'Maybe you should tell us what you know about this Alakis,' she said, 'and how we can get rid of him.'

Dominitia took a deep, shuddering breath and squeezed her fingers around the warm cup.

'I think…he thought he loved me once,' she said, 'back when we were lost. But it wasn't love, it was fear. He was afraid of loneliness. Hopelessness. Of being left alone in the dark with his pain. I met him when I ran from my Guild. Did you hear what happened in Asterheim?'

The woman hesitated.

'Bits and pieces. The stories contradicted each other by the time they reached here.'

Dominitia nodded and took a sip of tea.

'I was working in the Farming Guild when a message came. A secret message, going out to all mages, from Senator Gloriana. It said there was a ship leaving the city, and all mages were welcome on it. This was after the Barbican was attacked so mages were already in danger. But I was too scared to leave until the soldiers came, and by the time I realised I should have gone on the ship it was too late. I went to the only place I could think of, which was the Barbican, but it was in ruins. I only just managed to find some-where to keep warm and dry.'

Dominitia sniffed, wiping her nose with a cold finger.

'Eventually, Alakis found me and we lived there together for a while. He was the brave one, even though he was so much younger and so terribly afflicted. I wouldn't have survived those weeks with-out him, but then Sophine came back and we thought everything would be alright. But she didn't help him. She undid her spell, but it wasn't enough.'

'What spell?' asked Soren, the look on his face suggesting this wasn't the only part of the story he hadn't fully grasped.

'She'd bungled an incantation of some kind, something forbid-den, in the weeks before the Senate was destroyed. It did something to the students, made them lose control. Alakis was badly affected by it. When the Barbican was attacked, he lost himself, started throwing lightning from his hands and couldn't stop. It burned him badly.' She looked upward, as though she could see the light-ning infecting the sky through the Social's roof.

'So that's why…' the old woman began.

Dominitia shook her head.

'No. That was the start. I used to help him. I could find serenity on his behalf and pass it to him; it calmed the flashes of lightning that lived under his skin. It was a small thing, but he relied on it so much. But it wasn't a solution, and if Sophine couldn't help then he was determined to find it somewhere else. So he went for the forbidden books, the very books she'd used to put this…curse…on him. Then he tried to get us away through a portal, but he didn't really know how and what he made was…bad.'

'Bad how?' asked Soren.

'I can't explain it. I felt like we were being pulled through a scream, like a nightmare except we were the nightmare someone else was having. It was inside us and it was us. And when we came out, we were in Terminheim and Alakis was...different.'

'Different,' growled the woman, shifting on her chair. She held the tool across her lap, her gnarled hands kneading the leather grips. Dominitia nodded.

'The lightning wasn't inside him anymore, but I could feel it in the air around him. People we spoke to acted strangely, like they were struggling to concentrate. Looking back on it, I should have known something was wrong. I think maybe I did, but I was too scared to say anything. We asked for directions to the palace, and not even the soldiers or guards tried to stop us. It was like they were all dazzled by a light I couldn't see, and desperate to do what he asked to make it stop. So we walked right into the palace and he told a servant to prepare rooms for me. I didn't see him then until the storm began, and I went out into the palace...'

Overhead thunder roared, splitting the perpetual storm clouds as the roiling tempest continued.

The Social was silent now as every man and woman watched Dominitia as she told her tale. She could feel the eyes on her, feel the judgment in them. But she didn't care. A coward she might be, but she owed these people the truth of what she'd brought to their door.

'The throne room of the Lord Governor was quiet. People were standing around, but saying nothing. Looking at nothing. Some of them were slowly wrapping bits of wire around pieces of metal and wood, but they were vacant, like the Blanks. The Governor was standing by his throne, his face slack and empty, drooling on his robes, and on the throne was Alakis. I'll never forget it. He almost

194

looked like he was fading in and out of reality. I could see him and not see him. His eyes were pitch black and brilliant white, like flashes of lightning and the dark spots you get in your eyes afterwards, all at the same time.' She shrugged miserably.

'I ran. What else could I do? I ran. I don't think he even saw me. But he did later. The Blanks caught me. Put me in that prison, with the door open and unlocked. One last humiliation.'

'Unlocked?' asked the old woman.

'One of the Jack-o'-wires was there,' said Soren softly. 'He put it there and dared her to try to leave.'

The woman hissed and looked away, shaking her head.

'You poor girl,' she said. 'You poor, poor girl.'

'I feel like,' Dominitia said, in a sad, dead voice, 'I feel like Alakis was turned inside out by that portal. Maybe because he had those books with him in the portal, I don't know. But where before he was himself with a lightning curse *inside*, one which we could handle, afterwards *he* was the one on the inside. The lightning curse got stronger, much stronger, feeding on him. Wearing him, almost. And it's out there now,' she looked up at the roof, 'out there and in the Blanks. In the Jack-o'-wires. All feeding off Alakis.' She sniffed, feeling a tear run down one cheek.

'How do we stop him?' the old woman said, her tone matching the steel of the tool in her lap.

Dominitia let out a short sniff of a laugh and shook her head.

'You can't,' she said softly. 'No one can.'

***

Outside the sprawling warehouse-turned-refugee camp they called the Social, the rain thrashed and spat against the cold rocky ground.

Tools, cranes and heavy chains clinked and creaked in the furious wind and overhead, in the torn and demented sky, brilliant flashes of light illuminated dark roiling clouds.

Soren was talking to his people, standing on a workbench of some kind, fitted all around the edges with steel contraptions for the refinement of stone in various ways. It groaned as he moved, his heavy boots crunching dust and tiny pieces of rock beneath their tread. Dominitia cringed at the crunching, trying to breathe shallowly in case she inhaled the dust.

The Social was now nearly full, hundreds of people crammed inside the questionable shelter. All of these people had dared the patrols of Blanks and Jack-o'-wires to be here at this moment, and that thought alone frightened her. She desperately wanted to leave, to flee for the gates and the road west to Asterheim and away from this nightmare place, but she knew she couldn't. Her own terror kept her rooted here, her fate wedded to that of these rough, angry people. People whose city, if it could be called that given how it was mostly huts and rock, she had helped ruin with her cowardice.

'The Jack-o'-wires will slaughter us the moment they see us approaching the palace,' the old woman who had spoken to her before was saying. She shook her head, her thin white hair swaying around her shoulders.

'There are ways of approaching the palace that don't involve the roads,' replied Soren. 'We built that place, or Jonas did anyway. Jonas!'

At the back of the hall, an older man with a sagging gut and a greying beard, sitting on a stool far too small for his large backside, raised a meaty hand. He had the look of a powerful man long since past his prime, most of his muscle well on the way to fat by now but unwilling to admit it, the challenging gleam of youth still clinging to his wrinkle-edged eyes.

'You built the palace,' Soren prompted, nodding at the man.

'Every stone,' Jonas growled. 'With these hands.' He held them up. No one said anything, but Dominitia thought she was on solid ground in assuming he meant he'd been one of a team. A very large team that had taken a very long time to build a very large palace.

'But if you wanted to get back in, Jonas...' called Soren from his place on the workbench.

'Months it took,' huffed Jonas, ignoring Soren, his hands now on his thighs. 'And not a single offer of help from the palace boys. Not a one of them fit to wield a pick—'

There were some general murmurs of agreement and some laughs as Jonas recounted his epic struggle to raise the whole palace by himself. The old woman with the white hair sighed and looked at the floor as the crowd began to get louder. Dominitia had the distinct impression that this was the usual tone of conversation in the industrial sites of Terminheim; tales of heroic stonemasonry heavily spiced with criticism of the Lord Governor and his soldiers and courtiers, and probably everyone else in Astregoth who didn't hack their way through unyielding stone most of their life. In the rain.

'Jonas!' called Soren over the hubbub. 'What if you *had* to get back in? What if the freak causing this storm was in there, sitting on the governor's throne, waiting for an axe to improve his face? What if the roads were watched by Blanks and guarded by Jack-o'-wires?'

The crowd had fallen quiet again.

'Is that true?' asked a young man with a thin, wispy beard that Dominitia tried not to stare at for fear of offending him – but which was very, *very* thin. And very wispy.

Soren turned to her and gestured for her to get up on the bench with him. She hesitated, wanting to be literally anywhere else but in this room at this moment, but knowing she couldn't very well refuse. Reluctantly she clambered up, her wet shoes making a horrible paste of the dust on the bench that both squelched and crunched unpleasantly.

'I believe the storm is feeding off him,' she said to the now-silent assemblage. 'I think the Blanks and the Jack-o'-wires are feeding off the storm. It's how he can see us. It's how he controls them. He's connected to everything through it.'

'And he sits on the throne?' Soren asked gently.

'When I saw him last, he was sitting there, not moving. Not seeing. Like his body is the centre of it all but his mind is'—she paused and looked around at the roof and walls—'out there. If it's still his mind at all.'

She fell silent and shuffled her feet. The horrible crunching sensation made her cringe.

'It's all we have,' said Soren.

'It'll do,' added the old woman. 'It's more than we've had for days.'

'If you want to get into the palace,' growled Jonas from his stool at the back, 'you'll need to reopen the service tunnels. They're still there, first thing we had to dig when the site was excavated, to remove the bedrock to the dump sites.' He jerked his head in a vague direction that was evidently where the dump sites were. 'Used them after to bring the stone through for the lower floors, along with the gravel mix and cement—'

'Thanks, Jonas,' Soren said quickly, transparently trying to avoid getting into too lengthy a discussion of the palace's construction. 'So, these tunnels...?'

'Still serviceable,' Jonas said with a sniff of unmistakeable pride. 'Sealed off, of course. At both ends. But getting them open won't be hard.' He nodded off to his left, into the cavernous depths of the Social. 'Plenty of explosives, won't take much. We'll have to get the amount right, in case the tunnels collapse, but I can do that. I know how thick the stone is at the sealed ends.'

'Alright,' said Soren. 'Jonas, you're in charge of the demolition teams. Pick your men and go get the explosives you'll need for opening up the tunnel at the dump site and the palace. How long are the tunnels?'

Jonas shrugged.

'A mile? Maybe a little less.'

Dominitia shuddered.

'Will they hear the explosion in the palace? Will they know we're coming?'

Jonas laughed and jerked a thumb behind him.

'Have you heard the thunder, little mage lady? No one is going to hear a thing. Not until we blast our way into the freak's throne room anyway.'

The old woman stood up and peered around, trying to see Jonas over the heads of the people in crowded around.

'Surely the tunnels don't go to the throne room?' she called.

Jonas sniffed and stuck his lower jaw out.

'Well, no,' he conceded. 'They come out in the lower floors. Servant quarters, cellars. Food stores if I remember right.'

The old woman clambered up onto the workbench and leaned on Soren for support. She glanced at Dominitia with cold, hard eyes and gave a short nod. Then she addressed the crowd.

'We will have a fight on our hands,' she said gravely. 'We don't know how many Jack-o'-wires might be in there, and every single one of the staff, the soldiers and the Governor's family will be a Blank. We've all met them, and most of us have fought them. They're the reason our families cower in their homes and dare not venture out. Our loved ones are cold, hungry, and getting desperate. We do this for them. Every Blank was once a person, but they are not now. They will kill you as soon as look at you, so strike first and strike hard.'

Soren nodded and chimed in.

'The Jack-o'-wires are too much for any one of us to handle alone,' he said. 'I killed one earlier tonight, but only with help. Hit the heads, break those buckets or pots or basins, whatever they have. It seems to cut their power.' He looked at Dominitia. 'Is that right?'

She nodded, her eyes downcast.

'From what I saw tonight, I think so yes. The storm feeds them. The one I saw was animated by the same lightning that used to infect Alakis, and now infects the sky. When the bucket broke, it was like the lightning couldn't get in anymore. Like there was a string or a wire connecting it to the energy in the sky, and without the bucket, the string was cut.'

The bearded faces regarded her solemnly and nodded, murmuring to one another. She saw a burly man in a red knitted jumper in discussion with a huge, musclebound hulk of a man and gesturing, miming the shape of a tool of some kind. The hulk man was disagreeing, suggesting another kind of tool that would be better for the job. She turned her head and caught the old woman's eye. She shook her head with a smile.

'Stonemasons,' she said wryly, '*always* use the right tool for the job.' Dominitia tried to smile back, but it was a shaky affair.

'Friends,' called Soren. 'Wait a minute. Jonas needs some time to pick his demolitions, and then we need to get ourselves to the dump site. Shall we say we meet there at midnight? That gives us three hours or so.'

'Plenty of time,' sniffed Jonas, heaving himself off his stool and grabbing the two men closest to him by their shirt collars. 'You two, come with me.'

'And you, girl?' asked the old woman. 'Are you coming?' She cast a quick look up and down Dominitia, evidently not terribly impressed with what she saw.

Dominitia shook her head.

'If the choice is stay here where it's safe or—'

'Safe?' said the old woman. 'If we fail, what do you think will happen to this place?' She glanced around the Social. 'Those things will raze it to the ground and slaughter anyone they find. You might as well come with us, help us to win.'

Dominitia felt hysteria bubbling up inside her.

'How?' she cried. 'I can't do *anything*, I—'

'You used to calm him,' said Soren. 'You said that's what you used to do for him.'

'Yes, but how—'

'It calmed his affliction,' the old woman said. 'Maybe it still can. At a crucial moment, perhaps. We get to the throne room; you calm his mind. Give us a chance to end him.'

'I can't, I can't do that!' Dominitia wailed. 'What if it doesn't work?'

201

'Then you die there. In the light, with us. Instead of here, alone in the dark and surrounded by Jack-o'-wires.'

The words died before they reached her lips. She suddenly felt violently sick. Dominitia collapsed to her knees, ignoring the crunch of dust under her, and wept bitterly.

Chapter Thirteen

Someone had lent her one of the long leather capes with a hood that the men of Terminheim habitually wore to work in their inhospitable mines and quarries. It was old and smelt of stale sweat, but the rain thrashed harmlessly off it and even the wind seemed unable to penetrate it. Beneath the material, Dominitia was relatively warm and dry, so despite the constant crash of thunder overhead, she felt a little better. Somehow, the act of doing something, however futile it seemed, felt good. She was fairly sure she wouldn't be of much use but seeing the army of men and women in their hooded capes holding their heavy, sharp tools and axes, she began to think they might actually succeed.

The sealed entrance to the tunnel was in a sunken pit of earth, overlooked on both sides by large mounds of rock and compacted mud. The dump site, as its name suggested, was an unlovely stretch of open ground strewn with the detritus of building work. Poles, fences and bits of wire all sat in jumbled heaps amidst discarded rock and stone, and mounds of earth. Had it not been for the near-constant flashes of light from the tormented sky, it would have been impossible to see at this hour of the night. As it was, midnight in Terminheim was like a peculiar endless twilight, the world lit in hues of grey and blue, occasionally thrown into stark relief by a particularly large burst of lightning arcing between the growling, crashing clouds.

'Are you ready for this?' asked the old woman, whose name she had discovered was Ylinda. She was apparently something akin to a village elder, and well respected by the men.

Ylinda was standing by her side on a large hill overlooking the spot where Jonas and his team were fiddling with blocks of what looked like leather but which, she assured Dominitia, were bags filled with chemicals imported from Ceresheim and which were produced there as fertiliser for crops. Mixed in this particular way, they would explode on contact with fire. Jonas was moving with a surprising delicacy for a man of his size, carefully handling the bags with graceful, smooth movements. Dominitia kept her eyes on him, as though her vigilance might ensure that he didn't drop anything and vaporise them all.

'Not really,' she replied at length, forcing a wan smile. 'I'm not a fighter.'

'No one's asking you to be,' said the woman, gesturing with her tool, which she had explained was a rock-hammer. She took in the many men and women who had assembled with a sweep of the heavy-looking weapon. From their vantage point on the hill, there seemed to be hundreds of them. 'We have all the fighters we need. You're our secret weapon. And besides,' her tone turned softer, 'we couldn't have done this without the information you gave us. You've given us hope, and that's a powerful thing.'

Dominitia nodded, not really believing what the woman was saying. She watched as Jonas and his men stomped their way up the banks of the mud-mounds on either side of the tunnel, making flapping gestures at the assembled makeshift army. People started to edge back, some turned and scuttled away over the filthy hills, slipping and sliding. Dominitia turned as Ylinda began to pick her way over the uneven ground.

'Are we not safe here?' she asked, thinking they were much higher than anyone else and so if they weren't safe, surely no one was.

The old woman stomped on the hill with a grin.

'You don't want to be on a mud hill when an explosion goes off,' she said. 'They're only compacted earth, and they've been known to suck people down when something loosens them up.'

Dominitia balked and began to hurry after her.

'Down! Down everyone!' someone suddenly shouted. Dominitia turned in sudden horror, expecting to be engulfed in fire at any moment. Away towards the city, between the mounds of discarded materials, she could just about make out a running figure coming towards them, waving his hands. She recognised Soren's voice as he shouted and yelled over the crashing thunder.

'Get down! Blanks! Blanks are coming!'

Dominitia felt her heart freeze within her chest, not trusting herself to move as Ylinda dropped into a crouch beside her and pulled her down with one surprisingly strong hand.

'Keep still,' the old woman breathed into her ear. Dominitia tried not to scream and looked out across the dump site. Between flashes of lightning, the men and women of the resistance army seemed to disappear, folding to their knees and draping their dark leather capes around themselves. Suddenly there was no one, just the odd industrial tool or axe lying unclaimed on the ground to give any indication that a person had been there at all. In the driving rain, against the colourless landscape, they were all but invisible. Dominitia did the same, pulling her hood up around her head and kneeling on the hard, wet, unpleasant ground with her cape around her. She peered out from under the hood, watching the road in the direction Soren had come from.

Moments later they appeared. Three people, two men and a woman, each holding a long spear. They were dressed in mail shirts and leather armour but had no helmets. They seemed oblivious to the pounding rain and the terrible chill of the Terminheim night, trudging unhurriedly along the road.

'Maybe they didn't see him,' Dominitia said to Ylinda. The motionless form beside her said nothing, looking like nothing so much as a slick wet rock.

The Blanks continued their march along the road through the dump site, holding their spears as casually as was possible for mind-wiped puppet-soldiers. Dominitia felt panic welling up inside her as they stepped nearer and nearer to the lumpy form she was certain had to be Soren. He hadn't had that much time after bringing his warning...

The male Blank paused, resting the butt of his spear on the ground as he surveyed the rain-hammered landscape of discarded things and mud piles. Long seconds stretched. His foot was inches from the leather cape when it flew up and the man beneath it leapt to his feet.

Dominitia screamed, able to stop herself, as the Terminheimer swung a sharp-bladed axe and buried its point in the Blank's back. The other two Blanks leapt back, spears whirling to face the foolish man as he tried to jerk his heavy weapon free. Other men and women were leaping up, seeming to erupt from the ground in waves of yelling faces and swinging weapons.

The Blanks spun around, their eyes suddenly blazing with crackling energies. Almost as though in answer, the clouds overhead split with brilliant light and sharp growls of thunder.

Dominitia could almost feel the energy at work, something malign turning its attention to the plight of its puppets.

The screaming Terminheimers were upon the Blanks within seconds, swinging their massive hammers and rock-tools, bludgeoning the hapless soldiers to the ground. Dominitia allowed herself a shaky breath.

'They got them,' she said, turning a smile to the old woman. But her companion was getting to her feet, her face set and grim. The eyes she turned on Dominitia were scathing, but she said nothing.

'Move!' Jonas was yelling, jogging back to the tunnel entrance and waving his hands at his crew. 'We have to get this thing open *now!*'

All around them Dominitia could see frightened faces, people scanning the tops of the mud-dunes with fearful eyes.

'What is it, what's—' Dominitia began just as she saw a blazing figure crest one of the hills and stand looking down on them with inhuman eyes.

'Jack-o'-wires,' the old woman said simply. 'The Blanks called them.'

The misshapen thing of scrap and broken metal began to lope its way down the rough slope, its disturbing, impossible gait made all the more bizarre by the terrain. Its legs seemed to splay out beneath it each time it bobbed a step closer, its limp arms clattering by its sides. The head, which seemed to be fashioned from a metal vase of some kind, was lit from within by sparking arcs of tiny lightning. Its eyes blazed with cold purpose and dread indifference as its claws flexed and extended.

Down by the tunnel, Jonas was scrabbling away as one of his team worked to light a fuse. The man desperately clacked two stone objects together, sparks flying from his hands, but whatever he was trying to light was not cooperating.

'More of them!' yelled a voice. Dominitia looked around. A young woman armed with a long metal spike of some kind was pointing to the left. Another sparking, soulless marionette was bouncing over a muddy ridge, turning its bucket-head to stare blankly at the yelling humans. Dominitia slumped heavily to the ground as another appeared. Then another.

'Get up!' yelled the old woman, pulling at her arm. But Dominitia's legs wouldn't work. Nothing worked. She could only stare in horrified, terrified silence at the clattering abominations lurching hideously towards them.

Some of the men were running to the approaching monsters, yelling and roaring battle-cries as they swung their weapons. A few got some hits in before the indifferent puppet-things tore them to pieces, but most died before their blows fell. The Jack-o'-wires came on, one of them trailing an arm that had snagged in its tangled wire claws.

Jonas and his crew were running, spilling over the muddy ground and yelling. Suddenly there seemed to fall a moment of perfect silence, a motionless heartbeat of nothing, before the ground blew apart with a tremendous roar, louder than thunder. Rocks and earth were hurled up and out, clattering around the fleeing demolitions team and beyond. A ball of fire flashed into brilliant existence and then vanished just as fast, collapsing into smoke and dissipating energy.

The Jack-o'-wire was only feet away when Dominitia finally found her strength and let herself be pulled up by the frantic Ylinda. She could smell the unholy creation as they ran away, a hot smell of burning hair and decay, and only then did she realise quite how close she'd come to death.

'I'm sorry, I'm sorry,' she panted, repeating it like a mantra as her mind found a way to function through the fear.

'Never mind that'—growled the woman, shoving her towards the still-smoking entrance to the underground tunnel—'get in there and run.'

Dominitia ran for the tunnel and fled into its dark embrace, following the half-glimpsed heels of the men and women in front. She had no idea how many had made it, or how many had been ripped to screaming chunks by the Jack-o'-wires. She only knew that if Jonas didn't make it, they were doomed.

She slowed, stepping to one side and pressing against the wet sides of the pitch-dark tunnel as a thought occurred to her. People ran past, panting and screaming, not seeing her.

Dominitia reached into herself, remembering the very simplest of the abilities mages learned at the Barbican. Her mind was by no means calm, but this at least was something at which she'd had practice. Living in the dark ruins of the mages' fortress for so long had taught her how to do it without even thinking.

A ball of light, small at first, appeared in the palm of her hand. She smiled at it in spite of herself, and let it float up into the air. It brightened, then divided, then divided again. She sent a series of glowing, growing lights floating away down the dark tunnel, one left and one back the way she'd come. Gradually, the walls of the tunnel were revealed as the shadows retreated. People around her blinked at her in amazement, smiles of wonder briefly lighting faces clouded by horror.

The tunnel was wider than she'd realised. The hole blown open by Jonas and his crew was narrow, so she had thought the tunnel was large enough only for two or three people to walk abreast. As the light's intensity grew, she saw how wrong she'd been. The ground was smooth and flat, almost polished by the passage of many heavy wagons and loads of stone. Only the first hundred metres or so had an incline, the access route then evening out, presumably for ease of transportation. The tunnel had a high ceiling, glimpses of which the bobbing light that floated high above her head revealed. She could imagine tall wagons loaded with all sorts of equipment passing through this tunnel, and despite the dire situation, she was impressed. There was certainly more to Terminheim than huts and axes. At the very least, these people knew engineering on a level that no one in Asterheim could claim to. She felt another stab of guilt at the thought.

Back the way she'd come, another huge explosion rocked the ground, followed by the crash and grind of falling rock. Dominitia collapsed against the wall, whimpering with her hands over her ears.

Before long she felt hands on hers, pulling them away from her head. She looked up, into the silent tunnel lit by the ghostly shimmer of her conjured balls of silvery light. Soren looked down at her and smiled a thin, not-very-reassuring, smile. Behind him, the old woman Ylinda was in a heated conversation with Jonas.

'What do you mean we don't have enough?' she demanded, poking him in the chest with one bony finger. 'You said you had plenty!'

'For *two* breaches, Ylinda. Two,' said Jonas gruffly, spreading his arms wide. 'Why would I bring more than that?'

The old woman leaned back incredulously and put her hands on her hips.

'Why?' she repeated, her voice rising with each word as she continued. 'Well, I can think of one *very good reason why!*

'We didn't know we'd be attacked by a junk-yard full of Jacks!'

'No,' she yelled in a thin, strained voice, 'but you didn't even think about the possibility, which is what makes you an idiot!'

Jonas huffed and growled and stomped a few paces away, throwing his arms out as he paced.

'How much do we have?' asked Soren in the horrible quiet that descended.

Jonas shook his head.

'Not enough to get through the walls.' He made a vague gesture in the direction of the palace.

'We're stuck here,' said Ylinda flatly. 'Stuck here with nothing but these tools to dig ourselves out.' She hefted her weapon and looked at it doubtfully.

'There won't be time,' Dominitia said, surprising herself by speaking aloud. 'Those Jack-o'-wires will be here soon.'

'Here?' said Ylinda, looking at her through narrowed eyes as though concerned she'd hit her head. 'We're deep underground, child. They can't get in.'

Dominitia thought back to the prison. The glowing stone, the wire-and-railings claw stretching through it. She shook her head.

'No,' she said simply. 'They'll be here soon.' She looked at Soren, who frowned back for one moment of ignorant bliss before he made a groaning sound and put his hands to his head. Dominitia nodded sadly.

'She's right,' Soren sighed. 'Back at the prison, we saw one melt through the stone.'

'Melt through?' Ylinda asked, but without much conviction.

'We have *some* explosive left,' said Jonas from a few paces away, his voice subdued.

'You said it wasn't enough,' Ylinda snapped without looking around.

'Not to break the walls, no. But an explosion like that, in these confines…'

'Would it kill the Jacks?' she asked.

'Doubtful,' said Soren.

'Not the Jacks,' Jonas said softly, coming to stand near them. He held Ylinda's gaze meaningfully. She stepped back, shaking her head.

'No. *No*,' she said in a hushed, frantic voice. 'You can't be serious. There are *hundreds* of us down here!'

'And how many of us can face those things if they all get in here? Ten of them, twenty…you saw what *three* managed out there.'

Dominitia stood up suddenly. Soren, Jonas and Ylinda looked at her in surprise.

'Jonas,' she said, again surprised she was speaking aloud but the idea had taken hold and wouldn't let go. The bright prospect of her life was dangling like a gleaming mote of light just out of reach, and it was blanking out her fear. 'What is that explosive stuff?'

Ylinda frowned and looked at Jonas expectantly. The big man shrugged.

'Chemicals from Ceresheim. We import it in bulk—'

'She doesn't want to know how you import it, idiot,' said Ylinda. 'She wants to know what it is.'

'Ceresheim,' mused Dominitia. 'The grain belt. Farmer country. This chemical, what do they use it for?'

'Growing crops,' said Soren, with a tentative smile as he watched Dominitia. 'Some kind of fertiliser for the soil, I believe.'

'Yeah so? So what?' Jonas's voice was getting gruff again.

'May I see it?' asked Dominitia.

Jonas made a huffing, frustrated sound and turned away, returning with one of the leathery bags and putting it carefully on the ground. He made a gesture towards it and turned away.

Dominitia knelt by the side of the bag, smiling at the faint smell of animal manure and something sharp and tangy like organic decay. This was something she knew.

'I was a mage for the Farmers' Guild,' she said softly, running her fingers over the bag. 'I can't fight, I can't throw lightning or make portals. But I know crops,' she placed her palm against the soft leather and closed her eyes. 'I can feel them, I can tell what they want to do and help them do it. Crops want to grow, to throw off parasites. They want to bloom and reproduce and resist fires and floods...and I give them the power to do what they want...'

'So?' snorted Jonas, 'what does that have to do with—'

'These chemicals,' she said in a dreamy voice, her mind half floating through the chemical soup within the bag, moving from particle to particle and feeling the processes within, 'they're crops, or some of them once were. The organics and inorganics have been mixed, but I can feel their potential. Some part of them is still living...they still *want*...'

'What do they want?' whispered Ylinda.

'To *burn*,' Dominitia smiled, 'they want to burn.'

Chapter Fourteen

Dominitia stood in the gloomy tunnel, still lit by the silvery balls of glowing brilliance she had created. A few metres in front of her was a wall of cut blocks and mortar, the wall of the palace itself. The people of Terminheim were behind her, readying themselves for the fight to come. Ylinda and Soren were addressing them, reminding them of the mission which was, essentially, to kill Alakis.

The little bag of explosive chemical was slumped against the wall, looking very small and very inadequate. Jonas had thrown his hands in the air and given up trying to explain to her that there was no way this much chemical could bring down enough stone no matter how much she cajoled and persuaded it. She'd let him go, not knowing how to explain to someone who didn't understand mage-craft on a basic level how a very difficult process worked. She just hoped he was wrong.

She could feel the potential within the bag. The chemicals had been mixed in such a way that they positively yearned for release; she could almost hear them calling, begging for the touch of fire that would fulfil their desires and let them fling their energies wide and high in glorious combustion. The question was, how much could she stoke those desires and feed that potential and still direct it in a single, powerful blast? It would be no good if the bag detonated in a wide, fiery bloom, burning the Terminheimers in the tunnel to ashes and having no effect whatsoever on the wall. An ignominious demise if ever there was one.

No, she needed a single, fireless release of pure kinetic energy to crash its way through the stone and push up and out into the palace. With luck, she could take out the monsters prowling within the lower quarters, so at least they would have space to get themselves in position before more arrived. Her mind stroked and caressed, calling the organic components in the bag into alignment, subtly altering their potential and gently enhancing it in line with her own will.

A process not at all helped by Jonas, who was still pacing and muttering just behind her. She tried to shut him out, but then another voice joined the noise.

Someone was shouting from further back in the tunnel, someone in distress. Dominitia's eyes snapped open as she heard the word "Jack-o'-wires".

'We're out of time,' said Soren, his voice tight and gruff. 'We have to go, now.'

Dominitia let her mind make one last pass over the bag before retreating back inside her head. She sagged, her shoulders slumping as she exhaled hard. She turned to Jonas, pushing her damp hair back over her shoulder.

'It's now or never,' she said with a shaky smile.

'Will it work?' the big man asked, his eyes showing a hint of fear which made her feel much, much worse.

She shook her head and shrugged. Soren clapped her on the back and jogged a few paces away. Jonas turned to his team and called them over. One of the men had a length of wiry fuse and the two blocks he'd used previously. Dominitia shook her head and waved them back.

'No need,' she said, feeling more confident than she had in a long time. 'That bag doesn't even need a spark anymore.'

Jonas looked at her, then at the bag. His eyes narrowed in suspicion but he stepped back, gesturing for her to proceed.

'Circle save us all,' said Ylinda.

'They're almost on us!' yelled someone from far back in the tunnel.

Dominitia closed her eyes and let her mind drift back to the swirling, yearning liquid in the bag. It seemed to sigh at her touch and she smiled.

'Burn,' she whispered.

The bag erupted with a flash of light more intense than any lightning and twice as loud. The tremendous blast was followed almost instantly by the crack of exploding stone and the shriek of tearing metal. Rock, cement and stone was vapourised instantly as the shockwave swept through the palace wall and boiled up into the interior in a surge of superheated pressure. Walls were obliterated, rooms annihilated and staircases collapsed. Beyond the focused fury of the initial blast, windows shattered. Doors were blown off hinges. Dominitia kept her eyes shut tight, her mind bent completely to the task of directing the desperate, frantic energies outward and away from the tunnel. At the instant of detonation the impossible forces threatened to crush her, screaming against her willpower and defying their bonds, but she gasped and held on and the moment passed. The echoes of the blast faded and died, replaced by the crunch and crash of collapsing walls from beyond the hole and the shriek of screaming Blanks.

Dominitia fell to her knees and opened her eyes, panting heavily. She looked into the palace. The whole wall before her was gone, a thick layer of dust and silt covering the floor where it had stood.

The room into which she stared was huge, hundreds of metres across. It took her a moment to realise that the room had once been a series of smaller rooms, but the dividing walls were now obliterated, lying like children's toys scattered and broken in the gloom. Only the thicker, sturdier pillars of solid rock supporting the upper rooms seemed to have survived, but even they had ominous cracks running through them like dark threads. A staircase led up to the next floor, but only the top five steps remained. Through the hole she could see light and knew that was the only route they had now to the throne-room.

'Get up, Dominitia,' yelled Ylinda, pulling at her arms. 'You did well, but there are Jack-o'-wires behind us.'

'And in front,' muttered Soren darkly, pointing to the holes in the roof where other staircases and ladders had once ascended to the next floor. Clattering, disjointed things animated by filthy lightning were stumbling and falling through the holes, only to stir to abominable life in the confines of the wide-open basement of the palace.

'We're still trapped,' Jonas growled, hefting a large pickaxe. 'We'll keep them busy long enough for you to get to the throne-room.'

'Me?' Dominitia yelped.

'You need to calm him,' Ylinda said with gritted teeth, jerking her along like an uncooperative child. 'If you don't calm him no one will get near enough.'

'It's suicide,' Soren said from beside them with a lopsided grin, 'but then this whole thing was always a one-way mission.'

The four of them ran into the dark interior of the palace basement, lit now by the glimmering flashes of lightning animating the Jack-o'-wires. Dominitia gestured at her silvery balls of light and swept them into the cellar as the Terminheimers ran in. Behind them, the Jacks from the dump site were slowly jerking their way towards the hole in the wall.

Soren was the first to die. His axe swung and a bucket sheered in two, the clanking collection of objects it had animated collapsing to the floor like so much discarded household waste. He turned, looking for the second Jack-o'-wire that had been closing in on them, but his foot slipped on a tangle of wire and he fell to one knee. His axe dropped to the floor and clattered away as he scrabbled desperately to his feet.

Dominitia screamed a warning as the second Jack thrust a claw of fence-post and knives into Soren's chest with a burst of discharging energies. Soren gaped, eyes wide, for a moment before falling back to sprawl against the defeated Jack-o'-wire. Dominitia and Ylinda scrabbled back. The Jack turned its blazing, sightless gaze to them and took a lurching step forward.

All around them the people of Terminheim were dying. For every abomination they killed, at least four or five lost their lives. And more were coming, dropping from the roof and phasing through the walls. It was hopeless.

Dominitia tripped over a piece of broken stone, falling hard against the floor and gasping in pain. Ylinda, next to her, turned to offer a hand but snatched it back. She stared in horror at something over Dominitia's head and backed away. Dominitia could smell burning hair and decay, and her mind went blank with fear.

'Alakis!' she screamed, rolling onto her back and staring at the impossible marionette as it raised an inhuman hand blazing with lightning. 'Alakis!'

The Jack-o'-wire seemed to hesitate, its bucket-head tilting as though hearing something. It stumbled back a step, two steps, and collapsed against a wall. The blazing light went out. All around the basement, the abominations sat on the ground, legs splayed before them. The lightning fuelling them faded, the last arcs of snapping energy dancing along bits of wire and vanishing into nothing. Silence fell, but for the moans and cries of the wounded.

Dominitia rose to her feet and looked slowly around the room. At least a hundred of the Terminheimers who had entered the basement lay dead or wounded, the survivors huddled in groups back-to-back or running to the sides of their comrades.

'Dominitia,' a ghostly voice said, echoing around the expansive room like the haunting whisper of a dead god. 'What have you done?'

Ylinda looked at her briefly, her eyes wide, but Dominitia couldn't speak. She turned to look at the jagged ruin of the ceiling, which was glowing with a pale, dirty light. Tiny snaps of crackling lightning sparked to brief life in the air as the light intensified. Slowly, a human foot began to descend through the ceiling, phasing through it as the Jack-o'-wire at the prison had done. It was joined by a second, then a pair of legs wearing tattered rags that had once been clothes. Slowly, Alakis floated down through the roof, his body thin and emaciated and his clothing burned and torn. The mage's eyes were pitiless black orbs set deep in his bald head, and his teeth gleamed and flashed with the blueish energies that swirled around him.

'Dominitia,' Alakis hissed in that ghostly voice that seemed to come from the air around him rather than his own throat. He hovered a few metres off the ground, staring at her with those blank eyes.

'Now,' muttered Ylinda, by her side, 'do it now…'

219

A strange resonating sound echoed through the gloomy room, which Dominitia took a moment to realise was laughter.

'Do what, I wonder?' hissed the voice. 'What grand scheme have you pinned on poor, frightened Dominitia, Terminheimer? She will disappoint you. She always does.'

Alakis's thin body shuddered with amusement as he floated closer.

'You should have stayed where I put you,' he sighed. 'I didn't want to hurt you. Or these people.' He gestured around the room.

'You...didn't?' Dominitia's voice was small and pathetic and she hated herself for it. Alakis didn't seem to care. He simply shook his head.

'Not you. Not *them*. There is nothing in those books that can help me, not now. Not after this,' Alakis ran a hand down his tortured body. 'I am destroyed. And I will destroy those who did this to me.'

'No one did this to you, Alakis—'

One of the Jack-o'-wires twitched and blazed for a moment with unholy light as Alakis's face contorted into a mask of unspeakable rage.

'*They* did this,' he whispered in that ghostly echo, floating closer to Dominitia. She could see the pain etched on his twitching face, the bones sticking through his thin skin. 'Asterheim. Sophine. Rigel. Thaniel. The Senate. The priests. They chased me from my home. Made me a monster.'

He floated back.

'I wanted only to be left alone, to be free.' A spasm of pain made his limbs jerk as thunder crashed loudly outside. 'But the storm within became a storm without, and it is killing me,' he hissed. 'It *wants* to kill. It *needs* to kill. It feeds on life and grows stronger with every thrall, every puppet.' His eyes strayed to the Jack-o'-wires, which had begun to twitch and spark again.

'When it is finished with this place and we are strong enough, I will turn it on Asterheim,' Alakis said, in his painful whisper, 'and maybe that will be enough to sate it. Maybe then it will leave me alone.'

'Alakis you can't, these people are innocent—'

'And what was I?' Alakis screamed. 'Innocence is no protection in this world. It is an invitation to pain and death, called a virtue only by those who benefit from the naivety of others.'

The Jack-o'-wires lurched up, crackling with life once again. By Dominitia's side, Ylinda gripped her weapon and stepped back in horror.

'Run away, Dominitia,' snarled Alakis. 'Save yourself. You brought these people here to die, but you can leave.' He gestured with one hand, a yawning portal of black smoke ripping into the fabric of reality only a few feet from her. She glanced at it and shook her head.

'I…can't,' she said.

'Poor Dominitia,' Alakis mocked, 'always so frightened. Always so helpless. Is it innocence?' He shook his head slowly. 'No. How can it be when you never do anything that isn't, in the end, self-serving? You helped me because you needed me. You helped these people because you needed them. You are a parasite, Dominitia. And a coward. So run. Admit what you are and then tell me who the monster is.'

The Jack-o'-wires were spinning and lurching, ripping and tearing. One fell, its head split, only to be replaced by two more dropping through the ceiling. All around her, people screamed and fell.

221

The portal gaped before her, dark and unknowable. It could lead anywhere. To death, or to freedom. Alakis's words echoed in her head, the truth of them as sharp as any blade.

Beside her, Ylinda screamed a battle cry and charged the nearest abomination.

Dominitia looked at Alakis, at his sneering, mocking face. Tears ran down her cheeks.

She stepped through the portal.

***

Thaniel lay on his front in the rain and peered over the rocky ridge. Fifty metres or so away, the heavy walls of Terminheim stretched up to the sky. They were not as high as Asterheim's walls but looked far more solid. Cold, brutal stone seemed to ring the city, but the gates were open and beyond them, nothing stirred.

Eric squirmed next to him.

'Where is everyone?' he asked, pulling his sodden coat around him. Overhead the storm blazed its fury, seeming to flash and crackle from one point above the centre of the city, which Thaniel had a funny feeling was the palace of the Governor.

'I don't know,' he muttered, 'but something is very, very wrong here. Come on,' he stood up, reaching down for Eric's hand just as a ball of darkness erupted on the road a few metres from where they stood. Thaniel yelped and jumped back, summoning his powers and focusing his mind.

The ball of black mist expanded and groaned, yawning open like a gaping mouth of impenetrable darkness. Tiny arcs of black lightning snapped and crackled at the edges, which reminded him of Sophine's portals. He hesitated.

The portal stretched wide and vanished, collapsing in on itself. A girl lay on the ground, weeping and clutching at her long dark hair. For a moment he thought it was Sophine, but he'd never heard Sophine cry. Carefully, picking his way over the rain-slicked ground, he made his way to the girl's side. He gingerly touched her hand and she yelped, scrabbling to her feet and looking absolutely terrified.

Thaniel took a step back too. He knew that face, but his mind was blank.

'Thaniel?' she said, blinking at him. He nodded with a hesitant smile. The girl turned and looked back at the city, her shoulders slumping.

'I thought perhaps he'd sent me to Asterheim,' she said sadly. 'I thought perhaps I could do some good after all. But he's right. I am a monster. I left those people, all those people...'

'What's your name?' Thaniel asked, stepping forward and reaching out to the distressed girl. She jerked away from him and backed up another step, pulling her leather cape around her.

'I'm Dominitia,' she said simply. 'I came here with Alakis, and now he's killing Terminheim. I had a chance to stop him and I couldn't do it. He let me go.'

'Alakis is killing—' Thaniel repeated incredulously.

'He's gone,' Dominitia said bitterly. 'That storm, it feeds off him. It's like the lightning inside him got turned inside out and now,' she gestured at the lightning-wracked sky. 'It's alive. It infects people, and those it doesn't infect it kills. It gets stronger the more it kills, and Alakis has become...something else. The thing inside it. I don't know how much is even him anymore.'

'Come on,' said Thaniel, reaching for her arm. 'Let's get you somewhere safe.' His eyes strayed beyond her to the gates, where something flickering and bright was lurching along the road, followed by another.

She followed his gaze, looking around at the distant gate of Terminheim. She let out a cry of exhausted terror.

'Can you get us back to Asterheim?' she asked.

Thaniel shook his head.

'Not until we're clear of the storm. Come on, we can—'

She hesitated, then stepped away, her eyes becoming bright and fierce.

'No. Not this time. Alakis is coming for Asterheim, with an army of slave people and abominations made of junk and brought to life with lightning. He will come once he's strong enough, and from what I've seen that won't be long. If he sees you here,' she looked around again and swallowed. 'If he, or any of those things, sees you here, you'll be dead before you can get back.'

'Dominitia,' began Eric. She shushed him with a wave of her hand.

'Don't,' she said, 'I've been a coward for long enough. This time…this time I'm going to do the right thing. Take the warning to Asterheim. Be ready. I will buy you any time I can.'

Without a further word she turned and stalked away, striding back to the city from which she had just escaped. Thaniel looked at Eric, who stared back with wide, frightened eyes.

'We'd better go,' he said, turning back the way they'd come. 'We have to contact Sophine.'

He cast one last look over his shoulder at the retreating form of Dominitia as she approached the tempest-thrashed walls of the dark city.

He took Eric's hand and they ran.

Sophine stood in the middle of her office, looking at her body as it sat motionless in the chair behind the desk. If she had needed to breathe, she might have held her breath. As it was, the strange sensation of being outside her corporeal form carried with it the even stranger sensation of not needing to breathe. The in and out of air into her lungs was happening five feet away, in the physical shell in which she had lived her entire life and which she had never thought of as separate to herself until this moment.

She lifted a hand, wondering why it was she had a hand if all she was at this moment was a mind.

'Because I'm a spirit,' she said aloud. No words passed her lips, no air rushed through fleshy organs to form the sound. And yet she heard it. Expressed it. Fully expected that others could hear it, if they had stood with her in this strange twilight realm beyond the physical.

The world around her was almost identical to the world as she saw it through her physical eyes. The morning light still streamed through the window, the papers on her desk still fluttered slightly in the breeze. But the light was tinged a mournful shade of blue and the breeze did not touch her, and the shadows seemed deeper than in the ordinary world. Darker, as though they were less the absence of light and more portals down into a deep, unknowable place of shadow lying another level down beyond the one in which she stood. She forced her gaze away from those holes in the world, feeling a chill that had nothing to do with temperature.

In fact, it seemed she could not feel anything at all here. Neither warm nor cold, and the sofa had no substance when she touched it. It would be impossible to interact with anything in the real world after all.

She felt a twinge of disappointment as she glanced around the room, ignoring the roiling shadows which seemed to have deepened in the last few moments. The book had spoken of abilities one could use whilst projecting one's soul outward, but clearly that took a lot more study and effort than she had so far managed.

She was tempted to float further. She knew she could. A mere thought would have her flying across the city and beyond, to Terminheim even. Perhaps in this form the storm, or whatever Alakis's mind was doing, could not stop her. But she hesitated, glancing at her body and the darkening shadows.

Down by the desk, in the shadow cast by the window, the blackness was so intense that she felt an immediate flash of terror.

'I am not leaving myself here with *that*,' she muttered, unable to shake the thought of some nameless, bodiless entity forcing its way up through those shadows and into the vacant body by desk whilst she was flying around Terminheim.

Frustration followed quickly after that thought. She would have to leave Thaniel and Eric to it after all. To have come so close...

She let out a sigh of irritation and began to float back to her body, just as something caught her attention. Out here in the ethereal realm she could half-hear a thousand voices, thoughts and feelings from as many individual people whose own souls cast a faint reflection in the otherwise silent world. But one voice stood out.

'Rigel,' she smiled, recognising his familiar tones. She sensed he was close, not far from the city.

'You've come back,' she said, surprised at how happy she was at the thought.

Sophine let her spirit-form fly towards the sound, her smile widening as she came in sight of him. Far beyond the southern walls of Asterheim, there he was. He was getting off a horse and moving to stand with a pretty, curvaceous woman with thick curly hair. Her grin widened at the sight.

'My my, Rigel,' she laughed. 'Have you found a girl at last?'

She drifted closer, guiltily straining to hear their conversation and wondering if there was any way she could attract his attention.

Chapter Fifteen

On the second day after setting out from Ceresheim, Rigel and Sindel sighted the walls of the Hailfort. Asterheim was not far from that ugly fortress, and both of them sat in their saddles and watched the brightening horizon, not moving. They had taken their time getting here, walking at a leisurely pace which had infuriated Roan to no end. The bad-tempered horse had flicked and snorted and shaken his head most of the way along the road, but they had paid him no attention and stopped in most inns they came across "for a drink".

'I don't want to go,' Rigel said now, looking at the distance as the sun climbed higher into the morning sky.

'I know,' she said, sliding off her horse and moving to the road-side.

He kicked off his stirrups and jumped down from Roan's back, moving deftly to one side to avoid the brute's nipping teeth as he made a half-hearted protest. Rigel gave the horse an equally half-hearted thump on the nose and went to stand by Sindel.

'Last chance,' she sighed, not looking at him. There were un-shed tears in her eyes. 'You can always come back with me.'

They'd been over this so many times that he didn't respond at first.

'You know I can't,' he said heavily.

She said something in reply just as a peculiar sensation caught Rigel's attention. Almost like a rippling sound, with an echo of someone's voice…

'Sophine?' he said to the empty air, suddenly sure his friend was there somehow. Making some kind of contact.

Rigel jerked in sudden agony as something cold slid into his side. He gasped, feeling suddenly weak and rigid. Someone was holding him upright, someone pressing something against his body. *Inside* it. The intense feeling of violation was ghastly.

'Don't struggle,' said Sindel, her voice choked with emotion. 'Just relax, let it happen. You can't stop it now.'

Rigel managed a strangled cry and tried to grab at whatever it was sticking into him, but he was too weak and she had a grip like iron around his body. He looked down. She'd stabbed him with one of her knives, he could see the blood pumping over her hand as she held it deep inside his body. And then he was falling, slowly, being lowered to the ground like a child being put to bed. The grass was cool under his head, Sindel's beautiful face above him, her hair drooping down around it and framing it in luscious curls.

'Wh…why…' he managed to breathe, the times she'd saved his life flitting across his mind. The moments of bliss spent together. Her lips on his. His thoughts were becoming jumbled and unclear. Not far from him he could see Roan. The big destrier had his back to them, obliviously chewing grass.

'I'm so sorry Rigel,' Sindel said, bending to kiss him. Tears dropped from her face to his. 'You'll be in shock in a moment. It'll be like falling asleep. And you'll bleed out, so you won't wake. This was the most painless way to do it. I wish I didn't have to, I really do. I tried to get you to stay with me. Why couldn't you just stay with me?'

'I…I…please…' Rigel whispered, a terrible fear creeping through his dying body. He tried to summon his healing abilities, but he couldn't remember how. Something about silver threads…

'I was paid to keep you away from Asterheim,' she said, wiping her tears away. 'That was all. Keep you away. And so I hired those two thugs to jump us, to make you trust me. I thought if I helped you with Sidric, you'd stay happily in Ceresheim. But then I started to like you. I didn't want it to come to this, I promise.'

His vision was fading, darkness closing in at the sides.

'But a job's a job,' she sniffed between sobs. 'Even if the mark's a sweet boy like you. But I didn't want to kill you without giving you something in return, and we had a good time, didn't we?' She half-smiled, but tears were freely flowing down her face now. 'I'm so sorry, Rigel.'

Her voice was vanishing, echoing down a long dark corridor.

'Goodbye, sweet boy.'

And on the dusty road beneath the setting sun, half-a-day's ride from home, Rigel Wheatly took his last shuddering breath. Confused and frightened, cold and alone, he released it.

And died.

***

Sophine shrieked and jerked about impotently in the air as the woman knifed Rigel in the kidney with a long, sharp stiletto blade. Everything she'd read was a jumble in her mind; she couldn't conjure any energy or affect anything physical. The powerlessness made her panic even more.

Rigel collapsed to the ground, gasping. The woman was talking to him, crying. Sophine screamed and thrashed, unable to think through the frantic madness that had overtaken her. Then she was flying, soaring over the city and slamming back into her body with a physical jolt.

She was thrown violently against her desk and rolled heavily to the floor, the pain in her chest both physical and emotional. She panted, struggling to regain control of her emotions through the terrible shock. Again and again she saw the woman plunge the slender blade into her friend, saw his eyes widen, saw the betrayal in them turn to dreadful, soul-chilling horror as the certainty of death dawned.

'Rigel!' she shouted, scrabbling to her feet and throwing her hand out to conjure a portal with a snarl of pure, boiling rage.

Reality ripped itself in two at her command and she stalked through without hesitation, her eyes blazing with fury and the promise of death. Black lightning blazed at the edges of the portal, wreathing her in crackling energies as she bore down on the woman who had murdered her friend.

***

The heavy-set woman scrabbled back as Sophine came through the rift, jumping to her feet with a curious lurch. Sophine jerked her head aside as a stiletto blade, expertly thrown but slightly off target, whistled by her cheek. The woman, her face now set and her eyes focused, flung two more knives before Sophine had taken two paces. Her form was excellent and this time her aim was true, but she'd never tried to throw something at a distraught mage before.

Sophine stopped the blades with a thought and sent them screaming back to where they'd come from. She was rewarded with a shrill cry of pain from Rigel's killer. The woman collapsed, her blades embedded in one thigh and one shoulder. She tried to squirm away and Sophine raised a hand to conjure her dreadful killing power when her eyes alighted on Rigel's body. The woman was forgotten, terrible sorrow and desperate hope replacing all anger and thoughts of vengeance. Tears rose to cloud her vision and her throat closed in horror.

She collapsed to her knees by Rigel's body, her gaze running up and down his scrawny form, hoping against hope for a sign that he could be saved.

'No,' she whispered through the sobs she was powerless to stop. 'No, please. Rigel...'

The hope flickered and died in her heart as she knelt by Rigel's motionless body. She reached a tentative hand out to touch him. The ground beneath her friend was awash with blood. The grass glistened with it and the road nearby was stained red. It seemed to her that his entire body had been emptied, and his skin was cool to the touch already. Even in the few short minutes it had taken her to reach him, he had bled to death. She gently moved her trembling hand to his side and eased him up, choking anew at the sight of the wound the woman had dealt him. A single, extremely deep puncture wound from one of those hideous blades had been punched into his lower back. She didn't have to be a surgeon to imagine the passage of the blade, severing arteries all through his abdomen and up into his chest. It was a precise, perfectly murderous thrust that no mage, even Rigel himself, could have any hope of healing now.

He was gone.

Sophine rose on shaking legs, torn between wanting to wipe away her tears or the blood off her hand and knees. She stood for a moment, trying to collect her desperate, half-formed thoughts, then her eyes flicked to the woman who had done this to Rigel and the fog cleared.

'You,' she shouted through choked sobs, her vision still blurry with tears. Sophine swiped at her eyes angrily and half-stumbled towards where the woman was trying to crawl away backwards leaving a thin trail of her own blood in the dirt and grass.

'Why?' she cried, a dim corner of her mind screaming in horror as she slipped in Rigel's blood. 'Why did you do this? Tell me!'

The woman was floating into the air before she even knew she'd raised a hand. She forced herself to relax, just a little, realising that she really did need to know.

'I...' the woman coughed, struggling weakly. 'It was a job. I'm sorry...it wasn't...personal. I didn't let him...suffer.'

Sophine blinked, stunned by the sheer audacity of it.

'A job? A *job*?' she was shaking with rage, barely holding onto the restraint which kept her from crushing the woman there and then.

'To keep him away...I tried to keep him away...'

'And when he wouldn't you *killed* him?' Sophine was so outraged that it almost blocked out her seething hatred and need for violence. Almost.

A flicker of her finger made the woman shriek in agony, and she began to weep hysterical tears.

'Please,' she implored, 'I didn't want to do it. I tried to stop him, I asked him to stay with me! He...he loved me...'

Sophine felt a sensation so close to physical pain that she almost dropped the struggling woman. Rigel, poor innocent Rigel who had never met a girl he could talk to without mumbling like an idiot. The one person he found in all this miserable world turned out to be...

A terrible calm began to descend over her, a draught of icy cold suffusing body and mind. She moved her hand in the air, drawing the woman closer to her until she floated less than a foot from Sophine's face.

'I hope you were paid well for this, cutthroat,' she said in a dreadful, quiet voice. 'I will peel the flesh from you piece by piece, like an orange, and leave you here for the flies. Perhaps it will take hours. Maybe days. I will not enjoy it. But I will do it. For him. For what you did to him.'

The woman's eyes bulged and her movements became frantic, begging and pleading in half-formed words as Sophine lifted one finger to make the first of many, many cuts.

Thaniel.

Sophine blinked and shook her head as the thought of Thaniel forced its way into her mind. Thoughts of revenge and slow, deliberate murder were subdued against her will, replaced by an aching need to speak to Thaniel. To talk to Thaniel.

She gave a frustrated shout and flung the white-faced woman from her to tumble away on the ground. Sophine turned away and put her hands to her head.

'Alright, *alright!*' she yelled, trying to fight against the insistent urge that had taken root in her brain.

She turned her thoughts to Thaniel and knew instantly where he was. She could almost see him standing in the rain on a storm-blasted piece of rocky ground, Eric by his side. It was a combination of long practice and the peculiar working of the mind-stone that allowed her to almost negligently open a portal to the precise location.

The world ripped and a black hole yawned open, wreathed in dark lightning and crackling with the strain of defying reality itself.

Rain and wind poured through, thrashing against the sunlit ground on her side and soaking her clothes. She backed away, yelling at Thaniel to hurry. She turned away as he and Eric leapt through the portal and it sighed closed behind them with a faint sizzle of dissipating energy.

The woman was still struggling a few paces away on the ground, still bound by Sophine's iron will. Sophine barely noticed the captive, closing her eyes tightly against the scene she knew had to come. Her heart was already breaking for Thaniel before her friend turned to look around himself and saw…

'Sacred Circle! Rigel!'

Sophine kept her eyes closed as Eric's cries joined Thaniel's…the running of feet giving way to hysterical denials and then sobs of terrible, heart-wrenching loss.

'How did this happen? Sophine! How?' Thaniel's shouting was louder now. She turned as he approached, his face white with shock, his eyes wide in horror. She did not reply at first, unable to master her own emotions. Eric appeared behind Thaniel, placing a tentative hand on Thaniel's shoulder with a sorrowful look that she couldn't bear to see.

She turned and pointed at the struggling woman in the grass.

'She was paid to keep him from the city. Seduced him, it seems. Kept him close.' Her voice was quickly becoming a feral growl. 'Then when he insisted on coming home, she killed him. He bled to death here by the roadside, alone but for her. His killer.'

Thaniel was quiet, coming to stand by her shoulder. She could feel the intensity of the look he turned on Rigel's murderer even without glancing at him.

'Paid by who?' Thaniel muttered, in a voice so fouled by anger he sounded more beast than man.

235

'Let's find out,' she snarled, gesturing once more at the woman. The killer rose again into the air and turned to face them.

'Who are you?' asked Thaniel. Sophine was surprised, his voice seemed to have recovered a little.

'Sindel,' she gasped, 'my name's Sindel. I was a captain in the Grain Guard and—'

'I don't care what you were,' Sophine began.

Thaniel put a restraining hand on her shoulder.

'Sindel,' he said. 'Who hired you to...keep Rigel away from Asterheim?'

'A woman,' she said, the words spilling out as though they could save her. 'I never met her directly, but the man who paid me said she was one of the great nobles of Asterheim and that if I completed my contract, I need never be hungry or homeless again...'

'You were hungry and homeless?'

'Yes! Yes, terribly!'

'Thaniel,' Sophine said, her voice a warning growl.

He grunted a bitter laugh and looked at her.

'It'll do,' he said. 'Kill her.' He turned to walk away.

Sophine raised a hand and allowed the nimbus of energy to grow around it, connecting with Sindel's body, just as it had with Lord Balderwin's all that time ago.

'Please,' cried the woman, 'I can help save the city.'

Thaniel turned back at that, holding up a hand. Sophine hesitated.

'Go on,' he said.

'I was with Rigel in—'

'Don't say his name!' roared Thaniel, swiping at the air with one hand. The woman flinched as though struck, and a trickle of blood ran from the corner of her mouth. Thaniel stared at her, and she looked back with wide, fearful eyes. Her ample bosom heaved as she watched him, expecting death at any moment. Sophine waited, allowing Thaniel to make the decision. When he turned away, she felt a tiny flicker of disappointment.

'In Ceresheim,' Sindel said, spitting the blood away, 'I met Lord Orswell. He was fond of Rigel, put his hopes in him for reopening relations with Asterheim. If I go to him and tell him of the conspiracy against Rigel…'

'He'll what?' snarled Sophine. 'March on Asterheim and free it from the tyranny of the Senate? Don't make me laugh.'

Thaniel put his hand on her shoulder again.

'Wait, Soph. There is something she can do.'

She looked at him. Thaniel turned haunted eyes on her.

'What? What is it?'

'Terminheim. You were right. Alakis is there.'

She frowned as Thaniel turned to Sindel.

'Listen, cutthroat. We will let you live if you take a message to Lord Orswell.'

Sophine stiffened at that but said nothing. Her fingers ached to rip the woman apart.

'There is a mage, named Alakis. He was one of the damaged children in the attack on the Barbican. He has enslaved the population of Terminheim and plans to march them to Asterheim and destroy the city.'

Sophine forgot how to breathe for a moment.

'He…what?'

'He's gone, Soph. Whatever happened to him between here and there, he's been warped into something else. The curse he carried has consumed him and reached out to consume others. I met Dominitia, she told me everything.'

'And she…?'

He shook his head.

Thaniel looked up at the now-still form of Sindel.

'This affects us all, Sindel, and we need mages to defend the city. And the Grain Guard. Anyone Ceresheim can spare. Get that message to Orswell, and you live.'

'Just remember,' Sophine added, 'I can find you whenever I choose. There is not a hole in this entire country deep enough for you to hide from me.'

'I promise,' Sindel whimpered.

Thaniel looked at her.

'Let her go Soph. She's just a blade. The real killer is somewhere in there'—he gestured at the distant city of Asterheim—'in that nest of slimy degenerates Ariene calls a Senate. I say we take care…' he swallowed hard. 'We take care of Rigel, and then we deal with them.'

Sophine hesitated, feeling somehow hollow and robbed of her vengeance.

'Do we have time?' she asked. 'How long do we have until this…this slave army reaches the city?'

'Long enough,' he said grimly. 'Alakis was still mopping up resistance when I left.' His eyes strayed to the forlorn body of their friend and made a strangled, pathetic noise she couldn't bear to hear.

Sophine squeezed her eyes tight and gritted her teeth against the hollow, wretched feeling rising in her guts. She flung Sindel away from her with an anguished cry.

'Go then,' she shouted, 'before I change my mind!'

Sindel stumbled away without a backward glance.

Sophine turned away, back towards where Thaniel and Eric were standing by Rigel's body. A large horse had walked over to join them, and was looking down with what seemed to be sorrow at the corpse of its former master.

'Come on, my friend,' Thaniel said through freely flowing tears, kneeling to put his arms under Rigel's body, 'one last trip to make. And then…then you can rest.'

As he lifted the body, a piece of parchment fell from Rigel's belt to land in the congealing blood.

Sophine picked it up.

'Thaniel,' she said, scanning it. 'We know their names…'

Chapter Sixteen

The late Lord Balderwin's mansion was no stranger to Sophine's portals. The area by the front door had been cleared of any delicate items some time ago, leaving only a large sturdy urn against one wall which was more than capable of withstanding the sudden wind and the odd blistering storm of lightning. It was this urn into which Thaniel would void his roiling stomach each time he travelled with Sophine, but on this occasion, his guts forgot to heave.

The solemn procession stepped through the portal, barely noticing as it collapsed and faded behind them. Sophine held Rigel under his arms, Thaniel had his feet and Eric was helping support his back. The big horse had tried to follow them, but Thaniel had told him to stay behind.

Rigel was not bleeding anymore, so aside from the fact that his skin was dreadfully grey, he could have been sleeping. Thaniel's feelings flitted continually from misery to horror at the sight of his friend, with the occasional flash of near-hysteria. Sometimes it seemed Rigel was about to raise his head with a grin and the whole thing would turn out to be a stupid prank, because surely he couldn't actually be holding Rigel's body. His dead, bloodless body. Those moments were fast becoming fewer, as they struggled with moving the corpse into the reception room to the right of the door, and the banal reality of the world around him began to re-place the confused haze into which he had fallen.

They carefully lay Rigel down on the red-cushioned leather sofa and stood back, silently watching him. Thaniel wanted to speak, to say something either of comfort or recrimination, or simply something to break the silence. Words did not come.

One of the servants appeared in the doorway, a young woman with long blonde hair tied back in a ponytail and wearing white overalls. Her welcoming smile faded at the sight before her.

'Oh no,' she whispered.

By his side, Sophine squeezed her eyes shut and tilted her chin up with a sniff.

'Please fetch Lady Ariene,' Thaniel said thickly through a near-closed throat, dimly aware of Eric walking heavily to one of the thickly cushioned chairs at the side of the expansive, gold carpeted room and sinking silently into it.

'Sorry, my lord,' the servant replied in a hushed voice. 'Lady Ariene is not here. She has an appointment with Lord Barten at her estate.'

Sophine opened her eyes at that and glanced at Thaniel fiercely.

'Soph,' he said softly.

She shook her head.

'This is her fault,' she said. 'Her sons. Her husband. *Eric*,' she barked a short, humourless laugh. 'And now Rigel. Everyone around her dies and she carries on.'

'She didn't know...' Thaniel began.

Sophine cut him off with a wave of her hand, reaching to her belt for the paper Rigel had been carrying.

'No. But she should have known *better*. There's only one way to fix this hateful city, and I'm going to fix it.'

She started to push past him, but he held her by the shoulders. Her eyes blazed as she looked up at him.

'What are you going to do, Sophine?'

'I'm going to Ariene's, and then to—' She glanced at the piece of paper. 'Senator Jarethin's.'

'That won't fix *this*,' he said sadly, his eyes on Rigel. His grip on her shoulder relaxed as fresh tears arose in his eyes.

'No,' she sighed, looking at the floor. 'But it will fix the city.'

From his place behind them, Eric gave a hollow laugh. Sophine threw a poisonous look at him and stormed away into the hall. Thaniel gave Eric an exasperated glare and went after her, but it was too late. Her portal yawned open and vanished, taking her with it.

The urn rocked slightly and then came to rest in the empty silence. Behind him, Eric stepped into the hallway and put a hand on his shoulder.

'Than?'

He didn't trust himself to reply, instead simply put his hand to Eric's and clasped it.

'I'm going into the city,' Eric said softly. 'I'll go to the Mortuary Guild and see about...'

Thaniel nodded, forcing himself to turn around and smile.

'Thank you,' he said. 'I don't know that I could manage that myself.'

'You can come with me if you like? We could go together?'

He shook his head.

'No, I...I'll stay with him. He shouldn't be left alone here.'

Eric hesitated, his big brown eyes wet and gleaming. He tried for a weak smile, but the corners of his mouth wouldn't seem to let him. He sniffed and wiped at his nose.

'Nor should you,' he said, with a mirthless half-laugh.

'I'll be alright,' Thaniel said, running his hand over Eric's hair. 'You go. Clear your head. You'll need it, because mine's mush right now.' He smiled faintly.

Eric made a sound somewhere between a sob and a laugh and headed to the door. Thaniel watched him step through and pull the door closed behind him, leaving him alone with Rigel. He turned to the body of his friend and sat on the floor beside it.

'I didn't even get to say goodbye, Rige,' he said. 'I wish I'd been able to say goodbye...'

Thaniel bowed his head and wept until his shoulders ached. He wept until his chest spasmed and his lungs burned. Until the empty room echoed with the sound of his pitiful, wracking sobs. Then he wept some more.

***

Ariene slowly buttered a chunk of bread with a long, silver knife. The morning light gleamed from its edge, streaming through the open window of her favourite reception room overlooking the river. Though she did not know it at the time, this was a moment she would long remember.

Lord Barten was sitting opposite her in the hard-backed wooden chair he insisted on using claiming – foolishly she thought – that it was good for his back. Ever since the stab wound he had taken in that cursed stronghold Stonegate Castle, he had been plagued with abdominal and back pain. Rigel had been able to fix the wound, mostly, but the very dust of that place was inimical to mage-craft, and so something about the injury prevented it from ever being fully healed.

'I don't know how else to say it, Ariene. I want to step down,' he said bluntly. They had been discussing the problems faced by the city for some time now, with Ariene trying to put a positive spin on everything and finding it very hard. Relentless positivity did not sit well with her, but nor did the excessively defeatist drivel Barten was spouting.

'You hardly need to step down, Amir. You've barely stepped up.'

The remark was more cutting than she'd intended, but the stress of the last few weeks was getting to her. The factional infighting between the Guilds was a headache she couldn't seem to bring to heel, and until she could resolve them, she couldn't make progress on the petitions from the people and the workers. Grain supplies were in chaos, as were the fisheries. The workers at the docks had started behaving as though they were lords in their own right, controlling as they did the commodities that actually did make it to the city. The Travellers were on the verge of revolution, held in check only by the fearsome Overseer Skylock and her absurdly large hammer.

Amir, to his credit, did not reply to her spiteful comment. He merely watched her. She could feel his eyes on her even as she continued to spread butter on the bread, acutely aware that it was now in fact *more* butter than bread.

'I can't hold it myself,' she muttered. 'I have too many enemies. I can't get the senators to play nicely together without you.'

'You can't do that even *with* me, Ariene,' he said gently. 'We have to admit our failure here. They're right to want us gone. If the city needs caretakers, we are not the ones.'

She looked at him, wiping her fingers delicately on a piece of cloth. She could feel the sun on her face, the warmth so pleasant in such stark contrast to the bleak discussion.

'Without us it's over, Amir. There will be open warfare.'

'And there isn't now? They already targeted your mage and Orswell's.'

'Attacks against me aren't *warfare*, Amir. And why do you think they launched those attacks? To make me vulnerable. Force me to step aside. Do you want the city in the hands of the likes of Creswell? That debased slug Jarethin? Because if we step back, that's what will happen. The first rule of politics is that the ruthless hold the power. And they are ruthless.'

'Perhaps,' he allowed with a sad smile. 'But we can't stop it now. The Senatorial delegation has not found Thaniel. He's gone, and Rigel hasn't returned. Jarethin and the others won't wait. I'd be surprised if we even survived the week.'

'So you think we should step back to save ourselves?'

He shrugged sadly.

'We tried, Ariene. It's over.'

She took a bitter bite of her overly buttered bread.

'I can't believe that, Amir. I won't.'

Just then the door opened and in walked Sophine, trailed by a confused looking servant.

'Sophine!' called Ariene with a smile. 'Milly, some tea please.' The confused girl hesitated and left with a short nod, looking no less confused.

'Unlike you to use a door, dear,' Ariene said lightly. 'How nice to see you.'

245

Sophine smiled brightly, a ghastly rictus grin below hard, cold eyes. Ariene blinked and stood up slowly, sensing something very, very wrong.

'Lord Barten,' Sophine said, still wearing that horrible smile. 'I was just talking to some of Ariene's servants and there's something we can't quite figure out.' Her grin flickered and then reappeared, and Ariene's fear deepened.

'Sophine,' she said softly, coming forward to put a hand on the girl's shoulder.

Sophine shook her hand off and stepped away, still holding Amir with that death-grin.

'We were trying to think whereabouts Lord Jarethin lives,' she said conversationally, the easy tone at horrible odds with the manic gleam to her eyes. She fished out a piece of paper and glanced at it with a furrowed brow, moving with strange jerky movements very unlike her ordinary fluid grace. 'I know where Lady Aresbrook is.' She glanced knowingly at Ariene. 'An old friend of yours, isn't she, Ariene?'

The piece of paper had stains on it. Brownish-red stains.

'*Lord* Aresbrook is a friend,' Ariene said evenly, with a warning glance at Amir. 'I never much cared for his wife. Too young, too pretty, and too ambitious by far.'

Sophine was nodding her head, still with that barely-contained mania to her eyes.

'So. Lord Jarethin? Where does he live?' The conversational tone was strained now, the smile threatening to collapse at any moment.

Amir, however, was a dolt and a fool and answered her as though he didn't notice how very strangely she was acting.

'His estate is in the northwest, isn't it, Ariene? Near the corner watchtower actually, now I come to...'

He trailed off, finally noticing Ariene's furious stare.

'May I see that?' Ariene said, in a low, fearful voice, indicating the parchment held in Sophine's pale, trembling fingers. The girl thrust it at her, the pretence at civility vanishing in an instant.

'But of course,' she growled. Sophine turned her back and stalked away to stand in the shadows of the room, her arms around herself as though cold.

Ariene felt a cold dread seeping through her as she read the note.

'Amir,' she said softly. 'It's worse than we thought.'

Sophine made a short, bitter sound like the laugh of a long-dead ghost.

'Seven of our colleagues, including Jarethin, Creswell and Lady Aresbrook, were conspiring to stop food reaching the city and to stop any mages returning...' She read on and let out a strangled gasp, dropping the paper.

'They were to look out for Rigel too. They knew he would be going...'

'They manipulated you,' snarled Sophine from her spot in the corner. 'And you were too busy being a *mother to the city* to see it.' She spat the words with such deadly bitterness that a terrible certainty struck Ariene.

She sank slowly to the floor, her head swimming. Her skirts folded and crumpled around her on the wooden floor. Amir jumped to his feet and came to her side.

'Ariene?'

She waved him away, her breath coming in short gasps and her limbs icy cold.

'Whose blood is on that parchment?' she whispered, through a tight, choked throat.

Sophine turned, her dark eyes pools of shadow in the gloom. Ariene looked at her and knew beyond any doubt.

'No,' she cried, her chest constricting painfully. She clutched her hands to her heart and squeezed her eyes tight. 'Rigel...'

'They murdered him on the road,' Sophine said coldly, stepping slowly forward and watching her with those dark, pitiless eyes. 'I couldn't save him. By the time we got there, he was dead.'

Ariene rocked back and forth, barely hearing Amir's soothing platitudes as he held her shoulders.

'Not Rigel,' she whispered, only now realising just how much the young mage had meant to her.

'The woman who killed him was paid by them,' Sophine gestured at the paper. 'The same people who took Eric. Your enemies. Enemies of the city.' Her tone hardened even further. 'My enemies.'

'Make them pay,' Ariene growled. 'Burn them all.'

By her side, Amir stiffened.

'Ariene, what are you—'

She threw him off and rose to her feet on a tide of bitter, cold fury. She met Sophine's glaring eyes with a reptilian stare of her own.

'Kill them all, Sophine. Make them suffer.'

A flicker of a smile tugged at Sophine's lips, but her bleak expression didn't change. Without another word she turned away, gesturing at the empty air and ripping it open to reveal a yawning black void, wreathed in dissipating energy. The deadly mage stepped through, and the rift sealed itself behind her.

Amir was backing away from her, his expression one of utter disbelief.

'Ariene, are you mad? You've advocated the murder of seven senators.'

'It's no less than they deserve,' she spat. 'They killed my...my mage.'

His face softened a little.

'He was a son to you, wasn't he?'

She glared at him, her blood thumping in her veins.

'My son. My saviour. The one friend I had in this whole filthy city at a time when all I wanted was to die.'

'Even so...' Barten said tentatively.

She stalked forward and prodded him in the chest, and not gently.

'That boy was the best of us, Amir. The kindest...' Her voice cracked and she faltered, feeling his arms around her. She sank into his chest. 'The most loyal...a *good* person, Amir. How many good people are left?' Her voice gave way to sobs, wracking, heaving cries that shook her whole body.

Barten held her as she cried, smoothing her hair in silence and she wept.

'Ariene,' he said eventually, pulling back and tilting her face to look at him. 'You cannot let Sophine do this.'

She sniffed fiercely, stepping back and wiping her nose with one angry wrist.

'I can,' she said, though without much conviction.

He held her gaze.

'Think about what it will do to her,' he said. 'Don't let her fall into the dark.'

Ariene hesitated as she digested this. Amir's words seemed to cut through the fog of red anger and black misery, allowing room in her for more familiar thoughts and feelings. Her breathing started to return to normal as her eyes alighted on the parchment stained by Rigel's blood.

'What was the second name?' she asked.

***

Lord Jarethin's mansion barely deserved the name. Sophine had managed to locate it after a few minutes, having had to start the search by the city walls near the watchtower. Although she was good, she couldn't create a portal to somewhere she had neither seen nor had any accurate information about. Being in the right vicinity, however, she had only needed to open her mind and listen to the whispers that most people couldn't hear and...there it was.

She stood now at the gate of a surprisingly modest house, nestled in a relatively secluded spot in the further reaches of the Noble Quarter. It was built out of odd-shaped lumps of grey stone, and its walls stood only two storeys high, topped by crenelations that made it look like a miniature castle. But whilst the house was wide, sprawling in fact, with a wing to the right that looked as though it could house three families comfortably, it was still far smaller than one of the grander manses, like Ariene's or Balderwin's. She pushed the gate open and stepped lightly up the path, filled with dread purpose that chilled her soul and quashed all anger.

Today, she would end the infighting in the Senate. Today, she would send a message that those who remained would cooperate or die. Today, the mockery of democracy into which the city had fallen would be consigned to history.

A mirthless grin played around her lips as she knocked politely on the door. Nobody answered.

Sophine looked around, noticing a long rope on a pulley which disappeared into a hole in the wall. Impressed, she pulled it. Faintly, she could hear a bell ringing.

Before long, the door swung open and a small boy looked out. He was about seven, and dressed in soft-looking nightclothes even though it was now mid-morning.

'Hello,' he said cheerfully, with bright eyes. His black hair was tousled and glossy. Sophine crouched down next to him.

'Hi there,' she said. 'Is your mother home?'

'I think so,' the boy said. 'Shall I get her?'

Sophine shook her head.

'No. Go to her. Tell her she needs to get you to her chambers and lock the door, right now, because something very bad is about to happen.'

The boy went pale and peered round Sophine, fearfully looking into the estate's grounds.

'Come with me,' he said, with a heartbreakingly sincere face, holding out his little hand for her to take it. 'We can all be safe together.'

She gently enclosed the hand with both of hers.

'You're very brave,' she said. 'But I need to be here. Go now, to your mother.'

'And father?'

Sophine grimaced.

'No. Leave your father to me.'

The boy nodded and ran off, slipping a little on the polished stone floor in his thin, fabric house-boots.

Sophine stepped into the house. She did not have to concentrate hard to locate Lord Jarethin. She followed his thoughts up the stairs to a modest sitting room, surrounded by bookcases and furnished with individual soft chairs and low tables for entertaining guests.

A fat man in a red robe looked up as she entered and closed the door behind her with a soft click. He was big and jowly, with at least three chins hanging down past his neckline. He was seated on a long, low couch next to a large pile of papers, and slowly lowered a document on top of them as she came towards him.

'Good morning,' he said with a quizzical smile. 'I'm sorry I don't believe I—'

'Lord Jarethin?'

'Yes?'

'Rigel is dead.'

'Who?'

'Rigel,' Sophine said, vaguely amused at the man's sheer audacity. 'The mage sent to Ceresheim...'

'Ah yes that one. Dead, is he? Good, good.'

That was all she needed to hear. Sophine raised one hand, fingers clutched tightly together. A pale nimbus of white energy began to play around her fingertips. She felt her mind linking her hand with the essence of the fat body before her, binding it to her will.

'Some good may come of it,' she said softly. 'It's given clarity to some of us about the nature of politics in our city and the measures that must be taken to save it.'

'What on earth are you blabbering about? Who are you?'

Sophine chuckled.

'Perhaps you should have started with that one, Senator. That one and a cry for help, maybe, for all the good it would have done.'

'I don't—'

She opened her hand wide and Lord Jarethin came apart. Like the segments of an orange falling back from the centre, chunks of what had once been a senator slid apart and fell heavily to the floor. Papers scattered, soaked in a tide of steaming gore that splashed and soaked and pooled like a horrific, grisly river set free of a dam. Pieces of the former Lord flopped and bounced along, carried by the flow of what had once been bound within them.

Sophine turned away, stepping lightly to the door as the pale light faded from her hands.

She closed the door behind her and beckoned to the first servant she saw.

'Listen,' she said to the confused young man as he hurried over. 'Lord Jarethin wants this door kept shut, do you understand? It is not to be opened for any reason on pain of death.'

The boy blinked at her, looking fearfully at the door as though it might bite him.

'Make sure the other servants are aware,' she said, and marched away with such an air of dignified authority that she was sure he would do exactly as she said.

Beyond the gates of the house, reality ripped open once more.

'Lady Aresbrook,' Sophine said softly to herself in a lilting, sing-song voice, 'there's someone to see you...'

***

Sophine opened the door to the private study of the lady of the house and strode in. This time there had been no children to worry about, the ancient Lord Aresbrook having outlived the rest of his family years ago. The young new Lady Aresbrook had yet to reproduce, it seemed, and with every step Sophine took her chances of doing so dwindled considerably.

To say that the study room was opulent would have been an insult to opulence. Tasteless, ostentatious displays of outrageous wealth seemed to cover every available surface. Statues of fine marble stood haphazardly around the room; stuffed exotic animals stared with dead, glass eyes from the walls and shelves. Paintings and tapestries covered every available wall space and thick rugs in a bewildering array of colours covered the floor, some of them overlapping in a horrendous clash of patterns. Jewellery boxes overflowing with gold and gems sat like odd centrepieces on fabulously carved wooden tables, and heavy chests stood open with various glittering fabrics spilling out of them to drape negligently on the ground.

At the far end of the bizarre room was a large window overlooking the well-kept garden of House Aresbrook, in front of which were two enormous leather chairs with high backs and thick, soft cushions.

Both chairs were occupied.

'Hello, Sophine,' Ariene said from one of them. The woman opposite her did not say anything, and looked unlikely ever to do so again, sprawled as she was at an improbable angle in her chair. Her eyes were closed. An overturned glass was on the table, and one of the woman's hands clutched limply at her motionless neck. A red stain was seeping into Lady Aresbrook's shimmering green dress, fed by a tiny trickle of red from the corner of her mouth.

'They say poison is a woman's weapon,' Ariene said, taking a sip of her wine. 'But then again they have probably never met *you*, dear.' She smiled. 'I take it Lord Jarethin is...'

Sophine nodded stiffly, moving to stand by one of the jewellery boxes. She idly touched a necklace of glittering diamonds and ridiculous wealth.

'He is,' she said. 'I waited for him to confess and then...' She raised a hand and wiggled her fingers.

'And how do you feel now?' asked Ariene, her tone guarded.

Sophine shrugged.

'I...I don't know,' she said honestly. 'There was a boy at the house. Jarethin's son, I assume. I didn't feel it at the time, but now...'

Ariene said nothing, watching her from the seat by the window.

Sophine sighed.

'Now I feel it. I took that boy's father from him...'

'Not his real father,' Ariene muttered. 'Jarethin has no children, dear. His mistress though, I hear she does. Five or six, was he?'

'Something like that. Maybe a bit older.'

Ariene waved a hand and took a sip of wine.

'I wouldn't worry yourself then, dear. You didn't kill his father. And even if you had...'

Sophine looked at her sharply across the gaudy room.

'It would have been wrong,' she said firmly, surprising herself with the vehemence of her statement.

Ariene nodded.

'Yes. And yet here we are, on a murderous rampage to avenge Rigel. All the people on that list have people who love them.'

Sophine hesitated, looking at the woman in the chair.

'You killed her,' she said.

'Yes.'

'Why?'

'To show you the futility of it all. When you left for Jarethin's, after I calmed down, I realised I could drown the whole Senate in blood and still feel no better about Rigel. But I had another idea, so I thought I'd come here and...'

'And what?' Sophine's suspicions, long honed through association with the wily old senator, were well and truly aroused.

Ariene rose from her chair in a rustle of pretty silks and came slowly towards her. Her eyes flicked to the jewellery box, and she ran a finger through the gleaming metals and precious, meaningless things.

'Chaos will reign if we kill any more of them,' Ariene said softly, picking out a beautifully worked ring in the shape of the Sacred Circle and sparkling with gleaming gems. 'True chaos. Civil war. The kind that has been brewing ever since the fall of Lyoris.'

'It'll come anyway,' Sophine said softly, watching Ariene carefully.

The older woman nodded, slipping the ring onto her own finger and flexing it in the morning light.

'It will. Chaos is here with us, Sophine. The rules we have worked to, the rules others have flouted to hurt us, they serve now only to hold us back.'

Sophine's heart began to beat faster in her chest. Somewhere within the image of a dark-leather book, surrounded by wisps of darkness and faintly hissing, crept unbidden into her thoughts.

'What are you saying?'

Ariene looked at her with a level stare.

'Let the rules be damned, Sophine. Compromise has its place, but the time has come to save this city from itself. You were right when you said the city needs a queen, but the queen will need her mages. All of them.'

Sophine's blood thumped louder in her ears as adrenaline shot through her veins. The thought was hot, bright in her mind. Rigel, alive again, talking and laughing...

'You don't know what you're asking, Ariene,' she said, struggling to keep her excitement in check. 'This is the darkest magic of all. Necromancy...'

'An hour ago, we were willing to let this city kill itself,' Ariene said. 'Let's fix it instead. And you can't tell me that saving a life is darker than taking one.'

It was clever political sophistry, nothing more, and Sophine knew it. The darkness of necromancy lay in the violation of the natural order, whereas murder was simply speeding up the inevitable. But she nodded as though Ariene had made a good point, because she had already made up her mind.

'Meet me back at Balderwin's,' she said.

Ariene nodded fiercely. Then she gave a crooked grin.

'There's nothing like death to put life in perspective,' she said.

Chapter Seventeen

Sophine spilled out of her portal onto the flagstones in the court-yard of the Barbican. She scrabbled to her feet in confusion; she'd been aiming for her office. Her portals were never that inaccurate, normally. She hurried across the courtyard, waving to the children who had been playing outside when she'd materialised in an un-gainly heap. They waved back uncertainly; she could see the bewil-derment on their faces even from across the yard and almost chuck-led.

'Don't worry,' she called, surprising herself at how cheerful she sounded, 'no lessons today!'

The kids cheered and went back to their games as Sophine bus-tled into the main hall, heading for her office. Her mind was alight with possibilities, the licence to do the forbidden filling her with a thrill that had only the slightest twinge of guilt within it.

The book was just where she'd expected it to be, though not necessarily where she'd left it. She looked at it with eager anticipa-tion and reached a hand towards it.

Instantly, the book flipped open. Pages fluttered and flew, page after page turning rapidly until, almost the whole way through the book, they stopped suddenly. Little motes of dust swirled and floated lazily up from the long-abandoned script, dust that perhaps had been there for centuries. She knew without even looking that this was the part she needed. The very darkest of soul-theories. The art of returning the departed soul to a body.

The darkness of necromancy, as she'd noted before, lay in overcoming the essential truth that death was a one-way door. The book provided an analogy. Necromancy was the art of locating a glassful of water after it had been cast into a river, and then dragging it against the flow back to where one stood upon the bank. Who was to say whether what returned to the glass the same as what had left it? Another dire warning stated that death was a merchant and could not be cheated. Once the transaction was made, it could not be undone, only modified. And so the art of necromancy was about the exchange of one soul for another, and not simply returning a soul to a body.

Sophine muttered darkly about her thoughts on the principles of soul transference as she traced intricate designs and diagrams set out in the book. These were needed to channel the will of the necromancer to a specific end – the restoring of a single soul to a single very specific place and for the soul to take root in the specified body. The particulars at work were so precise, the consequences of failure so terrifyingly risky, that Sophine realised at last why this was considered so dark and deadly an art. It was not that the power to do this was inherently evil, but that the myriad of unintended effects that could occur if it was not carefully controlled were.

'Demons,' she whispered, reading a passage about the accidental granting of passage into the physical realm to beings of similar form to souls who, it appeared, had nothing better to do with eternity but to hang around necromancers trying to get through a weak spot in their spells.

The book seemed to hiss as she spoke the word, and she hesitated. In a moment of indecision, she slowly closed the book.

'What are you?' she asked, running her finger down its dark-leather spine. A horrible suspicion settled over her. What if Rigel's death and everything leading up to it, Alakis's corruption, the conspiracy against the mages…what if something had been influencing those events just a little. A touch here and there. To bring about this moment, where she in desperation turned to the darkest arts…

The book did not reply, and nor had she expected it to. She exhaled heavily. Until recently she'd not even believed in souls, let alone demons. She'd certainly seen no evidence of anything like one.

'Paranoia,' she said aloud, flipping back to the page she'd been reading and studying the diagrams once more. 'And besides,' she said, 'I'm *good*.'

***

Thaniel was sitting in glum silence when Sophine burst through her portal and hurried into the living room, barely glancing at Rigel as she came. He looked at her quizzically.

'Soph?'

She ignored him, glancing around the room with a frown. The blonde-haired servant appeared behind her.

'Can I get—' the girl began in a tentative voice, glancing with wide frightened eyes at Rigel's corpse.

'You'—Sophine whirled around to face the girl—'is Lord Balderwin's room still unfurnished?'

'I…yes?' said the girl, looking as confused as Thaniel felt.

'Good. No carpet? Floorboards?'

'Yes Miss Sophine, it was stripped and cleaned but no one ever wanted to use it so we…' The girl trailed off as Sophine turned away.

'Alright, thank you. That will be all.'

The girl glanced at Thaniel. He gave a short shrug and she slipped away.

'Than, give me a hand,' Sophine said. 'We need to get him to Balderwin's chambers and then I'll need candles…'

'Sophine.' His tone was harder than he expected it to be, but he couldn't help himself. 'What are you talking about?'

She walked slowly over to him, close enough for him to see the brimming, conflicted emotion in her eyes.

'Ariene told me to kill all the senators on that list,' she said softly. 'The city's on the edge of civil war and Alakis is coming. Ariene was all for letting it burn, but then…' she smiled faintly. 'Then she changed her mind. Told me that perhaps, if we're all about to lose, we might as well risk it all on one last gamble.' Her eyes strayed to Rigel.

He took a step back, holding her gaze.

'What kind of gamble?'

'I think you know,' she said, very quietly.

'Say it.'

She didn't look away, but the moment stretched.

'We're going to bring him back, Than,' she said in that soft, quiet voice. 'We're going to bring him back, and then we're going to defend this city from Alakis. And from itself.'

For a moment he said nothing, letting the implications of what she was saying sink in. She watched him carefully. He could imagine all sorts of ways she might react if he said the wrong thing.

Luckily, all he wanted to do in that moment was smile.

'Can you do it, Sophine? Do you really think you can...' He gestured at Rigel, unable to talk past the sudden lump in his throat. He started to choke up again, the sobs forcing their way past his self-control and reducing him to a blubbing mess. She took him in her arms and hugged him, and he let all the emotion of the last hours flood out of him.

'I promise you one thing, Than. I am going to try.'

He nodded without looking up, a fresh wave of sobbing stealing his voice.

After a while he pushed away and stood, blinking and exhaling, trying to get himself under some kind of control.

Sophine, meanwhile, bent to pick up her book from where it had fallen and gestured at Rigel.

'Let's move him,' she said. 'I'll need floorboards, chalk and candles for the ritual.' She frowned.

'And a soul,' she added.

Thaniel, who had been bending towards Rigel's feet, stopped. He straightened.

'A soul,' he repeated flatly. 'I thought you told me there was no such thing and I was being superstitious.'

She gave a weak shrug.

'Surprise?' she offered.

He narrowed his eyes at her.

'So what you put in that stone *wasn't* part of your soul?'

'Well,' she said, then broke off as a look of excitement crossed her face.

'What?' said Thaniel. 'What did I say?'

'Fragments,' Sophine replied. 'Do you still have the stone?'

'I...er...' Thaniel patted his pockets. 'No...' he winced. 'Is that a problem?'

'No,' she said, pacing around the room. 'I wasn't about to use my own soul anyway.'

'Why, what are we doing with this soul?'

'Sacrificing it.'

Thaniel's eyes widened and he shook his head.

'No, no. No, this is too much. Sophine, come on, even for Rigel—'

She whipped round to stare at him, and Thaniel felt a chill at the depth of purpose in those dark eyes.

'I'd do anything for him, Than. And for you. Never forget that.'

'I…alright…'

She released him from that glare and resumed her pacing. Thaniel exhaled a pent-up breath he hadn't realised he'd been holding.

'We aren't going to be sacrificing an *actual* soul,' she said, musing with alarming casualness about something he hadn't believed even existed until seconds before. 'But we can sacrifice a piece of one. Hilda placed a fragment of her essence in the book, I saw it when I was first reading about soul-theory. I was trying to find a way to see into Terminheim, and I thought astral projection was the way to do it. That's when I learned about fragmentation, like the stone. It was because I saw Hilda's fragment.'

Thaniel was stunned.

'Hilda. As in, *Hilda* Hilda. Mage Queen Hilda. That's her book?'

Sophine nodded.

'She put a fragment in it, I think, to help whoever came along to use the knowledge inside. Or maybe she did it when she worked necromancy…sacrificed a little piece of herself each time.'

'You *saw* her?' Thaniel was amazed. 'What did she look like?'

'Dead,' said Sophine shortly.

In spite of himself, Thaniel chuckled.

'Okay, I walked into that,' he replied.

'She was on a chair,' Sophine said, more seriously, still pacing. 'A chair made of darkness and smoke. I didn't think much about it at the time but now...'

'Darkness and smoke?' Thaniel looked with distaste at the book. 'Is that why I can hear it hissing?'

'You hear that too?'

He nodded.

'Hissing and whispering, like it knows I can't hear it but wants to talk to me anyway.'

She smiled.

'A good way to put it. Yes, I think whatever else Hilda had in mind, she wanted to keep that hissing under control.'

'But what is it?'

Sophine shook her head.

'I don't know. But the book deals with the very darkest of mage abilities, stuff that's so dangerous and emotive that it maybe...creates its own essence. I think the book is almost alive, a collective semi-sentient consciousness reflecting the dark soul-theories inside it. I wouldn't be surprised if Hilda put that fragment in there to keep it under control. A little piece of her will to stop it reaching out too far, to keep it from the wrong hands.'

'So after we use the fragment to exchange for Rigel's soul...' Thaniel said, hardly believing that he was even discussing this kind of madness.

'Then we'll probably have to destroy the book,' said Sophine. 'For our own sakes.'

He nodded.

264

'Or,' he said, 'you could put a fragment of yourself in there.'

'I could, but I don't know how often a person should do that. I already put a tiny sliver of my mind into that stone you *lost*'—she rolled her eyes at him—'so I think destroying the book is the best way.'

'What if one of us gets killed again?'

She shook her head.

'Let's not think about that just now.'

***

The room in which she'd killed the odious Lord Balderwin was almost unrecognisable when they entered. The bed, curtains and carpet had all been removed not long after the room had become unexpectedly vacant. The servants had apparently very much enjoyed destroying the heavy furniture and ripping the carpet to pieces once the stench of blood and offal had been sufficiently masked.

The floorboards creaked underfoot now, bare and rough and hard. Sophine's boots echoed as she crossed the room. She looked around, gauging the amount of space they had to work with and consulting her book, which she held in the crook of one arm. A bag of clinking supplies was over the other shoulder. After a moment's hesitation, she dumped the bag and book on a heavy dressing table that had been left in place and dragged it towards the back wall. The sound of it screeching its way across the wood was appalling and she winced.

Thaniel looked at her.

'Next time, ask,' he said with a wiggle of his fingers.

She pouted at him and surveyed the space.

265

'This will do,' she said, dropping opening her bag of supplies. 'Could you get them to bring him up?'

Thaniel left to go and instruct the servants to carry Rigel carefully up the stairs as she pulled out twelve long candles, and a number of other smaller ones, purely for lighting purposes. These she placed around the edge of the room. It was by now mid-afternoon, and the shadows had already begun to lengthen outside. Sophine had hoped to conduct the ritual in the light, but she certainly wasn't going to wait until morning.

Taking from her bag three sticks of chalk, which she'd been pleasantly surprised to find amongst the various supplies in Lord Balderwin's basement, she consulted her book once more and knelt to make the first of many marks on the hard wooden floor.

Behind her, the door opened and two men struggled their way into the room carrying the awkward form of Rigel between them.

'He's heavier than he looks,' one was muttering.

'Stiff too,' puffed the other one, trying to manoeuvre Rigel onto his side to better bend him around the doorframe. Sophine bit back a snarling order to be more careful and just seethed in quiet anger, whilst the men finally got themselves through the door and placed Rigel none too gently on the floor.

'Thank you,' she said through gritted teeth.

The two men nodded and puffed their chests out, clapping their hands as though to wipe off dust. She ignored them as they left, concentrating on her drawings.

The diagram was, in essence, a series of circles. An outer one formed of two lines, in between which certain symbols had to be placed, including six smaller circles. In the centre of this circle was a second, again formed of two concentric lines in which more symbols were carefully, painstakingly drawn. This was where Rigel's body would lie, the centre of his torso above the centre of the circle, but first additional lines and designs had to be added to this basic structure.

Thaniel returned and made his now-familiar strangled moaning noise at the sight of Rigel's crumpled body. She could hear him pacing about as she copied the design, adding lines connecting the six smaller circles and forming a series of geometric shapes in the centre of the circle. Triangles intersected with other triangles and diamonds, tricking the eye into seeing three dimensional patterns which shifted and altered as perception changed. She stared at the images in the book, then back to her lines, occasionally rubbing something out and trying again. She could almost feel Thaniel's wince every time she did so.

'I wish you'd stop pacing,' she muttered, rubbing at another small symbol that seemed to have more pointy bits in her version than in the book.

'What are all those anyway?' Thaniel's voice was hushed as he surveyed her work from the edge of the room. He had, for the moment at least, stopped pacing.

'They...don't mean much,' Sophine said distractedly, as she copied the symbol more precisely this time. 'At least not on their own. But the passages I'm reading are all guiding my thoughts and my feelings in a certain direction. Aligning them with ways of thinking that should give me the result I want. This symbol'—she paused as she added a small flick to the lower character—'is one the book uses to represent my intentions. I'm adding it here to reinforce the idea that the power I pass into this design must give effect only to what I want. Not what something else might want.'

'So it's a guestlist,' Thaniel said. 'Keeping your door from opening for more than one person.'

267

'If you like. All these symbols are just written versions of those mental ideas. I suppose I could have come up with my own if I was a skilled necromancer, but since this is my first time, I'm happy to be told what to think and how to represent it in chalk.'

'A skilled necromancer,' he repeated in hushed wonder. 'Sophine, what if Master Thomas could see us now?'

She exhaled hard, not quite a laugh, and shook her head.

'He'd want to try it for himself,' she said. 'Admit it, even you do.'

'I'll admit it,' he said. 'That just makes me all the more afraid.'

She sat back, peering critically at the last series of symbols.

'And so it should,' she said vacantly.

Carefully, taking care not to smudge the chalk, she tiptoed her way across the intricate design and came to stand by his side.

'Each of the circles around the outer edge needs a candle,' she said.

'Is that symbolic too?'

She shook her head.

'The light from them will be reflected in...well. Somewhere else. If the design is right and responds to my will the way it should, they should act as a beacon to Rigel wherever he is.'

'You don't know where he is, do you? The book didn't say.'

She looked at him fearfully.

'All I know is that this...beacon...shines across any number of places beyond our realm. It could attract all kinds of attention from all kinds of things. But if Rigel sees it, he should know it's for him, and the gateway in the second circle should open only for him.'

'There were a lot of "should"s in there, Soph.'

She nodded gravely.

'That's all I have, Thaniel. This is a risky thing we're about to do. I've done all I can, honestly.' She gestured at the chalk symbols and the carefully drawn lines. 'But I don't know if those will work.'

'You're the most skilled mage I've ever known, Sophine,' he said, his eyes running over the chalk. His face was deathly pale in the gathering shadows. 'If anyone can do this, it's you.'

The moment stretched as they stood in tense silence. Outside, the sun had dipped below the horizon, throwing them into the uncertain, blue-tinged gloom of dusk.

'Are we ready?' Sophine breathed. By her side, Thaniel gave a slow, grave nod.

Sophine yelped and almost jumped into the air as the door opened to her left.

'Ariene!' she cried, clutching one hand to her chest. 'Damnation, woman, can't you knock? I almost had a heart attack!'

Ariene had been staring at the arcane sight before her with wide eyes. Now she looked up.

'Sorry,' she half-whispered. 'What is all this?'

'The way to get Rigel back,' Sophine said. 'It's a doorway.'

Ariene shuddered and leaned back against the closed door, looking fearfully at the gleaming white chalk stark against the dark floor.

Thaniel made a gesture with his right hand, and a ripple of light flooded the room as the candles around the edge flared into flickering life. Then, almost as an afterthought, he made another motion with the same hand. Sophine heard the lock turn in the door behind Ariene and smiled faintly.

'Thanks,' she said. 'Now, let's get Rigel in position.'

Together, the two mages levitated Rigel's corpse from where it lay beyond the circle across to the centre. He alighted on the floor with a soft thud, his arms and legs splayed and his chest above the centre of the inner circle. Ariene made a choking, sobbing noise at the sight, and Sophine almost snapped at her to be quiet before realising that this was the first time the senator had seen Rigel since he left for Ceresheim.

'Ariene,' she said gently, 'are you going to be alright in here? You can wait downstairs if you need to, but I will need you to be quiet if you stay.'

Ariene pulled herself up and swallowed heavily.

'I'm staying,' she said, not looking at Sophine. She turned and walked to the other side of the room, where she stood with her arms around herself as if she was cold, watching.

Sophine edged her way around the circle, so that she stood at what she thought of as the top. She directed Thaniel to take up position at the opposite end. She lifted the book from where it lay on the chest of drawers and floated it across to lie upon Rigel's chest. For once, the hissing had stopped. The book was silent, as though anticipating what was to come. She forced that idea away immediately and made a last check of the circles.

'When I say, Thaniel,' she said finally, 'I want you to pass energy from yourself into the symbols and devices of the circle.'

'Which circle?'

She gestured at the whole design.

'The circle, all of it. Everything.'

'Oh, alright then.'

'What we're trying to do is light the beacon in the other realms to draw Rigel's attention. When he sees, he'll come. We should feel him here, which is when we then make the exchange.'

'How do we do that?'

'By burning the book and releasing the soul-fragment inside it.'

In the corner of the room, Ariene gave a sharp intake of breath but said nothing.

'The book spoke about more ritual symbols and devices to hold the…victim…in place whilst the transference was conducted,' Sophine said, ignoring Ariene's sensibilities, 'but since we're using a book, we shouldn't need to worry about that.'

'Another "should",' Thaniel remarked blandly.

'Should is all I have,' she replied. 'When you burn the book—'

'I have to burn it?'

'I'll be busy with opening the door.'

'Oh.'

'When you burn it, make sure it's gone completely. There must not be a single piece of it left or the fragment will remain inside. It has to be released, like a soul from a corpse or this won't work.'

'Trust me,' he said grimly. 'When I burn something, it burns.'

She nodded.

'Alright, let's begin.'

Sophine closed her eyes and reached within her to the swirling well of power she kept deep inside. Her nerves were not helping this time, jitters threatening to throw her off her concentration. But Sophine was no longer an untrained student, or a fearful victim of a spiteful spell. She relaxed her mind, letting her thoughts drift, filling her senses with the anger and fear Rigel's death had caused her.

Fiery heat bubbled up within her, and she fed it into the designs at her feet. She could sense Thaniel's mind at work within the chalk, tracing the lines and giving power to the intentions locked within. His power enhanced hers, and she bound her will into his as together they followed the design and lit each symbol in turn, imbuing the ritual with arcane meaning. She opened her eyes.

The circle was aglow; the lines and curves now gleaming blue-white as witch-light suffused them. The candles in the six circles flared blue, the leaping tongues of flame flickering hungrily at least a metre high before fading back to ordinary, albeit pale blue, candlelight.

The beacon is lit, she sent telepathically to Thaniel, through their connection in the swirling energies writhing on the floorboards. *Let's concentrate on Rigel – call to him.*

Their minds echoed across unknown planes, shrieking through places that had never known light and realms of dust and screams. Their calls rebounded from pillars of emotion and plunged into oceans of pain, spinning and arcing through endless eternities inhabited by ancient, unfathomable things of depthless malice. The beacon's light spread out with them, calling to the one for whom they had risked their very souls, had they but known it.

'Sophine,' she heard Thaniel gasp, somewhere in the real world, far beyond the impossible vistas through which they wheeled and danced. 'Sophine!'

She wrenched at her thoughts with a grimace of pure will, straining with every fibre of her body and the gleaming mote of her soul to free herself from the current that threatened to sweep her away into oblivion.

Her eyelids fluttered and opened, and she gasped, realising she was on the floor. Flames flickered on the ground around her, hungrily eating at the chalk lines.

'No!' she yelled, scrabbling to her feet and desperately trying to put the fires out. The energy in the circle was building, spiralling, bursting from the barriers she'd tried to build.

'He's here!' Thaniel yelled, still standing at the other side of the circle but edging back from it with his hands raised. The entire outer circle was aflame, sparking and shrieking as the energies within were released in crackling arcs of power.

'He's here!' he screamed again, and this time she understood.

'Burn it, Thaniel!' she yelled, beating frantically at her clothes which were now starting to catch fire. 'Burn the book! Bring him through!'

'I…I can't!' he wailed, 'I can't even see!'

The smoke was everywhere. Flame flickered between shadows, the heat suffocating and the air impossible to breathe. Sophine shrieked in agony as her leg continued to burn. She took hold of the burning material and tore at it, ripping it away. She could just about make out Rigel's body, lying on the still-intact second circle as the flames crept hungrily towards him. The thought flitted through her mind.

I failed. I failed him again.

Then the smoke parted and Ariene was there, ablaze head to foot and screaming. The burning woman bent to pick up the book and held it to her chest as she stumbled away and collapsed, a dark shape lost within a writhing curtain of fire. Her terrible shrieking ceased in a sudden flare of blazing flame.

The circle beneath Rigel glowed a cold, brilliant blue and an icy wind began to blow from nowhere. The flames consuming the room were beaten flat by the terrible, unholy gale, guttering and dying as the smoke swirled in the sudden tempest. A dreadful, charnel house stench like rotting meat filled the chamber as the blue brilliance of the circle flared even brighter and a half-heard whisper echoed through the air, like the ghostly sigh of something that had not spoken in aeons.

And then the room was dark and still. Smoke drifted thickly above where Sophine lay, gasping for breath and coughing. Her leg was a screaming song of pain and recrimination, but she barely felt it.

Not far from her across the room, sitting on the floor where the circle had been and rubbing at his eyes, was Rigel. He looked over at her and blinked.

'Sophine?' he said in a thick voice. 'What happened?'

A thousand possible responses flitted through her mind in the time it took for her to process that he was alive, but only one made sense.

'Fire,' she coughed. 'Ariene!' She pointed through the roiling smoke towards the approximate spot where Ariene had collapsed.

Rigel rose uncertainly to his feet as the smoke seemed to lift, rising into the air as though of its own accord. Sophine's grateful lungs drank in a few smokeless breaths before she realised it was Thaniel. He stood a few feet away, his hand outstretched and his comical concentration look on his red, seared face. With his other hand he had conjured a ball of light, which he now raised up to float just beneath the mass of smoke rippling below the ceiling, held there by his telekinetic barrier.

Sophine gasped in horror at the sight of Thaniel. Much of his long blonde hair was gone, burned away leaving only an angry scalp.

'Thaniel,' she said, struggling to stand on her burned and black-ened leg. 'I'm so sorry…'

He looked at her, his eyes seeming very bright in his smoke-stained, burned face. In spite of the pain he must have been in, he smiled.

'We got him back,' he said simply, nodding at the kneeling form on the other side of the charred, blackened room.

Sophine followed his gaze, still not quite believing what she saw.

Rigel had his back to them, his hands outstretched over the form of a young woman who lay on her side, completely naked. As Sophine watched, one last patch of black, charred flesh on the woman's hip seemed almost to rehydrate and flow back into the flesh it had once been, leaving not a mark on her body. Rigel dropped his hands and stood up.

He turned to look at them with a goofy smile.

'Even younger this time,' he grinned, 'wonder what she'll—'

He broke off, running a few paces across the room to gasp in horror at Thaniel's face.

'Hang on,' he said, still completely oblivious to the amazed stares they were both giving him. He closed his eyes and held his hands up, making curious little straining noises of effort.

Thaniel looked at her as the flesh of his face turned from angry, flayed red to scar-pink and finally back to his normal bronzed complexion. He held her gaze as his hair returned at an accelerated rate and Rigel switched his healing attention to her leg.

'Do you want to tell him?' Thaniel said, raising an eyebrow. 'Or should I?'

Sophine gave a short laugh and sighed in relief as the pain in her leg vanished.

'Thank you,' she said reverently as Rigel opened his eyes and smiled.

'Phew,' he said. 'I don't remember what we're doing up here but I guess it went wrong?' he looked around at the still gently smoking lines of chalk. He waved a hand at it. 'What was all that?'

'A ritual,' said Thaniel. 'A crazy, crazy ritual that only absolute lunatics would ever, ever attempt.'

Rigel looked at him, and Sophine almost went mad right then and there at the sight of the completely ordinary, entirely everyday humour in his bright, living eyes. She made a gasping, sobbing noise that made both boys look at her, and then flung her arms around his neck and gave herself over completely to tears and weeping.

She must have stayed like that for a minute or more before she felt Rigel's gentle fingers on her arms. He moved her away.

'It's alright, Soph,' he said, his face showing her that he still didn't know he'd been murdered. The heart-breaking innocence of it made her want to cry again, as though having learned how she now couldn't stop.

'Is anyone else hungry?' Rigel said, glancing at Thaniel with a knowing smile that almost set her off again. Thaniel could always be counted on to want to eat.

'If it's all the same to you three,' a rich female voice called from across the room, 'some clothes might be in order first.'

Sophine turned and stared wide-eyed at the undeniable, and undeniably naked, form of Ariene Gloriana. She had the slender, full figure of a woman of twenty and seemed absolutely unashamed of the fact. The young woman stood with one hand on one curvaceous hip, looking at them with such an arch air of senatorial expectation that Sophine had to laugh.

'Lady Gloriana,' she said, unlocking the door with a thought and ushering Rigel and Thaniel towards it. 'Let's find you something to wear before you ruin these boys for any other woman.'

***

'She...murdered me?' Rigel said, as they stood on the landing waiting for Sophine and Ariene to come out of one of the many bedrooms. The last thing he remembered was coming into sight of the city and getting off his horse. Sindel had been by his side...and then he'd been waking up in a smoke-choked room and desperately trying to bring Ariene back once more from the precipice of death.

'I'm sorry, Rige,' Thaniel said, putting his hand on his shoulder. 'She stabbed you with a thin knife like a knitting needle.'

'Yeah,' Rigel nodded. 'She had those. Really deadly with them too.' He gave an appreciative laugh.

Thaniel gave him a strange look.

'You admire her?'

Rigel hesitated.

'I think...I thought I loved her,' he said. 'She and I...well we...'

Thaniel's jaw dropped and he gave a theatrical gasp.

'Oh my gosh you did?'

'We did.' Rigel beamed, feeling stupid for feeling pleased, but not caring.

Thaniel clapped his hands together and bounced on his heels.

'That's great man, congratulations.'

'Thanks.'

'Shame she murdered you immediately afterwards but still, well done.'

Rigel laughed.

'Can't have everything I guess.' He looked away. 'Is she...did you...?'

'No,' Thaniel said quickly. 'No, we let her go.'

'You did?'

Thaniel eyed him.

'Are you insulted or happy right now?'

'I...don't know.'

'We let her go on condition she reported everything to Orswell, including Alakis and Terminheim.'

'Alakis?'

The door opened behind them and Sophine stepped out wearing a new dress of midnight blue. Rigel was impressed; he couldn't remember the last time he'd seen her wear a dress.

'You look nice, Soph,' he began, the words dying in his throat as Ariene followed her out.

The ninety-something year old senator, now in the body of a twenty-year-old, was wearing a bright red figure-hugging gown that reached to the floor. Her thick, black hair hung loose around her shoulders and a small tiara glittered on top of it. Her face was pale and smooth, with high cheekbones and full lips. Her green eyes gleamed. And yet the set of the features and the expression were, unmistakably, Ariene Gloriana.

'Ariene,' Thaniel breathed. 'You look incredible.'

'Thank you, dear,' she said, before pausing. 'I should stop saying "dear", shouldn't I?'

'Probably,' smiled Rigel. 'It makes you sound old.'

'Don't think you're off the hook here, Rigel Wheatly,' she said, narrowing her pretty eyes at him. 'I did not ask to be made fifty again, and I certainly didn't ask to be made twenty. In fact, I think I specifically said I didn't want to be young again, if memory serves.'

Rigel raised an eyebrow.

'Oh, I'm sorry,' he said. 'Next time I'm unexpectedly resurrected and commanded to heal someone on the verge of death, I'll be sure to ask them how old they'd like to be.'

'Do,' she said, without missing a beat. 'It's terribly rude to strip someone of their hard-won years.' And with that she swept past them with her chin in the air, making for the stairs.

They had almost reached the bottom when the front door opened and in walked an old man with a long white beard in a black outfit, closely followed by Eric. They all paused. Eric caught sight of them and froze, looking up at them in stunned silence.

'So,' wheezed the old man, leaning against the banister for support. 'Where is the body?'

Eric's face went from stunned to unimpressed in the space of a heartbeat. He nodded at the collection of people on the stairs.

'He's there,' he sighed.

The old man turned ponderously around and looked up at them, before turning back and fixing Eric with a disapproving stare.

'Young man,' he said, in his old, gravelly voice, 'I don't know what kind of joke this is but I assure you it isn't funny.'

Eric shrugged.

'It's *kind* of funny,' he said, breaking into a grin.

'I shall be sending an invoice for the wasted costs,' the man spluttered as he made his way to the door. 'Outrageous behaviour…never been so insulted…' He closed the door behind him.

Eric regarded them as the moment stretched.

'You couldn't have told me before I spent the whole day making funeral arrangements?'

'Sorry,' Thaniel said. 'It was sort of a last-minute thing.'

Sophine made a snorting sound. Rigel shoved her lightly.

Eric's eyes narrowed.

Chapter Eighteen

Dinner, when it came, was quite the spread. Sophine had told the servants to bring "everything", and they had hastened to comply. Loaves of bread competed for space amongst cooked cold chicken, hunks of salted meat and fruits of all kinds.

'Mistress Sophine,' said an older girl, after she'd placed a large bowl of cheese cubes in front of Thaniel. 'Will that be all?'

'Yes, thank you,' Sophine replied, reaching for a piece of bread.

'The chamber upstairs,' the girl said tentatively, 'is it…'

'It's fine,' Sophine said quickly, 'just don't go in there for a while. We opened the windows.'

It seemed a wholly inadequate thing to say, considering that anyone looking or listening would have seen the smoke and the glow of the flames, heard the unmistakeable crackle and roar of fire consuming wood, along with the shouting of the doomed occupants. The fact that they were all sitting here round the dining table must have been deeply confusing to the servants.

Rigel took a long, deep drink of his wine. It was fairly sour and burned his throat, but he didn't care. He felt as though his whole body was dry and needed filling, and so he intended to do just that.

Ariene was watching him with troubled eyes.

'Rigel,' she said, once the servant girl had departed and closed the door behind her, 'do you remember anything now?'

He shook his head and bit into a piece of bread. It was the tough and stale, and the best bread he'd ever tasted.

'What about…after?' Thaniel put in through a mouth full of cheese.

Ariene, seated opposite Thaniel, frowned at him and reached for the cheese bowl. Ignoring Thaniel's half-hearted protest, she made a pretence of putting some on her own plate and then left the cheese well out of Thaniel's reach. Once again, Rigel noted, she was not actually eating anything.

'There was nothing after,' Rigel said, with a shrug. 'Nothing I can remember, anyway. I was there, looking at the city, and then I was up there, in the burning room.'

Thaniel looked disappointed, though Rigel couldn't tell if it was due to the lack of information or cheese.

'You know, Ariene,' he said, with a mischievous grin, 'now that you're younger, you probably don't need to eat like a bird anymore.'

Ariene's eyes flared in sudden outrage, and she looked for a moment like she was about to say something. Then she paused, looking down at her plate.

'You know, dear, you might be on to something there. It's been a long time'—she said softly, reaching for a piece of bread—'since I've been able to butter bread *and* eat it. One gets to the point where the mere mention of food is sufficient to necessitate a trip to the shops to buy the next size up…'

She picked up a piece of bread and placed a large piece of cheese on top of it.

'But now…' she trailed off, staring at it.

'Go on,' Rigel laughed. 'Eat it!'

'Come on Ariene,' Eric smiled. 'Eat it.'

'Eat…it!' sang Thaniel with a broad grin.

'Eat it!' Rigel repeated loudly.

She ate it, chewing happily with a huge smile. The boys cheered and Sophine laughed.

They managed almost half an hour of pleasant chat before Rigel asked the question he'd been afraid to ask all along.

'Did you find the parchment I was carrying back when…when it happened?'

Thaniel looked down and sighed, as was his tendency when things turned serious. Ariene's mouth was full, but she nodded.

Sophine was the one to answer him.

'We did. It…there's a lot to tell you, Rige. It's hard to know where to start.'

'Start with Alakis,' Ariene said, wiping her fingers on a napkin. She looked at Rigel. 'He's in Terminheim, and he's gone mad.'

'He's enslaved the population,' Thaniel said quietly, toying with a piece of cheese. 'Says he's coming for us.'

'For us? Why?'

'Revenge. Anger. Pick one.'

Eric spoke up.

'We met a girl on the outskirts of Terminheim—'

'Dominitia,' Thaniel said.

'She said the storm had come from him, and that it was feeding off him. Whatever it is, that's what was infecting the people. She said Alakis was basically gone now, and when this storm had no one else to feed on it would come here.'

Rigel was horrified.

'And we're *having dinner?*'

'There's still time,' Ariene put in, with a glance at Sophine. 'Isn't there?'

'Probably a few days left,' she said. 'Alakis was still in Terminheim yesterday morning, around the time Rigel was...well. Around the time Thaniel and Eric came back and we brought Rigel back to the city. Even if he'd left right then, he wouldn't be here until the day after tomorrow.

'Enough time,' she added darkly, with a glance at Ariene.

Rigel looked at her suspiciously.

'Enough to do what?'

Ariene rose to her feet and composed herself with the air of one about to make a speech. Rigel smiled.

'The Senate is not fit for purpose,' she said flatly, leaning forward on the table with her head bowed as though scrutinising her plate.

Rigel was taken aback.

'What do you—'

She held a slender finger up to silence him, without looking up. He caught Sophine's eye; she looked smug.

Ariene replaced her hand and continued in that matter-of-fact tone. She still did not look up.

'The factions within the Senate have paralysed our city and our people have suffered because of it. They have vetoed every proposal that could have helped us, conspired with the Thanes of Ceresheim to starve and impoverish our people, and on top of that, have actively tried to murder one another to gain leverage. That there are not already riots in the streets is remarkable. And now war is coming.'

Rigel waited as the tension built.

'There is only one way to fix this,' she said, raising her head and looking at him. 'In place of a Senate we must have a single leader, to be obeyed without question, advised by councillors. Someone who can quash resistance, quell rebellion and get the wheels of state moving in a single direction. History will be the judge of that direction, but progress must be made now, or we all fall together.'

'And that leader?' Rigel asked, already knowing the answer.

Ariene drew herself up.

'Me. And you will be my councillors,' she gestured at them all with one slender arm.

'The assassin,' she pointed at Sophine, who smiled blandly back.

'The fighter,' her arm moved to Thaniel. He grinned broadly.

'Damn right,' he said.

'The conciliator,' she gestured at Rigel.

'And the thinker,' she nodded at Eric.

Rigel rose to his feet, feeling all eyes on him. He reached for his cup and raised it in salute to Ariene.

'To our new Echelarch, then. Long may she reign.'

They all lifted their drinks and toasted Ariene, who nodded at them.

'I suppose I should learn how to blush demurely again,' she mused, swilling her wine round the edges of her glass. 'One falls out of practice after the age of thirty or so, but it's quite the tool. You might try it, dear,' she said, nodding at Sophine.

'Demure doesn't come naturally to me,' Sophine said wryly.

Ariene laughed and wagged a finger.

'No one is naturally demure, dear. It is the province of the defeated and the manipulative, and either way, it's painful to learn.'

Rigel chuckled and shook his head as he sat down.

'Another one for the book, Ariene.'

She looked at him archly and declined to comment. Instead, she sat back down and reached for another piece of bread.

'So, how do we do this?' Rigel asked.

'Simple,' Ariene said around a mouthful of bread. 'In the morning, I'll call a meeting to announce I'm stepping down. Every single senator and minor official will want to be there for that. Then at midday, we walk in.'

Eric snorted a short laugh.

'We just walk in?'

'You have a better idea, I presume?'

'A few,' Eric said with a roll of his eyes. 'Starting with Lord Barten.'

Ariene looked nonplussed.

'Oh yes, Amir. I'd forgotten about him.'

'He's still Castellan of the Battlemasons isn't he? And you still have the Travellers?'

She nodded.

'Well, then. We have a couple of messages to get out before the morning summons, don't we?'

Ariene sighed and drained her glass.

'You do know the thinker tends to be the least liked, don't you, Eric?'

He gave a gracious nod and a bland smile.

'The great thing about being *the thinker*, ma'am, is that you don't need to care what other people think.'

She chuckled and rose to her feet.

'This is going to be fun; I can tell.'

***

The sun was high in the sky when Ariene stepped out of her carriage and stood looking up at the Senate building.

'It's funny how things go,' she said mildly to the four members of her new court, who stood flanking her. 'Not so long ago we came here to fix a mess and ended up destroying everything.' She nodded at the building. 'That included.'

'Hey, I said I was sorry about that,' Thaniel said, on her right. 'At least we put it back together.'

'*I heal buildings*,' mewled Rigel on the other side of her, in a tiny mocking voice.

Thaniel chuckled.

'I owe you a punch for that when this is over.'

'This time we'll do it right, Ariene,' said Sophine, from behind her. 'No more trying to carry on the way things were. We start again and we do it properly.'

'Looks like the cavalry is here,' said Eric. Ariene turned.

The streets around the Senate were filling with Battlemasons in armour, holding back from the courtyard before the grand white building with its pillars and heavy doors. No one inside would know they had deployed.

'I thought they had no right to deploy inside the city,' said Rigel curiously. 'How did Amir explain it to his generals?'

Ariene looked at Eric with a conspiratorial smile.

'Well,' Eric said, 'they can deploy in times of constitutional crisis and I'd say a coup d'état is a constitutional crisis.'

Rigel laughed.

'You're not serious. Even when they're the ones doing the couping?'

Eric shrugged.

'Nothing in the law says which side they have to be on.'

'That's absurd!'

Ariene chuckled darkly.

'Absurdity is ten-ninths of the law, dear. Now, shall we?'

As they headed to the steps leading up through the pillars to the heavy doors, they were joined by a contingent of armed men and women from the Travellers. In stark contrast to the ornate plate armour of the Battlemasons, these warriors wore leather and chain-mail, and for the most part carried light swords and daggers with one, very notable, exception.

Overseer Skylock of the Travellers' Guild was an enormous woman who towered over Ariene and her court, and carried a massive war hammer casually over one solidly muscled shoulder. She walked over to meet them as the procession made its way up the steps, clapping Rigel on the back and almost knocking him flying.

'Good to see you, Ariene,' Skylock said in her surprisingly feminine voice.

'You too, old friend.'

'So what's the plan today? It's not often my people have to pass so close to Battlemasons, so I assume something big?'

Ariene paused on the final step and turned to look up at the huge woman who commanded the peace-keeping internal security forces within the city, and without whom their gambit would surely fail.

'We're overthrowing the Senate, Skylock. I am to be made Echelarch and full control of the city, its Guilds and its forces will pass to me.'

Skylock looked at her for a moment, then raised an eyebrow.

'I see,' she said evenly, holding Ariene's gaze. 'Well, it's about time. Shall we?'

The large woman turned and headed to the heavy wooden doors, shoving them open as though they were made of paper.

'After you, my lady.'

287

The Senate was in uproar as they entered, senators of all factions and allegiances were shouting across the full chamber or huddled together in small, furtive groups. Few looked up as Ariene made her way down the steps to the dais at the centre. Fewer still noticed the Travellers filing in and taking up position all around the circular audience chamber, until a ring of chainmail and blades enclosed the squabbling nobles of the fracturing city.

Ariene reached the dais and turned to face the assembled lords of Asterheim. She was wearing her familiar blue Senate gown, but that morning she had sent for a tailor to take it in so that it fit her newly reinvigorated figure. Her favourite blue sapphire necklace glittered around her neck, and matching earrings danced above it. Her hair had been carefully arranged into a similar style to her ordinary look, so that she looked as much like herself as possible. Rigel and Sophine took up position on her left, Thaniel and Eric on her right, all four of them a discreet pace behind her.

'Very well,' she breathed to her councillors, feeling her heartbeat pounding within her chest. 'Let us begin.'

'Senators of Asterheim,' she called, feeling a mild twinge of annoyance at the fact that her more youthful voice had lost a little of its gravity and timbre. The noise began to die down as faces turned towards her.

Lady Aresbrook, whom Ariene had pretended to poison in order to save her life the day before, was seated next to her ancient husband. She was looking very pale indeed as she looked at the assembled mages, Sophine in particular, who herself was none too happy that she'd been tricked. Ariene let her gaze linger on the woman and the others with whom she had conspired as the murmur of voices died away.

Lord Barten hurried down the steps, making wincing apologetic faces as he came. Ariene rolled her eyes and twitched her head at him to get out of the way. He scurried to the side and stood awkwardly, shuffling his feet by the dais. Then he looked at her again, peering almost comically as though not trusting his eyesight. She gave him a tight smile and looked away, holding the audience with a steely gaze.

'Lady Gloriana,' said a familiar voice. Lord Cromantis rose to his feet. Neither one of her supporters nor one of the enemies, he was one of the well-meaning, no-nonsense fools who had unwittingly put Lyoris Mountebank on the throne not so long ago. He was a round-bellied, horse-faced man who ran the Grooms and Farriers Guilds. As ever, he was dressed in simple dark clothes except for his silver chain of office and looked very unhappy.

'I take no pleasure in this, but I must insist that you step down and surrender your joint stewardship of the Senate to another. Lord Jarethin and Lord Creswell are dead, murdered in ways which we know to be the work of your mages.' He looked boldly at Thaniel and Sophine, his chin tilted up in challenge as though daring them to strike him down. 'Lady Aresbrook was spared a similar fate by your own intervention, and I think we now know what happened to Lord Balderwin. You have not only failed to stop these murders, but I charge that you have profited by them. We need only look at you to see it.'

There was a general murmur at this, even amongst her supposed supporters.

'Will you yield the stewardship?' he demanded, staring at her. She had to give it to him; it was a strong performance and, if he was making a play for stewardship himself, then he would probably have succeeded.

Unfortunately for him though, she had other ideas.

'I will,' she said lightly, smiling. The Senate exploded into chaos, senators suddenly talking and shouting, others standing up to leave as though sensing the coming of the kind of momentous event that tends to result in a corpse or two.

Ariene turned her head and nodded at Thaniel. He raised his hand. Flickering flames appeared between his fingers. With a flick of his wrist, he sent a ball of roiling fire into the air. It flew over the heads of the senators and exploded in a loud roar of rippling flame before vanishing harmlessly.

The commotion stopped instantly, and fearful eyes turned to the dais. Those senators who had tried to leave were being directed to take their seats by unsmiling warriors in chainmail.

Lord Cromantis, still standing, looked around at his peers and then back at Ariene. His expression was now one of disbelief.

'I renounce the stewardship,' Ariene said, holding Cromantis's gaze.

By the side of the dais, Lord Barten stepped forward.

'I also renounce mine,' he called, waving at the assembled senators who may have missed that he was there.

'The Senate is leaderless,' Ariene continued. She paused, letting her eyes sweep the room. 'And what difference does that make? We have tried for months to get along. To cooperate. Some of us, at least.' She let her gaze linger on the faces of those who had conspired against her. They were staring at her in dismay and looked as if they wanted to be very, very far away from her.

'And what was the result? Squabbling. Fighting. Murder. You accuse me, Lord Cromantis, but I can answer every charge with a clear conscience. Members of this Senate have conspired with the Thanes of Ceresheim to starve our city. To prevent the return of any mages, even those who wanted to come home. To destabilise our leadership and to profit from the chaos.'

'Lies!' spat Lady Aresbrook, half-rising to her feet. Her husband, in his wheelchair, turned startled eyes on her.

Ariene gave her a flat look.

'Well,' she said with a chuckle, 'if anyone needs *further* evidence, I can provide it later.'

She gathered her thoughts as Lord Cromantis sat slowly back into his chair, looking disturbed.

'And now we face an army from Terminheim, led by a fallen mage under the cover of an unnatural storm. If we do not unite now, we will all die. Our city will be broken, our people enslaved.'

'What madness is this?' shouted someone else. 'We have heard nothing of—'

'Believe it,' Ariene growled. 'The Messengers have already told you of the storm, and anyone walking the walls will soon see it coming closer. That is the herald of the army that comes to us.'

The senators began to murmur again, fearful faces looking around for reassurance that none could provide.

Ariene exhaled hard and turned her head slightly towards Rigel. He touched her lightly on the shoulder.

'Go on,' he whispered. 'We're here.'

'And so,' she called, waiting for silence to fall again before she continued. 'And so, I have decided...'

They waited. Some of them knew what was coming, she could tell from the bitter, defeated looks they gave her and one another.

'That I shall assume the throne as Echelarch. You will grant me the powers I need to repel this invasion, return our city to prosperity and cleanse the rot from within it.'

'And if we refuse,' said Lord Cromantis, rising again to his feet with a pugnacious scowl.

She let her measured gaze tell him the answer before she spoke.

'Then we will all join Lords Jarethin, Creswell and Balderwin in death.'

Ariene looked very deliberately at the members of the faction that had opposed her, letting them understand in no uncertain terms what defiance would cost.

'Let me be clear,' she said in ringing tones. 'The Battlemasons are deployed outside this building. The Travellers are within it. Both await my word. My mages stand behind me. I already have the power to save this city. What I am asking for, my lords and ladies, is your blessing.'

Lord Aresbrook, the elderly husband of the flighty conspirator in the emerald-green dress, laughed ruefully and clapped his hands.

'You have it, my dear,' he called, through his chuckles, 'you can hardly do worse than we did.'

Some of her supporters, though wrongfooted by the very direct power grab, clearly saw their own advantages in a monarchy and so began to shout their support. Her enemies, knowing very well that not to do so was to die, added their voices.

Before long, the Senate rang to the sound of her name and she took a series of very deep breaths. Rigel put his hand under her arm to keep her steady and she cast a quick glance at him.

'Let's finish this,' he said, nodding to the shouting crowd.

'What do we do next?' she replied, her head swimming. 'They won't shut up...'

To her surprise, Thaniel stepped forward and raised his hand again. Flame spurted and flickered between his fingers and the noise died down. He remained in place, looking at the senators, but lowered his hand.

'Long live Ariene, Echelarch of Asterheim,' he said. The senators began to clap and cheer, until Thaniel flickered a little more flame and they fell silent again.

'Eric,' Thaniel said, 'what needs to happen now?'

Eric stepped forward, looking very timid and very pale. He cleared his throat a few times and looked around fearfully.

'Tell me,' Thaniel said softly, only for him to hear. 'Just pretend there's no one else here.'

Eric nodded and got himself under control.

'Well, the Farmers and the Fishers both need to open their stores, and turn control of the processing and distribution over to Citizenry to liaise with the Bakers and the other food producing guilds. The Armourers, Smiths and Masons all need to suspend orders and focus only on weapons and armour. And all other Guilds would need to be on notice that ordinary business is subject to the war effort, so the Castellan needs to appoint military liaisons to the Guilds to give direction and instruction...'

The chamber was silent as Eric listed more and more changes that needed to be made to give effect to true martial law, to bring all operations under the control of the Echelarch and to evacuate the eastern part of the city to temporary quarters in the west if the time came.

'And finally, the Echelarch must name her council to handle all those matters,' he finished.

Ariene stepped forward.

'So it is ordered. Castellan'—she looked at Barten—'appoint your liaison officers and have them report to the Guilds immediately, with suitable numbers of men to ensure compliance. The

293

remaining forces are to deploy outside the eastern walls at combat readiness within the day. Senators'—she cast her eye over the assembled nobles— 'go and prepare your Guilds for the transition. Overseer'—she looked at Skylock—'keep the peace in the streets. Full deployment. And prepare evacuation protocols for the east.'

She fell silent. No one moved.

She raised a hand, palm upturned.

'Go,' she said.

Chaos ensued as senators pushed and shoved their ungainly way out of the chamber. The commotion was painful to watch, the noise was deafening.

Ariene turned her back on the sight and gave a shaky smile.

'How did I do?' she asked her four councillors.

'You did great,' said Sophine. 'Now, let's deal with Alakis.'

Chapter Nineteen

'I heal buildings,' muttered Thaniel with a tired sigh. It was now mid-morning, and he'd covered barely half of the ground he'd hoped to by now.

The air felt strange, oddly close and warm but with a bitingly cold breeze. He could almost taste the lightning on the air, the conditions perfect for a storm. He looked over his shoulder, away from the city wall to which he'd been pressing his hands. In the distance, beyond Easterley Castle, where the green fields gave way to the rockier ground towards Terminheim, he could see Alakis's storm. Roiling clouds of black and grey tumbled and collided, lit from within by flashes of brilliant white. The rumble of distant thunder was a constant now, growing louder with every passing hour.

All around him the tents and banners of the Battlemasons stood, flags flapping in the wind. Men marched about, all looking very serious and some very frightened. As far as he knew, the Battlemasons had not fought an actual battle in a very long time, so whilst the red tents and splendid armour made them look like a force to be reckoned with, he couldn't help feeling a tingle of trepidation. There were hundreds of them, thousands even, which surely counted for something. The fortress of Easterley Castle beyond the walls and Stonegate within had both been emptied, with the majority of their forces deployed to help bolster the numbers before the walls. Ariene had reasoned that what approached was a horde, not an army interested in an orderly siege.

Above him rose the walls of the eastern city, stretching at least thirty feet high. They looked impressive to the naked eye, but as he'd learned on his laborious trek along the edge, they were far weaker than they appeared.

Every few metres Thaniel stopped, resting his hands against the stone, and sinking into that mindset that allowed him to visualise the threads and bonds within the masonry. Rock, pebbles, sand and other pieces of raw stone were welded together by the wonders of alchemy and occasionally mage-craft. It was his job to reinforce them, ahead of the bombardment they would no doubt take from the madness unleashed against them.

He walked a little further on, pausing to admire a soldier as he swaggered past. He watched the man walk away with an appreciative eye, then rested his hands on the stone and closed his eyes.

Through the darkness, he could discern the now-familiar web of gleaming lines that indicated the strengths and weaknesses of the walls. This section of wall appeared to have been added to, or reinforced, following the collapse of a previous structure. It was a complicated mass of overlapping lines which, whilst compacted together, were not connected well or at all. He sighed.

'A stiff wind would knock this over,' he muttered, concentrating his now-tired mind on the gleaming lines and urging them to realign themselves, forging connections between them that would keep them together should a blast of lightning crash into the wall. He idly made energy channels to dissipate the force from such a blast, as he had now done at least ten times.

'You there,' said a voice. Thaniel opened his eyes and looked around. The young soldier he'd been admiring was standing behind him. His heart sank.

'What are you up to?' the man asked suspiciously, his hand on his sword-hilt.

'I'm reinforcing the walls,' Thaniel sighed. 'As I told your colleague a little further down.' He craned his neck to try to see the officer he'd explained all this to not half an hour before. The man was not in sight.

The soldier looked up at the walls, then back at him.

'You a mage?'

Various sarcastic responses presented themselves for his perusal, but Thaniel merely nodded.

'I'll have to clear it,' said the soldier.

'You do that,' Thaniel said, turning away, and reflecting that perhaps the man wasn't quite so admirable after all. Not his face, anyway.

He continued on his way, trying not to think about how many miles of wall he had left to reinforce.

***

Far above where Thaniel trudged slowly around the walls being pestered by handsome soldiers, Sophine stood with her hands on her hips, looking critically at the glimmering barrier she had created. She vaguely remembered the last time she had tried to throw a shield over a wide area; it had been hard to maintain and quite weak. It hadn't lasted long.

This time, she couldn't afford to have maintenance of the shield be her main contribution to the coming conflict. Something told

297

her that she would be needed elsewhere. And yet, the storm was approaching, and beneath it the nightmare things that Thaniel had described as Jack-o'-wires. All beings of lightning, and all somehow connected to the dreadful affliction that had consumed Alakis. She had no doubt that the city would come under bombardment from lightning, whether thrown from the clouds or hurled from the ground, and so she was working on a way to keep the damage minimal.

'Try now,' she said to the young woman standing beside her. The Battlemason was young, one of the relative few who had been ordered to hold the walls. No one really expected the Jack-o'-wires or the enslaved population to try to scale the walls, but it was a possibility and so the less experienced were up here under the command of an old, battle-weary knight named Dirkling, whom Thaniel had recommended. When she'd reached the walkway at the top of the walls, Sophine had enlisted this soldier as her test subject.

The woman raised her sword doubtfully, looking first at Sophine, and then at the faintly glowing piece of air floating before her. Sophine nodded encouragingly, pushing her hair back from her face.

The Battlemason swung her sword, and the blade glanced from the disturbance in the air.

'You checked that swing,' Sophine said. The soldier gave a short shrug.

'Sorry,' she said. 'It just feels so odd, swinging at empty air. I'm afraid I'll hit the stone and blunt the edge.'

Sophine closed her eyes, feeding a little more energy into the little shard of shield she'd conjured. It glowed brighter.

'Better?'

The soldier gave a noncommittal half-nod, then swung the sword again. Sophine flinched as the blade shattered the barrier.

'Are you alright?' the soldier asked in a dispassionate voice, sheathing her blade but making no move to help Sophine.

'I will be,' she muttered. 'Thank you for your help.' She turned away, rubbing at her head. All around her the young, and some surprisingly old, soldiers of the Battlemasons walked here and there making preparations. She looked idly at their insignia, embroidered on their cloaks or emblazoned on flags and standards. A thought occurred to her.

...afraid it will blunt the edge...

'You,' Sophine called, beckoning at a young man walking past carrying a bundle of arrows. He looked at her, confusion spreading on his beardless, pimply face. She gave up beckoning and went to him.

'Can I have your dagger?' she asked, looking at the knife sheathed at his waist.

The youth almost jumped away from her, clutching his bag of arrows and shaking his head.

'Please? I'll give it right back...'

'Madam mage,' a gruff voice said behind her. 'Would you please stop accosting my soldiers? They all have work to do.'

She turned and looked up at a barrel-chested man with a thick beard and arms that looked as though they'd gone to fat, but which she suspected still packed a very powerful punch. His face was gnarled like old wood, and one of his eyes was a milky colour that matched his grey-white hair.

'Are you Dirkling? The commander here?' she asked, her eyes straying past the man to the flashing storm clouds on the horizon.

'A reward for a lifetime of service,' he harrumphed. '*Sir Rivan* Dirkling. I'm the babysitter.' He gestured around at the young soldiers atop the walls.

'Sir Rivan,' she smiled. 'Thaniel mentioned you. You know him?'

'I do,' the man said with no trace of a smile, 'now then, about this accosting...'

'I need a knife,' she said.

With a flick of his fingers, the man unsheathed a short blade at his hip and flipped it handle-first at her. She caught it deftly and nodded her thanks.

'So?' he said simply.

'I'll leave them alone.'

Sir Rivan gave a single nod and marched off, yelling at a group of young soldiers carrying crossbow bolts.

'You see anyone with a crossbow up here, idiots? Longbows, boys! Find the arrows for the longbows!'

Sophine gave a smile and knelt on the stone walkway, tracing the curve of the wall with her eyes and trying to use her fingers to measure out distance.

'Seven, maybe,' she muttered, wishing she had a book to refer to. 'Curse you, Alakis...'

Without a book she would need to come up with her own symbol to reflect what she was trying to achieve. A series of anchors drawn in the stone, each of them imbued with her intention in relation to the shield and each connected to the other. They would take the burden of the shield from her once it was up, and she could put as much energy into it as possible without worrying about having to hold it in place.

Scratching at the stone, she let her senses drift, remembering the shield she'd conjured during the attack on the Barbican. A shape occurred to her, one she thought she could remember and which seemed apt. With the tip of her blade, she etched the shape into the stone, thinking all the while of the energy shield and the maintenance of it. When she was done, she let the grooves she'd cut fill with energy like water in a well. Then she went in search of six other suitable points to anchor the barrier.

'Sir Rivan,' she called, seeing the old knight berating a pale-faced boy in ill-fitting armour. When he looked at her, she turned and pointed at the tiny glowing mark on the stone. 'Please don't let your soldiers cover those marks.'

The heavy-set man grunted and looked briefly at the boy he'd been shouting at.

'How many are there?' he asked, still eying the boy.

'Seven, probably,' she said. 'Or maybe eight.'

'Go, boy,' Dirkling growled at the terrified junior, 'fetch *seven probably or maybe eight* of your useless friends and go with that mage. Do what she tells you.'

He turned and stalked heavily away, his ancient armour clanking. Sophine beckoned at the boy.

'Come with me.'

***

Ariene was very good at looking like she understood things she clearly – to Rigel at least – did not. She had also perfected in only a few short hours the demure blush she'd mentioned, and the pretty deflection that the young could get away with and the old could not. Rigel watched her in amazement as she met Guild representative after Guild representative, experts all in their respective trades and all far more knowledgeable about them than she was. Each one, to a man, had left smiling, regardless of what she'd forced them to accept.

They had just met with the representative of the Farmers' guild, who had taken her assurance that not only was the grain supply from Ceresheim open again, but that for the time being, all costs of food would be subsidised by the city. On those terms, he had been more than happy to open the stores he had been desperate to preserve in case of real emergency to alleviate the starvation in the city. She had made similar overtures to the Tailors and Farriers, and any number of other Guilds that had responded to the crisis by hoarding what was left and charging extortionate prices for it.

'You mentioned Ceresheim,' said Rigel as he cleared the papers away from the last meeting and stacked them with the others at the side of the small office behind the dais in the Senate building. 'Are the supply lines really open again?'

'I certainly hope so,' said Ariene wearily from where she sat, sprawled in an uncomfortable chair by the desk. She pinched the bridge of her nose between thumb and forefinger. 'The Thanes have been dealt with and the senators are out of play here, so it should all be happening. We should be expecting to receive trade again within a day or two, shouldn't we? Ceresheim isn't that far.'

'And if Sindel managed to give that message,' Rigel said, 'they could already be on the way.'

Ariene was quiet, watching him put away the papers.

'What was she like?' she asked.

He laughed and raised an eyebrow.

'Fantastic,' he said appreciatively.

302

'Not like that.' She scowled in a way that made her look exactly like her ninety-year-old self. 'Young people, honestly.'

He chose not to mention how bizarre that sounded coming from a girl no older than him.

'She was nice,' he said instead, sliding a long, rolled-up piece of parchment into a box. 'She was good to me. Until she stabbed me. I think I'll always love her a little, despite that.'

Ariene made a sympathetic noise.

'First love. Always hurts.'

He sighed.

'Sometimes very literally.'

The door to the small room opened and Lord Barten stepped in. With a nod to Rigel he went to sit on the edge of the desk next to Ariene, rubbing a hand over his bald head. His brown skin gleamed with sweat.

'We're ready, Ariene. The Battlemasons are deployed and the walls are manned. How are things here?'

'I've unblocked the supply issues,' she said with a heavy, world-weary sigh that no twenty-year-old could have uttered. 'Food and provisions will make their way to the people and to the soldiers, and we should have enough replacement arms and armour for a very short siege, if it comes to that.'

'Good,' said Barten, the relief evident in his voice.

'But Amir,' Ariene said in a low, serious voice. 'We cannot survive anything more. There is no possibility our stores will stretch, so we make our best stand when first contact is made. No falling back, no strategic retreat. We win, or we die.'

'Understood,' he said. 'Listen, my scouts report that the...front line, if you can call it that, is less than a day away. We expect them to be here before dawn.'

'And Alakis?' asked Rigel.

'No sign of him,' said Barten gravely. 'It's a huge army, but the rear ranks are just people carrying industrial tools. No armour. No formations. It's a rabble.'

'And the front?' Ariene prompted.

'Those Jack-o'-wire things are with them.'

'How many?'

Amir scowled.

'Too many. One on one I would say our boys could beat them, but when there are all those slaves as well…'

'Is Thaniel done with the walls?' Rigel asked.

'I think so,' Amir sighed.

'Then I think it's time for a war council,' he said.

Ariene looked at him strangely.

'We've had plenty of war councils,' she said, gesturing around at the small office from which they had attempted to fix the mess of Asterheim. 'This is our war council.'

Rigel went to the door.

'I mean a *mage* war council,' he said. 'Something tells me this will be decided between us and Alakis. We need to prepare.'

***

Rigel found Sophine on the walls near Stonegate Castle, just as the sun was setting. He looked out, across the fields and countryside, past the darkening form of Easterley Castle to the swirling black clouds approaching. He could hear the thunder, and he thought he could even see the rain.

'They'll be here soon,' he said to Sophine. She was standing, leaning on the wall and looking out just like him. Her face was set and grim.

'We need a plan,' he added. She turned to look at him, as though she wanted to say something spiteful, but instead she smiled.

'I'm glad you're back,' she said.

Rigel returned the smile, deciding not to ask what bleak thoughts she had been having before he interrupted her.

She moved away from the wall, indicating a small patch of ground beneath her. A small picture was glowing there, a pale white nimbus suffusing the sigil she'd evidently etched with the knife she held. A few paces away, a very nervous looking young soldier hopped from foot to foot, glancing between Sophine and the gleaming symbol.

'Shall we see if this works?' she said with a yawn.

'Oh I see,' he said, 'there are more of these?'

'Nine of them, as it turns out. Each one with its own little guardian,' she winked at the nervous soldier who looked about fifteen years old. He blinked and stammered something neither of the mages caught.

Rigel looked at Sophine.

'Nice idea.'

'Thanks,' she said, with a quick mischievous glance at the soldier. 'Got the idea when I resurrected this one,' she confided to the boy, nodding at Rigel.

The soldier went white at that and backed away a pace. Sophine laughed.

'Alright then, here we go,' she announced, closing her eyes and dropping the knife to the ground.

Rigel waited, watching her arms slowly rise above her head. The strain on her face was alarming as she struggled with the forces she was trying to control. He had only seen her conjure a shield once before, and it had cost her a lot.

The symbol in the rock blazed a brilliant white and the soldier yelped. Rigel looked away from the searing light as Sophine let out a half-scream of effort and dropped her arms. For a moment, just a brief second, nine beams of light connected the sky overhead with the walls, a strange shimmering haze appearing between those beams like the surface of rippling water. And then it was gone.

Sophine dropped to her knees by the still-gleaming sigil.

'It...I think it's done,' she panted.

'How do you feel?' Rigel asked, taking her arm and helping her up. 'Are you still maintaining it?'

She shook her head.

'No, I threw the shield into the sigils. I can't feel it at all now.'

'That's good,' he said. 'Isn't it?'

'If it works,' she said. She picked up the knife from where she'd dropped it earlier. She turned to contemplate the view over the wall, then hurled the knife over the side. It bounced off a hazy disturbance in the air and rebounded back at them. Sophine ducked as it flew over her head and clattered to the floor.

'Guess it works,' said Rigel. 'Did you feel that? The impact I mean?'

She shook her head and shrugged.

'That's the best I can do. Let's go and see if Thaniel's done with the walls. Then we can figure out what to do about Alakis.'

Later that night they sat in the vacant seats by the dais in the Senate building, as the rumble of thunder and crash of lightning got steadily louder.

Rigel and Thaniel silently watched Sophine's body as it continued to breathe and its heart continued to beat.

'She's really not in there, is she?' Thaniel said, with evident distaste.

Rigel shook his head.

'It's really creepy,' he said. 'I'm still struggling with this...soul business.'

'Me too,' said Thaniel. 'When she first learned about it, she denied it. Said it was about minds and fragments of your emotion. But it's souls. We have actual, real souls that can...' he gestured at Sophine's body. 'Leave,' he finished lamely.

Ariene yawned, her eyes looking raw and tired.

'Can't stay at this much longer,' she said. 'Amir said they'll be here before dawn.'

Sophine's body shuddered and jerked upright. Ariene yelped, suddenly looking much more alert.

Sophine began to splutter and cough, but waved Thaniel away as he moved to help her.

'Alakis,' she said, as she got herself under control. 'He's not with the storm.'

'You could see in?' Rigel asked.

'Not clearly, it's still a huge amount of energy. But it's wider now. Dissipated. I saw the Jack-o'-wires...' she shuddered. 'If those things get into the city...'

'They won't,' said Ariene. 'What about Alakis?'

'I managed to get around the storm,' Sophine said, gratefully accepting a cup of wine from Eric who gave the rest of them an exasperated look.

'He's in Terminheim still. The storm is much, much weaker there. I think it's almost tethered to him. He wasn't moving. He's sitting on the Lord Governor's throne in the dark, and there are holes in the walls and floor like someone tried to blow the room up.'

'He's alone?'

'Alone. Not moving. It's like he's one of those puppet things himself.'

Ariene rose to her feet.

'And if Alakis dies?'

Rigel nodded.

'Then the storm dies. The slaves are freed.'

Ariene looked at Sophine.

'You agree?'

She nodded.

'Everything started with him. I don't think he would have stretched the storm that far if it didn't need to be tethered to him. He'd just have sent it on ahead. Plus it looks like he's keeping himself out of harm's way and maybe this is why. He knows if he's attacked, it all falls apart.'

'Very well,' Ariene said. 'Thaniel, Sophine, my fighter and my assassin. Go to Terminheim, and deal with Alakis. Rigel, you stay here.'

'But—'

'They can't go until Alakis's forces are engaged here,' she said, talking over him in a very Ariene Gloriana no-nonsense tone. 'If he senses an attack, he'll be waiting for them. And that means we have to face them outside the city walls, and I would like one of my mages on hand when the danger comes. Particularly the one skilled in healing and time manipulation.'

Rigel struggled to think of a reason to protest. He glanced at Thaniel, who looked away, and at Sophine. She nodded at him.

'She's right, Rige. We can't all go. What if...if Thaniel and I fail?'

'What if you fail *because* I wasn't there?'

She raised a sardonic eyebrow.

He sighed heavily.

'Alright fine, I'll stay here.'

Ariene nodded and started up the steps.

'Get some rest,' she said over one elegant shoulder. 'Tomorrow the battle begins.'

Chapter Twenty

The sky, in the west at least, was beginning to lighten. Turning from that pitch darkness of night into the navy-blue that heralds the coming of dawn. In the east, however, night still ruled.

Rigel, Thaniel and Sophine stood with Ariene on the battlements above Stonegate Castle and looked out over the plains and fields. The unseen shield above them spat and sparked as the rain beyond pattered gently against it. Storm clouds above rolled and crashed, fierce flashes of lightning illuminating the edges of ominous black shapes in gleaming silver for seconds at a time. The occasional fork of jagged energy jabbed down, as though probing at the barrier. Each time the lightning was shattered, its power absorbed by Sophine's carefully laid defences. Each time one of the symbols etched in stone flared and burned all the brighter.

Sophine glanced at one of the glowing icons as another lightning strike was repelled. The little image flashed a brilliant white for a moment, before fading again. The crash of thunder overhead almost seemed to have character now, a frustrated angry god outraged at their defiance.

'I don't know how much longer those will hold,' Sophine said, eyeing the symbol warily.

'You think it's absorbing power from the attacks?' Thaniel replied, the childlike hope in his voice making Sophine wince.

She shook her head.

'I didn't build it that way. Eventually it'll weaken and then...'

'The outer city has been mostly evacuated,' said Rigel. 'If the storm gets through the barrier, we'll still have some time.' He didn't sound at all sure of what he was saying, and no one replied.

'They're here,' said Ariene simply. She nodded out over the battlements.

Beyond the lines of the Battlemasons, who had arranged themselves with cavalry at the front and infantry behind, gleaming figures were lurching through the darkness. They were close enough now that Rigel could almost make out the bizarre, misshapen limbs and the peculiar gait, as though bobbing along held up by invisible strings. The storm overhead roared its hunger as they came.

'Jack-o'-wires,' Rigel breathed. 'How can there be so many...?'

Thaniel shook his head.

'If every citizen of Terminheim was compelled to make even one...'

'Hundreds,' said Ariene. 'Thousands.'

Standing near them, off to the side, Sir Rivan Dirkling raised a hand.

'Range,' he said in his gruff voice. A young man next to him holding a longbow held the tip of the arrow he had notched in a small brazier of leaping flames. The oil-soaked rag tied to the arrow flared into blazing life and the archer wasted no time in pulling the string back and loosing it into the air.

The glowing point of the arrow arched up, over the heads of the assembled Battlemasons and out into the night, landing with a thud a few hundred metres away from their lines.

The ghastly apparitions did not slow, did not react. They came on, a wave of crackling energy and silent, twisted limbs. They were approaching the diminishing light of the arrow.

'Range reached,' Dirking growled. 'Give the order.'

Thaniel raised his hand and unleashed a gleaming gout of flame up into the air. It rolled and plumed, fading away into the slowly lightening morning. In response, hundreds of arrows from hundreds of archers flew from the walls, plunging into the approaching horde.

Rigel let out a growl of frustration. Even at this distance, he could see the damage had been minimal. The creatures continued their ghastly loping tread, some stuck with arrows through their chests, some with limbs sheared off. A few had fallen, lucky strikes impaling their makeshift heads or cutting through whatever was holding them up. But not enough. Not nearly enough.

The silent enemy was close now. Rigel could see the cavalry jostling with movement, men with plumed helmets riding along the front lines with banners raised to snap in the air above their armoured destriers.

'The cavalry is about to charge,' Ariene said. 'You've done what you can do here. Go.'

Sophine and Thaniel looked at Rigel, and he nodded at them but did not trust himself to speak.

After a moment Sophine turned and gestured at the air. A portal tore itself into being, wide enough for two and crackling with energy.

'Hurry,' Rigel finally said. 'I don't think we'll last long here.'

Thaniel looked at him grimly and clasped his shoulder. Then, without another word, Sophine and Thaniel stepped through the portal and it evaporated into nothing behind them.

***

The clash of battle and the roar of the storm was off to their left as they exited the portal. Sophine looked around the twilight landscape into which they'd stepped.

'Not as far as I'd hoped,' she muttered. The walls of Asterheim were only a few miles behind them. Above where they stood, the storm was still rumbling but less angrily out here away from the battle.

'How many jumps will it take?' Thaniel asked fearfully, his eyes on the distant darkness with the hideous flashes of gleaming lightning.

'I don't know. I just don't want him to know we're coming,' Sophine said shortly. They'd been over this many times, weighing up the different approaches. Whilst it might be possible to skirt around the storm and try to punch straight into the throne room in Terminheim within the space of two or three portals, the energy and power involved was immense and there was every chance that Alakis, his consciousness altered and enhanced by the tempest to which he was connected, would feel or see them coming. Multiple smaller jumps, with as much time as they dared between them, should ensure they could take him by surprise.

And, of course, making a portal to anywhere non-specific was an inexact art at best, so the shorter the better.

'We'll head that way,' she said, pointing at the crest of a small hill. 'We can take a bearing from there and jump to the next point.'

'This is going to take too long,' Thaniel fretted as they began to run over the grassy field.

'Rigel will hold them,' she panted, wishing she was fitter. 'He *has* to hold them.'

***

Rigel watched the third cavalry charge with growing horror. The tactics were sound, he knew, but to see them turn out to be so ineffective was demoralising in the extreme.

He had asked Sir Dirkling about the charging knights, and knew their spears were designed to be dropped shortly after impact amid the chaos of the reeling enemy, giving the knights time to wheel their horses and retreat along with their fellows to regroup for another devastating charge.

Not only that, but the mounted, heavily armoured men and horses, bristling with lances as long as two or three metres would, to most enemies, be a terrifying sight. A wall of gleaming steel and blades hurtling at speed into their ranks caused panic, which was why the mounted cavalry charge was the cornerstone of any truly powerful military.

But the Jack-o'-wires had given no indication that they even noticed the deadly spears or heard the thundering hooves. The first charge had smashed into their ranks, with each knight impaling one, two, or maybe even three of the warped monstrosities on his lance, but only killing one if he was very lucky.

And most had not been lucky.

Rigel's heart had thumped wildly as the knights of the first rank turned their horses expertly and rode away, leaving Jack-o'-wires stuck through, some joined together on lengths of abandoned lances. The enemy did not slow, they merely hobbled. Some clicked unnatural blade-claws and snapped the shafts embedded in their crudely fashioned bodies.

By now, with the warriors of the third charge riding hard for the relative safety of the Battlemason ranks, a frightening number of cavalrymen lay dead and forgotten behind the approaching ranks of Alakis's mindless monsters, trampled beneath unnatural feet. Having failed to kill anything or create any sense of panic, it was as though they had simply ridden three ranks deep into the open arms of the enemy. Pulled from their horses or cut down where they sat, it was an ignoble end for such brave soldiers.

Something was happening below, an altercation between the plume-helmed officers of the cavalry and the infantry commanders. Eventually the cavalry officer rode off, yelling commands to the remaining mounted men. One by one, they slid from their horses and belted on their swords, moving with their lances to stand in the ranks of the infantry.

The Jack-o'-wires were less than a hundred metres away.

By Rigel's side, Sir Rivan turned to the ten boys he had selected as runners.

'That's it, lads,' he said, in voice heavy with bitter resignation, 'give the order.'

The ten boys ran off, to deliver their orders to the archers. No more arrows. Banners would be raised by another team of youngsters standing nearby, but the morning gloom was still unnaturally dark so there was no guarantee the archers would see them.

'I can't stay here, Ariene,' Rigel said, wincing as another crackling thunderbolt smashed against Sophine's shield.

'I know,' she replied sadly, watching as the cavalrymen joined the pikemen at the front ranks of the infantry lines and brandished their weapons at the enemy. The Jack-o'-wires were almost upon them.

'Just...' she added, looking at him and touching his cheek. 'Come back alive. I can't lose you again.'

He nodded, then headed as fast as he dared back along the walls, making for the stairs that would take him to the open gates.

All around him men ran, carrying orders and reports, shouting over the thunder. Rigel almost slipped on the steps where someone had spilled the noxious pitch-oil mixture they'd been carrying to the large vats on either side of the gate. He hoped *that* wouldn't be needed.

'Sophine,' he muttered as he headed through the gate and ran beyond the shield into the driving rain, racing to the back lines of the infantry, 'hurry…'

***

Terminheim loomed on the horizon. Thaniel gave a shout of triumph and pumped his fist in the air as they stepped through yet another portal.

'We're nearly there, Sophine!'

He looked around, and his excitement died. Sophine was sitting on the stony floor, breathing hard.

'I just need to rest, Than,' she said panted. She shrugged off her long, rain-soaked coat. It was only then he realised it wasn't raining here. They were beyond the fury of the storm.

'Rest? Soph…' he gestured helplessly at the shape of the squat city on the edge of sight, dark against the brightening morning. The grey clouds above it rippled faintly, but no rain fell and only the occasional gleam of pale light suggested a hint of lightning.

He squatted next to her, touching her shoulder.

'We're nearly there, Sophine,' he said, peering at the city and trying to judge the distance. 'We can reach it with just one more portal, I know we can.'

'But…Alakis…'

'Look around you, Soph. The storm is weak here. I'd say it's barely hanging on. All his power and thought is back there'—he looked at her sternly before adding with deliberate emphasis—'where Rigel is.'

She gave him a hateful look, her cheeks flushed and red. Sweat beaded on her brow.

'He won't feel it. Get us there. If you need to pass out or throw up or both then fine but do it there. I can deal with Alakis myself. You've done your part as Ariene's assassin. Let me do mine as her fighter.'

Sophine smiled weakly and gave a short laugh.

'I don't think that's…quite what she meant…'

'Maybe not. But we have to do this. Rigel is in the middle of a battle right now, against those things…'

She took his arm and hoisted herself up, wincing and grimacing with effort.

'Alright,' she said. 'One more portal.'

She closed her eyes.

***

Rigel yelped and jumped back as a whirling thing of blades and wires spun past him and sliced into a soldier, parting armour with a swipe of its claws. The man tried to parry, but the monstrosity moved unnaturally fast, its disjointed limbs flexing and whipping at strange unpredictable angles. Rigel shouted and threw a blast of unfocused energy at the demon marionette, rocking it aside and giving the man a short reprieve. He nodded his thanks and bent to pick up his fallen shield, just as another soldier took the Jack-o'-

wire's misshapen metal head off with a precise swipe of a sword. The capering puppet collapsed instantly, returning to the junk parts from which it had been fashioned.

All around him, the soldiers of Asterheim struggled to keep their shields between themselves and the insane, spinning figures. Hundreds of men were dead or wounded, their cries adding to the cacophony of clashing battle and the endless crashes of thunder. It was lighter now as the night gave way to morning, though the battlefield was still shrouded in the shadow of the unnatural clouds and the thrashing rain.

Rigel looked round just as a shape of blades and bits of whipping wire threw itself at him. He tried to jump, but the mud was slick beneath his feet and he fell heavily on his back. A thin piece of jagged metal ripped through the air where his head had been moments before, and the Jack-o'-wire stumbled. He kicked at its disjointed leg and knocked it aside, scrabbling to his feet on a tide of adrenaline.

The thing righted itself and turned its head slowly towards him. This one had a spade for a head, with jagged eye holes, clearly punched through with something heavy and blunt. Crackling arcs of white light danced around the edges of the holes.

Rigel blinked, taking in the bizarre construction. The spade had been crudely jammed into the mass of wood and nails and other commonplace items that formed its body, and wrapped in fence wire. The utter insanity of what he faced banished his panic for a moment, and he found a brief space to think.

The nightmare marionette lurched at him again, but Rigel threw out a hand and reached within himself for the power that had saved him so many times before. This time, though, he held it in a tight grip, directing it up, out and around the soldiers around him.

Time for the Jack-o'-wires slowed, their limbs and blades crawling through space at a fraction of their normal speed. Rigel gasped with the weight of the tide of time pressing against his mind. He gritted his teeth as he held it back, forcing the flimsy barrier to wrap and contort itself in a very specific way.

A hush fell over the battlefield as soldiers blinked and shook their heads at the strange phenomenon.

'Soldiers of Asterheim!' Rigel bellowed as loudly as he could, the strain beginning to become almost too much to bear. 'Strike at the heads! Strike now!'

The cry was passed on, soldiers suddenly emboldened and wasting no time in hacking at their immobile enemies.

Ordinarily, it was virtually impossible to move or affect something frozen in time. But this time…

The head of a Jack-o'-wire to his left exploded as a wide-eyed soldier swiped at it with a clean stroke of a sword. The body did not collapse, did not move, and the man stepped back fearfully. He looked at Rigel.

'Time won't be frozen long,' he said, through a strained throat. 'But the heads are out here with us. Destroy as many as you can…'

All along the line, the cavalrymen, pikemen and infantry of the city chopped into the defenceless makeshift heads of Alakis's insane killers. Buckets were sheared, spades chopped, pots and pans knocked from their crude moorings. Exuberant cheers and fierce yells accompanied the din of steel on steel and cracking wood.

Rigel's head felt like it was being crushed between two stone walls. He couldn't keep the tide back any longer. He bit down hard and sank to his knees, his whole body shaking with the effort of maintaining his hold on his arcane power. He could feel blood running from his nose and his skin starting to heat up. He cried out in pain as the heat became burning and he fell back, the spell was broken.

All around him, the leering shapes of Jack-o'-wires crumpled into heaps of discarded trash, imploding where they stood as their lack of heads caught up with their bodies. Time flooded back in an overwhelming wave, releasing the pressure on Rigel's skull. His skin steamed in the rain as he lay gasping on the ground.

He had given them less than two minutes, enough for each man to kill ten or so of the monsters. Hundreds had been destroyed, all along the line, and those that remained seemed to pause. The storm overhead swelled and roiled, arcs of lightning now spearing down against the walls of the city with renewed fury.

Rigel tried to get to his feet, but slipped again in the mud. His body was trembling with the effort of the last few minutes, and he didn't see the capering lightning-wreathed marionette dancing towards him until it was almost upon him.

He stared at it, knowing there was nothing more he could do. He was spent. The horrific demon construction rushed at him, rusted pieces of jagged metal outstretched from disjointed fence-post arms.

A ripping sound to his right distracted it for a moment, before three large pieces of jagged rock crashed into its bucket-head and smashed it apart in a short burst of energy. The Jack-o'-wire collapsed to the ground and Rigel blinked at it in wonder, as pieces of its discarded body flew into the air, spearing towards its fellows and ripping their unholy heads from their bodies.

The ripping sound had become a roaring growl that he knew very well. Wind blew from the portal which Master Thomas came striding through, his perpetually disapproving face managing a small smile as he reached for Rigel's hand. Behind him, Madam Raftopolis and three other teachers from the Barbican stepped grimly through, pieces of rock hovering above their upturned palms. As Rigel took the hand and pulled himself up, the mages flung their projectiles with deadly precision, killing scores of Jack-o'-wires with each powerful cast. The collapsing, disintegrating bodies became new projectiles, and scores more fell as yet more mages stepped through the portal and added their power to the counterattack.

Rigel looked at Master Thomas with astonishment. His old mentor wore a rough travelling cloak of homespun cloth over a tunic and trousers, and he cast a frown at the sky as he was soaked through by the rain.

'Bloody weather,' he said.

Rigel laughed shakily, looking around as the tide of battle was turned by the arrival of fifty or more mages. The Jack-o'-wires seemed to sense the threat, turning from the soldiers to launch themselves at the small enclave of sorcerers threatening their flanks. They died by the hundreds.

'How...' Rigel began.

Master Thomas smiled, jerking his head to the south.

'Orswell,' he said simply.

Rigel wanted nothing more at that point than to fall to the floor and cry. Instead, he pulled his old teacher in for a hug and gripped him tight.

'Thank you,' he sniffed. 'Thank you.'

'Thomas,' Madam Raftopolis said sternly, marching up to them. Her face looked a lot less lined and her hair looked a lot healthier than the last time he'd seen her. The mage-tutor's eyes gleamed in the flashes of the lightning overhead. Then she caught sight of Rigel.

'Rigel?' she said in amazement. 'But…'

She looked at Thomas, and Rigel could see the dawning suspicion on her face.

'Don't worry,' he said hurriedly. 'I really was dead.'

Both of the older mages looked closely at him then, their faces wearing almost identical expressions of guarded concern.

He laughed.

'Long story,' he shrugged.

Madam Raftopolis watched him for a moment more before turning to Thomas again.

'Thomas, the…puppet things…are all gone. But there's another wave approaching.'

'More Jack-o'-wires?' Rigel said, his heart sinking.

'Is that what they're called?' she said with a sniff. 'No, not them. These are people. But they look…strange. No armour, and they seem to be armed with hammers and axes. Tools.'

'The population of Terminheim,' Rigel said, nodding. 'Alakis's slaves.' He turned to Master Thomas.

'Pull your people back to the city, Master. I'll round up the officers and get them to do the same. We don't need to hurt those people unless Sophine and Thaniel…well, unless we have to.'

'You have that power?' Thomas asked in respectful surprise. He raised his eyebrows.

Rigel nodded with a weak smile.

'I'm one of the four councillors of the new Echelarch, and I speak with her authority while martial law is in place.'

Thomas blinked at that.

'Well, well,' he said. 'I've clearly missed a lot.'

'Oh,' Rigel smiled, 'you have.'

Chapter Twenty~One

Terminheim was empty and silent beneath the perpetual gloom of the clouds. Thaniel ran as fast as he could through the deserted streets, trying not to worry about Sophine. When he'd left her, his friend's face had been ashen pale and she'd been shaking with exhaustion. He knew that the navigation around the terrible fury of the storm had drained her almost completely, and he could barely comprehend how hard it must have been. Sophine could make portals in her sleep, and so for it to have done this to her...

There was no chance either he or Rigel could have reached Terminheim, he knew that now. Which meant the whole plan rested on him. He leapt over a jagged piece of rock, his boots crunching gravel to dust as he ran on.

The palace loomed ahead, a squat structure of stone and wood, like everything else in this charmless city. Something had happened to it though. A section of walls on the western side had fallen in, the outer wall and some of floors connecting to them having collapsed too. As he ran towards it, he allowed his senses to drift a little, letting him see the tormented threads of the building's construction waving forlornly in the light breeze. He could see it clearly now. Someone had blown a hole in the basement and knocked out the supports holding the upper floors. It was a wonder that so much of those floors still stood, but he could see they were bound with the silvery threads that marked a mage's work.

Thaniel climbed gingerly to the edge of the pile of rubble and looked up into the palace's ravaged interior through the blasted hole in its side. No candles burned; no movement caught his eye in the shadows. The palace seemed empty, and yet he knew Alakis was here somewhere.

Thaniel breathed out slowly and focused his mind, taking hold of his body and levitating it like a stone. He drifted up the side of the building, concentrating hard and forcing the thought of falling out of his head. Two floors up he nudged himself forward, and alighted on the edge of the torn wooden floorboards. He took a gentle step, only letting go with his mind when he was sure his feet were on solid ground. The floor creaked as his weight settled onto it, and he winced.

A door stood in front of him leading, he reasoned, into the middle of the palace. From there he figured, it would be a shorter distance to the throne room than from any other entry point.

He did not expect the door to open into the throne room itself.

Thaniel froze as the door revealed the shadowy heart of Alakis's stolen kingdom.

The room was long and wide, and largely empty. A carpet of faded red that looked almost black in the gloom crunched softly under his feet as he made his way forward. A musty smell of damp and corroded fabrics wafted through the air as he walked.

All around the room, pillars of stone and wood stretched between floor and ceiling, hung with banners and tapestries that swayed gently in the light breeze from the open door behind him. On the wall opposite where Thaniel had entered, he could see another door, leading away into the palace. A third was set in the wall to his right, opposite the series of tiered steps, which led to a large dais against the wall to his left.

Upon that dais sat a throne of heavy wood and set with polished stones. And upon that throne…

'Alakis,' Thaniel breathed, his heart pounding in horror at the sight of the boy he had known. His skin was almost translucent now. Even at this distance, Thaniel could see the veins beneath the gossamer thin flesh, lit still by intermittent sparks of light from within. Alakis's hands rested on the carved wooden arms of the throne, his body leaning forward and his head down. He did not move, but the air around him seemed to shimmer as though through a heat-haze. Thaniel fancied he could almost see Alakis slipping in and out of reality, as though no more corporeal than the storm which fed upon his mind.

Sudden movement to the right made Thaniel jump. A trio of Alakis's Jack-o'-wires were lurching to their feet, animated by sparks of arcing energy that snapped along their repulsive bodies. Thaniel eyed them with distaste, then stretched a hand towards them.

He closed his fist, slamming the abominations together in a vice of telekinetic force. He held on, grimly crushing the monsters, until one by one their makeshift heads tore loose of their bodies and they fell into piles of spare parts.

Thaniel turned away and jumped in alarm as he looked back at the throne.

Alakis was staring at him, his head raised and his eyes black pools of midnight within his near-transparent skull. Lightning flashed inside his jaw and he winced.

'Thaniel,' he said, in a voice like the grave. His mouth did not move, the voice echoing around him as though whispered by the walls themselves.

'Alakis,' Thaniel replied guardedly, thinking fast. 'I've come to ask you to—'

'You've come to destroy me,' the voice sighed. Alakis seemed to unfold into the air, rising slowly. Rippling light danced through his opaque body.

'Die,' the ghost-voice hissed.

Thaniel leapt to the side as Alakis unleashed a blast of pure, brilliant white energy at him. The floor where he had stood seconds before exploded, the carpet catching fire instantly as jagged pieces of the floorboards flew up and clattered away. He tried to throw a telekinetic blast back in response, but Alakis made a lazy gesture and knocked it aside before hurling more blistering energy at him.

This time Thaniel tried to parry with a hastily thrown shield, like Sophine's, but the blast shattered it and threw him to the ground. Thaniel screamed, the violence to the shield like a physical pain in his head.

'You should not have come here,' breathed the ghost-whisper. 'I am—'

Another voice, just on the edge of hearing, cut the ghost-voice off. The floating apparition that had once been a mage turned to look at the wall against which its throne sat.

'Alakis...'

Thaniel followed that pitiless black gaze through the aching throb in his head. Suspended halfway up the wall like some hideous trophy or the artwork of a deranged and depraved mind, was a person. She hung limply from pieces of steel and wood embedded in her clothes and – Thaniel gagged as he realised – through her body, pinning her to the wall. Her head was raised, though barely, and she looked weakly across the room at Thaniel.

'Dominitia!' Thaniel cried.

Alakis made a gesture and overwhelming force slammed him to the ground. He could feel the impossible weight of Alakis's enhanced will slowly crushing him, though whether by design or because he simply didn't know his strength Thaniel couldn't tell. He cried out in pain.

Dominitia was trying to talk, slowly, haltingly. Saying something in whispers and gasps too low to hear. Alakis frowned and floated closer.

Thaniel craned his head. From where he lay, he could see her fingers moving, slowly tracing designs in the air with hands that looked so impossibly pale that Dominitia had to be close to death. How long had she hung on that wall?

Something in the air began to change, becoming lighter somehow. The crackling tension and power surrounding Thaniel seemed to falter a little.

The echoing ghost-voice shrieked.

'Stop! Stop that!'

Alakis raised a hand, palm first, towards Dominitia, but his light was fading and he jerked in the air.

Her voice was stronger now, repeating something like a mantra with desperate gasps of half-formed words. Her eyes were closed and her hand continued to trace the patterns in the air.

The energy pinning Thaniel to the floor vanished as Alakis tried to unleash a blast of energy at Dominitia. But he crashed to the floor and the blast went wide, setting fire to a pillar instead. Alakis let out a soul-rending cry as he hit the ground, all light gone from his body, and now the shrieking and moaning came from him, not the echoing ghost voice from the walls. Thunder crashed overhead in sympathetic fury.

Thaniel got to his feet in an adrenaline-fuelled lurch.

'Now, Thaniel!' cried Dominitia, from where she hung like a pitiful scarecrow.

He didn't hesitate. A piece of the broken wood lying near the still-burning hole in the floor snapped into the air and flew with deadly precision at Alakis, burying itself deep in his translucent skull with a sickening thud. Alakis began to twitch and writhe, the fallen mage rippling with light, blazing arcs of energy crackling and dancing around his flailing limbs.

And then with one howling burst of dissipating lightning, Alakis stopped moving and caught fire. Hungry flames consumed the body instantly, smothering it in a curtain of orange flame and leaving nothing but ashes.

Thaniel hurried to Dominitia's side and began to telekinetically pull the iron bars and wooden stakes out of her clothes and limbs. Her eyes were closed, her skin gleaming near-white, her clothes were soaked in blood. He didn't stop, floating her gently through the air to his waiting arms and then carrying her to the door.

On the threshold of the collapsed floor beyond, he looked up into the sky. The clouds were dissipating, allowing a watery sun to peer through.

Without a word, Thaniel wrapped Dominitia and himself in a shroud of telekinetic power and lifted them into the air.

***

Ariene sat with her head in her hands as she listened to the reports from Rigel and Master Thomas. The Ceresheim mages had arrived just in time to destroy the hideous things everyone insisted on calling Jack-o'-wires, even though the term gave her the creeps, but now the slave-people were almost at the gates. Rigel had given the order to pull their forces back inside the city, and she had to admire him for that. But to have an enemy army outside, even a slave one, and nothing in the field to combat it disturbed her greatly.

The storm had seemed to grow in power the more of the filthy puppets had been destroyed, as though once freed from the bother of animating them it had more strength with which to smash lightning at the walls. Everyone grimly acknowledged that Sophine's shield would not last much longer. Already the odd strike had penetrated the barrier and slammed into the eastern city amongst the Guild offices. Three or four were already ablaze.

'If I may, Lady Ariene,' Master Thomas was saying, 'I will send the mages we have to the fires. They can put them out quickly and get back here within—'

'This isn't ordinary lightning, Thomas,' she said exasperatedly. 'If I let your mages go out there and they get struck, what then? I'd rather let the fires burn than sacrifice anyone else to this insanity.'

'Ariene,' said Lord Orswell, who had just arrived with a reasonable sized force of Grain Guard and his personal household guards, whom he had tasked with assisting the efforts at the gate. 'If you let those fires burn, then you'll lose far more.'

'I don't see how,' she said petulantly, although she did. She saw very well.

'You know this leadership business isn't everything it's cracked up to be,' she remarked. 'I haven't even sat on the throne yet, and I already hate it.'

'The mark of a good ruler,' smiled Master Thomas.

She sighed.

'Alright, go then. Get the fires under control. But only those of your mages who you trust to protect themselves.'

He bowed, a little too low and a little too long for it to be sincere, and then left. She scowled.

'Ridiculous,' she muttered angrily. Then she cocked her head. 'You hear that?' she asked the room at large.

Rigel, Orswell and Sir Rivan Dirkling looked at one another.

'Nothing...' Ariene breathed. 'No thunder...'

Just then the door burst open and one of Dirkling's runners appeared in the office.

'My lady!' he cried. 'The storm...!'

'Yes, I know,' she snapped, rising to her feet with an irritable wave of her hand. 'I have ears. What does it mean?'

'Mean, Lady?'

'Oh, never mind,' she said, flapping a hand at him. The boy vanished.

'I see youth hasn't changed you, Ariene,' remarked Orswell with a light smile.

'People don't change with age,' she muttered, pushing past him. 'We're not apples.'

Rigel chuckled.

'One for the book.'

'To the blazes with your book, you insolent wretch.' She swept from the room.

***

Sophine was sitting on the cold rocky ground, staring at the walls of Terminheim, when Thaniel dropped out of the sky next to her. She yelped in alarm and he gave her a tight smile.

'Sorry,' he said.

'So you fly now?' she remarked, standing up. She looked at the girl in his arms and grimaced.

'Dominitia. Is she…?'

He shook his head.

'I don't think so, not yet. But close. And no, I just levitated us.'

'Just,' she repeated wryly, glancing up at the clearing sky. 'So it's over?'

He nodded.

'Get us home, Soph. Dominitia needs Rigel.'

She turned away, ripping open reality with a gesture.

'Let's go,' she said.

***

Ariene was standing with her advisors on the wall, watching the terrified, confused people of Terminheim file in through the great gates of the city. Rigel had assured her, following a cursory inspection, that although they looked wide-eyed and shaky, that was mostly due to having been so rudely awakened standing, soaking wet, in the shadow of Asterheim's walls far from home and with extensive amnesia.

Once she'd been happy that the spell holding them had been broken and that they were no longer a threat, she'd given orders for them to be housed in the evacuated parts of the city until arrangements could be made to send them home.

Just then, the air split apart with a familiar screeching yawn. Wind blew in unnatural gusts and a dark orb materialised on the city walls just next to where she stood. She stepped neatly aside as Sophine and Thaniel came through, and the portal vanished.

'Oh my,' Ariene said in horror, at the sight of the dying girl in Thaniel's arms.

'Where's Rigel?' asked Thaniel shortly, without preamble, looking around at the small crowd of people standing with her in some confusion.

'Master Thomas?' he said.

'Hello, Thaniel,' the older man replied in a tone that spoke volumes about the appropriate time and place.

Rigel pushed his way through and enfolded Sophine in a hug. Ariene reached out and tapped him on the shoulder.

'Ahem,' she said, nodding at the unconscious girl. She turned away as Thaniel lowered her to the ground and Rigel bent to administer to her.

The sky was clear now, not a trace of the roiling storm clouds was left. She closed her eyes as the sun warmed her face.

'It's over,' she sighed.

***

Rigel stood with the others on the dais in the crowded Senate building as the new Echelarch was affirmed by unanimous vote. In lieu of a throne, they had simply brought a chair, a nice one, from one of Lord Balderwin's more opulent and gaudy rooms. It had a plush seat, ornately carved arms and a high back, and looked pretty close to a throne, he thought.

Ariene did not look at all comfortable, fidgeting and changing position while the senators stood one by one to say "aye" to the question put before them by Lord Barten. Standing behind the throne and off to the right, Rigel shared a grin with Thaniel.

Sophine and Eric were on the other side of the throne, and in a seat in the front row sat Dominitia, smiling.

Lord Barten stepped up the dais and turned to face the crowd.

'By unanimous consent, I hereby decree that Ariene Gloriana is named Echelarch of Asterheim. How says Ceresheim?'

Lord Orswell rose from his seat in the front row and bowed to Ariene.

'As a duly appointed representative of Ceresheim—'

Ariene made a slight snorting sound at that and Rigel hid a grin. Orswell was nothing of the sort; he could imagine the look on the Moderator's face when Orswell had set off with fifty of the city's new mages.

'I hereby confirm the vote of the Senate.'

'How says Terminheim?'

The appointed speaker for Terminheim during this elaborate piece of theatre was an old woman named Ylinda. She had seemed to speak for most of the people when she'd recovered her wits, and had given Dominitia a very large and very emotional hug as soon as she'd set eyes on her. She rose now to confirm the vote of the Senate on behalf of Terminheim.

Barten turned to Ariene, a broad smile on his face and mischief in his eyes.

'Lady Ariene, will you consent to being our Echelarch?'

'Do I have a choice?' she muttered in a voice only her councillors could hear.

Rigel chuckled.

'Nope,' he replied quietly.

'Thrones are like toilets,' she sighed, 'a thin veneer of dignity over a pit of pestilence.'

'One for the—'

'Oh, do shut up,' she growled. Then raising her voice to address the Senate she finally replied to Lord Barten.

'I accept,' she declared.

'Long live the Echelarch!' cried Lord Barten, turning away to throw his hands up at the crowd of senators as he repeated it over and over.

They took up the booming chant, and the walls rang to the sound of her name.

Acknowledgements

I'd like to say thanks to my family, for believing in me. My mum, for reading with me. Dad, for telling me stories. And my brother, for guarding my soul against spiritual corruption. Riches to the conjurer indeed.

Steven D. Jackson is a British novelist, who lives on the South Coast with his husband and son. You can find him on Facebook, on Twitter @SDJackson85 or Instagram @steven_d_jackson.

If blogs are still a thing when you're reading this, then he has one at sdjackson.blogspot.com.